⁊ PRIƷONER ⳩

IN A RED-ROSE CHAIN

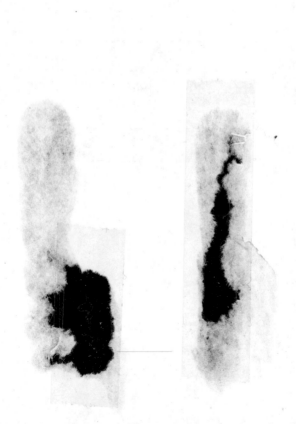

PRIƒONER
IN A RED-ROSE CHAIN

JEFFREY MOORE

THISTLEDOWN PRESS

Canadian Cataloguing in Publication Data

Moore, Jeffrey S.
Prisoner in a red rose chain
ISBN 1-895449-92-8
I. Title.
PS8576.O6141117P75 1999   C813'.54   C99-920114-X
PR9199.3.M618?P75 1999

Cover photograph by Karekin Goekjian
Typeset by Thistledown Press Ltd.
Printed and bound in Canada

Thistledown Press Ltd.
633 Main Street
Saskatoon, Saskatchewan
S7H 0J8

Canadian   Patrimoine
Heritage   canadien

Thistledown Press gratefully acknowledges the financial assistance of the Canada Council for the Arts, the Saskatchewan Arts Board, and the Government of Canada through the Book Publishing Industry Development Program for its publishing program.

A
YORKSHIRE
Tragedy.

Not so New as Lamentable
and true.

Acted by his Maiesties Players at
the *Globe.*

VVritten by VV. Shakſpeare.

AT LONDON
Printed by *R.B.* for *Thomas Pauier* and are to bee ſold at his
ſhop on Cornhill, neere to the exchange.
1608.

To the memory of my mother and father

Leading him prisoner in a red-rose chain . . .
— *Venus and Adonis*

PART ONE

ONE
(YORKSHIRE, 1970s)

O, I smell false Latin . . .
—*Love's Labour's Lost*

"I've got an idea," Gerard announced twenty-two years ago, and it suddenly seemed I was on the edge of a cliff. "An exquisite idea, something we've never done before—that no one, I dare say, has done before . . . "

I looked up at Gerard's red face and eyes that mesmerised. Whatever he asked I'd do; wherever he went I'd go too.

"I'm going to blindfold you with this," said Gerard as he unknotted his necktie, "and you're going to choose any book in the room, any one at all, at random. But you must touch the spines and covers carefully, and listen to the voices inside you. When you feel something, when you sense you've chosen the right book, let me know immediately. Is that clear?"

I nodded. Gerard was wearing an African mask, which made his voice sound muffled and strange.

"Can you see anything?" he asked as he fastened my blindfold.

"No, it's all black."

"Right then, off you go."

"What does 'at random' mean?"

"It means you can pick any one you like."

"Right." Arms outstretched, I stumbled round the room, breathing in its smell of long-unopened suitcases, tripping over objects, groping for books. Often I hesitated, volume in hand, waiting for a "feeling" of some sort.

"Be patient, lad. Be absolutely certain. You wouldn't want to select the wrong one now, would you?"

I shook my head. And then back on my quest I went, in darkness, the floorboards whining under my tread. I discarded several books from among the hundreds on the floor and walls, afraid of somehow selecting "the wrong one" and disappointing Uncle Gerard. Maybe this one. No, I didn't *feel* anything. What was I supposed to feel?

From a shelf at floor level I picked up a heavy volume and turned it over in my hands. It had a grainy cover and raised bands on the spine. I didn't really feel anything, to be honest, but when I heard church bells chime (a wedding?) I took this as a sign, a good omen.

"Uncle Gerard, I've found it! This is the one, I'm quite sure of it!"

I heard the rattle of loose boards and the squeak-squeak of Gerard's rubber-soled slippers. He took the book from my hands.

"Let's open it up and the let the future in, shall we? No, keep your blindfold on, Jeremy, we're not finished yet. What I'm going to do is flip through these pages and you're going to stick your finger in whenever you feel it's the right moment. Do you understand?"

"You mean at random?"

"Precisely."

I could hear the sound of turning pages, smell their mustiness. I waited. Yes, I definitely feel something coming on! I can sense something! I thrust my hand out and felt the book close on my hand like a trap.

"Now take off your blindfold and look at the page you chose—that you were *destined* to choose."

The page was thin, like tissue paper, and the characters were very small. I grew hot, and could feel myself starting to tremble.

"I want you to rip that page out of the book," said Gerard. "Go ahead lad, tear it right out, don't be afraid."

I did so, but not cleanly; the fragile page ripped in a jagged slant. I needed two hands to make amends.

"Now fold it up and put it in your breast pocket. Good. You must never lose that magic leaf, Jeremy, it's your *anting-anting*, your flying carpet—it will take you wherever you want to go. But be patient because it will choose the time, and that time may not be for months, years. Now go. And don't mention this to anyone, ever. You must promise on all you hold sacred that what happened today will remain our secret forever. Do you promise?"

"Yes Uncle, I give you my word as a gentleman. It'll be our secret—and torture won't drag it from me."

ဆ

I always called him Uncle, though I knew we were just pretending. Gerard was my mother's boyfriend, who came to live with us in York when I was about three. He was much older than my mum and with his wisdom and experience prevented her, I'm told, from having a nervous breakdown when my father left us. I can't say with certainty how nuts Mother was because I was curled up in her abdomen at the time. Abortions were not so common then as now, but even if they had been I think my mum would have kept me—she was of that sort, or maybe just lacked the courage. Gerard helped her along (us along) during the stressful pregnancy and sort of moved in three years later, as I said. But he wouldn't marry my mum, not Gerard Gascoigne, no matter how many times I asked him to. "Marriage is not a word but a sentence" and "Fast women and slow horses were my downfall" were his two stock answers, neither of which I understood at the time. Either, come to think of it, would make a good epitaph.

When I was around seven, my mother met someone at church who *would* marry her. Ralph Stilton was his name and he was a lopsided beanstalk of a man with thin eyebrows and crooked front teeth and a high voice he would try to push down. He wore colours like oatmeal and brown gravy and sang in the choir with bug-eyes and a mouth opened superhumanly wide. I didn't care for him, in other words, and he didn't care for me—or especially for Gerard. "He is *not* your uncle," Ralph liked to remind me, "and he'll set you no shining example, you can be sure of that. That man has led a life of epic dissipation, he has. A scoundrel of the deepest dye is what he is, one jump ahead of the police. Aye. Lord knows how your mother got mixed up with that bounder, that heathen . . . "

Epic dissipation. Scoundrel of the deepest dye. What grand expressions, so . . . heroic-sounding. For days I muttered them over and over like mystical runes. And then asked Gerard what they meant. I don't remember his answer but I do remember him exploding with laughter—and me laughing along with him, in stitches. Oh, I understood that dissipation and scoundrels were not good, but I didn't care. Gerard was my idol, my ideal. Ralph, who did his best to find me other, higher objects of worship, soon barred me from seeing him again.

For days I screamed, sulked, threatened to kill myself. And then became the docile, dutiful son—"a very decent stamp of boy," I overheard Ralph say. Had I seen the light, the error of my ways, Gerard's epic dissipation? No, I simply discovered the art of deception. Like rabbits out of hats I produced alibis for Saturday morning visits with Gerard: friends, school outings, football practices, cricket matches at St. Peter's. Gerard was my coach ("What is a lie but truth in masquerade?" said he); he taught me to lie and with practice I became quite good at it.

"You and mum split up," I would say, "but *we* never did, did we, Uncle."

Our last lie was the most farfetched, and in spite or because of this, the most successful. It depended on a certain Mr. Dragonetti, who was once Ralph's brother-in-law (he divorced Ralph's sister), a white and wispy man who was always rushing about in odd clothes and speaking nonsense, which made everyone think he was a scholar. He may have been (he did know Latin). Gerard said only that he was "fond of alcohol but not very good at paying for it, and fond of horse races but not very good at predicting their outcome." He owed Gerard, as a result of these two failings, large sums of money. This, then, was our plan: I would develop a sudden interest in learning Latin and Mr. Dragonetti would offer to teach me, on Saturday mornings, in exchange for help in his back garden.

My leery stepfather, especially at the beginning, would accompany me to Mr. Dragonetti's front door. Once he even asked to see the garden. "All in good time," Dragonetti replied, "all in good time. *Vincit qui patitur.* I shall be delighted to show you my . . . my delphinia and eryngia when everything's properly tended. Your son's been invaluable—he's got a real green thumb, that lad." As Ralph walked back home, Dragonetti crawled back to bed and I flew out the back door.

Through the phantom flowers I ran, across the paved garden, over the fence and along the City Walls, from Fishergate Bar, across Skeldergate Bridge and the chocolate waters of the Ouse, to Micklegate Bar, the monarch's entrance. From there it was a short run—and winds could not outrun me—to the flat of my illegal guardian. I would clap the lion-head knocker three times before letting myself in. The battered oak door, like a dungeon door, creaked on its hinges, I think by Gerardian design. It was lockable but never locked.

With its sloping roof and exposed wooden beams, the flat could have had charm, but didn't. It was too dark, too dirty, too full ("Oceans of room," Gerard would protest, "Oceans!"). Its furniture, some of it dust-sheeted, seemed not to have been chosen so much as left. Books of all shapes and sizes were scattered amidst untenanted cabinets, overburdened suitcases, locked steamer trunks, faded costumes and props, unfinished canvases, and a swarming, higgledy-piggledy mound of flea-market curios and arcana.

In the "kitchen" was a picture of two large birds perched on a branch (with a TV antenna), minding two pints of beer:

> Toucans in their nests agree
> GUINNESS is good for you
> Open some today and see
> What one or Toucan do.

I loved this. Below it, amidst exotic postcards fixed with Sellotape, was a faded yellow card with cursive lettering and red ornamented borders. It was not as funny, even if Gerard seemed to think it was:

What is home without
Plumtree's Potted Meat?
Incomplete.
With it an abode of bliss.

In the bathroom, often in the bathtub, was a slightly limping rocking horse that Gerard promised one day to mend. "Magic Wanda" had brass fittings and swing irons and stirrup covers made of real leather; on her belly was a brass plaque from the British Rocking-Horse Society indicating full pedigree, dam and sire. In "my" corner was a toy chest, whose constantly replenished stock included a gas mask, water pistols, catapults, lead soldiers, a cream-coloured Royal Ascot badge, a bag of Barker and Dobson's Fruit Drops with something else in it (regimental buttons?), Happy Family playing cards, Moon Traveller fireworks, and an African mask that scared me even after the hundredth time Gerard wore it.

A strict routine was in effect on these Saturday mornings, perhaps the only one in my young life I never wanted to see upset. Gerard, when not in gas- or African mask, would greet me with a grin in which one eye closed up more than the other, and a handshake that hurt. Then it was "spying and tales" conducted from the flat's only source of light, a large dormer window. As we stuck our heads out and gazed at the spires of York Minster, Gerard would recount some spellbinding tale or chapter in mediaeval history. I don't know why the view of the Minster inspired him so—he had no use for religion. Often, he would direct his gaze towards more residential architecture, through a telescope, so perhaps it was not the cathedral that inspired him.

I was never really sure what Gerard did for a living. His window stories contained some inconsistencies. After being "slung out" of Rugby, Gerard once recounted, he sailed to Africa and ran guns in Zululand. In another version he became a jockey after graduating from Eton. Yet another time he was a Shakespearean actor and never went to school at all. I believed all three stories until Ralph pointed out that Gerard went to a state school in York, that jockeys are rarely six feet tall, and that Zululand was incorporated into Natal in the 19th century. What I know for certain is that Gerard travelled a lot ("I've knocked up and down a bit," said he), especially to France, and that he worked in "mathematical" fields. Mother said that he once worked as an actuary for Great Northern Life, and I know that he worked as a tic-tac man at the racecourse in Pontefract, near Leeds, because I twice saw him in action, relaying the changing odds by hand signals. He had two boxes of business cards, one set with "Mathematician" under his name, the other with "Turf Accountant".

After the window stories came the Games, usually involving words or chance. I kept a record of these games in a book filled with musical staves that Gerard gave me on my seventh birthday. On the marbling of the front cover was a patch over someone else's name. It was a big book, quite beautiful, bound in green moiré silk that shimmered when you tilted it. We called it the Book of Saturdays. It was empty, except for these notes on the last page:

Sometimes we would make anagrams in this book— Gerard was constantly making anagrams, a sign of schizophrenia so they say—with random words from a *Manchester Guardian* or *Yorkshire Post*. But Gerard insisted on "pertinent" anagrams—they had to relate to the word in question. I was not good at this, though once devised **"THE EYES: THEY**

SEE". If my anagrams were not pertinent, my uncle would say "Jeremy, you're being impertinent!" and I would laugh, without knowing why. Gerard was always pertinent. On 11 March 1972, for example, he wrote: "MARRIAGE: A GRIM ERA; MOTHER-IN-LAW: WOMAN HITLER; DESPERATION: A ROPE ENDS IT."

On our last Saturday together we played a new game, a very simple one, which Gerard approached with uncharacteristic gravity. He may have known it was to be our last.

"I've got an idea," said Gerard. "An exquisite idea, something we've never done before . . . "

ༀ

Please don't imagine, as I did for so long, that the contents of the Page will somehow set in motion the events that follow. Life's not like that. Its course is not printed on a sheet of paper, ripped from a random book; only mystics and children would think otherwise.

Normally I would walk home, ploddingly, but on this last Saturday I ran quickly, zigzagging in and out of camera fields along the Walls, then back across the locks of the Foss. I went straight to my bedroom, got into bed and pulled the covers over my head. I was bathed in sweat, my heart beating its drum.

I held the Page for a few seconds in the dark. *You must never lose that magic leaf. It's your anting-anting, your flying carpet . . .* I took a deep breath, counted to eleven and turned on my bedlamp. The Page was folded unevenly in four; I stared at it, afraid to restore it to one. I took another deep breath and my door swung wide open.

Ralph, standing in the doorway as I frantically slid the Page beneath the sheets, looked from my flushed face to the blankets, perhaps suspecting organ abuse. "How are your Latin lessons going?" he asked. I grunted. How nice of you to knock.

"Your mother and I would like to see you downstairs. Smartish."

"What's an anting-anting?"

"A what? Is that Latin?"

"Never mind. Could you close the door on your way out, Radulfus?" (Gerard had re-christened Ralph with his Latin name.)

"Don't you ever speak to me in that tone, young man. And my name is not Radulfus. So downstairs, then—and sharp about it." Radulfus stood there, staring at me, daring me to defy him. Or perhaps he was hoping to see what was under the sheets.

I lay in bed, waiting for his footsteps to recede, and then tiptoed to the door. I closed it gently before scurrying back into bed, throwing off the covers and quickly unfolding the Page.

"Jeremy!" trumpeted Ralph from downstairs. I glanced over the contents before carefully refolding the Page and slipping it into my breast pocket. "Jeremy!"

In the front room Mother was sitting in her favourite blue armchair, an Angora shawl round her shoulders and mauve wool on her lap. She looked as though Ralph had just belted her, though I knew he'd never do that. I sat down in ominous silence.

"Mother, do you know what an anting-anting is?"

"You've already asked me that," said Ralph.

"I'm asking Mother."

"Neither of us know—"

"It's like a good-luck charm, isn't it?" said Mother. "Something that protects you from all harm?"

More silence. Mother counted her stitches. Ralph rocked on his heels, his chest bent inward, the line of his torso like a question mark. He removed his glasses, wiped them with his handkerchief, returned them to his nose and examined me as if I were some strange specimen of insect. He then hitched up his trousers, cleared his throat, and announced something that made no sense.

"We're what?"

Ralph lowered his chin, trying to pull his voice down with it. "I believe you heard me—I said we were moving."

"But . . . but where are we moving . . . to?"

"North York."

"The North York Moors? Why are we moving up there?"

"We're not moving up anywhere, except perhaps up in an aeroplane." Ralph smiled, evidently pleased with this verbal cartwheel, then paused for dramatic effect. "We're going west young man, not north, and a canny bit farther than the Moors, I'm afraid."

I immediately thought of Gerard and our secret Saturdays. "To West Yorkshire? You mean Leeds? Bradford?"

"Lord no, who in their right mind would move to Leeds or Bradford? We're going much farther than that. We are going, in fact, to the New World—to North York in Canada."

I looked at my stepfather's pasty face and imbecilic grin. I looked at my mother who was now knitting furiously. (It was at this point in my life, I'm almost sure, that I began to stutter when upset.)

"C-Canada?" I cried. "W-why in the world are we going there? I don't want to go to stupid bloody Canada and I'm not going! And that's final. What about my Latin lessons?"

"Your 'Latin lessons', as you have the effrontery to call them, are one of the reasons we're moving, young man. And don't look so innocent. You know perfectly well—"

"I'm staying," I replied firmly.

We moved the next Saturday (things had obviously been brewing behind my back). North Yorkshire to North York: Ralph the optician's bookkeeper liked things symmetrical. On the plane, between trade magazines, he pointed out that Toronto, of which North York is a suburb, was once called York. Now isn't that an odd coincidence? And that one city has a York University, the other a University of York. And that the most famous hotel in each is the Royal York Hotel, and that . . .

"God, how amazing," I said. "How bloody fucking amazing."

Ralph stopped speaking, looked at Mother with his mouth open, then back at me. "Why, you cheeky young bastard!" he exploded, while cuffing me in the ear with a magazine full of statistics. "You cheeky young bastard!"

I put my arms over my face, like a shield against arrows. "Better a bastard than your son," I muttered.

"Why you little . . . Twelve years old and cursing like a convict. Not surprising either. Not surprising in the least, hanging about with that . . . depraved man all the time. Well, that's all in the past now, thank God for that! Gerard Gascoigne will set you no shining example, you can be dead sure of that. A chancer, a real oiler that one. There's rumours about that man, Jeremy, something that happened in—"

"Please don't," said my mother to Ralph, placing her hand over his. "Let the boy be."

I unfastened my seat belt and climbed over Ralph's big feet, towards the aisle.

"And where do you think you're off to young man? Jeremy, your mother and I would like an answer . . . "

I didn't know where I was off to, to tell you the truth. To look for a parachute? I headed for the airplane toilet. I fiddled with one door, and then another, and blushed crimson as a stewardess showed me how they opened. Inside, I stood in front of the mirror, shaking, teardrops running down my face. From my breast pocket I pulled out the Page and blearily roamed its lines, these lines I've read a thousand times:

> and after his mother's death all pregnant women and their husbands were slaughtered, along with thousands of milch cows, so that even the calves might know what is was to lose a mother. Early in 1828 Shaka's stepson and banished daughter stole into his kraal as he slept and stabbed him to death with his own scarlet assegai.
> **Shakespeare, William,** also spelled SHAKSPERE, byname BARD OF AVON, or SWAN OF AVON (b. 23 April, 1564 d. 23 April, 1616), English poet, dramatist, and actor, widely regarded as the monarch of English letters and the greatest playwright of all time . . .

Down the page and overleaf Shakespeare continued, and then:

> **Shakespearean apocrypha,** works dubiously attributed to William Shakespeare, e.g. *Fair Em*, *The Passionate Pilgrim*, "A Lover's Complaint," *A Yorkshire Tragedy*, *Love's Labour's Won*. See Shakespeare.
> **Shakespearean sonnet:** see SONNET and DARK LADY.
> **Shakhtyorsk,** city (1957 pop. 51,000), Ukrainian Soviet Socialist Republic. A mining town on the Donets Coal Basin, famed for its high-quality anthracite coal. In Ukrainian legend it is known as the "City of Fool's Errands".

shaking palsy: see PARKINSON'S DISEASE.

Shakuntala, in Hindu mythology, daughter of Visvamitra and Menaka, and heroine of Kalidasa's erotic drama *Shakuntala* (c. AD 400). In this idealised tale of love lost and regained, which many regard as India's greatest literary achievement, the infant Shakuntala is abandoned on the banks of the river Malini and raised by the hermit Kanva. While hunting, King Dushyanta watches the maiden from behind a tree and falls irretrievably in love with her. After days of indecision and heartache he seduces her, asks for her hand in marriage, and gives her a ring as pledge before returning to his throne. A son is born of their union, whereupon mother and child set out to find the king. While bathing, Shakuntala loses the ring and King Dushyanta, enchanted by a curse, does not recognise her. The ring is

The page ended there, with the word "is".

TWO
(MONTREAL, 1996)

The doors of Fate lie open in all places.

—Shakuntala

Years later I was moving again, and again I felt like crying: behind hot stinking columns of cars I'd been taken to the wrong street, the wrong section of town, and I had this dread feeling it was my own fault. Or the fault of the Page.

"Stop!" I cried when I saw a sign.

"You don't want to live around here," said the cab driver as he pulled into a decrepit alleyway. He rolled down his window and hawked a fluttering wad of mucus onto the pavement. "Not that house, anyway."

"Keep it," I replied. I slammed the door, sidestepped the sputum, and walked over to read the sign. *Sous-sol à louer,* it said. No, I was not going to live underground. I glanced this way and that. Next door, across the alleyway, was another sign, or rather a piece of driftwood with wide-brush kindergarten characters that dribbled down like blood, spotting the ground below. I opened the wrought-iron gate, tripped on a patio of uneven flagstones, and rang the bell.

And rang again, looking this way and that, wondering what the hell I was doing. A weather-beaten barbecue leaned drunkenly against the fence, drooling out a frothy brown liquid; blotched houses across the street stood lopsided and rotting, like Ralph's teeth. I sighed and thought of what I was leaving—a gorgeous high-rise and girlfriend—and wondered how I'd obtained either. I suppose I was at that age—do men ever outgrow it?—when beauty is enough. I couldn't afford my mountainside apartment but it was beautiful; I couldn't relate to Sabrine on any level but she was beautiful too. Others agreed and when I caught her in the apartment pool, nude, treading water in the arms of the night porter, I decided that would be the end of that. When Sabrine went back to France for a holiday (with the night porter), I got into a cab to look for a new life. Even the driver said I was looking in the wrong place.

The door opened. A stout man with a bull-neck, bushy grey eyebrows and turtleneck trousers gave me an inquiring head jerk, but before I could open my mouth he turned his back to me and shouted in a foreign tongue. A stout woman with a bull-neck, grey moustache and stained windbreaker eventually emerged, greeting me with a scowl. I assumed she would act as interpreter, as he appeared to have little English and no French. She, however, had no English and no French. The conversation that ensued would be difficult to transcribe without choreographic notation. Evidently the top floor, the third, was vacant. I went up with them to inspect it.

Sometimes one tries to conceal one's shock. It may be out of politeness, or it may be to save face (after being informed of a risibly exorbitant price for a mountainside apartment, for example). When the door opened to the third-floor apartment, I tried to give the impression that this was about what I expected. "Right, OK, fine," I said, nodding intently. But I couldn't keep up the pose, I just couldn't.

The wood floors, painted over in Martian green and bordello red gloss—the colour of the sign outside—were studded with bits of stray or regurgitated food, squashed insects, scorchburns, runic magic-marker graffiti and petrified animal shit. Cycloned about were empty bottles, or shards thereof, mostly of generic gin or *dépanneur* wine, as well as empty tubes and solvent bottles, damp piles of magazines, and withered stalks of stinking dead brown plants. The walls were poxed with mildew and soot—and tiny perforations, as if from automatic rifle fire. In the kitchen, travel posters with Central American seascapes were held up with hockey tape, white and black. The sink contained a decade of dishes and a grey-green liquid with the viscosity of pus. The windows were glaucomatose with grime. The bathroom housed a network of copper, steel and plastic pipes of Byzantine complexity, joined with U-bends, Y-branches, T's and traps, wrapped with a mile of yellow electrician's tape. They appeared to connect a half-size, corroded brown bathtub to the bathroom sink, the faucets of which, for reasons lost to history, had been ripped out of their sockets. The toilet had problems too: its flushing lever was stuck and its seat, strangely, was wired shut. I went out onto the balcony to recover from the stench. The landlord joined me. He explained with a shrug and broken English that the previous inhabitants had been there for six months and then vanished. They were from "the forest".

I inquired about the price, said I would "sleep on it", then prepared to vanish as well. Naturally, I had no intention of sleeping on it or, for that matter, of setting foot in the neighbourhood again. For apart from its squalor, the area—and the apartment—had bad vibes. Some places make you feel uneasy and this was definitely one of them. This place had storm clouds, black cats and broken mirrors all rolled into one.

The next day I returned and said "I'll take it." Why? If you'd asked me then, I'd have mumbled something about the apartment's "potential" (it had none), its laughably low rent (peppercorn rent, as we said in York), its suitability as a pit-stop, a stop-gap (*a pied-à-merde*). All subterfuges. For there was another, much stronger reason.

While the landlord and I had stood on the balcony discussing the habits of tree-dwellers, I glimpsed below us a black-haired woman opening the gate of the house next door. She walked to the door of the basement apartment for rent, took a key from a silver chain hanging from her hip, and paused. In telepathic concentration I stared down at her, willing her to look up, sensing that obscure forces were stirring within her, as they were within me. She doesn't see me looking at her, I said to myself, but she feels it through her whole body. She looked up. I nodded, held my shoulders back manly and straight, turned to reveal my profile. I was in this pose when the door slammed behind her.

ભ

Please don't mistake me. This was not one of those tediously common unrequited love at first sights. It was actually unrequited love at third sight. The first happened soon after the swimming-pool episode, during a Jane Campion retrospective at a woman's film festival. I went with Sabrine.

We had made a mistake about the time, as it turned out (*I* had made a mistake), arriving exactly one hour early. To entertain one of us, Sabrine verbalised her thought waves for the hour. Here and there I piped in the odd "Really?", "Are you serious?"—perhaps a bit off cue. A bore has been defined as one who mentions everything: *L'art d'ennuyer c'est de tout dire*. In this, Sabrine was an artist. No detail, not even the most wildly peripheral, was left out. She touched on all subjects and rested on none. She put words and images in my head I did not want put in. She bitched about everything, including the movie we had not yet seen.

As she was apparently telling a funny story, other people began to trickle in. The theatre gradually filled and then over-filled: people sat in the aisle wing-seats and in the aisles themselves. And yet the seat next to mine remained empty, even when I removed my coat from it. This Sabrine found quite funny, suggesting first that I stank, and then (implying a huge sacrifice on her part) that nobody wanted to sit beside a man at a woman's festival. About twenty minutes into the film, in any event, someone sat down beside me.

This was my first sight of Milena, in shadowy profile. Her head was a mass of dishevelled hair, a night-black thunder-cloud that hung over her eyes; her nose was prominent, slightly aquiline, her lips full, her complexion on the dark side. Egyptian? Sicilian? Persian? With her came a gentle hint of body odour, a fragrance more alluring than any perfume (at least when given off by the right people). I looked at her—peripherally, imperceptibly—and then turned my head and gawked. I couldn't help it: she was sending out these rays, these insidious rays that went through me like faint vibrations. It was the future impinging on the present. She, obviously, was impervious to whatever I was sending out. Minutes before the end of the film, as Sabrine whispered something inconsequential in my right ear, Milena left.

We took the métro home, Sabrine and I, but only after a fight: Sabrine wanted to take a cab. By the exercise of an iron will I got my way—at the expense of being called a *grippe-sou*, a skinflint. I generously offered to pay for her ticket. As we walked through the turnstiles, Sabrine remarked that the film (*Sweetie*) was one of the worst she had ever seen, and I remarked that it was one of the best I had ever seen. We then heard and felt the rumbling of an approaching train. If I had been alone, or with anyone else, I would have run to catch it. But Sabrine was not one to run for trains, and I respected that.

From the top of the escalator I spotted someone tall dark and handsome waiting on the platform below. This was my second sight. The moving stairs suddenly stopped. I grabbed Sabrine's hand and pulled her down the stationary escalator as she squealed in protest. On the platform I dragged her like a skidding recalcitrant child, or dog. We made it, not to the mystery woman's car but to the one behind, and only just. I jumped into the car before the doors closed; Sabrine jumped too, but half-heartedly, as they were closing. Her arm and skirt were pinned. She cursed, the doors reopened, and a voice emerged from tinny speakers: *"Lâche les portes, le beigne!"* (literally, "Let go of the doors, you doughnut"). There was some laughter in the car at this, which only fueled Sabrine's rage. Sabrine did not liked to be called a doughnut in any circumstances, but least of all when I was the one at fault. As she explained this to me in a molten river of French invective, I strained to see through the double door panes into the next car. This time I got a much better look at Milena as she stood in the unforgiving fluorescent lights.

Tall—at least 5′8″, 5′9″—and almost anorexically thin, she stood in an empty car holding a hardcover book in one hand and the bar above her with the other. She wore an oversized white T-shirt with the sleeves ripped off (revealing unshaven underarms), a torn black-satin vest, faded black jodhpurs laced from the knee down, and brown ankle boots. Her long black hair was a wilderness, that just-out-of-bed or just-boffed look that is sometimes planned but probably not in this case. Minutes later, I can't say how many, Sabrine pushed me out the door and onto the platform, where I stood dazzled and beglamoured ("drooling", said Sabrine) as my dark Juliet accelerated past us. Her eyes never left the pages of her book.

And so like Newton, who suffered for years from an after-image of the sun, the result of incautiously staring at it through a telescope, I suffered for months from an after-image of Milena, from incautiously staring at her.

THREE

Tis in the nose of thee;
thou art the Knight of the Burning Lamp.

—*Falstaff*

That the forest people had fouled their nest was one thing, that they'd made renovations while on drugs quite another. The first few days of my new life, when I wasn't hunting for the dark lady, were filled trying to unfoul the nest and undo what they had done. One of my first tasks, not surprisingly, was to unwire the toilet seat. This I did, and made a rather unpleasant discovery: a waterlogged turd, of unknown authorship, in a surprisingly well-preserved state. It was in the exact shape of a dotted, lower case "j". I fixed the flushing lever and, feeling quite proud of myself, flushed.

As I watched the circling contents rise and overflow onto the floor, I screamed out a number of obscenities, including an appropriate "Shiiiit!" A belching/vomiting sound answered me: my buzzer. I slammed the bathroom door, trudged down the stairs, opened the door and squinted up at someone two and half yards high. I could've walked between his legs. "Raphael," he said. "I want Raphael." He looked shockingly short of sleep. I grunted and closed the door in his knees, or at least tried to. Like a contortionist, he slipped through an opening as narrow as my views on unannounced guests.

"Uh, excuse me? I don't know who Raphael is . . . I'm the new tenant . . . "

"*Tengo mucho hambre*," he said dully.

Not a disputable point: his hunger-hallucinating eyes shone. "Yes, I'm sure you're hungry, but you see I just moved in yesterday and well, quite frankly, I don't have any food myself. The only thing I could offer you is some salt. Or perhaps some non-dairy creamer . . . Wait, what are you doing?"

He was climbing up the stairs. "*Tengo mucho hambre*," he replied, shrugging his shoulders. Yes, so you said. He entered the kitchen as if he'd been there before, opened a cupboard and removed a tin of Brunswick sardines. "I eat?" he asked politely.

"Um, well OK, I . . . forgot I had that."

Before I could find a can opener he was mangling the tin with something red and metallic: a Swiss Army knife. I watched in nausea as he tilted his head back and poured the oil into his mouth, watched him dig out the last fragments of fish with a skeleton forefinger. He turned to look at me.

"*Hueles a la mierda*," he spluttered, his face full of fish like a seal.

"Pardon?"

"*Hueles a la mierda*. You smell like shit."

"Right, I . . . I've had some plumbing problems and—"

"I crash?" he inquired. There were specks of fish on his cheek and oil dribbled down his acne-potted chin.

I decided to be firm. "No, you can't 'crash'," I replied with all the manliness I could muster, which was not a lot. "I don't know who you are, I don't know who Raphael is, apart from the painter, I have no connection with the former tenants and . . . "

With oily fingers he opened up his knife blade and took a step closer to me; I finished my sentence into his woolly chest.

" . . . and so you see I can't really . . . receive you."

"I go wash," he said. "OK?"

Fine. Be my guest. I'll wait here for you. I whistled casually as I wiped oil off the floor. I poured myself some apple juice. He was very quiet. What was he up to? I could hear no movement of water. I tiptoed over to the bathroom door and was about to knock when I heard rhythmic suction sounds. Where on earth did he find a plunger? I went back to the kitchen and drank more juice.

The apartment was now stone silent. What was he doing? I returned to the bathroom and knocked softly on the door, which was open a fraction of an inch. No answer. "Hello-o?" I peered in. The floor was now clean and dry, but he wasn't on it. He was sound asleep in the bathtub, his spindly legs buckled, his open-mouthed head ensconced in a pillow of towels.

My first thought was that I had just washed those towels; my second was that I should feel sorry for him. Which I did. Poor bastard. So I left him there to sleep and went to my bedroom to do the same. I tossed and turned for what seemed like hours, trying to figure out my role in this low comedy, this theatre of the absurd. Why should I feel sorry for him? Because he's tired, homeless and hungry. Fine, he's like a stray cat, a tall one, and now he lives here. I'll feed him fish.

I dressed and went outside, onto the landing, to mull things over. Head in hands I sat, waiting for a plan to emerge from the muck of my mind. I looked down, across the alleyway, toward the dark lady's subterranean chamber. Should I ring her bell, borrow a cup of sugar, ask her what to feed a giraffe? I returned to my new roommate.

Who was no longer in the tub. Or anywhere else. The door in the kitchen, I observed, was slightly ajar so he had obviously hared out the back exit and down the fire escape—after realising just who he was up against. I shot the bolts, wedged a chair beneath the door handle, deadlocked the front door. I removed the towels from the bathtub, hosed down the enamel, and then made a quick run of the place. Nothing appeared to be missing, and in fact something had been added: a Swiss Army knife, slick with oil.

ೞ

The next two days I laboured, performing virile home-handyman tasks. When I realised I had no understanding of even the most rudimentary DIY principles, I called a plumber, a carpet-layer and an electrician. This sudden recognition of my limitations came to me in a kind of epiphany, in a glimmer of insight from atop a stepladder, after a stream of electricity travelled up my arm and left me sitting on my ass.

I also called the cable man, who arrived almost immediately with the largest gut I have ever seen. As I watched him staple the cord to the quarter-round, his enormous trousers slipping to reveal the cleft of an enormous bum, I thought of one of Uncle Gerard's stock sayings: "Television is a medium because it is neither rare nor well done." As soon as the cable man left I tested this dictum out, watching television for the better part of twenty-four hours. I remember in particular a dial-a-psychic infomercial with a fat fraud in a fairy princess outfit, and a cable channel called Télé-Rencontres, a dating service with pictures and post-box numbers and a list of qualities desired in prospective mates. The most frequently desired quality, I quickly discovered, was "a sense of humour." He or she "must have a sense of humour." I wondered what this meant. Is there a generic "sense of humour"? I've noticed that those who laugh at everything, like asylumites, are usually described as having "a good sense of humour." But I understood the thrust. We all need someone to laugh with; things are not as funny alone. Sabrine laughed a lot, but never in the right place.

There was another commercial I remember, in which a bad actor improved his hearing via a sound amplifier worn like a Walkman, priced at three easy payments of $39. "What'd you say? I-I can't hear you" was followed by "You're comin' in loud and clear!" Its potential users were many—the hard of hearing, nature lovers, eavesdroppers. I laughed steadily the first few times I saw it. And then phoned the toll-free number and ordered one. The operator, from Utah (I asked), informed me that for a very limited time I could buy a second Supersound 2000 for half price *and* they'd throw in a mood ring. I laughed again, with my best derisive laugh. And then accepted her offer.

ଔ

On my seventh day at the apartment I rested, sunning myself half-naked on the balcony for hours. This was my plan: to go out in the evening and attract females with a sleek, all-over bronzing. This was my revised plan: to go out in the evening and attract females with a bright red nose. On my way out I splashed on some Andron, a cologne containing a synthetic version of androsterone, found in male armpit and genital perspiration, and in urine. According to Gerard, when the Royal Shakespeare Company sprayed select theatre seats with it, the majority of women followed their noses to those seats. I bought some while living with Sabrine; she said it made her sick.

On the "Boulevard" (the main drag) I started with some ritualistic window-shopping—past the Ukrainian bakery, the Jewish tombstone-maker, a Lebanese bicycle shop called Prince of Tyre, a Greek barber shop with vintage spiral pole— to "Retouches Chez Harry", a clothing store of sorts owned by Harry Därt, who was from one of the Baltic countries. Harry's display window, streaked with the dried runnels of acid rain, was empty, except for some yellow newspapers and a dead moth hung in a web. I pressed my face to the glass to see if any changes had been made inside. None, none since the seventies: a row of flowered shirts with seven-inch collar points—all in the same colour and pattern—and a row of boys' red-vinyl ski jackets, topped with Miss Havisham layers of dust. In between the rows, half-hidden by clothes, Mr. Därt worked twelve hours a day at a battered oak desk, sewing by hand or with anachronous machines till he dropped. On the door, beneath a superfluous "Provost Alarm Systems" decal, was a small hand-written sign that said FOR SALE. But said it sadly.

On I went—past more declining shops of ageing immigrant tradesmen, whose sons were not following in their footsteps, whose stores were being bulldozed into the future—to the cat bookstore. On the rare occasions this nameless shop was open, columns of books clogged the entranceway. If this didn't discourage you from entering, the air inside did. Thick with dust and fur, it had a fierce smell emanating from a box of kitty litter in which multiple deposits from a half-dozen free-roaming cats piled up like abstract sculptures. The owner, a dour introvert with a grey brushcut and wire-glasses, seemed not to notice this, or for that matter, much of anything else. His eyes were normally trained on a half-dozen German philosophy books, each open on his desk, with a styrofoam cup, lit cigarette or purring cat as bookmark. It was only with the greatest reluctance that he attended to inquiries or sales or book thieves. On this particular day the store was closed, but the cats were there, sleeping and shitting. On the window was a newly-installed sign that said À VENDRE/FOR SALE.

My last ritual stop was a pawnshop named Rumrich's. Or its skeleton: only the lettering on the window remained (the apostrophe, in conformance with the law, had been eradicated). Only once had I entered—Sabrine had wanted to see a bracelet with a timepiece—and I ended up buying that and a grandfather clock. The clock was not cheap, even if Sabrine and the owner said it was.

"It belongs in museum of horology," said Mr. Rumrich. "And I ain't kidding."

I nodded. Only they could afford it.

"*Elle est superbe*," said Sabrine.

"*Oui, elle est superbe*," agreed Mr. Rumrich. "*Comme toi, ma belle.*" He appeared to be licking his lips.

"Its price is rather high," I pointed out.

"And it'll be higher next month. Nothing's going down except ourselves. Want some advice? *Voulez-vous un conseil?* If it don't eat bread, leave 'em lay. That's my advice. Hold on to things—sooner or later someone will pay top dollar for them. If it don't eat bread, leave 'em lay."

"My uncle thought the same way," I said.

"A pack-rat, am I right? A pack-rat? I'll bet he's a rich man today, am I right?"

"Well no . . . I mean yes, as a matter of fact he is."

"Doesn't surprise me. Doesn't surprise me one iota. Nothing's going down except ourselves. Hey, guess what the most valuable thing in my shop is. Come on, take a guess! Is guessing a crime? No one's gonna arrest you, no one's gonna slap handcuffs on you for guessing, am I right? Come on! *Devinez!* What's the most valuable thing?"

I guessed the grandfather clock and Sabrine a mahogany Chippendale-style lowboy.

"No," he said with a broad smile, "it's me—Herman Rumrich!" We all had a good laugh at that one. Mr. Rumrich enjoyed the joke so much that he repeated it. "You get it?" he asked. According to a sign on the window, Mr. Rumrich was to be replaced by a death-metal club called NAIL.

The gentrifying, gently dying Boulevard. Whose quaint ethnic shops and pre-Bauhaus buildings were being transformed by palm-rubbing real-estate barons into bistros and discos for women with big Florida hair and men with turtlenecks and chains. A 19th-century building with capitals, pediments and pilasters was gutted and glitz-lit and turned into JOIE DE VIE, a three-floor disco for the single-again. A 1940s-style Jewish stationer's, where everything was cheap and nothing taxed, was now a cement cave with a permit called TRANSAXION, a minimalist environment in which young suburbanites could exchange their parents' money for cocaine.

I sighed, wondering if I was turning into an anti-modernist, a fuddy-duddy, championing old ways like some Verdun veteran. I was also starting to sweat; it was an equatorial night, thick and soupy. Round in circles I walked, skirting and flirting, leering and lusting, knowing it was pathetic, doing it anyway. I was beyond rationality, practically in *musth*, that potentially hazardous state of frenzy to which elephants are liable in rutting season. Male elephants, that is.

A woman in a short skirt passed by on a bike and I walked into a No Parking sign. It didn't hurt and no one saw me. On a street of open-air terraces with "Victorian" cobblestones and lampposts, I read a poster for some long-dead event while watching a waitress bend over to wipe a table. She was wearing a man's white dress-shirt, tied in a knot at the waist, and red pantyhose. But no skirt. As I gaped I heard a voice. *"Monsieur Davenant, ça va bien?"* she said. Oh shit.

Arielle was a former student, a keen, pretty, gregarious type with great white teeth, great blue eyes, and hair of honey-blonde. She was an executive on some student committee—something to do with ethics, I think. "*Ça va bien,*" I replied, "*et vous Ariane?*"

"Arielle. What happen to your nose? It is bleeding?"

"No no, it's just . . . I hit a . . . it's probably the air pollution."

"And it's very burnt too."

"Yeah, I was out . . . playing a bit of tennis—"

"It's shining. Like a big red bulb."

I nodded.

"Like Rudolph . . . "

"Yes, fine."

" . . . the red-nose reindeer."

"So what's new?" I asked.

As Arielle drew closer I made some rapid, though keen, meteorological observations. She dabbed my nose with a paper napkin and agreed it was a hot night. I asked her if I could buy her a drink when she finished and she said yes. Be finished in an hour. Great, see you then.

And so I roamed the streets again, killing time, wondering why I do the things I do. I watched a weathered old owl slide her lips along a mouth organ, back and forth, up and down, pell-mell, helter-skelter. She looked at me through thick glasses that made her darting eyes as big as golf balls. Into a rubber shower cap, which was primed with pennies and Monopoly money, I tossed a golden loon in the hope she would stop playing. She stopped playing, looked down, smiled at me with the teeth of a corpse. As I smiled back I felt a hand on my shoulder, which made me jump as if stung by a bee; I turned round to the bulbous-nosed face of a bagman—with Ancient Mariner eyes staring out of cavernous sockets. Her protector? When I fumbled in my pockets for silver he waved his hand dismissively, explaining he was the Prophet from Pluto and a follower of Kulla, the Sumerian god of bricks. I nodded, and he ran off to hail a passing cab, roaring with laughter when it stopped. He hailed two more, perhaps for my benefit, grinning back at me each time. I nodded appreciatively.

At the appointed hour I returned to the restaurant and from a barstool watched Arielle count out her money. Yes, she's an attractive woman. No, I'm not going to try anything stupid. "Be finished in a sec," she said with an outrageously beautiful smile.

We walked back up the Boulevard, pausing again at my favourite stores (which didn't seem to impress Arielle), to a Portuguese bar called Dame de Piques. With its yang decor of stuffed stags and owls, Woolworthscapes, wacky signs, beer logos and varnished wood, it was one of those hip-by-accident places, so uncompromisingly uncool it was cool to be there. At a table next to the sidewalk I learned that Arielle wanted to be a United Nations interpreter, that she loved English idiomatic expressions, and jokes. I have trouble listening to formula jokes but did my best, piping in canned laughter on cue. My face muscles began to ache. I told a joke that Uncle Gerard told me when I was around five, the only one I can ever remember. You may know it: "What time did the Chinaman go to the dentist?" (Just say I don't know.) "Tooth hurty." Arielle laughed, flamboyantly. Her face muscles were probably aching too.

As she headed for the toilet, I opened at random a *Cosmopolitan* she had left on the table, under a dog-eared *English Phrase Book*. In an article entitled "How to Be a Great Date", women were advised to:
  • Be flamboyantly amused by his witty asides.
  • Say 'That's absolutely fascinating!' at least once before the evening's over.

As I was leafing through the perfumed pages, lingering over lingerie, Arielle sat down with a smile and lipstick on her long teeth. She said she loved Magic Mountain and Homer (the video game and Simpson, as it turned out) and hated rolls of toilet paper that had too much glue holding down the first square. "I know what you mean," I said. "You end up shredding the damn thing, through the middle layers, leaving big borders on the side. I used to do it as a kid, sometimes on purpose—it annoyed the hell out of my stepfather."

Arielle laughed. "That's absolutely fascinating!"

After another round, and more anecdotes about as interesting as that last one, I suggested we leave. "Soft words butter no parsnips," she replied.

"I'm sorry?"

"Parsnips. Soft words don't butter them."

I nodded at her sagacity. Sometimes you correct non-native speakers, sometimes you don't. Besides, I wasn't at all sure what that expression meant.

"Mere words," she added, "will not find salt to our porridge."

We walked up the Boulevard in silence. Arielle pointed. A few yards ahead, in front of a restaurant, was a commotion of some sort, possibly a fight. No, it wasn't a fight. A group of oversized T-shirts and slipping waistlines were tossing a girl with flaming red hair into the air and shouting in unison, "*Un!* . . . *deux!* . . . *trois!* . . . " At *dix-huit* they converged upon her, smothering her with kisses—eighteen from each I would imagine. That's a lot of kisses. It was a beautiful, poignant moment. How lucky she was. So young, so befriended.

"I wish *I* was eighteen again," I said. "How old are you, Arielle?"

"Eighteen."

We continued on, in nervous chatter. The only English-speaking "bloke" Arielle had gone out with had called her a "Pollyanna" and a "goodie-two-shoes". "What does that mean?" she asked. It meant, I told her, that she was an optimist, and a fine dancer. She seemed pleased. "He also say I have face like walrus." Which end of the walrus? I wondered. I looked at her drooping incisors. "Walruses are cute," I said. "Where are we going now?" she asked.

On the way to my apartment, which was on the way to hers, I saw a familiar dark shape gliding up the opposite sidewalk. My pulse quickened. I suggested we cross the street. Arielle said something in opposition and I looked at her with bewilderment and despair. I can't go alone, I thought, you *must* go with me. I grabbed her hand, and pretending to be drunker than I was, pulled her across the street, a jaunty song on my lips. Arielle, good sport that she is, laughed all the way. But before we got to the other curb I knew it wasn't my dark lady; it was a mirage born of loneliness, desire, red wine. I closed my eyes. I reopened them and saw the same raven image, this time on the other side of the street, approaching like a promise, like a genie out of a bottle.

"*Regard, c'est Milena,*" said Arielle. "*Salut Milena!*"

Milena, looking splendidly ruffled, had the straight-ahead gaze of someone who wanted no diversions, of someone too bound up in her own or the world's problems to know or care what she looked like. She was a paradox incarnate, at least to me: her tall angular form made you think of a model, but the more you looked the more you saw a kind of anger in her body and a depth in her gaze that models rarely have; her expression somehow blended anxiety with boredom, wired energy with world-weariness, sensuality with coldness. *Milena,* said Arielle, rhyming it with *arcana.* It was the first time I'd heard her name; it's been a basso continuo since.

With dark ill-omened eyes she smiled at Arielle and then at me, but didn't speak and didn't stop. I turned and gazed as she floated by. And then casually asked in a clear castrato who she was.

"She's a friend—she and my sister are friends. A bit bizarre, but really nice."

"What nationality is she?"

"I think she's Indian. East Indian. Or part. Why?"

Indian! Shakuntala. The Dark Lady. "No reason, I . . . I've seen her somewhere before. You'll have to introduce me."

A block from Arielle's apartment, where we parted as a concession to a jealous boyfriend, Arielle smiled her thousand-watt smile and told me she had a wonderful evening. "I had a wonderful evening too," I said, hugging her tight. "We'll have to do it again some time."

When I arrived back home, Milena's basement light was on.

FOUR

Like water in a marsh, my mind will not leave her.
—Shakuntala

The entire spring went by and summer came, and I never saw that light on again. Yet not a day went by that I didn't think of her, didn't watch for her from my balcony, didn't tremble with the feeling that she was someone I'd been waiting my entire life for.

I'd almost given up hope when something happened that seemed to put my life into another orbit: my landlord died. I don't mean to be flippant here—Wolodko Golash was a good man, I liked him a lot. I liked the way he doted on his wife, the way he listened, cared, after all those years. I liked the way they joined hands the moment they stepped outside, comrades in arms, allied against the world.

Twice Wolodko invited me in for a drink (cherry brandy followed by an obscure beer called Champlain, served warm), and while we drank he told fascinating tales that were intended, I gathered, as exemplars of spiritual living. They all ended parabolically: "You pray to God, you believe to God, he help you. I believe to God, he help me. You nice to people, dey nice to you—you make r-rough to people, dey make r-rough to you." In the Ukraine, Wolodko was drafted into the Polish army, fought on the front lines ("I never shoot no one because I don't know them") and was captured by the Germans. He spent two years in a POW camp and nearly died of starvation. When the war ended he worked on a farm in Lower Saxony, and then on another in Lincolnshire ("English vedy polite peoples, just like you, Jeremy . . . You believe to God, you pray to God, he help you"). When Wolodko arrived in Canada, God helped him get a job at Woolworth's, where he toiled invisibly, glad to have a job, cleaning, grubbing, stocking, standing it, for thirty-seven years.

On the night of our last conversation, as I lay in bed, I reflected on the things Wolodko had said, on his absurdly hard life and my easy one. I couldn't get to sleep. The next day I heard the wail of a siren, getting frighteningly louder and louder. When it stopped, the ambulance's swirling lights made wild patterns on my walls and ceiling. I closed my eyes, feeling sad in every way, knowing who they'd come for, expecting it somehow.

ⓞ

I looked at the digital 7:45 AM that glowed green in the semi-darkness. Maybe it's really PM, I thought. Yes, it's got to be PM. This is just an evening nap. I hit the off button, closed my eyes, and rolled over to go back to sleep. But my conscience would have none of this: it knew it was AM, knew that today was the day of my landlord's funeral and that I ought to attend. I didn't really argue. I felt sad for Wolodko's utterly dependent wife and I was convinced, moreover, that my destiny was at stake—their birthplace, I was certain, appeared on the Page.

I hit the snooze bar twice before getting up, ears ringing, at 8:05. The funeral service began at the ungodly hour of nine. I splashed water into my eyes, shoved a towel into my face, stumbled over to my bedroom closet. Opening the door I got a nasty surprise, almost like a bucket of ice water: a cascade of magazines, one by one in rapid succession, fell from the top shelf, hitting me first on the head and then in the face as I looked up to see what had hit me. What had hit me was the top half of a complete set of *Hustlers* from 1992-95, along with a few scattered polaroids tucked between their pages. They belonged to the former tenants, who I expected would return at any moment to retrieve them. It was only for this reason that I decided to keep them.

What does one wear to a funeral? I pulled out a white dress shirt that was unusual in that it had both fresh packager's folds in the cuffs and year-old streaks of grime. I put it on. A jacket and liquid paper would cover everything. I rooted around for a black tie and pulled out one I'd never seen before, one that may have been worn for a year around someone's waist. The phone rang. I picked it up and put my ear against a dial tone. I slammed the receiver down. I wrapped the tie round my neck, grabbed my black coat and liquid paper, and abseiled down the stairs.

It was that preternatural time before a storm, when daylight dims, when wind and rain impend—nature holding its breath. Normally one of my favourite times. As I reclimbed the stairs to get my umbrella I realised my keys were inside. Frustrated, annoyed, I slammed my hand against the door pane and the glass cracked. I stood there, examining the fault line, unable to believe what I had just done. What had made me strike the glass so hard? Sleep deprivation? My bombsite of an apartment? My vein-openingly lovelorn life? I pressed against the pane with both hands, harder and harder till it gave way, then screamed out obscenities as my right wrist grazed a jagged edge. I reached through the splintered glass with my left arm, unlatched the door, and scrambled up the stairs for something to stanch the flow of blood. It was only a trickle but I was sure I was going to pass out.

Should I go back to bed? Call an ambulance? If I go to the funeral they'll bury us both. I wrapped a whitish sock round my wrist and secured it with a rubber band that snapped in my hands. In a rage I put on another and flew down the steps and out the door, slamming it behind me, causing more glass to fall.

It was now even darker, a reminder that I had again forgotten my umbrella. Fuck it, it's not important. Yes it is, I'm not giving in. I counted back from ten and reascended the stairs. The telephone was ringing, but dead when I answered it. I redescended the stairs, umbrella in hand, and slammed the door for the third time. My Polish and Italian neighbours were now out on their balconies, perhaps wondering whether to dial 911. One of them, temple-tapping, shouted out something as I ran by.

The rain came down, not straight down but in diagonal sheets and sidelong gusts. My umbrella was soon inside out. On the Boulevard I walked backwards, tacking against the wind, searching for the yellow beacon of a cab. Nothing. As I cursed I saw her, on the other side of the street, in the entrance of a restaurant. Her. She was talking on the telephone but looking at me. I walked towards her.

"Where have you been?" I said, knowing she would only see my lips moving. "I've been looking for you for centuries."

Milena pointed to herself with a questioning look, said something into the receiver, covered it with her palm. Through the open door, into the rain, she cried, "If you're talking to me, I can't hear you!"

Gasping for breath, my heart out of its groove, I bleated out something with no recognisable words.

"Come out of the rain," she said.

I folded the umbrella, a flowered "woman's" umbrella whose ribs were broken, and stepped inside the door. What am I doing? This is not like me. I don't even know her. Milena, wearing a man's raincoat and bemused expression, waited for me to state my business. I nervously tried to straighten my hair (which forms waves after rain), cleared my throat, and uttered more gibberish.

"I beg your pardon?"

"M-my name's Jeremy you live beside me you know Arielle your name's Milena and you're an Indian." An auctioneer could not have said this faster.

A puzzled smile creased Milena's face. "I'm not sure . . . I'm not sure if caught all that. I do know Arielle. I'm not an Indian. And . . . what was the rest?"

"Your name's Milena and you live beside me."

"It is and I don't. Did Arielle give you this information? What happened to your wrist?" She asked these questions casually, with the same half-smile and an accent I couldn't place.

Blood was seeping through my sock-bandage. "It's just . . . a stupid accident." I held up my wrist and adjusted the elastic band.

"They say it's best to cut vertically on the wrist, not horizontally," said Milena. "And preferably in a hot bath."

I smiled but couldn't think of a rejoinder. I am not good at the art of repartee, never was and never will be. No, not quite true: once, as a child, according to Gerard, I made a retort that was astonishingly quick and deep, an unforgettable quip that arose from a flash of understanding tantamount to the insight of genius; unfortunately, he couldn't remember what it was. I looked down at the puddle I was making on the floor and then up at the telephone. "Oh, sorry . . . I forgot you're on the phone—"

"Don't worry about it. It's only my sister—and she's talking to someone else. So where you going all dressed up on a Saturday morning?"

I thought of Saturday "mourning" and tried to resist saying it. When I'm nervous, puns come to me unbidden (polysemania it's called). I also stammer. "No, I'm g-going to a funeral. So I g-guess it's Saturday *mourning*. M-o-*u*-r—"

"I'm sorry to hear that."

"Well, it's not someone . . . all that close." I looked up slowly, from the puddle to her face. She was examining my bandage with eyes that suggested oversleep or no sleep at all. On her cheek was a crescent-shaped scar. She caught me staring and I looked away.

"Well, m-maybe I'll see you some time," I blurted like a saxophone. "I mean if . . . maybe." There was another silence, interminable.

"I work here Monday, Tuesday and Wednesday night," she said finally.

"Well, maybe I can . . . we can . . . I'll come in and . . . maybe if sometime."

Milena smiled as a roll of thunder came down between us. "Do you want my umbrella?" she asked, loudly, nodding towards a black portable beside the phone.

"No, I'm fine, this is fine, thanks." I unfurled my skeleton umbrella and plunged back into the storm, hoping to conjure a quick cab. Perfect timing. Taxi approaching. I whistled smartly and closed the umbrella as the cab shot past me. Another one, as luck would have it, was close behind. The driver didn't see me right away but sharked to a halt when he did, skidding through the puddle I was standing in. I stepped back cravenly, but not before a wave of water curved up from the tires and drenched me from the crotch down. I was flabbergasted. I could not believe that this had actually happened, that life could be so slapstick, especially at a moment like this. What's next? A pie in the face from the driver? But maybe Milena hadn't noticed. I turned to look. She was talking into the phone and smiling. "Shaking with laughter" is perhaps more apt. I jumped in the cab and waved gleefully through the rear window, as if I'd planned the whole sequence for her amusement. And for that of her sister.

ↀ

The church was in the lower east end, in a dismal blue-collar/welfare zone hurting from plant close-downs and government cutbacks. I felt vaguely uneasy there, imagining single mothers and defaulting fathers and reflexively angry offspring, all of whom would feel much better if they could just punch me in the face. The Church of St. Nicholas, a Ukrainian Catholic church built in the 1950s, stood unhelpfully in the middle of all this, an isolated fortress.

In what was now a light drizzle I stood fidgeting outside its main portals. No one was yet inside the church and only a handful of people, all old, outside. In small clusters of umbrellas they chatted quietly. No one so much as glanced at me. From windows across the street draperies moved and heads appeared, in anticipation of another death parade. Their own would pass by soon enough, I reflected, and mine too.

After affecting interest in the arabesques of the church facade, I spotted my landlady forcing her frame out of a black limo, in widow's weeds and a veil that only partially concealed her ruddy complexion, puffy eyes and tears. I was moved by the sight, and yet I couldn't get a quote from Jimi Hendrix out of my head: "Mourning's self-sympathy—the person who's dead ain't cryin."

Lesya was escorted into the church, after which the others filed in slowly and silently. I entered last, with some trepidation: a lapsed Protestant and born-again pagan, I had never attended a Catholic service, let alone one of Byzantine rite. Was I expected to participate? I didn't like the look of the kneeling boards, so I chose a pew without them near the back. I was not feeling good about this. I did not like funeral services. The fuming censers, moreover, were making me nauseous, my wrist was soggy, my pants soaked, and my bottle of liquid paper had leached into the lining of my coat pocket.

I looked around at the sparse turnout. I was probably the only non-nonagenarian. What would happen to this place when all the old Ukrainians died? As the priest spoke in another tongue I drifted off into Milenaland. I had not been exactly dashing. More like a ninth-grade nerd with a crush. But wait—what did she say? *I work here Monday, Tuesday and Wednesday.* Yes, she did say that, didn't she? What an amazing thing to say! Very encouraging. Very forward! *Do you want my umbrella?* God. There's a double meaning in that . . .

Some incomprehensible yodelling began, with echoes here and there from the congregation. We stood up and sat down, sat down and stood up. It went on far too long. I eventually remained seated and closed my eyes. Images of my mother's funeral flowed like lava through my mind and I tried to stop them, tried to think of something that would stop them. I gazed up at the stained glass but couldn't escape my mother's softly focusing eyes and dark drooping hair.

"*Who do you love most in the world?*" she would ask, leaning over me, before I fell asleep.

"*You, mother.*" I would reach out to touch her hair like polished ebony, which glistened and shone all around me, and she would smile a rueful smile. She knew I was lying. If only I'd loved her more!

"*And what will you be, Jeremy, when you're grown?*"

"*I'll be a gypsy knife-grinder and a trainer of race horses and we'll live together forever, just you and me and Uncle Gerard . . .* "

People were rising again as I looked up at the stained glass, to a panel of white and red roses. I closed my eyes and saw the shimmering rose window of York Minster, its image dissolving into the parade of the cock and the fox, the monkey's funeral and monkey doctors . . . Eve appeared, in the Great East Window, with engorged breasts and erect nipples . . . Images shuffled like cards in a deck until thoughts of my mother flared up even brighter, like flames. I tried to run from them, tried to find someone to run to.

"*You're the smartest man in the world,*" I said to Gerard in the cathedral, as it pelted rain outside.

"*Now let's not be hasty, son. I wouldn't go quite that far.*"

"*Are you the second smartest?*"

"*I shouldn't think so—though I am pretty high on the list.*"

"*Who's the smartest person in the world?*"

"*Well, that's a bit of a tall order, that one, can't answer that one I'm afraid.*"

"*But if you're so high on the list . . .* "

"*Right, I see your point. Hang on. Do you mean living?*"

"*Right.*"

"*Your mother. For choosing me as her dearest friend, and yours . . .* "

The sound of people stirring drew me from this lost realm. A queue was forming in front of the black-draped catafalque, now ringed by blazing candles. As the line slowly encircled it, each person, in turn, kissed the closed coffin. Reluctantly I got up to join them and was last to place my lips on the cold, shiny wood. As I did so, I wondered whether you were supposed to go that far, to actually put your lips on the wood. I returned, quickly and self-consciously, to my forlorn pew at the back. All Ukrainian eyes were now upon me.

Outside, cars and limousines, wipers in motion, waited. I caught Lesya's eye and walked over to condole and say goodbye, but before I could utter a syllable she grabbed my arm with her black-gloved hand, vice-like, and unleashed a torrent of Ukrainian, forgetting in her grief what language I spoke. She stared at my puzzled face, waiting for an answer, then began again in Neo-Esperanto: "OK, mount you now, vous . . . " She pointed to the sky and then to the limousines.

The burial plot, I gathered, was on top of the mountain. "Yes, all right," I sighed. I walked towards a cortege of long black limos and hesitated, not knowing which one to get in. A spidery man who looked like Vincent Price appeared from nowhere, motioned me to follow and then opened a door of a car at the end of the line that was only slightly bigger than a fridge. Vincent had the faintest of smiles, but didn't look at me. I wedged myself in beside a vast woman with a mink hat and moustachioed scowl who remained silent the entire ride, even after crushing me on sharp turns.

The burial grounds were right out of Poe. Though not yet noon, darkness had descended, and the rain had turned to an opaque mist, blurring the summit of the mountain. We parked, tilted in a ditch. After a chain reaction of car doors shutting and umbrellas opening, I walked towards the plot.

More requiescat chanting followed, after which the coffin was lowered into a puddle. Each of us, in turn, tossed ashes into the soggy grave. When my turn came, the last before the widow's, I was ankle-deep in mud.

ɔȣ

Back at the church I again tried to say goodbye, and again Lesya took my hand, squeezing it white. The rims of her eyes were raw and her mouth twitched, as if struggling against more tears. She seemed on the verge of saying something but no words came out; when I tried to console her, she covered my English with Ukrainian. I nodded, pretending to understand, as she slowly guided me towards a sand-coloured building beside the church. *Centre communautaire ukrainien*, said its sign, not quite concealing the English underneath.

Arm in arm we entered, walking down the aisle like bride and groom, towards long, cloth-covered trestles crammed with food. Too much food, too many chairs: someone had grossly miscalculated. My instinct was to flee, but as I hadn't yet eaten, and as I spotted a young Ukrainian woman serving the feast, I sat when told to sit. Lesya continued on, to the head table, to her place beside the priest.

No one joined me at my table and no one spoke to me, except Daira, the serving girl. With her encouragement I ate like a swine and drank, unaided, two carafes of wine. I was growing sadder and sadder—*vin triste*—as I watched the grieving widow beside the priest. What was going through her head as she ate and drank and gazed upon her black-garbed guests?

ఞ

Sprawled out on my bed that evening, watching the ceiling move, I sensed that something inside me had changed. I had scarcely known Wolodko, and yet his death gave birth to a morbid obsession. When I looked at people that day—and the days after—I could see the corpses waiting within. My own corpse too, in every mirror. My dead mother, though I had far from forgotten her, now appeared in bursts of light, most hours of most days. Superstitions had played only a minor part in my life—my adult life that is—but now they guided my existence. I touched wood whenever I thought about death or heard the word or its cognates; I picked up pennies off the ground; I made wishes with thistledown; I felt compelled to kick certain cans, cigarette packs, sticks or stones—if I didn't a gnawing feeling would force me back, sometimes hundreds of yards, to kick what had to be kicked, pick up what had to be picked up; I slept only on my right side, as I did in York (to face the Minster and Gerard); I had flashes of foreboding and flickerings of supernatural insight. Something was going to happen. Something terrible, or wonderful, was going to happen.

And the Page—how it now assumed oracular importance! There was a time, especially in North York, when I'd tried to fit the Page into my life, jam it in like a door-wedge, but after moving to Montreal I let the door close behind me. I had grown up after all; I was not a mystic, no longer a child. But after meeting Milena, and leaving Wolodko, the Page regained its power, its hundreds of words and numberless images reverberating inside me like a gong.

FIVE

Dishevelled locks, drops of sweat on her tired face,
slender drooping arms . . . lips so pale and unadorned.

—*Shakuntala*

I *work Monday, Tuesday and Wednesday.* Yes. I would go
back to the restaurant, back to redeem that miserable
performance, that inglorious exit of mine. I would go, but
fortified with alcohol. I would go, so as not to seem hard
up, on Wednesday.

I went to see Milena on Monday, arriving minutes before
her shift. She was sitting on a barstool, reading, and didn't
look up from her book. I stood skittishly behind her, armpits
afire, trying to remember the two openings I'd rehearsed on
the way. When I accidentally cleared my throat, she turned
round, smiled, closed the book. "Hi, how's it going?" she
said.

"Fine," I improvised. "How are you?"

"Not bad." Silence. "Why'd you stop the other day? I've
been puzzling over that. Who are you anyway?"

That was one of my lines. "I'm . . . my name's Jeremy
Davenant, I just moved into the neighbourhood, I've seen
you around a lot . . . and I've never seen anyone like you."
I winced, knowing this didn't sound very good.

"How was the funeral?"

"Fine."

"How's your wrist?"

57

"Fine."

She nodded, while unwinding the plastic strip of her cigarette pack. "So where'd you move to?"

How could she not remember me that fateful day? "Rue Valjoie."

Milena quickly dislodged a cigarette and put it in her mouth. She ripped out a match but didn't strike it.

"In fact," I continued, "I'm pretty sure you saw me the day I moved in."

"I don't think so . . . "

"I was on my balcony. You looked up, I smiled at you."

Milena shrugged her shoulders, lit her cigarette. "Want one?"

I shook my head. "I also saw you a few days ago, on the street, when Arielle said hello to you."

"Arielle? Oh yeah, I think I remember. Like a drink?"

"You also sat beside me at *Sweetie*," I persisted.

"You're kidding. Would you like a drink?"

I asked for a draft, which she reached over the counter to get. How could she not remember me? How could she not remember the elementary particles ricocheting between us?

"An anagram of 'there we sat' is 'sweetheart'," I said, perhaps a bit too fast. This was another of my rehearsed lines.

"I beg your pardon?" said Milena, turning her eyes from the beer pulls.

"An anagram of 'there we sat' is 'sweetheart'. We *sat* together at *Sweetie*."

Milena looked at me blankly.

"So how long have you been waitressing?" I asked.

"I'm not a waitress." She set a pint of nut-brown ale before me.

"Well, I mean, how long have you been doing . . . whatever you do?"

"I work in the kitchen. Not long." She looked me in the eye; I looked away.

"Do you do anything . . . besides that?" I asked.

"No, it's my sole activity in life."

"What I mean is, are you a student or . . . "

"No. I used to be a painter."

"A painter? Really? Cool. What kind? Post-deconstructionist? Techno-cyber?"

"House. How do you know Arielle?"

A fiftysomething blonde with dark roots and tweezed eyebrows here interrupted us, asking Milena to make some Greek dish.

"I've got to go," said Milena.

"So do I."

She looked at my untouched glass. "OK."

I stood there wobbly-legged, like a puppy orphan, gazing into her eyes. Take me home, take me home.

"Was there anything else?" she asked.

"No not really. No. Well yes actually. Would you like to see the Virginia Wolves on Saturday?"

"No thanks."

"Oh."

"We could do something else though."

"When?"

"Saturday. Drop by before Wednesday and we'll set it up."

"I'll drop by on Wednesday."

Milena was already halfway to the kitchen. I watched the indentation in her cushioned barstool return slowly to normal, gulped down my beer and left a tip that could have bought two more. On my way out I glanced at the book she was reading: *Valentine*, it was called, by George Sand.

ಆಃ

I went back to the restaurant on Tuesday. The woman with blonde on black, when pressed, informed me that Milena wasn't working that day.

I went back to the restaurant on Wednesday. The woman with blonde on black shook her head as I entered.

I didn't see Milena on Thursday either, but I did see a friend of hers who lived nearby, a slingshot away, diagonally across the street. I was at the top of the stairs with my (predecessors') garbage when he appeared in the pre-dawn like some chirping bird, whistling and humming as he watered his plants in a cherry-red jogging suit. As I dropped my green bag onto the sidewalk he shouted something I couldn't make out.

I was on my way up the stairs when he said something else. He crossed the street, picked up the bag and carried it over to me. "I don't want to be a fussy Freddy, a pernickety Nicky, but garbage day's tomorrow. You're the N.K.B., am I right?" He laughed, as if he'd made a joke of some kind.

"The what?"

"The new kid on the block. How's the apt?"

"Don't ask."

"A fixer-upper?"

"A handyman's dream."

"Need some help? I used to be a plumber."

"No thanks, I'm . . . finished."

"You're up early."

"I'm going to bed."

He walked over to the stairs and raised his hand towards me. "Victor's the name." He held on to me as I told him mine, sliding our handshake into a soul clasp. His hand was as soft and moist as the salad inside my garbage bag.

"What do you do for a living, Jeremy? Sorry if I'm being nosy—my mother's nosy and it's very possible I got it from her. You might be interested to know her name, her maiden name. In fact, you might like to guess." He was still holding my hand.

"Well . . . "

"Parker. Do you see why that's interesting?"

"Yes."

"Nosy Parker. That's her and that's me. I'm always asking people what they do for a living. It's none of my business."

"I teach."

Victor let go of my hand but stood there nodding, looking me in the eye for an embarrassingly long time. "Those who can, do. Those who can't, teach. That's what Mother used to say. You may have heard it before. No offence intended." He winked at me.

"None taken. I was just thinking you left out the last line."

"I did? What's the last line?"

"Those who can't teach, teach university."

Victor screwed up his face, as though in pain. "Good one." We stood there looking at each other. His ears were like violins. His hair had the colour and texture of a denuded corn cob. On his chin was the pale suspicion of a goatee. Was it my turn to ask what he did for a living?

"What do you do for a living, Victor?"

"I work underground. For *Barbed-Wire*."

Barbed-Wire, a weekly street paper with a low news-to-ads ratio, could only winkingly be described as "underground". I waited for him to tell me what he did there. Perhaps he delivered them.

"I ply," he added, "the penman's trade. You may have seen my column."

"Your column? What's your last name?"

"Toddley."

My mouth dropped, I think. Victor Toddley was famous—
he was the city's Sensitive Male, a writer of Ann Landers
columns for the New Millennium Man, one of those cheer-
leader columnists who not only love writing but are forlornly
bad at it.

"Are you familiar with my body of work?" he asked.

"Yes. Very impressive."

"Yes, so I'm told." He laughed again. "So where do you
teach?"

I nodded towards the mountain. Victor winked. "I go to
a university myself. Guess which one."

"Which one?"

"U. of L."

"U. of L.?"

"University of Life."

"Right."

"So what do you teach?"

"Shakespeare, mostly. In translation . . . "

"The Bard!"

" . . . and in film. I just bluff my way—"

"The Bard! Zounds! Forsooth. I'm impressed. How'd you
end up choosing the Bard? I'm mean in this age of cyber-
space and everything."

"Fate, I guess."

Victor looked at me as if he wanted to hug me. "Say something from Shakespeare. Say something Elizabethan.
Something fitting."

*Methink'st thou art a general offence and every man should
beat thee.* "Well, there's a lot . . . maybe some other time."
With my garbage bag I quickly ascended the remaining stairs.
"I really have to get some sleep. Nice meeting you."

"The ironic thing," said Victor, climbing up after me, "is
that I'm working on some literature myself. I record my

dreams. Date them, fill in the gaps with my imagination. It's a book of dreams, a noctuary in your parlance—Graham Greene had one."

I looked at Victor's earnest, sweating face and for an instant softened. I'm sure he's a nice guy; I'm sure he's got a heart as big as a house. He's a dork but he's still part of life's rich pageant. "And you think the public will be interested in your dreams?" I asked.

"Promise not to steal this? I recount all my dreams in second person, present tense. Second person. You know, like you you you. You are doing this and you are doing that—"

"Right."

"*Second* person. *Present* tense. It's an advertising technique. Want to take a look? It covers all the bases—tragical, comical, tragico-comical, you name it." Victor was now trembling with excitement, like a chihuahua. "There's this one hilarious sequence, for example . . . "

I tried, I really did, to follow the run of the scenario but almost instantly foundered. Poodle balloons were involved. When he exploded into laughter, so did I. "That's very funny," I agreed.

"You may wonder how I got the idea in the first place."

Not at all.

"Well, it's a long story . . . "

It was. At the end of it he grabbed my hand, pumping it like a well handle. I wiped my hand on my shirt, he went off jogging, I to bed.

೮ನ

I know. This all sounds a bit one-sided, doesn't it—a dimension or two short, vicious caricature even. Maybe it is, a little. But not much. Toddley's forty going on fourteen, he's the indestructible cartoon radio that can never be turned off.

He's the type that talks loud with his Walkman on, that claps his hands when his plane lands. He's the guy in high school who wore an ironed crease down his jeans and because of this had his head held down a toilet bowl while his hair was scrubbed with a wire brush. That I was murderously jealous of him (on which more later) is beside the point.

ᛗ

On Friday I walked up and down the Boulevard, one eye on the lookout for dark dishevelled women, the other on my reflection in store and car windows. Eventually, I realised what an idiot I was and became resigned and realistic. If Milena wants to keep our Saturday *rendez-vous*, she knows where to find me. If, that is, I happen to be in. There's a lot of fish in the sea. I'm certainly not going to hang around waiting for someone I don't even know.

Having some class preparation to do for the fall, I decided to stay in all day Saturday. I set up shop in the bathroom, from whose window a certain basement apartment could be seen. Around three o'clock my buzzer gave me yet another coronary jolt. I cursed. Since the sardine episode, it had taken on the sound of a leper-bell; I had no intention of answering it again. But wait, what if it's Milena? I went out to the balcony and looked down. It was not Milena; it was a man with white gloves and a pane of glass. A glazier. I descended and instructed him to do what had to be done and to charge me, not my landlady. As he pulled out bits of broken glass lodged in the frame, I walked back up and into the bathroom. Urrrgh! said my buzzer. I went out on the balcony again. My landlady, wearing a black frock and a perm wig that may have been a size too small, was waving her arms at me, up and down, back and forth, like a crazed conductor. I ran down the stairs.

After some unguessable charades (was I getting shit for breaking the window?) and gibberish involving the word "TV", I said "I don't understand." Lesya frowned at my stupidity and motioned me to follow. I followed.

At Lesya's you got the red-carpet treatment: the phrase is exact. Her runners and carpet remnants were fire-engine red, the same colour as her plastic brocade draperies and table-cloth. The walls were mainly pink. Religious icons infested every room, as did doilies, antimacassars, Woolworth trinkets and ailing sepia photographs from the Ukraine—including a fetching one of her on horseback. On one wall was a row of mostly upside-down books bookended by stacks of 78s, and on another, above a vintage radio and Russian sewing machine, was a faded and fold-marked map of the Ukraine.

Lesya pointed to the blank screen of her colour TV, a lo-fi Westinghouse console with portals. When confronted with dysfunctional televisions, I always say "It must be the flyback transistor." Before I could get these words out, Lesya got down on her hands and knees and began crawling along the floor. What's going on? Has she misjudged my age? Am I expected to hop on? After some straining and grunting, she found the television cord and plugged it in.

After it warmed to life, the force of the sound practically threw me against the wall. This, evidently, was the problem. I showed her how the volume bar worked. She slid it back and forth and smiled. I then showed her how the on-off switch worked, wagging a disapproving finger at the electric outlet below. As she smiled again, I felt a tightening in my throat. The television was obviously her husband's domain. She said, "Tank you, Cheremy, tank you." I looked away, towards the television screen, and stared sadly at it for almost a minute before realising that the colours were off: the faces were livid pink and lime. Toddley colours. I showed her how to adjust the hue. When she saw the changing colours, she started to giggle. Lesya's favourite show (I learned later) was now in progress: General Hospital. She was not to be disturbed between three and four, which is why she was now ushering me out. At the door, she handed me two lumps wrapped in aluminum foil. "Perogui," she explained. I thanked her and she pointed at a rip in my black jeans. "I do?" she asked, making sewing motions with her hands. "Uh, well no thanks." She pointed at a missing button on my shirt. "I do?" "No . . . well, OK thanks, I'll bring it to you . . . soon." I put my hand on her shoulder and kissed her on the cheek. She smiled like a bashful schoolgirl. I smiled too, feeling sad in unnameable ways. I will try to help you, I said to myself.

○3

Late Saturday, past midnight, my buzzer sounded again—but this time with a sweet, promising tone. Milena! It had to be Milena! I looked down from the balcony but saw only darkness. I flew down the steps—after making adjustments to my hair in the hall mirror—and opened the door. Two shadowy figures were standing on the landing, or rather swaying, arm in arm. One was honey-haired Arielle. The other, taller, head resting on Arielle's shoulder, had short dark hair. Her boyfriend? To say they'd had a few is to recklessly understate.

"*Salut, Jérémie,*" said Arielle, "*j'ai une surprise pour toi.*"

"Yes, this is quite a surprise," I said lukewarmly, "but you see I can't really . . . receive you guys right now. I'm expecting someone any minute—"

"*Un rendez-vous galant?*"

"No not really, well in a way, yes."

"Anyone I know?"

66

"No no, I don't think so. I mean you *may* know her . . . she's a bit late . . . "

Arielle laughed. Her companion's head slowly righted itself. My heart began to thud. The head belonged not to a boyfriend but to a girlfriend, and she did not have short hair; she was wearing a dark bandanna, which Arielle may have rigged. "Come on in," I said in a canine frequency. Even drunk, Milena was sending out those rays, those lethal rays.

"No, we can't come in," said Arielle. "We were just walking by. I just wanted to present you two. Do you want to go for drink?"

"Come on in," I repeated.

We walked up the stairs, I behind Milena, Milena's behind before me. As we reached the half-landing she almost fell over backwards, but with some awkwardness I managed to steady her, leaving my hands on her hips perhaps longer than was strictly necessary. It was the first time I'd felt her body beneath my hands. Arielle guided Milena into the living room, where she leaned against my grandfather clock, her head lolling to one side. A spasmodic grin appeared on her face as she watched the movement of the pendulum. She then mumbled something about "profiteers and pirates," and might have pursued the theme had she not keeled over and passed out on the couch.

"So, can I loosen you two up with a drink?" I asked.

"I'd love to," said Arielle, "but if that's the good hour I can't rest. I told to Ramon I am coming home one hour ago. He's going to be steamed. Milena, we gotta go now—"

"Hold on," I said, as she headed towards the poisoned Sleeping Beauty. "Maybe we shouldn't disturb . . . I mean is she . . . How did you . . . end up here?"

Arielle yawned. "I am walking in the face of Dame de Piques and see Milena and her sister who look like they've had a few drink. So they like wave the hand and direct me to come and join themselves, right? So we like yack for a bit and blah blah blah and then her sister she go to the toilet and she doesn't come back, isn't it? Me I'm thinking she left with some guy—Milena call him King Leer—who was fixing her all night long, I mean staring her all night long, I think he is musician or something. Anyway, Milena ask to her I mean ask to me about this guy she meet in the rain that knows me and which she can't remember the name of, and so we talk about you. And she is supposed to meet you, she thinks. She keep bringing you up so I say 'Let's go.' Except she can't really see by that time. Anyway, here we are. Didn't you ask me to present you? Aren't you tinkled pink to see us?"

Arielle, her eyes sparkling, was alight with triumph. I felt like taking her in my arms. "*Tickled pink*," I said. "And *introduce*, not 'present'. And yes, I'm happy to see you. Very happy." I turned towards Milena. I was trembling slightly and trying to conceal it. "Are you sure she's OK? She's not done anything else or . . . "

"Just wine. '*Red red wine, stay close to me-e . . .* '"

"Right. Does Milena live next door? Arielle, does Milena live next door?"

"'*Don't let me be alone . . .* ' No, a friend of hers used to live next door. His name is Denny. Maybe she will tell you about him some time."

A *friend?* "A boyfriend?" I asked.

"Milena?" said Arielle, who didn't appear to hear this important question.

"Is Denny her boyfriend?" I repeated.

Arielle shook Milena gently by the shoulders. "Me-lay-na. Me-lay-na. I don't think she want to move. Maybe you can like, call a cab when she will wake up. I'm not sure where she is living—not far, near to the park. Or we could maybe like try to carry her to my place. Except that Ramon will be sleepy sleeping . . . ”

Ramon, I took it, was Arielle's boyfriend. “Is Ramon Hispanic by any chance?”

“*I was lo-ost . . .* ’”

I repeated the question.

“You're telling me,” she replied.

“Does he like fish?”

“*‘Now I'm fo-ound . . .* ’ What? Yeah, I guess he like fish.”

“Is he tall and thin?”

“No. Why?”

“No reason. Listen, I don't think it would be a good idea, necessarily, to . . . to move Milena. At this point in time. I mean right now and everything. At this juncture. We should probably . . . I mean she's in no . . . and anyway, Ramon would definitely wake up and probably get mad and . . . stuff.”

“*C'est ça,*” said Arielle, nodding. She then broke into helpless laughter, I don't know why. “OK,” she said finally. “Call a cab later. I have to go now. I have to hoist the blue peter.”

“I'm sorry?”

“The blue peter. I have to hoist it.”

“You have to go.”

“Exactly. I phone you tomorrow, OK? Be good, *hein?*”

I walked a singing Arielle to the door, my arm round her shoulder. When she reached the bottom of the stairs, I yelled down after her. “Wait. Arielle!”

“*Oui?*”

“Thanks . . . thanks for the . . . you know, introduction. I'll see that Milena gets home all right, I really will. You're the finest person in the Western hemisphere.”

Arielle laughed as she stumbled out the door. I darted back to Milena and fell to my knees, not knowing quite what to do. So I simply watched her sleep. Except for the blue bandanna, and a brooch with what looked liked a miniature assegai running through it, she was dressed approximately the way she was in the métro that fateful day: faded black jodhpurs laced at the leg with knotted shoestring (now ripped at the knee), brown round-toed boots, ruffled T-shirt, wrinkled vest. The unmade-bed look. She had minute flecks of what appeared to be red paint on her eyelashes and forehead, a beauty mark on her cheek, a small vertical scar on her wrist (a suicide attempt?), and the smell of wine, tobacco, sweat. On her slender brown arms were what looked like track marks, needle marks. *I have seen you before*, I said to myself.

"Milena, Milena," I whispered. Her name resonated inside me like a mantra. "Milena." She stirred. "Would you like a coffee?" She opened her eyes. "Can I get you anything?" She shook her head. "Would you like to go home?" She closed her eyes. "Would you like to sleep?" Silence. With my heart bounding spasmodically I took her in my arms; instinctively, like a trusting child, she wrapped her arms round my neck. I was dizzy, weak-kneed, intoxicated by her proximity as I carried her to my bedroom and laid her down gently on my bed. If she had come in from a storm, I thought to myself, and if this were a movie, I would undress her and clothe her in my pyjama top, looking away as I did so. But there was no storm, nor shelter sought, it was not a movie and I had no pyjamas.

I spent the night on the sofa—that much was like a movie. For hours I was kept awake by Milena's radiating presence, her troubling nearness. I could sense, then and there, that we were separated, not only by the gulf of drunkenness and sleep, and distant beds, but by something more fundamental, something I couldn't yet understand. To reach the centre of her, I felt I would have to survive endless trials, make my way

amidst yawning crevasses, along the brink of erupting volca-
noes, through flames and impenetrable darkness. *I have seen
you before*, I whispered again as time whirled backward
through my brain.

∞

When I was twelve and a bit, a family from Dublin—a single
mother and two, maybe three children—moved into a block
of flats nearby, and then left two, maybe three months later.
One of the children was a dark-haired girl almost exactly
my age (one day my junior) who was difficult to talk to
because she was so pretty and clever and confident. One day,
from our kitchen window, my mother and I saw her sitting
on the pavement out front, head bent, possibly crying. My
mother said, "I wonder if she's all right—be an angel and
see." "I'm sure she's all right," I said nervously. "She looks
better now, really, and anyway I wouldn't know what to say."
"Go on dear, there's a good boy." I went out and skirted
round her without saying anything, while looking back from
time to time at the kitchen window. As I was about to ask
her if she was all right, she wiped her tears with the hem of
her dress, and in a micro-second flash I saw the white of her
knickers. She said that her dog had yanked his leash from her
hand and run away. She pointed to our neighbour's yard. He
had wriggled under the fence, she explained, and when she
tried to climb over it, some old lady (Miss Adams-Vaughan,
our next-door neighbour but one) screamed at her. Now,
normally I was afraid of Miss Atom Bomb too, but not on
this day. Without a moment's hesitation I went off to capture
the mutt and, by extension, its owner.

When I returned—with muddy shoes and trouser cuffs—
and handed her the leash, she kissed the grinning, gyrating
dog on the snout, over and over. She then kissed me, leaving

71

a patch of dog saliva on my cheek. She was very grateful, being "scared half to death" that Crab was going to get hit by an automobile. I didn't see how this was possible from my neighbour's backyard, but agreed that it could have happened. I was about to shuffle off when she asked me, in her soothing Irish lilt, if I wanted to come and see her the next evening. She was babysitting her younger sister, or sisters. Why not pop round? I desperately wanted to see her again but said, "I don't know." She told me where she lived. "I know," I said.

The following evening, as I was sitting at the dinner table with butterflies that stole my appetite, Ralph, in fine form, advised me that I was not to leave the table until my plate was clean. I didn't answer. "You're mooning," said Ralph. "You don't have a pick of notice these days."

"He's not feeling well," my mother interjected. "Are you, dear."

"I just want a bit of fresh air," I mumbled.

"I *want* doesn't mean I *get*," said Ralph, in his false baritone. Mother excused me and Ralph assured me that everything would be waiting for his lordship when he returned. Thank you, that's very kind.

I hopped on my bicycle and rode in all directions, trying to pluck up courage, before tapping—softly, apologetically— on Bernadette's front door. I had already turned to leave when the door opened and beautiful Bernadette, in a deep-blue nightgown, her hair a stormy sea of dark waves, stood smiling before me. I could barely speak as I stepped into her private world.

Mercifully her little sister soon appeared, a welcome distraction. She was clutching one end of a piece of rope while Crab, with his teeth, clutched the other. Eyeing me sideways, Crab held fast, his huge tail thrashing the air.

"You get back into bed, Violet, right this instant!" said Bernadette.

"No. I don't want to. Who's he? Mother said no visitors."

"I'm going to count to ten."

"I'M GOING TO COUNT TO TEN."

"I'm serious."

"I'M SERIOUS."

"Oh please don't start that infernal game again. You're not being in the least clever."

"OH PLEASE DON'T START THAT FERNAL GAME AGAIN. YOU'RE NOT BEING IN THE LEAST CLEVER."

"I didn't say 'fernal'."

"I DIDN'T SAY 'FERNAL'."

Crab let go of the rope. "Woof woof woof ruff ruff ruff . . . "

"Crab, stop it!"

"CRAB, STOP IT!"

"Violet is the sauciest girl in the world."

"VIOLET IS THE SAUCI . . . BERNIE IS THE SAUCIEST GIRL IN THE WORLD."

"You're a . . . you're a monstrous brat."

"YOU'RE A . . . YOU'RE A MONSTER BRAT."

"I didn't say 'monster'."

"I DIDN'T SAY 'MONSTER'."

"Woof woof woof ruff ruff ruff . . . "

"Crab, shut up!"

"CRAB, SHUT UP!"

The rest of the conversation was held in Violet's bedroom, out of earshot (except for Crab's remarks). When Bernadette came back—with a prancing dog at her flank—she for some reason asked me when my birthday was. I told her, and she seemed pleased. On the kitchen table we played a game of draughts, followed by noughts and crosses, even though I hated both games. When Bernadette asked if I enjoyed them, I said "Oh yes." She said she couldn't bear them, but didn't know what else to suggest. I said I couldn't bear them either and we both started to laugh. She asked me if I had ever had a drink—"you know". I said that I had drunk champagne, "many times". Bernadette went to get a bottle with no label on it and poured out two glasses of a yellowish liquid. It was homemade wine, I think—but warm, as if it had been out in the sun all day. After two glasses, which we drank as if in a race, Bernadette suggested we play a card game—poker, to be exact.

"What's that?" I asked.

"Well, it's a game I used to play in Dublin with my two cousins. I don't have a real set of cards so we'll have to manage with these."

She dealt some strange cards and talked about the Major and Minor Arcana and the four suits of swords, wands, cups and pentacles. Whoever got the Lovers card or the Hanged Man under certain circumstances had to take their clothes off—or something like that. It turned out to be too complicated to explain, or perhaps I was too nervous or tipsy to concentrate, so she said she'd just take off her clothes if I'd do the same. I nodded, my heart rate rocketing. I glanced at her deep-blue nightgown with pink carnations, wondering what was underneath.

"I'll roll it up seven times but that's as far as I'm going," she said. With a look of intense concentration, she made a fold in her nightgown of about an inch. She looked at me before repeating the procedure, rolling up the hem like a window shade, counting aloud to seven. She then let the hem drop, smoothing it back down with her hands.

"But I didn't see anything," I said tremulously. "Go to ten."

"I'll go to eight."

"At least nine."

"I'll go to eight."

When Bernadette reached seven, after again meticulously measuring each fold, she paused and looked up at me with a faintly embarrassed smile. "Last one." She made a fold of a fraction of an inch, said "eight," and then let the hem fall.

"Hold on," I said, "that's not exactly fair, that last one was just a puny one. Do it properly. Do one more!"

"I'll do one more, but remember you're next."

I gave her a vague nod.

"Are you afraid?"

How could anyone of my age, of my sex, admit to fear? "Not in the least."

"You promise to go after me?"

"I give you my word as a gentleman."

"All right then, I'll go to nine."

This time there was resignation in her voice. She threw her head back and looked at the ceiling as she counted quickly to nine, making large, uneven folds. She continued folding, without counting, up past her budding breasts. She then quickly rolled it back down.

"Now it's your turn," she said, her face flushed.

"All right, but I must first go the loo." My face was flushed too.

"Last door but one—on the left."

In the bathroom I rearranged my unpractised genitals and then looked into the mirror, wondering how I was going to get out of this one. What did she expect me to do? I splashed cold water on my face and flushed the unused toilet. On my way back I kicked Violet's door. She appeared seconds later.

"You go to bed this instant!" said Bernadette.

"Someone knocked on my door."

"You're a liar!"

"No, *you* are!"

"I am not, you are!"

"No I'm not!"

"Yes you are."

"No I'm not."

"Yes you are."

"No I'm not."

"Oh, please Viol!"

"OH, PLEASE VIOL!"

"Go to bed this instant!"

"GO TO BED THIS INSTANT!"

"Woof woof woof . . . "

And so on. Violet, after uttering a few words she shouldn't have known, stomped back to bed.

"She's got a wicked tongue on her all right," said Bernadette, as Violet slammed her door. She sat down, her legs sprawled over the arms of a chair, and looked me over. The diversion I had set up clearly hadn't worked, for she immediately asked me to uphold my end of the bargain, so to speak. "Don't be a coward, Jeremy," she giggled.

"I am *not* a coward." But of course I was. I stood there, mute, feeling awkward and silly.

Bernadette was now drinking from the wine bottle's neck. "Come on, then. I don't have all day." Before I knew what was happening she had jumped out of her chair, dropped to her knees before me, and was pulling down the zipper of my trousers. "Wait, I don't know if . . . " I was trembling with excitement, with . . . I didn't know what. Blood rushed from my brain to my loins as her hand grazed my erect boyhood. I immediately came in my pants.

A fumble of apologies later, I meekly crept downstairs, this time tiptoeing past Violet's door and noiselessly opening and closing the bathroom door. "Congratulations," I whispered to the mirror, "you're now a member of the club. You finally know what it feels like to fornicate."

Bernadette was listening to King Crimson's "21st Century Schizoid Man" on a portable record player when I returned, which we listened to over and over while she rubbed Crab's belly. It was Crab's favourite song, she explained. She started to dance alone and then said "Oh shit." With exaggerated grimaces Bernadette pointed out the window, then grabbed my hand and ran with me to the door. "Hope to see you again soon, Jeremy. Maybe tomorrow, or the day after." She kissed me on the lips and pushed me out the door. But tomorrow never came, nor the day after, and a week later she was gone.

∞

I drifted into sleep, into a night of tormented, sheet-twisting dreams, the last of which ended with the sound of a flushing toilet. The bathroom door opened and someone stood beside it.

"Bernadette?" I whispered. "Is that you?"

"Did you say something?" the ghost replied.

I opened my eyes. "No. I think I was . . . How are you?"

"What am I doing here?" said Milena.

"Arielle brought you here."

"Oh." Milena stared off into space. "Why did Arielle bring me here?

"Well, I think that . . . I don't really know."

"We were . . . at Dame de Piques, right? I was supposed to see you on Saturday or something, wasn't I? What day is today? I think I fucked up." There was a slight lilt to her voice, and "fucked" almost rhymed with "looked".

"You didn't fook up. You're here now."

"Oh God, I must have been really drunk. I'm sorry. Things are not . . . going well. I don't drink. Often."

"No problem."

"And I even took your bed."

"It's OK, really."

"You can have it back. I should go. What time is it?"

"I don't know. Early. Hold on, I'll check." I took my pocket watch out of my jeans, which were doing the splits on the rug. "It's only nine . . . seventy-five."

"I feel like shit."

"Do you want breakfast?"

"I don't eat breakfast."

"Do you want to go back to sleep?"

"No."

"Do you want me to take you home?"

"I'm not six years old," she answered, and it was like an elastic band snapping in my face.

"Do you want some coffee?" I asked.

"Yes."

"Okay, I'll get dressed and make some."

I remained in bed, waiting for Milena to leave the room, but as she lingered I had no choice but to display the rippling interplay of muscles in my upper and lower abdomen. She went quickly into the bathroom, where I could hear her kneeling before porcelain. I dressed and waited for the prayer to end. The door finally opened and wan Milena walked back to the bedroom.

"Are you all right?" I called out from the living room.

A muffled, subaqueous groan rose from the blankets.

"The sight of me in boxers trigger that?" I shouted.

"Mm."

I glanced inside the bathroom and then bedroom, where Milena was sprawled out on the bed, face-down, the sheet pulled over her head. "Are you OK?" I said.

She turned over, pulled the sheet off her face, looked at me through a mass of hair. "Oh, God, I don't think I flushed." She pronounced "flushed" as in "pushed".

"Don't worry about it. You want me to make some coffee? Or do you want to go somewhere? Or do you want to go back to sleep?"

"Do you have any cigarettes?"

"No."

"Let's go somewhere."

In the bathroom I flushed the toilet and sprayed out half a can of Lysol. I urinated (on the sides of the bowl so as not to be heard), took a whore's bath with mango-scented soap, carefully dishevelled my hair, put Murine (who chose this name?—it means rat-like) into my eyes, mouthwash with myrrh into my mouth, raspberry balm on my lips. My deodorant was in the bedroom so I applied Andron liberally to my armpits. And to the toilet bowl. As I walked out of the bathroom, Milena was about to enter. "I'll just wash my face," she said.

"No wait, I'll . . . get you a clean face cloth."

"Don't bother." She entered and shut the door. I could hear the sound of water hitting the sink, full blast, followed by the sound of breathing, of hyperventilating. As I stood there eavesdropping, wondering what to do, the door opened and hit me in the leg. Milena, oblivious, sleepwalked back into the bedroom. I finished dressing, primped in two mirrors, took two vitamin E, tiptoed back to the bedroom. Milena was on her back this time and seemingly sound asleep. Again, the sheet was stretched over her face like one of Magritte's lovers. I closed the door, and went out in search of cigarettes.

It was a Sunday morning in the world outside, as still and empty as a ghost town. The streets were rainwashed, images and colours Pre-Raphaelite in their vividness; flowery perfumes, as sweet as new love, emanated from the front garden. I had never felt the neighbourhood in this way, and never would again.

At a new French *charcuterie* I exchanged pleasantries with the owner, who was from Nancy. In another decade I had spent a weekend in Nancy but for some reason stretched these two days out to sound like years. I alluded to the River Meurthe, which I don't remember having seen. He looked at me as if he knew I was full of shit. After paying for six croissants, four styrofoamed coffees and seven lottery tickets, I walked two blocks to the *dépanneur*, the local inconvenience store.

It was inconvenient in that it had no fixed hours: its openings and closings depended on which drugs its owners were on, stimulants or sedatives. It was also hard to find things, as most of the goods were in the aisles, in their original boxes. Business, nevertheless, seemed to be booming, the major attractions being easy credit and contraband Mohawk tobacco and alcohol. Standing in line, looking at the columns of cigarettes, I realised I didn't know what brand to buy. Export A, Craven A, Matinée, Du Maurier . . . Was there an officially cool way of asking for the black-market material? A gesture? Wink, fold arms like Indian chief?

The door opened noisily to a man in a fawn-coloured fedora, fiftyish, who may have had vision problems because he didn't appear to see the long queue in front of him. He went directly to the counter and asked, or rather demanded, a "cartoon" of Lucky Strike. No, he had no money to pay for it. Yes, he was on the list. The owner consulted a beaten spiral notepad and then handed him a pack of Lucky Strike. "No no, a cartoon!" said the man as he scratched at an open sore on his mouth with a nicotine-stained forefinger. "I don't have all day," he added. The owner, calm and unhurried, gave him a carton and then looked at the next customer. "Hey! I'm not finish!" said the hatted man. "Matches! More. Come on!" He stomped out of the store with heels that clicked; we shall be hearing more from these shoes.

As I passed by Victor Toddley's house, where Victor was now lounging out front in swim trunks, I decided that a hairy back and a set of large tits was not a happy combination. Either item he could expose, if he liked. But not the two together. The value of the surrounding real estate was depressed enough.

"What ho, goodman neighbour!" he said, in a voice I hadn't heard before. "How now, sirrah!"

I looked blankly at him. A grin was tugging at the corners of his mouth. "That's Elizabethan," he said in an expulsion of air.

"Right."

"How goes it?"

"Great."

"That's the ticket." He rubbed his hands together in a pantomime of hunger, lifted the lid of a cardboard box and pulled out half a pizza, which drooped over his hand. Like hummingbirds, Victor ate twice his weight in food daily. "Want some? Veggie-pizza."

"No thanks, I . . . I'm just about to eat."

He held up a paper cup. "Diet slushpuppy?"

"No I . . . I've got someone waiting for me."

Victor winked. "Male or female? Hope I'm not being nosy again, I know it's none of my business. I don't care either way."

"Female."

Victor nodded. "Your significant other? Your main squeeze?"

81

"I wish."

Victor laughed. "Ever taken a ride on the marriage-go-round, Jeremy? I know it's none of my business . . . "

"I've no wife. Not yet."

My landlady, of good peasant stock, was out working the fields, bent over in her front garden, her beige fortrel rump a giant mushroom in a wild garden of weeds, Jack-and-the-Beanstalk vines and six-foot flowerless plants. She smiled broadly at me as I greeted her, on my way up the stairs, with a confident *"Dobry den!"* I also said something like "Take care" or "Don't work too hard," and she said "Same time to you." Even if you said "Happy Birthday" or "Nice dress," Lesya would say "Same time to you." She pointed towards something in the sky: a satellite dish on a rooftop (I think). "Trouble," she confided in hushed tones. "Dey make trouble." For Lesya the world comprised two types of people: those who cause trouble and those who don't, the vast majority being the former. "Trouble. Dey make trouble," she repeated. The "r" was trilled.

Upstairs, a shock awaited me: Milena was no longer in my bed. "Milena? Are you still here?" No answer. "Milena?" I made a cursory run of all the rooms. She had vanished. I went to the bedroom for a final check, and even lifted up the sheets. Desolate, inconsolable, I sat slumped on the edge of the bed. "Figures. I knew it, I knew this would happen. The bitch!"

"Did you say something?" said Milena, as she walked in from the balcony.

"No, I mean yes, I thought you'd . . . I was just talking aloud, I mean thinking aloud, humming aloud actually. I went out and got some coffee and then I . . . "

"Then you what?"

"Got some smokes."

"What time is it?"

"About ten thirty, I think." I checked my watch. "Yeah, around that." It was after eleven.

"I'm off. I start at half eleven." The vestigial accent—Irish?—resurfaced.

"Here." I handed her the paper bag, which she peered into.

"Kanawuckie Strikes. A carton? I don't know if I have enough to pay for all these. Do you smoke?"

"Well . . . not really. I'm mean I've smoked cigarettes before. But you can have them all. They were dirt cheap."

"Don't be stupid. I'll pay for them. Got any matches?"

"Yeah, I'll get you some. I didn't know what brand to buy!" I shouted from the kitchen. "I hope those are all right."

"Perfect. I'll give you some money—"

"It's okay, don't worry about it."

Milena walked into the kitchen, hand in back pocket, and dug out some crumpled bills. "Don't be stupid," she said. "Take this, I'll owe you the rest."

"No, really, it's all right—"

"Take it and shut up."

I took it. Milena smiled wanly as I handed her a book of matches. "You're too nice," she said, "nicer than I deserve. What's that god-awful stench in the bathroom?"

"Stench? Oh, that. I might've spilled some . . . aftershave."

Milena looked at my unsevered bristles. "Can we go out on the balcony?"

On rickety office furniture, foul remnants of the forest people, we looked out on the resplendent morning. Victor was no longer there to blot the landscape. I quickly ate four croissants and smoked, inexpertly, two Lucky Strikes; Milena had zero and three, respectively. She was not in a talkative mood and her head was bowed most of the time, which I first attributed to shyness and then to malnutrition and the wrath of grapes.

"Are those yours?" she asked wearily.

I followed her gaze to the lottery tickets I'd placed beneath her coffee cup. "Yeah, I bought us some tickets. You never know."

"I *hate* lottery tickets. I think it's stupid for people to spend their whole fucking lives depending on chance, I hate anything to do with gambling, with what it does to people. The hardest hit are the poor—everybody knows that. And minority groups and women and teenagers."

Milena's change of tone, of countenance, were the equivalent of a scratch across the face. I took a few seconds to recover, and to reflect on what she'd said. How can you *hate* lottery tickets? I was in the middle of a probing question when Milena cut me off. "I need a patch," she said.

"Pardon?"

She placed her long delicate fingers on the frayed knee of her jodhpurs (and bare skin). "A patch."

"It's not ripped in the name of fashion?"

"Hell no, it's annoying. It's cold in winter. And it hurts when you kneel down."

"You don't sew?"

Milena frowned.

"I can do it for you," I said.

"You can sew?"

"Yeah, and I've got just the right material for a patch. Give them to me."

"You mean take them off?"

"Yes."

"No."

"I'll get you some jogging pants."

"No."

I went to get Milena some jogging pants. She rolled her eyes when I handed them to her but, to my astonishment, began to undress. She remained seated and didn't bother with the jogging pants, except to casually drape them over her lap. I gulped. And then ran, with staglike swiftness, back into the bedroom, where I cut a large square from a black denim shirt. It was old anyway. I told Milena I was going to use my land-lady's sewing machine, be back in a jiff.

Lesya smiled when she saw the ripped knee, and without a word laid down her gardening tools. I followed her inside to her czarist sewing machine, which was already threaded with black thread (funeral repairs?). Sitting on a yellow pages, humming softly, she looked up from time to time as I bobbed up and down nervously, as if I had to pee. In minutes she had expertly sewed on the patch. I kissed her on the cheek and she said, "Tea Cheremy?" "Uh, no, some other time . . . " "OK?" she asked, pointing at my bandaged wrist. "Yes, I'm fine, it's nothing." I took out a bill from my wallet and she wagged her finger at me while shaking her head. So I asked her out to dinner. She shook her head again. "No restau-rant, no like." She motioned me to follow her into the kitchen, where she put her finger on a wall calendar with a picture of tulips. I examined the square on the calendar. "Tuesday?" I said, "we have a date this Tuesday?" She shook her head again, as if playing twenty questions. "It's your birthday on Tuesday?" Lesya frowned at my denseness and dragged her finger down the column. "We eat together every Tuesday? Is that what you mean?" Lesya nodded. "Here?" I asked. Lesya nodded again. "It would be a pleasure, Lesya, I'd be delighted, I'll . . . bring the wine or . . . whatever you drink. Vodka, I guess. Vodka?" Lesya started to laugh. "Thanks again, Lesya, you're a real sweetheart." "Same time to you," she replied. I kissed her on both cheeks then bounded back to Milena like a dog bringing back a stick.

Milena looked impressed. Now can we get married? I was thinking as I watched her examine her new knee. "Now can we get married?" I said.

Milena looked up at me, woodenly. "Got any more matches?" She stepped into her jodhpurs while I lackadaisically lit up two more Lucky Strikes, straining to appear calm. She zipped up her fly and then gulped down her third cup of coffee as I held onto the railing with my head down, feeling dizzy from tobacco and the sight of Milena's bare thighs, from the rogue strands of dark pubic hair escaping from her white panties. I squeezed my eyes shut. A sound from below: in the garden something was moving, possibly an animal. Lesya. I turned to look at the basement apartment next door, whose jalousies were now shut. Would it be indiscreet to ask about its occupant? Probably.

"Who's Denny?" I asked.

Milena abruptly raised her head, her face clouding dramatically. I looked into her deep dark eyes, her two mourning eyes. I was obviously trespassing. She looked away and set down her styrofoam cup, which fell over on its side.

"How do you know about Denny?" she said softly, watching the empty cup trace an arc on the table.

"Arielle said that he lives next door and that he's a friend of yours."

"What else did she say?"

"Nothing."

She tapped her cigarette, looked down into the garden. "I don't really feel like going into it now. Maybe some other time. I should go."

"So when's 'some other time'?" I asked, following her to the door.

"Oh I don't know. Should there be one? Sure you're up to it?"

"Yes."

"Okay, I hope you won't regret it. What day's good for you?"

"I'm free to the end of the millennium."

A smile flitted across Milena's lips as she pulled out a pen from her bag. "Mr. Popularity. What's your phone number?" She wrote down my number in a large book, possibly a diary (at least she appeared to write it down), and then scribbled on the matchbook I had given her. "Here," she said, tossing it to me.

I examined her slanting, swirling digits. "Are you busy after work, Milena?"

"Yeah, I'm uh, seeing my sister . . . and I have to pick up a prescription." Two excuses, Milena was perhaps unaware, are always less credible than one. "I'll phone you. I will, really. Thanks again. I hope next time we'll meet under more . . . auspicious circumstances."

"Is this a zero?" I asked.

With an indecipherable smile Milena nodded, and then leaned over to air-kiss me on both cheeks. She had a long, elegant neck and grace in every movement. A dark swan queen. She glided down the cascade of stairs and slammed the door shut.

Dazed, motionless, I remained briefly on the half-landing before racing to the balcony, where I watched Milena get smaller and smaller, like a toy figure, a matchstick figure, too small to be real. She didn't turn around. I looked in the other direction, down towards Denny. The jalousies were now open.

☙

That evening I began a diary, in the last half of my Book of

Saturdays. Eleven words (the writing is illegible): *I love Milena. I love Milena. I cannot live without her.* As I was writing, everything became clear to me: I had crossed the threshold of another world; meeting Milena was the beginning of my life or the end.

Six

I had rather be a toad, and live upon the vapour of a dungeon
Than keep a corner in the thing I love for others' uses.
                                              —*Othello*

T he police came the next day—not to my house but to
  Denny's basement apartment next door. From my
balcony I watched them ring and ring and then go around to
rap on the side window. No one answered. What was going
on? Should I phone Milena? From my left breast pocket I
drew the matchbook she gave me, then dialled her scrawled
numbers.

No answer, even after twenty rings. I dialled another
number, Arielle's, for more information on Denny. When she
instantly put me on hold, I laid down the receiver and went
to the bathroom, where I spotted something Milena had left
behind: a half-empty bottle of pills called Zoloft.

I picked up the phone and waited. A loud grating sound—
my buzzer—made me jump a foot. Milena! It had to be
Milena! I raced into the bathroom to adjust my hair, bolted
out the door, and with the dexterity of a stuntman placed my
nose against the bottom landing after rolling down the stairs.
I bounced up, unhurt, tried to regain my cool. I pulled the
window curtain to one side. A hand, pressed against the glass,
made me jump another foot—the hungry Hispanic, returning
with another red knife! The hand on the pane dropped.

It belonged not to the Hispanic but to Jacques de Vauvenargues-Fezensac, who used to be my best friend. The aristocratic surname is typical of him (he had it legally changed from Dion). I should probably describe him now, and get it over with.

It was at my first faculty meeting that Jacques made his grand entrance into my life. He sauntered in late with a lord-of-the-manor air, sat down beside me without looking at me, spoke with eloquence on every subject on the agenda, carved up everyone with wit and style in both official languages and then invited me, before the meeting ended, to go for a drink. Why he singled me out for this honour, why I was judged worthy of his acquaintance, is more than I can say—normally Jacques' mind worked like a bouncer, limiting entry, checking credentials, throwing people out. His invitation may have had something to do with the alcohol I could smell on his breath, or perhaps with my having a British passport, with our being near-compatriots. For despite his name, Jacques de Vauvenargues-Fezensac was as British as they come: his mother was from Upminster, his education from Winchester and King's College (Cambridge), and his voice and manner from some degenerate earl.

In addition to being alcoholically inclined, Jacques had an immune deficiency problem—or so, later, a co-worker informed me. Jacques and I were becoming close, inseparable even, and I was devastated by the news. But when I awkwardly tried to commiserate, after much beating about the bush, Jacques laughed, saying it was all vicious invention, spread by a colleague named Haxby. "I trashed the dear professor's translation of a Ducharme play in *Barbed-Wire*," Jacques explained, "so he gave me a fatal disease in return. Plus Haxby thinks I'm gay—the ultimate transgression."

Was Jacques gay? I know now, but didn't then. Then I thought of him as rather sexless, maybe because he once described himself as a "bisexual with asexual proclivities." He did, however, like to delve into the sex lives of others (mine in particular) and he did own a substantial collection of photographed Near Eastern depravities. Be that as it may, there was another rumour making the rounds, a murky marks-for-sex scandal involving Jacques and one of his students. It may have had some truth to it because Jacques quickly fell foul of Dr. Crépin, our former director, who sacked him.

Even after his dismissal (especially after, it seemed) Jacques spent like a sultan, more than he could possibly have earned writing theatre reviews for the alternative presses. In his greatcoats and neckwear and high boots, all made of what he called "noble" materials, he was the demonic dandy of the boulevards. Some found this look pretentious, the pose of an artist, but I thought it rather suited him. Jacques was an aesthete, a servant of beauty, a brilliant failure incapable of creating anything himself but good at judging a decor or setting a tone . . .

"About fucking time," he said as I opened the door. "Next time leave a deck of cards. I'll play solitaire on the steps."

"What do you want?"

Jacques walked in without answering and looked up, into the gloom, towards the top of the stairway. "How do you propose we get up there, Davenant—with crampons and a rope?" He made his ascent and entered the bathroom. I waited.

The toilet gurgled and the door opened. "This flat," said Jacques, looking around, "is perfectly foul." He grimaced, as if he stood in a sty. "Your bathroom, if that's the word for it, smells like a Turkish cathouse. Your phone's off the hook. And turn on some lights—what are you, a bat?"

I turned on some lights. And then recounted, in round numbers, the events of the previous night and morning. Jacques closed his eyes, shook his head. "What a risibly squalid life you lead, Davenant. There were, I trust, countervailing rewards? A new mattress partner, perhaps?"

"Fuck off. Do you know what Zoloft is?"

"An antidepressant. Why?"

"No reason."

He nodded towards my bandaged wrist. "Toying with suicide, are we? Zoloft didn't help?" He looked back at my face. "Or did you try to end things by setting your nose on fire?"

"No, the sun . . . my wrist I—"

"Hang up the phone."

I hung up the phone.

"So what does this new little friend of yours, this Milena creature, look like? Another of your wild raven-haired gypsies? Really, Jeremy, your Dark Lady fantasy is a bit—"

"She is dark, as a matter of fact. She's East Indian."

"Excellent—like the real Dark Lady, Lucy Negro, Elizabethan England's most celebrated whore."

I sighed. "Yeah, and you're Shakespeare's 'fair young man', Southampton, the narcissistic nobleman who buggered young boys."

"I'm flattered by the comparison. So continue. What does this East Asian Dark Lady look like? Mahatma Gandhi?"

"Tall, slender, pirate queen style, raggedy hair."

Jacques nodded. "Mad-lady hair, you mean. I know who you're talking about."

"No you don't. She's a woman of dusky beauty—of unparagoned beauty. A black diamond."

Jacques' eyes rolled. "So opposites attract? She has a sister, right? A wing nut, pop tart? Bit of a local porn star?"

"Her sister's a porn star? I think you've got the wrong one. What do you mean by 'pop tart'?"

"A groupie."

"No idea, never met her."

Jacques scratched at his underarm. "Milena. Right. Ex-junkie, big beak. Mad bitch with tropical armpits, tall as a Zulu, am I right?"

"Why do you say she's mad?"

"So you admit she's a bitch—"

"I do not admit—"

"She's mad in both senses of the word: she's a paranoid Marxist who's angry on a full-time basis, who walks around waiting to be offended."

"I think you've got the wrong—"

"A warrior diesel dyke, a feminist separatist. Wasn't she the one who tried to burn down Cinéma La Chatte? Not that that's a bad idea . . . "

"Next thing you know she'll be demanding the vote."

Jacques paused to look at me. "Jeremy, does that sort of thing pass for wit back in Yorkshire?"

"I don't know anything about her politics—or her for that matter. We haven't talked about anything. The only thing I ever saw her reading was a book by Sand."

"George Sand? Which book? The one in which she recommends champagne before a golden shower?"

"Jacques, why does every topic degenerate—"

"And naturally it was love at first sight, am I right?"

"There's something about her. Something she just . . . emanates, I don't know. She's unique."

"All women are the same."

"Don't be an idiot."

93

"You'll never get anywhere with her. She wears a suit of armour."

"How would you know? Maybe there's a chink."

"Not for men."

"You'd like her—she's very smart, very nice, very natural. I like that; I like girls who use fewer beauty products than I do."

"Call her a 'girl' and she'll have your nuts in a jam jar. Just remember this: if they don't love you first—and most—forget it."

"Oh please. How do you know her anyway?"

"I don't know her . . . that well. But I do know you're not her type."

"Oh really? And what, pray tell—"

"If you're not underdogging it, Jeremy, Third-Worlding it, you're just not in the running. If you're not in some minority—"

"I *am* in a minority. You, frog boy, are in the m-majority, remember?"

"Your stammer, I admit, might work to your advantage."

"F-fuck off."

"If you're not black or lesbian or insurrectionary . . . "

I plugged my ears, like a child. I didn't want to hear any of this. Jacques is a jackass. Milena is perfect in every way. Our union was preordained. I'll join another minority if necessary, a better minority, I'll join the Canadian Marxist Party, I'll dole out soup in Mozambique. Why is Jacques so venomous? Has he been spurned? Is he jealous? Does he want me for himself? Is that the phone ringing?

"Don't answer it," said Jacques.

I walked over to the telephone. "Why wouldn't I answer it?"

"Because it's interrupting an edifying conversation and because you have an answering fucking machine. What are you, Pavlov's dog, a bell rings and you—"

"Hello?"

"Jérémie? C'est moi, Arielle."

"Arielle! It's *wonderful* to hear from you."

"Oh, well . . . thanks, I . . . sorry to put you on hold. I was talking to *maman* in Trois-Pistoles. So Milena's all right, you got her home all right?"

"Yeah. I mean no. I mean she was in no real condition to . . . she sort of passed out. She stayed the night."

"She stay the night? She is still there?"

"No, she had to go to work." I glanced at Jacques, who was standing in front of my bookcase, scrutinising spines. "Who is she exactly?" I said to Arielle.

"What do you mean, who is she?"

"Is her sister a groupie?"

"No, well sort of, yeah, in a way. Why?"

"Would you say she's a mad bitch?"

"Her sister?"

"No, Milena."

"No I wouldn't. Jeremy, what are you . . . "

"Is she a warrior feminist?"

" . . . talking about? Yeah, she's a feminist, a Next Wave feminist. So what? You don't have anything against feminists, do you?"

"No. All intelligent women are feminists. You're a feminist, aren't you?"

"No, not really."

"Oh. Sorry. What's a Next Wave feminist?"

"Ask her."

"Is she a paranoid Marxist?" I was looking at Jacques as I quoted him. He was wearing his patented smirk.

95

"I don't . . . think so. Sounds like it didn't go too good between you two."

"No, really, it went fine. Things went . . . fine. I want to see her again. So tell me more about the guy next door, Denny."

"I don't know much about him. He's a friend who's . . .

"Her boyfriend?"

" . . . dead. He killed himself a few weeks ago."

"Oh, Jesus."

"She's taking it really hard. Vile say she's in a fog since a long time."

"Oh, God. Shit. That's so . . . sad. Who's Vile?"

"Her sister. Violet. The groupie, remember?"

"Was Denny Milena's boyfriend?"

"I don't know. I don't think so. Ask her."

"I will. By the way, thanks for the . . . you know, coming over last night, that was really . . . cool."

"Have you fallen for her, Jeremy?"

"Me? Well, I wouldn't say . . . I wouldn't necessarily go that . . . Yes, I have."

"Have you got her in the sights of your love gun?"

"Where'd you get that expression?"

"The Young and the Restless."

"You must never use it again."

"I've got another call."

I recradled the phone and turned to face Jacques. "It's *her*," he said, as if pointing to her from a witness stand. "I was right as usual. Surely you're not planning on—"

"A friend of hers, some guy named Denny, committed suicide next door."

"Denny? He was a friend of hers? Dennis Tyrell? I heard about that. In fact I knew the guy—he was a cash-man, carried wads of cash in his pocket, used to buy me drinks. I was the only one who could keep up with him. I also heard it wasn't suicide. I wouldn't go near her."

"Jacques, why are you so—"

"You've made the textbook error, Jeremy, of falling for someone you don't know. It's the sort of thing that should be killed off early, drowned like blind kittens. Take it from someone who knows."

"*You*? I can't imagine you falling for *anyone*. Apart from yourself, you don't like anybody for Christ's sake—"

"Oh, and you do. I'm sorry, I forgot I'm talking to one of the great lovers of mankind, one of the world's leading seraphs. Confess, Jeremy: all Yorkshiremen are meanspirited and uncharitable—"

"I'm sick of that fucking myth—"

"All descended from monastery robbers and horse thieves and sheep shaggers. I don't really know Milena that well, I admit, but I've learned to trust my initial impressions because they're never wrong. You're free to disregard them, of course. As Auchincloss once said, 'It can be great fun to have an affair with a bitch.'"

"Why exactly did you come here, may I ask?"

"To stain your porcelain. And offer you a titillating afternoon."

I said I did not feel like a titillating afternoon.

"We are going to play billiards. I am in need of cash."

I said I did not feel like playing billiards, or providing cash. "Especially to a flaming asshole like you, Dion."

Silence. Jacques, while raising an eyebrow, slowly turned to face me. "My name is no longer Dion. And I detect—correct me if I err—a note of animus creeping into your tone."

"You're a fuck of a detective."

"The better the advice, the worse it's wasted." Jacques headed for the door.

"Hold on," I sighed.

ℭℬ

In the pool hall, as in most other realms, Jacques belonged to a class more exalted than my own. Around the five straight-triple-vodka mark, maddeningly, Jacques would enter a phase of dexterity and precision that is granted to mortal humans seldom. And this despite driving the ball so hard—as if he were punishing it—that you thought it would either crumble into powder or sail across the room, as it sometimes did. Jacques had no "touch" shots in his arsenal, and didn't seem to need them. In his words he was a "Wizard with a Wand"—"as unstoppable as the tides." On this occasion, as on most, he lived up to his own mixed metaphor. With a clutch of pensioners watching (and cheering for the Wizard) he sank the last ball, an unneeded black, with a midcourse correction from his cue.

It's what happened after that matters most. I paid for three lost games and enough alcohol to fuel a Concorde while Jacques went to find a cab. He was sitting in the back seat waiting for me when I came out, his arm out the window, his fingers drumming ostentatiously on the roof. The air was dank with mist. I had barely opened the door when Jacques complained, as he was forever complaining, that I hadn't had enough to drink. "You are the temperance expert," he declared, "and that is your only area of expertise." While pulling on a stand-up air bass, he began to grunt along with the jazz on the radio, and I stuck my head out the window to ignore him. If I hadn't, I may not have seen a hand waving spastically from inside a passing cab. It was only when our cars stopped abreast at a red light that I recognised Victor's smiling face, a pink smudge of mirth. I waved back and said, "Jacques, look, it's your colleague at the *Wire*."

"Toddley? So it is. Life in the fat lane. Is that a female he's with? Perfect, a situation ripe with comic possibilities. Toddley! You studmuffin! Out painting the town beige? Where you off to? A bump-off under the mirror ball?"

Victor, with a lopsided grin, rolled down his window and uttered something that appeared to be in another language. The light changed and his taxi sped off.

"Toddley's French," said Jacques, "is about as good as my Apache." He tossed some bills onto my lap and then opened the door of our moving cab. "*Chauffeur, arretez!*" he commanded.

"*Mon sacrament,*" cursed the driver after Jacques almost slammed the door into the back seat. Through the rear window I watched my drunken friend weave his way through oncoming cars, taunting them, waving his jacket at them like a deranged matador.

At my destination, rue Valjoie, I spotted Victor closing the door of his cab as mine pulled in behind his. I almost asked the driver to keep moving. "Don't worry about the change," I whispered, not to be generous with Jacques' money but to make a quick getaway. I closed the door ever so gently and practically tiptoed across the street.

"Hey nonny nonny!" yelped Victor, as I lifted the latch of my gate. "Hey Shakespeare!"

I turned round with a mask of sunny surprise and looked at the person standing next to him. *Milena.* "How now, my liege?" said Victor, grinning like a butcher's dog. With an inane smile I wiggled my fingers then looked on in horror as they crossed the threshold of Toddley's bachelor pad. From my balcony I watched his fog-shrouded front door until dawn. I felt like Othello's younger brother. Toddley would have to go, there's no getting around it.

SEVEN

My unsteady mind runs back,
Like the silk of a banner carried into the wind.
—*Shakuntala*

I was singing a Lennon-McCartney song when my stepfather killed my mother. It was the spring of '79, my last year of high school, and Mother was two months pregnant. She was summarising a letter from a friend on a ferry headed for Ryde, on the Isle of Wight, and I was singing, from the back seat of the car, "*She's got a ticket to Ryde, she's got a ticket to Ra-ha-hide . . .* " I stopped singing when Father hit a Dodge van head-on. Almost head-on, that is—he swerved so that Mother got the brunt of it.

After days of numbness and denial, and then weeks of crying like a baby before going to sleep, I developed a dark theory that my mother's death was no accident, that it was all cleverly plotted by Ralph. One, their marriage was in tatters; two, Ralph didn't want children; three, my mum (like me) couldn't stand North York; four, she was still in love with Gerard (which Ralph must have known); five, a life insurance policy, probably with a double indemnity for death by van. I may have been watching too many movies.

Soon after the funeral and soon before I graduated from Sackerson Collegiate, Ralph asked me where I wanted to live. I told him York. The next day he presented me with an open ticket to Paris, my second choice. Travel abroad would "allay my grief and expand my horizons." We both knew this was crap. He knew I was on to him and wanted me out of the way. I was happy to go, mind you: Ralph and I had spent our North York years in a state of semi-disguised mutual aversion. And I'd never be able to prove my homicide theory anyway.

Gerard was away from York at this time, engaged in some of his vague business, so I decided to remain in Paris—at least until Gerard returned home. He would have wanted it that way, I reasoned, wanted me to learn French. Through a connection of his I found a small apartment—a garret, of course—in an 18th-century building on the rue de Bellechasse. The owner, a dotty viscountess, was prodigiously charming the first time we met; the second time she asked me to be out by the end of the month.

The month, fortunately for me, still had four weeks to run and before they ran someone came to rescue me. I was mounting my spiral staircase after classes one evening when I noticed someone sitting on the next-to-last landing. Before I could get a clear look the thirty-second light expired, plunging the stairwell into semi-darkness. At the landing I pushed the *bouton d'allumage* and went from shock to elation at the speed of light.

I rushed into Gerard's arms and then felt embarrassed for having done so. We stood on the landing, talking excitedly in light and dark, before he reminded me that we could talk more comfortably, and in continual light, inside. We resumed our conversation in the communal kitchen while Gerard prepared tea that had come all the way from China. As the kettle began to sing, Gerard headed for the communal toilet. "When I makes tea," he said in Dubliner tones, "I makes tea. And when I makes water I makes water."

In the kitchen he sat back down and winced as he put his leg up on a chair. "Knee," he explained. "Had to hit the old silk over Haute-Saône—damn thing wouldn't open." I looked at him and we both laughed. Gerard had a saturnine face, with heavy and sombre eyebrows, which a smile lit up like sun through clouds. Impeccably dressed in old-fashioned tweeds, he looked like some decommissioned captain of industry. I glanced at his patterned brown shoes, ancient but polished, which I had greatly admired as a child.

Gerard poured the tea. "I'll square things with the viscountess, lad, don't you worry about her. Awfully sorry, once again, to hear about the accident, your mother's accident. *O matre pulchra!* A rare jewel that woman, a real . . . thoroughbred. When I met her at the Theatre Royal, lad, everyone was in love with her, aye everyone . . . "

I opened the fridge door, pretending to look for something inside as my throat tightened. Gerard continued to talk, his voice cast low, but almost none of his words registered. If only it could all be turned back, I thought for the millionth time, if only our car had taken a different route! I had not loved her long enough!

" . . . *but let's not burden our remembrances with a heaviness that's gone,*" Gerard intoned as I pulled out some unnecessary jars, put them on the counter, and then put them back in again. "*Romeo and Juliet,*" he added. *The Tempest*, I thought but didn't say. When I finally turned to face him, after wiping my eyes, he was smiling and holding up a manila envelope with a red string tie. "Happy Birthday, lad."

I forced a smile. Gerard was always doing this sort of thing: in each of my seven years in North York, ostensibly for my birthday but at various times never near my birthday, I would receive a parcel plastered with British or French or

South African stamps. I quickly unwound the string, and pulled out a piece of parchment paper. It was in Latin.

"What's this?"

"Read it."

"*Senatus Universitatis admisit* . . . It has something to do with university . . . *cum omnibus juribus, honoribus et privilegiis* . . . A diploma of some kind. The University of North Shrewsbury? That's an obscure one."

"It's in South Africa."

"It's really nice." I wasn't exactly sure what was so impressive about it. Perhaps it was an antique. Gerard offered no clues—he just smiled with squinting eyes. "Who does it belong to?" I asked. "It's blank."

"Bang on. I knew you'd get it."

"Get what?"

"We'll fill in that bottom line soon enough, won't we lad?" He winked at me.

"We will? With your name?"

"Don't be daft lad, not mine. It's not for me. It's not my birthday. It's not my graduation."

"It's not my birthday or graduation either."

"Cottonwool in your brain-box, Jeremy? We put your name on it, date it, and you get that teaching post you've always dreamed of. Isn't that what you said in your last letter? Well here's a helping hand. You don't want to languish in a library, do you?"

"I must have been sixteen when I wrote that letter. And besides, I'm only in first year."

"Are you happy here? I thought you said you despised your professors."

"Just one of them."

"Your Latin teacher?"

"No, I like her."

"The Voltairian? The one's who's always attacking Shakespeare?"

I nodded.

"But apart from him you like it here?"

"I like it here, I just don't like all the junk theorists and obscurantists—Saussure, Lacan . . . they grow like weeds here in France. They've ruined the study of the arts."

Gerard laughed. "So who's forcing you to listen to them? Be a teacher, not a student."

"Be serious. I'd never get away with it. What about references and transcripts and . . . whatever else you need?"

"Leave the rest to me. I have, shall we say, a bit of pull at the university's registrar. You'd be surprised how many people have done this sort of thing before you. All academics falsify—or wildly exaggerate—their achievements. The fact is, universities simply don't check up on this sort of thing. Ask anyone."

"Who would I ask?"

"Take a shortcut, lad. I don't mean right now necessarily— get the undergrad stuff first. But for God's sake, don't go any further until you talk to me. Remember, you can easily read the books on your own. You're a bright enough lad, I've taught you well enough. All the Ph.D.s I've met are ignorami."

"What if they wrote to one of the . . . judges, or whatever they're called?"

"Referees. I'll be one of them. Give them my address in York. We'll choose another who's dead. And I already told you I've got connections in high places. But who's going to check anyway? If you were going to lie about your university, would you pick the University of North Shrewsbury?"

"But no one'll ever have heard of it."

"Precisely. No one's likely to trip you up with a 'Do you know Professor so and so?' or 'What college did you go to?'"

"And you think I could get a teaching post with a degree from North Shrewsbury?"

"They'll love it in America."

"I'll keep it as a souvenir, but I don't want my name on it. Thanks anyway."

"You know best. Let's to the Hallebardier, shall we?"

 C3

The Hallebardier was a bistro on rue des Fosses-St-Bernard, near the Sorbonne (it may still be); it had "mediaeval" beams and wainscoting and bogus halberds and battle-axes. Gerard claimed to have fought in the Resistance with the proprietor, and when we arrived they talked with ease about dishes from Gascony and the Auvergne. "There is no sincerer love than the love of food," declared Monsieur Du Bartas, in English, with a wink in my direction. I never know how to react to a wink.

We sat in silence for the first few minutes, as Gerard always maintained that one cannot talk and look at the menu at the same time. When the waiter came Gerard ordered the *tablier de sapeur* ("fireman's apron"), which Monsieur Du Bartas explained was tripe pounded into a flat sheet and fried; I ordered, or rather Gerard ordered for me, an air-dried meat called *brézi cervelas remoulade*. Of course I've forgotten all this. Gerard, who never forgot anything, described this meal in a letter to me. For no convincing reason.

"Bistro" comes from a Russian expression meaning "fast", an etymology evidently lost upon our hosts. While waiting, we drank a white Arbois, drawn unfiltered from a cask and served in heavy glass jugs (the *sommelier* knew without asking what Monsieur Gérard required). Just before our fourth, Gerard raised his glass and said: "The first is for thirst, the second for nourishment, the third for pleasure, and the fourth—the fourth, lad—is for madness."

As we touched glasses Gerard said, "Oh, I almost forgot." He set down his jug and rummaged through all his pockets before producing, from his mac, a folded piece of brown paper. On it was the phone number of a "comely lass" of my age I should get in touch with. She was the daughter, he explained, of a "dear friend" of his from Normandy, wink, wink. Her name was Sabrine.

The meal, when it finally arrived, was delicious but I hadn't much of an appetite. I was preoccupied.

"What about my thesis?" I asked suddenly. "Won't they ask to see it?"

"Remember the words of T.S. Eliot: 'Immature scholars imitate; mature scholars steal.' Go to the library, find some obscure thesis, file off the serial number, put yours on. They're all bum-fodder anyway."

This, I gathered, meant they best served as toilet paper. And I was almost sure Eliot had been misquoted. Wilfully. It was Gerard's conviction, I think, that epigrams improved on misquotation. Or misattribution.

"Sometimes, one simply has to lie or steal," Gerard continued, his mouth full of food. "There's nothing wrong with that. Remember, Galileo did it."

"Did what? Stole a thesis?" I waited for Gerard to swallow.

"He lied. He denied publicly that the earth moved round the sun."

"What the hell does that . . . "

"Disraeli as well . . . "

" . . . have to do with anything? And anyway, Galileo also said, right after, *E pur si muove!*"

"How about Shakespeare? He stole plots, incidents, ideas, entire sentences. Molière too. Thank God they hadn't a conscience like yours! Think of what the Bard lifted from Samuel Daniel or Sir Thomas North . . . "

"Oh come on, like borrowing a cup of sugar . . . And what was that about Disraeli—he also denied that the earth moved around the sun?"

"He was a perpetual plagiarist."

"Nonsense."

"And look what he went on to accomplish! Follow his lead, you can't go wrong. Look at Sterne—he stole his best stuff in *Tristam Shandy* and then denounced plagiarism in words stolen from Burton."

"I don't quite see—"

"All I'm saying is that of all the forms of theft, plagiarism is the least dangerous to society. That's not original, but never mind. Remember Emerson: 'A ship is a quotation from a forest.'"

"What the hell does that . . . It's just that if I stole a thesis I would be pretending to be someone I'm not."

"Precisely."

I smiled. "But Radulfus always stressed that you are who you are, that you shouldn't try to be someone else, otherwise you're an impostor and—"

"Ralph's a shit-can. We're all impostors. All actors and liars. Ralph Stilton included."

"I just don't think I could do it, that's all. End of subject."

EIGHT

One must obey one's teacher.

—*Shakuntala*

On the 6th of September, a decade or so later, I was sitting in a large cupboard euphemistically called my office, looking over my new schedule: two classes on Wednesday—one in the afternoon, one in the evening—with an M.A. tutorial sandwiched in between. That was it. It was the perfect schedule, the envy of the department, obtained not as a reward for merit or seniority but for extravagant proposals of marriage to Madame Plourde, the Director's sexagenarian secretary.

Junkmail littered my desk and mailbox: memos regarding (missed) faculty meetings, colleagues' book launchings (how I hated to see these); a thesis proposal (my tutorial student, a retro-hippy, was eager to compare "A Whiter Shade of Pale", "White Room", and "Knights in White Satin" with Shakespeare's *The Winter's Tale*); overdue assignments from the previous semester; and two letters. One was from Dr. Clyde Vincent Haxby, LLD (Oxon.), the star of our department, its sole international player, the one who was spreading rumours about Jacques and the only one on the hiring committee—so I was informed by Haxby himself—who opposed my nomination. He basically wanted information about my "doctoral thesis", the meddling bastard.

Accidently paperclipped to his note was an ice-blue airmail letter that bore the distinctive bite of Gerard's typewriter, whose periods made holes:

```
                Saint Aubin-sur-mer, France
My dear Jeremy,
    I didn't have your address with me,
so trust this letter finds you at the
university. It's simply to inform you
that I shall be arriving in New York
City on or around 15 October. Some
time thereafter I shall hire a car and
drive up through the Adirondacks (via
Saratoga) in order to visit you, if
that is convenient. You may reach me,
by telephone or post, at the American
Express office in Elmont, New York.
Audaces fortuna juvat.
    As always,your scoundrel of the
deepest dye,
    Gerard
```

Why so formal? If that is convenient? Is he kidding? Elmont. Which rhymes with Belmont. I phoned the American Express there and left a message.

"Oh, by the way," I said, "is there a big race in October?"

"At Belmont?"

"Yes, at Belmont."

"Hold on. Yes, the Breeders' Cup."

"And at Saratoga?"

"I wouldn't know."

I hung up and stared at the floor. I remembered Gerard telling me that the very first time he bet on a horse, at the age of four, he won—probably the worst thing that could have happened to him. For among his many subsequent losses (at least according to Ralph) were his family lands near Knaresborough.

"I strongly suspect," said Ralph, in one of his many lectures on the evils of gambling in general and of Gerard in particular, "that it was those very lands that made your mother get involved with that . . . bounder. She had you to think of, remember. Oh, they weren't all that much, I'll grant you that, but they'd have generated a fair living sure enough. Gascoigne was left with good prospects, make no mistake about that, but of course he had to throw everything away, didn't he. So let this be a lesson to you, Jeremy. The only way to make money from following horses is to walk behind them with a shovel and bucket."

My mother wouldn't confirm any of this, so I don't know if it's true or not. At the time, I refused to believe it and screamed at Ralph till I was hoarse. Why was I so upset? It was perhaps the thought that Gerard could have been my stepfather, that he had thrown not only his lands away but me too, that somehow he had done it on purpose, that he didn't really want me. Why didn't he think of *me*?

I looked at my pocket watch. My class had already begun. I sighed and dragged out my dog-eared lecture notes. Same old crap. I really should update them, or acknowledge my sources. I looked at the computer printout. Not bad, only 16 students. *Salle 222.* I shoved everything into my knapsack and ran out the door without locking it.

Salle 222, to my surprise, was an amphitheatre. With a stage, podium and microphone. At the door I paused to look through the meshed window, surveying my prisoners. Lots of them. The "16", evidently, should have read "61". Some faces were familiar, including Arielle's.

On stage I again looked out on my flock, this time with professorial hauteur. Inquisitive faces stared back at me. Two members of the audience—my tutorial student Galahad Rawdon and a smiling Arielle—were now heading towards me. With his shaggy locks and congenitally dark circles under his eyes, Gally looked like a cousin of the panda, or racoon. Or some gentle herbivore fond of marijuana leaves. Like pandas and racoons, Gally had no reason to be at a university. He asked me how I liked his proposal. I told him he had the green light. "You mean the white light," he quipped.

"What is this, Law 101?" I said to Arielle. "Who are all these people?"

"Must be your reputation."

"I'll get rid of most of them, wait and see. Are you taking this course?"

"*Je ne sais pas encore.* I am not inscribed yet. That's one of the reasons I am coming to talk now. Would you mind if I am taking it?"

"No, of course not. But are you sure you want to?"

"*Pas complètement.* I might have to leave before the class end so I give you this now." She handed me a piece of lined paper folded in half, sealed with scotch tape. "Don't open it now or you risk to lose your concentration." She smiled and headed back towards the stage steps.

"Oh, Arielle." I summoned her back with a jerk of the chin. "After I say the words '*neo-classical concerns for decorum and dignity,*' put up your hand and ask me what I mean by 'decorum'."

"*Quoi?*"

"When I say neo-classical concerns for decorum and dignity ask me what I mean by 'decorum'."

"Neo-classical concerns for decorum and dignity. *D'accord.*"

I slit the scotch-tape seal and unfolded a page that had been ripped from a spiral notebook. On it was a scrawled backhand message in red that appeared to have been written in a speeding vehicle, or by an animal. There was something disquieting about the handwriting—it was like a ransom or bank robber's note:

I slowly deciphered it: "*Jeremy. I lost your number. I'll be at ~~The Jailer's Daughter~~ Noctambule ~~tonight~~ tomorrow night if you want to drop by. Milena.*" Had the microphone been on, my students would have heard the booming of my heart. I stared at the last word. I couldn't read Milena's name, whisper it, think of it without dizziness. I refolded the page and slid it into my breast pocket. I looked out at my audience, a rolling sea of rustling paper, coloured binders, creaking seats, moving torsos. I turned on the microphone, adjusted my lapels, cleared my throat. I waited until there was a hush, and extended it for dramatic effect. I then said something in a broken, pubescent voice as feedback squealed through the speakers. Bursts of laughter. I wrote my name and office number on the blackboard, descended the podium, distributed the syllabus and bibliography. Compose yourself, Davenant. *Un, deux, trois . . .*

Did she sign it "Milena" or "Love Milena"? With an attempt at academic gravitas, I reclimbed the stairs to my position of vantage. I reached into my breast pocket. Just "Milena". I placed my notes on the lectern, and again waited for a respectful silence.

"Genius," I began anyway, "is not often recognised in the age in which it appears, but it was in Shakespeare's case. In England, that is. England's closest neighbour, France, was not even aware of Shakespeare's existence, let alone genius, until more than a century after his death. Voltaire, in 1730, could boast that it was he who introduced Shakespeare to Europe . . . "

I scanned my captive audience. Some were bent over their desks, madly transcribing my every word; others were lost in reverie, gazing out the window or at the large institutional clock above me.

"In Voltaire's own words: 'I myself was the first to speak of this Shakespeare, I was the first to show the French a few pearls that I had found in his enormous dunghill . . . '; 'It was I who discovered this barbarous mountebank, this buffoon who has flashes of wit and does antics . . . who did not even know Latin . . . this savage drunk whose plays can please only in London and Canada . . . '"

I looked up from my notes.

"You know, it's funny that despite the 'enormous dunghills' that Voltaire found in Shakespeare, he wrote one play that followed the basic plot of *Othello*, another that of *Julius Caesar*, two with *Hamlet*-like ghost scenes, and another with scenes redolent of *Macbeth*. It's also interesting to note that Voltaire's plays are almost never performed . . . "

I looked down at my notes. "But that . . . is a side issue that need not detain us. Voltaire's criticisms, it should be remembered, are rooted in a set of dramatic conventions radically different from our own and from those of Shakespeare's time, which reflect neo-classical concerns for decorum and dignity . . . "

I looked peripherally at Arielle; she had her back to me, whispering to someone in the row behind her. I went closer to the microphone.

"Which reflect neo-classical concerns for *decorum* and dignity."

Arielle turned around and raised her hand. "What do you mean by . . . dignity?"

"Good quest . . . Right, I should . . . perhaps clarify this." For Christ's sake, Arielle. I walked over to the side of the stage in what I hoped would pass for professorial absorption, and set my notes upon a lectern. "Perhaps I should repeat that question for those at the back."

I looked down at a smiling Arielle, whose great teeth gleamed like pearls. While feeling in my pocket for Milena's message, I rephrased the question.

" . . . Thus the term 'decorum', in the context of 18th-century theatre, refers to one of the many accepted dramatic conventions of the era which . . . "

" . . . And so, not surprisingly, Shakespeare's sexual or scatological wordplay not only violated the decorum of neo-classicism, but also the unity of action, separation of genres and possibly even verisimilitude . . . "

Blah blah blah. On an overhead projector, after a few moments of inept fiddling, I projected the following:

I. (Venus in *Venus and Adonis*)
I'll be a park, and thou shalt be my deer;
Feed where thou wilt, on mountain or in dale:
    Graze on my lips; and if those hills be dry,
    Stray lower, where the pleasant fountains lie.
Within this limit is relief enough,
Sweet bottom-grass, and high delightful plain,
Round rising hillocks, thickets obscure and rough,
To shelter thee from tempest and from rain . . .

II. (William Empson, *Seven Types of Ambiguity*)
"It shows lack of decision and will-power, a feminine pleasure in yielding to the mesmerism of language, in getting one's way, if at all, by deceit and flattery, for a

poet to be so fearfully susceptible to puns. Many of us could wish the Bard had been more manly in his literary habits."

The class was getting noisy. "For next class," I announced, "I want you to (a) find translations of this passage from Shakespeare or do your own, and (b) comment on this quotation from Empson. Are there any questions?" I let my eyes roam over the faces ranged beneath me.

Silence, then two or three overlapping voices: "Does this have to be handed in?" "Does this have to be typed?"

NINE

Your bum is the greatest thing about you . . .

—*Measure for Measure*

I n bed that night I held my two messages side by side, in communion, in covenance, two messages from the two most important people in the world. It had to mean something—the page was turned, the magic door opened, my life was finally unfolding as it should. Was it not? (It was not.) I took two Dormex and my mind drifted chemically toward sleep.

My buzzer wrenched me from a dream in which I was holding Victor Toddley's head down a toilet bowl while scrubbing his hair with a toilet brush. Annoyed, understandably, at the interruption, I stumbled out onto the balcony where I could just barely make out, in the fierce sunlight, a man in a blue uniform. A policeman? I clomped down the stairs and opened the door. It was the mailman, with a ponytail and bermuda shorts, who handed me a small package and asked me to sign on a line that he had marked with an X.

Good things, as we all know, come in small packages. I knew what it was right away. I dug my fingernails into the filament tape and with samson strength pulled at the flaps of the box. I then went to get a knife. Under styrofoam pellets and polystyrene bubble wrap were my two Supersound 2000s. And one Mood Ring.

Unfortunately, the Supersound 2000s needed a special battery, which the swines had not supplied. I wanted to over- hear a conversation immediately. My disappointment dissolved when I saw the Mood Ring. It came with a chart:

IF THE STONE IS COLOURED:	YOU ARE LIKELY TO BE:
Black	Tense, Inhibited or Overworked
Reddish Brown	Under Stress, Anxious
Light Green to Bright Green	Average, No Great Stress
Blue Green	Somewhat Relaxed
Bright Blue	Relaxed, Free & Easy
Deep Indigo	The Ultimate Mood
CAUTION: Ring Should Not Be Immersed in Water	

I was struck by the beauty of this, I admit. My only doubt was whether one would be enough. I put the ring on. It went from black to reddish brown and stayed there. My goal, which Milena would help me to attain, was Deep Indigo. I wanted to be Deep Indigo. I wanted the Ultimate Mood. I quickly dressed and practically sprinted to Pharmaprix, where I bought a 9-volt battery and, on a whim, a box of two dozen condoms.

All day long I carried around Milena's note like a talisman, unfolding it from time to time to examine her red hiero- glyphs. I thought of going to a library for books on graphology but reconsidered, fearing what I might find in that careening, cacographic hand.

ஒ

I'll be at Noctambule tomorrow night if you want to drop by. I should probably describe what kind of people go there, or better still, I'll let Jacques do it. In an article for *Barbed- Wire*, from which he said I was not to quote, he began:

*Café Noctambule, a stygian coffee-house-bistro
with a shoe-box cinema at its rear, is the haunt of
artwrecks—those threadbare, world-weary intro-
spectors who, stimulated by caffeine and nicotine,
write bad poetry conspicuously . . . [Noctambule]
also attracts studied eccentrics with steel suitcases
(containing air?), kindergarten anarchists, rad
gynocentrics, herbivorous GenXers and cartoon-
reading cyberpunks . . .*

    I should perhaps add that Jacques spent a great deal of his
time there, and so did I.

    My heart was racing as I looked around for Milena. She
was there, her back to me, alone at a table. I went to the
washroom to look in the mirror and think up wry openers.
When I came out, slowly so wind currents wouldn't disturb
my improved hair, I noticed that Milena was not, in fact,
alone. Sitting across from her was a male wearing layers of
flannel and plaids and a Medusa nest of dyed-blonde dread-
locks. He was ridiculously handsome, like a Viking hero in
a comic book. On the chair beside him, the only chair avail-
able, sat a distressed and bestickered guitar case.

    As I stood fidgeting by their table he spoke, like a ventril-
oquist, with a huge hand-rolled cigarette in his mouth. In the
first lull I slipped in a "Hello, Milena." I had to repeat it.
Milena turned her head slowly, and with the voice of one
who answers an interrupting telephone, said "Oh, hi." She
then introduced me to "Drew Bludd." Drew sent tobacco
clouds in my direction as if he were smoking out a nest of
wasps; I stood in awkward silence, wondering whether I
should find another chair or go home. Milena picked up her
knapsack and beer and said, "Good luck on the video, Drew."
She then nodded, while squinting through the smoke of her

dangling cigarette, towards an empty table in the corner. She led.

"Which chair would you like?" I asked, as Milena ground the butt of her cigarette beneath her heel.

"Does it matter?" she answered, sitting down.

I guess not. I sat down and we looked at each other in silence. "Is that his real name?" I said finally. "Drew Bludd?"

"It is now."

"Is he in a group?" My voice, I thought, sounded a bit squeaky.

"Yes."

"What kind of music?"

"Philo-performance fusion, based on Kierkegaard."

"Really? What's the name of the band?"

"High Mass of the Funky Ass."

I nodded. "I think I've heard of them. Can I get you a drink?"

"You're so chiv." Milena stood up halfway, stuck her hand in her back pocket. "Here's some money."

"No, it's all right."

"Take it."

"You feel uncomfortable when people offer you things, don't you?"

Milena didn't answer right away. "I don't like chivalry— the courteous facade of the chauvinist swine, as they say."

"You can buy the next round."

"Whatever."

When I returned with the drinks, another woman was leaning over our table, supported by her elbows, in close conversation with Milena. I paused to examine her sheer black stockings just over the knee, laddered and tattered, and a yellow tartan mini-kilt that almost covered her buttocks.

"Jeremy, this is my sister Violet. Vile—Jeremy."

Violet straightened her torso. "I think I seen you before. You used to go out with Sabrine, right?" She had a languorous voice, the equivalent of a bored shrug, and a slight accent like her sister's. There was a physical resemblance as well—except for the pale, posthumous look and the nose, too small and perfect, like a plastic doll's, through which a trio of silver nose rings ran. I had seen her before too.

"Yeah, used to," I said, straining to match her tone. "You know her?"

"I know Bonze."

Luc (or "Bonze", as he was called) was a skinhead from France who had a brief stint at my old apartment as a night porter. "Really? Is he still around? I heard he got deported."

"They'll never get Bonze, he's way cool, he's . . . "

"A neo-Nazi," said Milena.

" . . . moved in with Sabrine," said Vile. "And the baby. I guess you're like, online with all that."

The last time I slept with Sabrine two hearts beat inside her. I sighed. "Yeah I . . . moved out, I . . . moved out."

"You must have been like, majorly bummed out."

It was a shock, but a healthy one: Sabrine and I were floundering together, sinking like stones. "A bit, yeah."

"So where'd you move to?"

"Rue Valjoie," said Milena gravely. "Beside Denny."

"Oh, so this is the guy you . . . um, described." Vile looked at me with squinting eyes.

The three of us sat in leaden silence. I was dying to ask about Denny, but didn't dare. I instead cast furtive glances at Vile, at her black-lined cat eyes, black lipliner and white oval face. Her hair, painstakingly tousled and flamingly orange, hid much of it.

"There he is, I'm outta here," said Vile. "It's been real. Ciao Milly. Ciao whatever your name is." In black Marine boots she clomped over to Drew Bludd, who ignored her.

Milly? Milena was called Milly? *When will we be married Milly, when will be wed? When will we be bedded in the same sweet bed?* More silence. I glanced sideways at Vile's cadaverous charms and impossibly short skirt. I glanced at Milena, who was watching me. I was determined not to talk about my life with Sabrine, or hers with Denny.

"Denny was a friend—a friend of the family—who hanged himself a few weeks ago," said Milena, eavesdropping on the voices inside me. "I was the one who found him."

Desperation: a rope ends it. "Oh God, I . . . I'm really sorry, I . . . That must have been just . . . I don't know, just . . . "

"It was."

"God. So I guess that's why the cops were there a few days ago."

Milena's face darkened. "I guess so. Listen, I'll be right back." She walked over to the Drew-Vile table and whispered something into her sister's ear. A few more sentences at normal range passed between them, then a pack of cigarettes, then a small plastic bottle.

"Let's change the subject," said Milena, as she sat back down. "Where you from?"

I was about to ask the same question. "York originally, then Toronto. How about you?"

Milena opened the fresh pack of cigarettes and popped one in her mouth all in one seamless motion. She then rummaged through her knapsack and frowned.

"You're matchless, Milena. Here." I struck a match from the book Milena had written her number on. She watched the flame burn towards my finger before leaning over it.

"I thought you didn't smoke," she said, exhaling.

"I don't."

"You're just prepared. Like a Boy Scout. So you can be a knight errant to women in distress."

"Right."

"You strike me as the deluded romantic sort—no offence intended."

Obviously offence was intended. "Deluded?"

"You're probably always falling in love."

"Not always."

Milena gave me an indulgent smile before inhaling a full one-third of her cigarette. "Why exactly are we here tonight?" she said, her words riding a stream of smoke.

What do you mean? You're the one who set it up, you're the one who wrote me the bloody note. "What do you mean?" I said.

"I mean how did I . . . encourage your attentions? I'm just curious, I didn't mean to sound rude."

I paused to think of an appropriate response. None came. "By not encouraging them, I suppose. I don't know, I've never really seen—met—anyone like you before, I really haven't. You're one of a kind. And I've never said that to anyone. No, I'm serious. There's a look in your eye—you have a look of . . . well, hidden depth or mystery or something."

A smile hovered on Milena's lips. "Hidden depth or mystery or something?"

"Complexities, difficulties, neuroses. Interesting neuroses. Like you're harbouring important information or some dark secret."

Milena laughed. "All women harbour dark secrets. Who was it that said a girl of fifteen has more secrets than an old man, and a woman of thirty more than a chief of state? You sound a bit masochistic if you like to pursue that sort of thing."

"Why did you write me that note?"

Seconds passed. Milena tapped her cigarette on the ashtray unnecessarily. "I don't know. Because I couldn't resist your good looks, I guess. Because I said I'd phone you. Because you're a teacher—I might've been impressed by that. I felt like I had to report back to you, that it was like an assignment or something."

I smiled. And then gazed into my beer. Good looks? Is that what she said? Is she myopic? I took a drink. "How'd you know I was a teacher?"

"Arielle. I bumped into her yesterday afternoon. She asked if I'd seen you. I told her I'd lost your number and she insisted I write you a note, that she was seeing you that night in class."

"Oh." This took a bit of the lustre off things: Arielle the matchmaker strikes again, strikes a match. Thank God for that. "So are you a student?" I asked.

"No. You already asked me that. I dropped out of high school. You got any brothers and sisters?"

I laughed. "You really want to know?"

Milena smiled. "Yeah, unless it's a dark secret you're harbouring."

"I'm an only child."

"Really? My sister's only a child too."

"Isn't she . . . " I paused, suspecting there was a joke I'd trampled on. " . . . older than you?"

"No."

"Younger?"

"Very good."

"So there's just the two of you?"

"I had another sister who died when I was young. Where do your parents live?"

"How'd your sister die?"

"Where do your parents live?"

"My mother died a few years ago. My stepfather's in Toronto. I've never met my real father—he left before I was born."

"I'm sorry to hear that." Milena's face and voice softened. I lowered my eyes. I could never think too long about this, my under-parented state, without getting mired in self-pity. "Yeah, I'm the 'bastard boy of York'. King Henry VI, Part—"

"That can't be easy, no family to turn to, both parents . . . gone. It's when the second parent goes that you finally begin to accept your own mortality, or so they say. Do you get along with your stepfather?"

I shook my head, scratched at my beer label. "'You exist because your mother was careless,' was one of the first things Ralph said to me, and I've never forgotten it. He once calculated the weekly cost of the food I ate, and the gasoline and oil I used when borrowing the car, to two decimal points. I don't know, I always thought he was temporary, that he'd eventually fuck off, and I think he thought the same of me. He was always too present, too much of an adult—he seemed to have been born an adult, forgotten his childhood like an amnesiac. His imagination, if you could call it that, always needed a great deal of firing . . . Am I boring you?" Milena was looking in Drew's direction.

"No, sorry. I'm . . . rapt. Where did we leave our hero?"

"With his wicked stepfather, I think. My uncle was actually more of a father to me. Now he had an imagination. Ralph couldn't stand him so we moved. At least that's the way I saw it."

"How about your mom?"

"What about her?"

"What'd she think?"

"Of Uncle Gerard? Well, after her marriage I think she just sort of went along with her husband. But she never really said that much about Gerard, she always seemed to avoid the subject, though she did once say that she suddenly began to mistrust him, I can't imagine why."

"Is Gerard still alive?"

"Very much so."

"What's he do?"

"He lives on his wits."

"Meaning?"

"He's a con man."

Milena smiled.

"And a gambler."

Milena's smile disappeared. "Why the fuck is everyone in my life . . . " She closed her eyes, took a deep breath. "Never mind, he's not in my life." She began scratching away at her beer label. "And never will be." Milena's mood and demeanour had changed, as it had when I brought home the lottery tickets.

"Milena, are you all right? It upsets you that—"

"I'm sorry. Tell me more about your mother. What was she like?"

"Gerard's really not a typical gambler—"

"What was your mother like?"

"I hope you can meet him one day, in fact." I stared at Milena, tried to secure eye contact, but her eyes were burning a hole through the cigarette pack that she revolved in her hands. What have you got against gambling? I wondered. Is it worse than any other way of making money—commerce, for example, or playing the stock market? "Milena, what have you got against . . . " A voice inside me, and Milena's expression, stopped me, told me to move on, and quickly.

JEFFREY MOORE

What was the question again? "What was my mother like?
She was the most beautiful woman I've ever seen."

Milena lifted her eyes towards mine.

"Apart from you. She was beautiful in a lot of ways. The
way she held you, for example, her softness, her touch . . . I
still dream about it. And she was amazingly thoughtful,
always thinking of others first, in a way that you don't really
see any more, not in our generation at least. She never
complained. What else can I say? She was uneducated but
cultured, extremely graceful. A natural grace like yours,
Milena."

Milena lowered her gaze again, opened and shut the lid
of her cigarette pack.

"She was actually an actress—amateur mostly—before she
got pregnant with me, but for some reason never went back
to it. Ralph certainly didn't encourage her, to say the least,
probably because that's how she met Gerard. She was always
deferring to her husband—which used to annoy the hell out
of me. It was ironic too, because her mother was a suffragette."

"Her *mother* was a suffragette? One of the originals?"

Gerard had supplied this information so it was probably
false. "Grandmother?"

"That's amazing, very cool. Go on."

"There was something . . . sad about my mother, I never
really understood what. I always thought it had something
to do with Gerard, some secret about him, about them, I
don't know. She could be a bit flighty sometimes, in another
galaxy—sometimes you'd be in mid-sentence and she'd start
singing or humming softly. It was a bit unsettling. But most
of the time she was absolutely fine. And she was always—I
can't remember any exceptions—wonderfully kind and soft

127

and generous. I really miss her. I suppose I've never gotten over her death."

"How'd she die?"

"My stepfather killed her."

"Your stepfather killed her?"

"In a car crash."

"You mean it was his fault?"

"Some guys in a van crossed over the solid line, into our lane, hit us head-on."

"So it was an accident."

"I guess so. What about *your* parents? Tell me about—"

"What do you teach?"

"You're not answering any of my questions."

"We'll get to me eventually."

"I'm in Comp Art."

"What the hell's that?"

"Comparative Art. It compares one art with another, one's nation's art with another's, or one art with some other non-art discipline. Most of it's a crock."

Milena nodded but made no comment.

"So what do you want to do in life?" I asked.

"I'm not through with you yet. And I hate that kind of question. So what made you come here in the first place?"

"To this neighbourhood, or this province?"

"Yes."

I came to this neighbourhood because of you, because the Page and my lucky stars led me to you. "I don't know why I came to this neighbourhood."

"And this province?"

Gerard once asked me the same question. I don't remember my answer but I do remember he approved, on the grounds that Quebec had the lowest marriage rate in the

Western world. "I came to this province because it's French-speaking," I said finally.

Milena looked at me, waiting for me to expand, perhaps disappointed by my answer. I should have said something grander, more ideological, poetic.

"I love the snow here," I added wistfully. "Nature's detergent bleaching the stains of life . . . "

Milena here collapsed into laughter, which turned into a coughing fit, a deep smoker's hack. She took a sip of beer, then emptied her glass in two swallows and wiped her mouth with her sleeve.

"So you came here because of your parents?" I changed.

"Yeah."

I nodded. Long silence. Milena is a tough interview.

"What sign are you?" I asked.

"Fuck off," was the handsome reply. "Astrology is crap." A new cigarette appeared magically between her fingers, which she lit with its predecessor, no more than a burning filter. Milena smoked her cigarettes thoroughly—and swiftly, as if in a tournament. I examined her more closely: hair tied at the back; dark circles under her eyes; little or no makeup.

"Don't look at me like that," she said sharply.

We sat without speaking, listening to a scratchy song by Édith Piaf. This couldn't be worse, I thought to myself, she's mortally bored, we'll never meet again.

"Want another beer?" Milena reached over and turned my bottle to examine the label, which my nervousness had scratched to shreds.

I watched her glide like a swan to the bar, use sign language with the bartender, then disappear into the Femmes. I finished my beer, scratched off the rest of the label, glanced at my mood ring. Reddish-brown. I looked over towards Drew and Violet, who seemed to be looking my way, laughing. When I nodded Drew looked right through me, while Violet pulled at her earlobe and made a series of motions with her hand, as if I were deaf and dumb. What was all that about? I turned to see if she was motioning to someone behind me.

"Christ almighty," said Milena, from the other side, jerking me back round in my chair. She set down, or rather slammed down, two bottles of beer.

"What's the matter?"

"Nothing, just some drunken asshole."

"You got propositioned?"

"Yeah. Well, more like prepositioned. He asked me if I wanted to 'get it on, babe, go for the old in-out.'"

Prepositioned. That was very clever, very quick. Why can't I say things like that? I was about to ask her more, and the drunk to step outside, when the lights suddenly dimmed. Three men walked onto a stage three inches high and treated us, after equipment problems, to the kind of music that occasionally veers towards a tune. According to Milena, it was called speed jazz or thrash jazz, she couldn't remember which. "Want to go?" she said. On our way out I waved tentatively to her sister, who was slouched in her chair and didn't wave back.

On the Boulevard, when Milena stopped to light another cigarette, I asked her if she would quit smoking if someone she was in love with asked her to. She laughed and laughed as if I had made some clever joke. I joined in the laughter, wondering what was so funny: the preposterousness of her giving up smoking, or of being in love? "That's a good one," she said.

We continued walking, in total silence, to Dame de Piques, where we sat in more silence, or rather in loud music that replaced words and thought, that shook our table. I am not at my best in bars, partly because I have trouble with utterances that are shouted into ears, without modulation, coloration. When I shout, moreover, my voice slides into a register that very few can understand.

"Your sister," I shouted, "a few minutes ago, it was weird . . . "

"Pardon?"

"Your sister! She was motioning towards me, some sort of sign language."

Milena shrugged her shoulders, as if she couldn't hear or couldn't care less. "I like this song!" she replied.

I paused to determine what song it was. Right. An old suicide anthem by Blue Oyster Cult. "I'll be right back!" I said.

When I pushed the washroom door in, as it invited me to do in misspelled French, I pushed air instead and almost the face of the person exiting—a man with a passing resemblance to Leonard Cohen, who used to live in the neighbourhood. Back at our table, I told Milena that I had almost pushed Leonard Cohen's face in, and had used the same urinal.

"Ooh, I'm impressed," said Milena.

"You don't like him? I thought all women were in love with him. I know Arielle is."

"I'm supposed to be impressed that you joined your urine with his?"

"I wasn't actually bragging—"

"He doesn't exactly spin my tires. I got a collection of his poems a few Christmases ago."

"Shit?"

"One of them went something like: *I didn't realise until you turned to go that you were carrying a masterpiece—your ass. Sorry for not being seduced by your face or your words.*"

Milena paused to remove something from between her teeth. "Just about sums up every man I've known."

I reflected on this as the waitress set our drinks down and changed Milena's ashtray for an unused one.

"Do you do drugs?" Milena suddenly asked, perhaps thinking of the sugar and caffeine about to course through her veins. Like Parisians, Milena dropped sugar-cubes into her coffee redundantly, well past the point of super-saturation.

"Occasionally. Not often."

"You seem too temperate to do anything dangerous," she remarked, while over-tipping the waitress.

I beg your pardon? Come again? *Temperate?* Now what the hell does that mean? Is that a slight? Has she been talking to Jacques? "How about you?" I asked.

"I don't do anything. Anymore."

I waited for Milena to continue, but she remained silent, looking not at me but at the table behind me. I thought of what Jacques had said about her. A full minute passed.

"What's your sister's name?" I said, jumping theme. "The one who died."

Milena raised her eyebrows. "Bernadette. Why?"

"Bernadette? Are you serious? I think I met her. In fact, I think I met Violet too. In York. Bernadette was twelve, we played cards and drank white wine . . . "

"I think you've got the wrong—"

" . . . and played strip poker and . . . Vile kept interrupting us, and your dog Crab was there . . . "

"We never had a dog named Crab. You're definitely thinking of someone else."

I sighed. "So what's your last name?"

"Modjeska."

"Modjeska? What nationality are you?"

"Canadian. Although I lived in Ireland for a few years. Age five to twelve."

"Ireland? Modjeska's Irish? How'd you end up living in Ireland?"

"My mother thought I should be with her."

"No, I mean . . . How'd you like living there?"

"They were the best years of my life. And they weren't very good."

I nodded, took a sip of my microbrew. "So your parents are Irish?"

Milena sighed as if weary of telling the story. "No. My mother was from India, my father's Czech. I know it's confusing. Listen closely 'cause I'm not going to repeat it. My mother emigrated to Canada, my father emigrated—or at least ended up—in Ireland. My mother went to Ireland on a holiday with her Canadian boyfriend, met my father, then dumped her boyfriend." Milena paused to extract things from her knapsack, including a bent cigarette. "God knows what the two had in common—maybe their dialects, which aren't that far apart."

"Czech and Hindi aren't far apart?"

She lit her cigarette, shook the match out. "No. Romany and Sanskrit aren't. My father was a Roma and my mother a Banjara."

"Roma and Banjara? You mean gypsies?"

Milena nodded. "Believe it or not. Though they never used that word."

"Amazing. So how'd your father end up in Ireland?"

"He was excommunicated from his band. He had friends in Ireland. Anyway, they got married in Canada, had us kids, then we went back to Ireland. And then something weird happened, something that changed everything. The two men—my father and my mom's ex-boyfriend—met up again, in Ireland. My mum thought they were going to kill each other, so we moved back to Canada."

I paused to think all this over. "And that was the last time the two men saw each other? In Ireland?"

"No. They met up again a year later in Canada."

"And the shit hit?"

"No, they became best of friends. Drinking buddies. They're both alcoholics." Milena's expression darkened.

"Does he . . . do your parents still live here?"

"My mother died years ago. I don't know where my father is, exactly." Seconds passed. "He's around."

"My mother is . . . dead too," I said slowly, solemnly, as if this coincidence were fraught with great significance.

"I know, you already told me."

"Right. So I take it you don't get along with your father."

"How perceptive."

"Why?"

Milena remained silent, flicking an imaginary ash. I was trespassing again.

"And how about your father's friend?" I asked. "Your mother's ex. Is he still around?"

"Denny? He's dead. He used to live beside you. I found him swinging in a closet. Any more questions? Let's get out of here, I'm tired, I'm going home."

TEN

Death to those who do not laugh!

—Shaka

Two sleepless nights later, after that rather shaky dress rehearsal, the curtain rises on the same two characters: I walking aimlessly in the park at night, immersed in thought; Milena sitting atop a picnic table, legs spread wide, pulling on a cigarette, gazing at the ground.

I almost rubbed my eyes in disbelief. "Milena! What are you doing here?"

"Looking for four-leaf clovers. What does it look like?"

"You live around here?"

"Over there." She nodded to a beautiful stone house in need of paint and repair across from the park.

"You're not afraid to sit in the park late at night?"

"Yeah, but I do it anyway. How about you? You're not afraid to be walking around in the dark?"

"I'm getting used to it. Where do you live?"

"You already asked me that."

"What's that book sticking out of your bag?"

"None of your business." Milena pulled out a giant paperback from the outside pocket of her knapsack. "But I'll show you anyway." She handed me *An Anthology of Bantu Literature*. "You teach this stuff, don't you?"

"No."

"Arielle said you had a course on South African lit."

"One semester I replaced somebody . . . for one class."
Milena nodded. I think I had disappointed her. "But I . . . I
do know something about the subject."

"I've got a good video on some of the writers. A friend
taped it for me—Victor Toddley. I think you've met him."

Toddley. "Right. Nice guy. Do you want to watch the video
now?"

"Oh no, not now."

"You sure?"

"Positive. And anyway, I don't have a video machine."

"Get the tape, we'll watch it at my place." I looked at my
watch. "The night is young, a mere adolescent. It's not even
midnight."

"No, I don't think so."

"Come on, it'll be fun. I'll crack open some champagne—
we'll drink stars. And who knows, the world may end
tonight."

Milena smiled bleakly. "I don't think that would be a good
idea."

"Okay, forget it."

Milena examined the top of the picnic table, like an ento-
mologist following the path of some insect. "Okay," she said
finally, after a sigh. "But you have to wait outside while I get
the tape."

We went around to the back of Milena's building, into a
dark alleyway, where the smell of gasoline warred with the
stench of rotting garbage. There I waited as Milena climbed
over the fence. Through the slats I watched her take the fire-
escape steps two at a time, watched her pause at the top of
the landing and then pry open a window. Her apartment
lights were on.

"Go to the front door," she yelled down to me. She then
climbed through the window.

I went around to the front and waited. Why do I have to wait outside? Who or what is she hiding? Why did she climb through the window? I looked up to where I thought her bedroom would be. Would she cast down a rope ladder from the balcony of her moated tower?

A car stopped on the other side of the street, its headlights illuminating a man in a pale fedora, leaning against a tree, staring at me. He looked eerily familiar. A creaking sound made me jump: the front door opened and Milena emerged, wearing a dark sweater with glass buttons that sparkled, which I noticed not because of their iridescence but because they were inserted in mismatching slits.

"I'm always leaving these inside," she said, dangling a chain of keys in front of me. "I should just leave the fucking door wide open—come on in, open house, help yourself. 'Cause there's nothing to steal. Nothing left to steal, I should say."

"You got robbed?"

"A few months ago I came home to an empty apartment. All my books, all my clothes were gone—I didn't own much else."

"Shit. Sounds like you've had a great year."

"Divine."

"Did you see that guy watching us over there?" As I pointed, the man's hatted head withdrew behind the tree like a tortoise into its shell.

"Yeah I saw him. Let's go."

I chose a roundabout route to my place, through two alleyways; Milena, after eyeing me warily, lagged slightly behind. We walked without words through patches of light and dark, our long shadows streaming forward. At a brick wall lit by a meshed yellow bulb, I stopped and pointed at some sprayed red graffiti: WAR IS MENSTRUATION ENVY. Milena nodded. We

137

continued on in tense silence. She's regretting this, I said to myself, she's definitely regretting this.

As we approached my home theatre, I prattled on to distract her from the apartment next door. I spoke of intergalactic noise, a new cyber laundromat, a change in my garbage day. I fumbled with my downstairs and upstairs locks, worried Milena's thoughts were with my dead neighbour. Inside, in the living room, after glancing in a mirror, I asked her if she was all right.

"Fine. Why do you ask?"

"No reason, I just thought that being . . . never mind."

"Denny, if that's what your getting at, was a boor. He meant nothing to me—I couldn't stand him. He's better off where he is."

I didn't know what to say to that. What would be appropriate? "Would you like a drink?" I said.

"Yes, I would."

"Champagne?"

"What for, so we can celebrate the swell year I've been having? I don't think I've ever had champagne."

"All the more reason." I bustled off to the kitchen and returned with the bottle and two glasses. And a polaroid camera. "We'll toast the goddess Fortune in foaming goblets," I said, borrowing one of Gerard's lines. I held up the camera to take a picture of her.

Milena held up her hand like a traffic cop. "Don't you dare. Jeremy, put the camera down! I'm serious."

"Why, what's wrong with a few—"

"Just put the fucking camera down, OK? Don't *ever* do that again. Don't ever stick a fucking camera in my face without asking, is that clear?"

"Yeah, fine. Sorry." Jesus Christ, what the hell was that all about? Seconds ticked away on the grandfather clock as I smouldered and Milena watched the moving pendulum. "Milena, I don't understand what—"

"You don't have to understand. It's later than I thought. I think I should go."

"The clock, it's . . . a bit fast. But you're free to go."

Milena looked at the floor, bit her lip, seemed to hesitate. "I'm sorry . . . my temper, it's something I'm working on. One of the many things."

We both watched the moving pendulum, like hypnotics. Her gaze then shifted round the room, resting briefly on my Shakespeare bust, Zulu mask and *Shakuntala* miniatures, then on a photograph of my mother that I'd tricked her into laughing for by doing a demented ballet leap, and finally on the champagne flutes in front of her. "My God, you're equipped. How bourgeois."

"They were a gift from my uncle. Would you prefer to drink it out of the bottle?"

"All the same to me."

"Cheers."

"*Baxt, sastimus.* Luck and health."

After clinking and sipping I said, "A friend of mine remarked, rightly I thought, that women always look awkward when swigging out of a bottle." This was one of Jacques' observations.

"What's that supposed to mean?"

"Nothing. You think that's sexist?"

"Yes. And a bit sweeping, wouldn't you say? Give me that."

Milena grabbed the bottle from me and, left-handed, took a swig with uncommon dexterity. She then handed the bottle to me. I took a manly chug and then wiped the champagne from my chin and neck.

"I did that on purpose," I spluttered. "OK, there might be some exceptions. I could also say that, generally, men are more awkward than women when they dance. Is that sexist?"

"I'm saying that those are subjective things, and generalisations. And I guess you know what Blake said about generalisations."

I nodded. I'd check it later.

Milena said, "What other ones do you have, pray tell? If you say men think and women feel, or men must work and women weep—"

"Women like ice cream more than men."

"Oh God."

"It's true—go into any ice cream parlour and look at the ratio. And the men are only there because they've been dragged in by their women."

"*Their* women?"

"You know what I mean."

"What's your point, that women—"

"I have no point. It's neither good nor bad, it's just a harmless observation. Oh, women also like strawberries more than men. And herbal teas and heat . . . "

"They like heat more? Men like the cold?"

"no and boys don't like suckers as much—"

"Oh come on—"

"Well, at least they don't really suck them—they just crunch them. They don't like sticks hanging out of their mouths. Girls like to suck them."

"That's fallacious."

I looked up to see if she were making a joke. She didn't appear to be. "Maybe," I said.

"Boys like to suck too," she said.

"Puns are a feminine thing, according to Empson."

"What? Puns are a *feminine thing*? Who the fuck is Empson? That's bullshit."

"Women go to fortune tellers more than men."

"Where do you get all this information? Is this like, scientific?"

"Women like cats more than men."

"That may be true," said Milena, "and there's a reason for it."

"Let's hear it."

"Women don't feel the need to dominate—they don't mind that cats won't take orders, won't fawn all over them, follow them around, lick their faces when they get home. Poets love cats, soldiers love dogs."

"That's a generalisation. Women also use more -ly plus adjective constructions than men. That's been documented."

"What do you mean?"

"Well, like 'stunningly divine', 'amazingly stupid', 'unbelievably happy', 'obscenely—"

"I get the point. Whose conclusion is that?"

"A study was done."

"A study was done. That's absolutely ridiculous."

"Women also use more exclamation marks."

"Oh please! If we do, it's probably because we have to shout to be heard. Because men are becoming more and more deaf. Same reason we use the 'ly'. For reinforcement. So big deal. So what? What are you trying to say?"

"I'm not trying to say anything. It's just, I don't know, interesting. Forget it."

"I will." Milena's face took on a slightly puggish, belligerent look and her eyes blazed, as if I'd done something less acceptable than infanticide. Things were not going well.

But things change, don't they? After her second and third glasses of champagne, and under the spell of my rarefied wit, Milena started to relax. She even took off her boots.

"Nice apartment," she said, looking around. "I didn't really notice it last time I was here."

"Thanks." I described how it looked when I moved in— "They defecated on the floor, in the same room they dined," I embellished—but Milena's sympathies seemed to lie with the tree-forters from the lower latitudes. I also told her about the longitudinal sardine-eater who slept in my bathtub, but even after I exaggerated the danger I was in, the story failed to carry the desired punch.

"From your description," she said calmly, "it sounds like a friend of mine."

"Take a look at this." I handed her the weapon left at the scene.

"What about it?"

"He was secreting that on his person."

"A Swiss Army knife. Nice one too. Corkscrew, scissors." Milena played with the knife, pulling out all its blades and instruments with her nimble, angel-harpist fingers.

I turned on the television, inserted the video and was about to push "Play" when Milena said "Wait." On Vermont ETV were two guerezas—two monkeys with long, silky black-and-white hair from Zanzibar.

"I'm reading a book about primates," said Milena. While she described the book, by a feminist who thought we had much to learn from their sexual habits, we watched two guerezas copulate. "Among other things," said Milena, after the act was completed, "I learned that the female spider monkey's clitoris is twice as long as the male monkey's penis."

"Really? God, no penis envy there, eh?"

"Penis envy exists only among males."

"My aunt in England used to have a monkey. She ordered one from Guyana, of all places—in South America."

"I know where Guyana is."

"I remember her insisting that it be female, and in fact sent one back because it was male."

"Why?"

"Well, she claimed that the major portion of the male's day was spent jerking off."

"Like his human counterpart?"

"Do you think men do it more than women?"

"I wouldn't know. I don't think there should be any stigma attached if they do—maybe it calms them down a bit, gets rid of their aggression, or some of it."

"Masturbation gets bad press, doesn't it?"

"Yeah, and I don't like when it's used as a metaphor for self-indulgence or futility or something."

"So how often do you masturbate?" I asked.

Milena paused, examining the bubbles in her champagne. "About the same as a female monkey I imagine."

"How many times have you masturbated in the last twenty-four hours?"

"Are you serious?"

"Yes."

"None."

"In the last forty-eight?"

"None."

"In the last week?"

"None . . . of your business. How about you?"

The video needed rewinding. While I attended to this, Milena channel-surfed, pausing at a black-and-white Truffaut movie from the sixties, when women's bras were pert and pointy. "Torpedo tits," said Milena. I pressed "play" and then sat as close to Milena as I dared, wondering about her breasts. The video, called "Great Bantu Writers of the 1930s", was ill-recorded and missing the first few minutes. Not likely harnessed by a bra. Parts of the video were interesting, to damn with faint praise, and Milena seemed happy to be watching it. Certainly not pert and pointy. As my eyes began to ache from peripheral strain, I heard the word Shaka. *"Shaka mighty cub of Phunga and Xaba, borne upon the shoulders of the sun and suckled by the tender moon herself . . . "*

Shaka, whose name you may recall from the Page, was the subject of a number of "praise poems" of the era. In North York I had made some notes on the 19th-century Zulu king—twenty-seven pages worth—in my Book of Saturdays. He was about as psychotic as they come.

" . . . Shaka, without question, was one of the greatest Zulu chieftains ever—a brilliant military strategist, the Bonaparte of South Africa. And his men worshipped him—when he ordered them to jump off a cliff, they did so, promptly and unquestioningly. Among his remarkable innovations in the art of warfare . . . "

The *art* of warfare. Surely that's not the right word. And why would he ask anyone to jump off a cliff? He would also ask his people to laugh, I remember from my notes. When things were not going well at home or in battle, Shaka would order everyone to laugh. Those who didn't, or didn't do it convincingly, were executed.

" . . . Nearby, young women stood like statues, enraptured, wearing the briefest of Zulu skirts, waiting to begin a passionate love affair with one whom all desired . . . "

Shaka, according to eyewitnesses, had an extremely small penis. He also had approximately one thousand concubines whom he caged in huts, out of profane sight and reach. All offspring were killed.

"For Shaka had so much knowledge of a woman's heart . . . ?

And other organs as well. One of his pastimes was cutting up pregnant women so he could see the foetus.

" . . . that magic charms were unnecessary . . . "

Another was padding elderly women from enemy clans with straw, igniting them with a torch, and heaving with laughter as they ran off.

"Your name shall endure, great Shaka, guarded eternally in the hearts of all generations . . . "

When the video ended abruptly, scrambling before the actual end, I felt pressured to make some cogent, professorial remarks. In lieu of this, I used my favourite classroom technique: muddy the waters and drop names in.

"What these Zulu poets and novelists are doing," I began, "by presenting Shaka the warrior as valorous and god-like—an heroic idealisation having little or no resemblance to the historical figure—is in essence erecting a mythical structure that . . . that well, has little or no resemblance to the historical figure . . . as I said. Rousseau's primitivistic suppositions are relevant here. Rousseau's almost fanatical dedication to the natural man led, I think, to a kind of adulation of the noble savage that . . . Defoe, of course, comes to mind here, and Diderot, and Chateaubriand in particular . . . "

Milena was looking me in the eye. I looked away, towards my mood ring: black. Should I cut my losses, quit while I'm behind, admit I haven't the faintest idea of what I'm talking about?

"There is also, conversely, the Ugly or Ignoble Savage—Polyphemus in classical antiquity and Shakespeare's Caliban are the prototypes. Johnson and Voltaire were both anti-primitivists who were . . . well, against primitivism and . . . ”

If there was a thread in there, I'd lost it. Milena's stare made me lose it. I excused myself and fled to the bathroom. When I returned, face freshly-scrubbed and underarms re-deodorised, Milena looked at me for a few seconds in between hauls on a cigarette.

“Good video,” I said. I looked round the room, bit my fingernails, emptied her ashtray, filled her glass, straightened what was already straight, asked her if she liked Albert Brooks. She'd never heard of him. I put on *Defending Your Life*. Fifteen minutes in, she dozed off. I watched the flickering images without anything registering—psychic blindness it's called—while drinking the dregs of refrigerator wine.

After some hesitation of near-Hamletish proportions, I placed my hand inches from her thigh, but quickly drew it back. I could not bring myself to touch her. I began to think, once again, how utterly beyond my reach she was, how far my mad dreams were from ever being fulfilled.

After gulping down my wine I risked my arm around her shoulder, as lightly as humanly possible. She jumped as if bitten by a snake. “Sorry Milena, I didn't mean to . . . to wake you, I . . . do you want to sleep here tonight?”

“No, I should go.”

“Oh.”

“I hope I haven't misled you.”

“Misled me? About what?”

“About . . . me, about who I am. About staying the night.”

“Of course not.”

“You understand?”

“Perfectly.”

“I should go.”

“I'll walk you home.”

"It's not necessary."

I walked her home. Birds were singing and it was almost light when we arrived at her front door. In clumsy fashion I tried to kiss her on the lips and ended up kissing her eye. She thanked me for the champagne and said she'd call me the next day. I nodded. I knew she wouldn't.

ELEVEN

Thou misshapen Dick!

—*3 Henry VI*

The next day I had what is commonly known as "that sinking feeling", though in this case it was more like "that diving-into-an-empty-swimming-pool feeling." It had nothing to do with Milena. It came from opening my agenda and seeing a red circle around the 6th of October, the day of the annual Comp Art party.

The Department of Comparative Art, a mongrel born of the former Comparative Literature and Comparative Philology Departments and later infused with some tired blood from Film Studies and Art History, embraced twenty-odd professors and lecturers, "odd" being the operative word. The fall celebration gave all of us, particularly the untenured profs and junior aspirants like me, a chance to kiss the director's ass. Normally the exercise was held in the staff lounge, but this year the new director, Dr. Sobranet, decided to hold it *chez lui*.

I knew I shouldn't inflict this on anyone else, but I also knew I couldn't go alone—partly because misery loves company but mostly because I needed protection from certain colleagues: Daphne De Witt, for one, an expert in Dutch art and literature and the private lives of everyone who crossed her rather wide path; Philippe Forget, for another, a Quebec folklorist drudge who was madly in love with me (or

148

so I thought); and especially Clyde Vincent Haxby, the psychoterrorist who wrote me about my so-called thesis.

Milena, true to her word, phoned in the afternoon. I was stupended. "What are you doing tonight?" she asked.

"A faculty party." I described the fall tradition as enticingly as I could without sounding ironic.

"Gosh, Jeremy, that sounds really exciting. Maybe you should take some spare underwear."

"Will you accompany me?" This question had the most pathetic ring to it. Obviously she would decline. An anti-ivory-towerist, Milena would not want to piss away an evening with pedants. She declined.

"We just have to clock in an hour or two," I assured her.

"I'd rather drink lava."

"Or even less."

"No thanks."

"You may regret this."

"How's that?"

"Because we may, while blindfolded, pin a paper tail onto the outline of a donkey."

"Don't forget the spare underwear."

As I was debating whether to ask Arielle to go, or even Vile (two interesting possibilities, each with its strong disincentive), Milena phoned back. She agreed to go, provided (a) she didn't have to "dress up" and (b) she could "bangout" whenever she wanted. I agreed to each provision. Though burning with curiosity, I asked for no explanation of her change of heart.

It was the hottest October 6th in history. We sweated in our long cab ride to the city's west end, and sweated in the vestibule of the Director's mansion, where an olive-skinned maid had left us. After glancing this way and that, I suggested to Milena that we bangout then and there, that we sprint

149

down the street to retrieve our taxicab. For in the next room it appeared a reading of a will was about to occur. Even those under forty-five looked sixty-five, as if they'd aged since arriving.

Dr. Sobranet, a bald man with a narrow horseshoe beard, welcomed us in a booming voice, with forced party joviality. A beard can often act as a counterbalance, diverting one's attention from the baldness, but in Sobranet's case it served only to make his face look upside-down. I introduced Milena to him and his elegant wife Claire, who appeared suddenly with a plastic icebucket and smile, and then disappeared as suddenly. Sobranet ushered us into the living room before going back for another doorbell. We walked towards an empty corner.

... *Of course his juvenilia is less clouded by a feeling of— how should I put it—of бсртбпекп тении* ...

... *une phase docimologique qui permet de formuler un pronostic général* ...

... *they'll do anything for a price—they published my husband, didn't they?*

... *many of the university's operating synergies are going unrealised* ...

... *I'll name my first-born after you if you get me off that fucking committee* ...

... *Da com on more under mist hleothum Grendel gongan. Godes yrre baer* ...

"Maybe we can skip out the back door," I said.

"What language was that?" whispered Milena.

"Old English, I think. From the lips of that lunatic Haxby."

Milena glanced towards the man in question. "Why's he a lunatic? Who is he?"

"He's a man of prodigious learning, known round the world. He speaks every dead language and publishes at least one incomprehensible article a month. He's also an inquisitioning little red-tapist who's out to get me for some reason. It's a long story."

"Let's get a drink."

"Worse, he's an Oxfordian."

"You don't like Oxford?"

"Yes, I do. What I mean is that he's one of those lunatics who think that the 17th Earl of Oxford wrote Shakespeare's plays."

"Like Sigmund Freud."

"Uh, yeah, exactly."

"Let's get a drink."

A woman with long silver hair, early forties, walked into the room with Sobranet as we walked out. Her face—I liked this about her—projected irony and calm dignity. Milena asked in a whisper if her name was Celerand, and when I said it was, Milena admitted that she was "one of the reasons but not the only reason" for accepting my invitation. After hanging up, she remembered that Barbara Celerand was a lecturer in my department. Ms. Celerand was also one of Montreal's most prominent feminists.

"You scoundrel," I said.

Milena was smiling, but flustered all the same. "No, really, I didn't know she'd be here. How could I know? I agreed to come . . . even without knowing . . . "

"Sure Milena. I'll introduce you. She's one of the few I like here."

"No don't." But it was too late—I had already waved Barbara over.

Milena had little to say beyond a few faint monosyllables addressed to me. Barbara and I, while gagging on the industrial-strength perfume clouds around us, talked about missed faculty meetings and then non-sexist language. When I asked if feminists objected to the words "remiss" or "menu", Milena rolled her eyes, but when Barbara smiled so did Milena. "For that," said Barbara, "you shall be penalised. Get Milena and me a drink. Now."

In the crowded kitchen I was attacked by Daphne de Witt, the Dutch giantess, who released the arm of some wizened emeritus and kissed me drunkenly, leaving specks of mushroom vol-au-vent on my face. She swallowed. "We were just talking about you, Romeo! Where's your doublet and hose? I heard your French girlfriend dumped you. Beautiful girl, what's her name again? Sandrine? So who are you sleeping with now? That Indian girl over there? How old is she? Remember the Dutch rule of thumb: a man's wife should be half his age plus seven." Daphne here paused to sample another vol-au-vent, saying she shouldn't. I waited for her to swallow. "You'll never guess," she began again, "what happened to me on a beach in Maine . . . "

I didn't try. Near the denouement of her tale she said, "I bet you're not even listening, I bet you prefer the silent type, am I right? You like the silent type, am I right Romeo?"

"I brook no babbling."

This was the wrong thing to say, as it got me a resounding thump on the back and a nearly dislocated shoulder. "You're a funny boy, Romeo. A very funny boy. Always ready with the word jokes, ya? A regular Joyce or Swan of Avon ya? Romeo, you're a bad boy. I left messages for you in your box—weeks and weeks ago. You're a rogue. A naughty little boy. Who's the gypsy girl? Your fiancée? Is she the silent type? She's a luck-y woman, very luck-y woman to hook a handsome man like you. You go for long locks, ya? I'll have to grow mine now. And maybe dye them black too, ya? Fine, fine . . . "

The latter words, always twinned, were Daphne's punctuation mark, more like a semi-colon than a full stop. She was our most brilliant scholar, at least in my view, but off the page she was out of control. She picked up a dessert tray arrayed with cakes and pastries. I honestly thought I was about to be pied.

"May I offer you a Berliner?" she asked. "I made them myself."

"A what?" I followed her eyes to a pastry with a hole in it. "In Dutch they're called Berliners?"

"In German. Do you remember—no, you're much too young—did you hear about the speech by John F. Kennedy in Berlin when he said—"

"'Let them come to Berlin?' That one?"

"Yes, he also said '*Ich bin ein Berliner*'!" She said this with a creditable Boston accent. "You remember?"

"It's a famous speech." I took a sip of wine.

"Exactly, it's a famous speech. But you see, he should have said, '*Ich bin Berliner*', because by adding the article, what the President really said was: 'I am a doughnut!'"

I actually managed my first movie spit-take, spraying wine into the air. At least some of it—the rest entered my windpipe. As I coughed and spluttered Daphne put down the dessert tray and, from behind, wrapped her arms around me like a Sumo wrestler. "Rotterdam remedy," she explained.

Gasping for air, heels off the ground, I spotted Barbara and Milena in the next room. Milena spotted me too. I tried to look as dignified as I could, in the circumstances. "You can put me down now," I wheezed.

Daphne put me down, into the path of two bookworms whose names and specialisations I've forgotten or never knew. They engaged me in conversation while I was blue in the face. We talked about the cosmos and *A Brief History of Time*.

"Who's the hunkalicious man?" Daphne whispered in my ear, interrupting my explanations, and minor emendations, of Hawking's theories.

"The what?"

Daphne turned me ninety degrees. "Him—the major hunk, with capital letters." A few feet away was the new lecturer on American cyber art, a sweaty individual I wouldn't describe as a hunk. More like a skunk. I waved him over, introduced them, then slipped away unmissed.

Barbara and Milena, engrossed in conversation, took their drinks from me without acknowledgement. I nodded a lot to give the impression we were a trio. Barbara said something about "Bachelors" and "Masters", a subject of that day's newspaper.

"Both are sexist," said Barbara, "throwbacks to the days when universities catered to the male clergy. It doesn't make sense to call a woman a 'bachelor' or 'master'."

I glanced at Milena, who was nodding in agreement.

"Are you a bachelor or a master?" asked Barbara.

"I never got out of high school," Milena replied.

"Most degrees mean bugger-all," I piped in. "Even doctorates are a dime a bloody dozen . . . " Barbara's smile made me balk. "Oh, sorry Barbara, no offence intended."

"None taken," she replied. "I don't have one. A Ph.D. is taken seriously only by those who do. You're working on yours, aren't you?"

I nodded vaguely. I had told everyone, including the Director, that I was. "Finishing up, final sprint," I would say if anyone asked about it.

"What's your thesis on again?"

"*A Yorkshire Tragedy*," I said in a near-whisper.

"Pardon?"

"*A Yorkshire Tragedy.*"

"Right. I've forgotten where you're doing it."

"I've forgotten as well. Why don't you jog both our memories?"

I turned round to the chilling face and hornet eyes of Dr. Clyde Haxby. He and Barbara were now looking at me, waiting for my answer. I mumbled the name of my school. Haxby gave me a slow, shrewd glance. "Yes, of course, North Shrewsbury. In South Africa. How are things progressing?"

"Finishing up, final sprint."

"You must have been there at the same time as Frederyke Jennen, and Bartho Dekker. *Terloops, het jy toe my brief gekry?*"

Oh shit. Surely this wasn't a question in Afrikaans. I smiled, retardedly.

"*Ah, bonsoir Madame Sobranet,*" said Haxby, "*comment allez-vous . . .* " I was saved by the Director's wife, who appeared with two new lecturers in tow, one of them Daphne's Major Hunk. As she was introducing them to Haxby I tried to slip away to the bathroom, but was intercepted halfway by lovelorn Philippe Forget.

"*Jérémie. Salut! Que ça me fait plaisir de te revoir!*" As we shook hands his eyes pierced me with telepathic declarations of lust.

"*Moi aussi.*"

After a few seconds of silence, and then crucifying attempts at conversation, Clyde Haxby ambushed us from behind. Haxby was always doing this sort of thing, creeping up behind you in his crepe soles, like a cat on padded claws. He told us a joke, the punchline of which was in Old Norse. As I chuckled knowingly, the Director came over with a tray. He asked me if I would like a flan, "*un flan de poireaux.*"

"*Qu'est-ce que c'est qu'un flan au juste?*" I asked.

"*Un flan? Eh bien, un flan c'est un flan.*" His voice ended with a sharply rising intonation as he shrugged his shoulders dismissively and walked away. For a moment I thought I was back in Paris.

Haxby enlarged: "A flan is just an open pastry, really. Usually filled with fruit, but sometimes with leeks or spinach or cheese, or even *fruits de mer*. The name derives from the metal tin with which it's made."

"Oh, I see." I was in no mood for one of Haxby's lectures. I turned to talk to Philippe.

"It has a rather long history, in fact." Haxby again. "Fortunatas—the Latin poet—mentions them. He also mentions that St. Radegonde made flans but ate only the coarse outer crust."

"Why wouldn't Radegonde eat the rest?" asked Philippe.

"It was an exercise in mortification."

I burst out laughing. The image was very funny. Haxby, a devout Catholic, was not laughing and neither was Philippe. I excused myself, my lips tightly closed, and on my way back to Milena conjured up images of poor Radegonde working in a hot kitchen all day, carefully preparing succulent flans with fruit and whipped cream and then chewing on the rye dough perimeter. But calling it a well-spent day.

As the evening dragged on, the Director decided to liven things up with a parlour game, one of his own invention called "Initial Impressions". It was quite simple, he explained. One person would start by giving his or her initials and then the name of a literary author, or character in a literary work, with the same initials. The next person would give another name with these initials or, failing to do so, was out. The sex of the person starting the round dictated the sex of all ensuing characters or authors. The last person to give a correct answer won that round, and a new round would begin with the next person's initials. Disputes were resolved by a vote or literary dictionary. The grand-prize winner was the winner of the most rounds and the prize, our host announced with fanfare, was a bottle of Lanson *champagne rosé*.

The Director began dividing us up into three groups of five, despite a clear void of enthusiasm for the idea. Some wanted all artists to be included, not just authors—are we not in Comp Art? That would be for later rounds, explained the Director, a Comp Lit man. Some managed to opt out, Milena among them. I tried to join her, but was prodded into one of the sheepfolds by the Director.

I made the fifth in a group that included Barbara, Daphne, Philippe and the old man I saw in the kitchen, a dusty ex-dean of four score and more, who may have been at the wrong party. Last to sit down, I was first to start, as no one else seemed to want to.

"J.D. John Dryden," I said in a confident voice.

Daphne, next in line, suggested that after the initials were announced we be given a few minutes to reflect. Everyone agreed, and then began jotting down names. I laughed. And then did the same.

"John Donne," said Daphne, after the allotted time.

"Joaquim Du Bellay," said Philippe.

"John Dashwood," said Barbara. "From *Sense and Sensibility*."

Good Christ, I thought, what a memory. The dean, up next, stared at a wood button on his cardigan. I got his attention and he said, unaccountably, "Cotton johnnies, always snuggly good!" We soon discovered that he was deaf as a post and unaware he was competing in a game. So we bellowed out the rules to him, causing the other groups to look our way. The dean eventually nodded and said, louder than he knew,

"Jerusalem Delivered!" Seeing our puzzled looks, he continued, "You know, *Gerusalemme liberata*, by Tasso. Published in 1580—without his consent, I might add!" He folded his arms across his chest. We decided to move on.

"John Day," I said. "Who may have collaborated with Shakespeare." This was a good one, I thought; no one will have heard of him.

"'Day was a full-blown flower in heaven,'" said Barbara.

"I beg your pardon?"

"A line from Swinburne's sonnet on Day."

"Of course."

"John Drinkwater," said Daphne. Her tongue flicked out, thirstily.

"James Dickey," said Philippe. He seemed to accentuate the first syllable of the last name. Or maybe I imagined this. "The author of *Deliverance*." I thought of the sodomy scene in the woods.

"John Davidson," said Barbara. We all laughed. "No, not the American TV star. The Scottish poet."

It was the dean's turn. I gave him a little nudge, as he appeared to have dozed off. "It's your turn!" I yelled.

"Four no trump!"

"John Davies," I said.

"Who?" asked Daphne and Philippe in unison.

"The Elizabethan poet," I explained. "Or poets—there were two of them. One of them praised Shakespeare as 'our English Terence' and the other wrote a poem that Shakespeare plundered for *Julius Caesar*." I smiled, in anticipation of applause.

"Fine, fine," said Daphne. "Johan Daisne. Dutch. He's like Joyce. In *The Man Who Had His Hair Cut Short* there's pages and pages about this girl whose body is rotting, her flesh putrefying, the stench—"

"Jean-Paul Daoust," said Philippe, "the Quebec performance poet."

"James Douglas," said Barbara. "Sir James de Douglas."

"But wasn't he an actual Scottish chieftain?" I asked, displaying my well-known mediaeval scholarship.

"True, but he appears in Scott's *Castle Dangerous*."

"Right."

"Wasn't he in *Henry V* as well?" said our host, Dr. Sobranet, who was now making the rounds, shoving his oar in. "Shakespeare's your domain, isn't it Davenant?"

Everyone turned to me. My face felt like a sunset. I made a sound that was not human.

"I beg your pardon?" said Sobranet.

My memory could not have been emptier. "There may have been . . . there was an Earl of Douglas in . . . " Here I laughed and for some reason mumbled a phrase in Danish, the only one I know, which means "How much does this cost?"

"I'm not sure I caught that," said Sobranet.

I gulped down my entire glass of wine. Barbara Celerand turned to the Director and said, "James Douglas's son, the bastard son, is in *Henry IV*. Isn't that what you said Jeremy?"

"Yes. *Henry IV*. The bastard son." I looked up defiantly at Sobranet. "Not *Henry V*." You fool. He nodded and trundled off to the next group.

It was the old dean's turn. One by one he examined our expectant faces "I'm off to the john!" he cried.

"I'm out," I said. I had lost my concentration.

"Fine, fine," said Daphne. "Jan De Hartog. He's Dutch too. Give me the dictionary and I'll prove it." And she did.

"*Je suis* out," said Philippe. Only two players remained.

"I can't think of anyone," said Daphne.

We all looked at Barbara, who could win with a correct answer. "Jim Dixon," she said.

"Who's Jim Dixon?" asked Daphne and Philippe.

"*Lucky Jim*," I said. "Lucky Barb. You've won."

"It's the dean's turn," she replied.

We played three more rounds—without the dean, who seemed to have disappeared. Barbara suggested I check the bathroom to see if he was all right, see if he still had a pulse. I checked, couldn't find him. Our host, who appeared with two sweating bottles of Cul de Beaujeu, assured us the dean was alive and well, asleep in the master bedroom. He asked in a whisper if we would mind taking Professor Haxby into our fold, as he had won every round in his group and "alienated" everyone in the process. We politely agreed. Daphne volunteered to change places with Haxby. I watched her as she seated herself next to a standing Major Hunk, within fellating range.

In Daphne's place Milena sat, and in her ear I spoke of my two admirers, of getting caught between the hammer of fat Daphne and the anvil of fag Philippe. Which I realise is not the preferred nomenclature.

"You have the sensitivity of a cod," replied Milena. "Asshole."

"What?"

"Everyone's an object of ridicule for you. Why is that? Is it to make you feel better about yourself?"

"What? What are you talking about?"

"You're weightist and homophobic. Not to mention conceited."

"I'm what? Weightist? What the hell . . . you mean fatso-phobic?"

"Yes."

"Oh, come on . . . and homophobic? I'm not afraid of gays. Are you kidding? Me of all people? Some of my best friends are homophobic. I mean homosexual. I was j-just . . . joking about Philippe. And about Daphne too. I like them both, I really do. It was a joke, I was . . . come on . . . "

I rambled on, red-faced. What was she talking about? Clyde Haxby materialised suddenly in his Hush Puppies, burgundy briefcase in hand. After making a quip in some extinct tongue with gutturals and kennings, and after I laughed volubly, he sat stiff as a ramrod next to Philippe, tapping his fingertips together. Barbara congratulated him on his champion performance in the other group, and he waved his hand dismissively, uttering more gibberish. The dean, looking more rumpled, rejoined us.

Someone suggested that Milena start up the next round. She shook her head. "*Vas-y*," said Philippe. "I don't want to," said Milena. "We need you," said Barbara. "We women are outnumbered."

Milena sighed. "M.M.—Marilyn Monroe." She said this half-heartedly, perhaps thinking it would exempt her from further play. But it was taken as a joke. We waited for another name.

As she hesitated Professor Haxby said, "Let's not embarrass the poor girl—she's obviously not read anything."

A few seconds ticked away, awkwardly. Milena stared at the floor, her face changing colour. Should I interject here? Defend her honour? Hand Haxby my card, tell him to choose his seconds, meet me at dawn?

"Maid Marian," said Milena softly. More awkward silence. I examined the flowered curtains.

"Good, from *Piers Plowman*," said Barbara.

"Yes, and a romance by Peacock," added Philippe.

I nodded. When someone pointed out it was my turn I said, "Let's take a break to think about this." My mind was a fog. Why didn't I say something to Haxby? Because of that letter he sent me? Christ. And what did Milena accuse me of? Weightism? Homophobia? I turned to look at Milena, who did not seem pleased. Her teeth were set and her eyes launched lasers. She emptied the last few cigarettes from her pack, tore off the front panel with more force than was necessary, and began scribbling madly on it. I looked around. Everyone was jotting down names except a smiling Haxby, whose folded hands rested on the table. I had lost my concentration, my thoughts gone with the wind.

"Margaret Mitchell," I said.

"Mary Macleod," said Barbara.

"Who?"

"The Gaelic poetess."

"That's right," said Haxby. "Let's see, I think I'll go with Malachi Mulligan. From *Ulysses*, of course."

"Who?" asked Barbara. "Is this a scoop? Was he actually a she?"

"No, of course not," said Haxby.

"Women only in this round."

"Oh yes, I forgot. This will prove more difficult, won't it? Let's see. Oh—Molly Mog. The titular protagonist of a crambo ballad by Gay." He paused here to look at Philippe. "Possibly in collaboration with Pope and Swift. The intent of the crambo poem, you see, being to exhaust the possible rhymes with someone's name, in this case a pretty young wench—an innkeeper's daughter, actually—"

"Marquise de Maintenon," said Philippe. He didn't appear to know who she was. Haxby did.

"She was the mistress and second wife, morganatic of course, of Louis XIV. She was also the widow of the deformed novelist Scarron . . . "

I here made the mistake of asking what "morganatic" meant.

With a raised eyebrow, Haxby explained. "Well, naturally it's from the Latin *morganaticus*. You, Davenant, are no doubt familiar with the French *morganatique*. Well, the term evolved from the Latin phrase *matrimonium ad morganaticam*, the last word linked to *marganaticum*, and of course the German—Middle High German—*morgengâbe*." He stopped here, as if this answered my question.

"Morning gift," said Barbara.

"Precisely," said Haxby. "Given by the husband to his wife upon marriage."

"So her husband gave her something in the morning . . . " I began.

Haxby laughed. "What it signifies—"

"What it signifies," said Barbara, "is that the wife gets shafted. She gets nothing else besides this gift, and neither she nor any of her children have any share in the husband's possessions or titles—"

"It's also called a left-hand marriage . . . " said Haxby.

"From the French *gauche* and the Latin *sinister*," said Barbara.

" . . . from the German *Ehe zur linkenhand*. In the ceremony, you see, the bridegroom gives the bride his left hand instead of his right. There's a morganatic marriage, come to think of it, in Disraeli's *Vivian Grey*."

"This is all very interesting," said Philippe, "but is she acceptable?"

"No," said Haxby, "the Marquise wrote no works of literature."

"How about Madame Murasaki then?"

"She neither. Her name is Murasaki Shikibu."

"I'm out then."

We looked at the dean. "Magic Mountain," he said in a voice audible to everyone in the room but himself.

"Mary Magdalene," said Milena, quickly starting the next round, and interrupting Haxby's objection to the dean's answer.

"Mary Magdalene?" Haxby repeated. "I suppose so—bible as literature and all that."

Barbara pointed out that Mary Magdalene also figured in the "Digby" plays. Haxby looked at her without comment.

"Margaret Mead," I said.

"Unacceptable," said Haxby.

"I'm out then."

"I too," said Barbara. This I was disappointed to hear. Haxby was smiling. "Maud Muller," he said. "The character in, and title of, John Greenleaf Whittier's poem. 'For all sad words of tongue and pen, The saddest are these: It might have been.'"

We all looked at the dean. "The Mysterious Mother!" he ejaculated. "By Walpole of course. Its theme of incest was rather shocking at the time but Byron quite admired it!"

Philippe, by this time, had explained the dean's handicap to Haxby, who remained silent. It was now back to Milena. I had my fingers crossed, both hands touching wood. Only she and Haxby remained, if you excluded the dean. She eyed her Lucky Strike panel, which was filled with backhand scribblings.

"Marianne Moore," she said finally.

"Excellent!" I shouted.

"Don't be condescending," she said quietly.

"Mary Russel Mitford," said Haxby, "who at the age of ten—that would be in 1796 or '97—won £20,000 in a lottery, which her father proceeded to gamble away . . . "

It was the dean's turn, but he was headed for the bathroom again, hand cupping crotch.

"Mary McCarthy," said Milena.

"Mina Murray," said Haxby, his fingers drumming on the table. "From *Dracula*."

"Marie Majerová," said Milena.

A few seconds drifted by. *Who the hell is that? Should I check?* Examining his fingernails, Haxby said, "She's Czech, is she not? Marxist-socialist?"

"Among other things," said Milena. "Her main theme is the subjugation of women."

Haxby smiled. "Mary Moore. 'He might have had my sister, my cousins by the score, but nothing satisfied the fool but my dear Mary Moore.' Yeats, of course."

I burst out laughing at Haxby's "Irish" accent. He turned his head slowly towards me, cocked an eye, but said nothing. *Come on, Milena.*

"Melissa Murray," she said, reading from her cigarette pack. "I think she's Irish too." We checked. English poet and playwright. Wrote *The Falling Sickness and Ophelia*, a reversal of *Hamlet* in which Ophelia falls in love with her maid.

Haxby took off his glasses, polished them, put them back on, X-rayed Milena's chest. "Right. Mary Monck, who wrote a few literary trifles. Wife of George Monck, 1st duke of Albemarle, who fought . . . "

"Mary Meigs," said Milena.

" . . . against Irish rebels." Haxby paused. "Mary Mig, did you say?"

"No, Mary Meigs," said Milena.

Haxby looked at each one of us, clockwise, with a skewed smile. "Who the devil is Mary Meigs?"

"She's a distinguished Canadian lesbian writer," said Milena. "I'm surprised at how ill-read you are, Mr. Haxby."

Professor Haxby's mouth, although clearly forming words, produced no sound. As if signalling for help, he cast glances at Philippe and then Barbara, both of whom simply smiled. He sat there, no longer with his impeccable posture, but slouched, like a crumpled paper bag. He cleared his throat, shot an uneasy glance in the direction of his briefcase, bit his lip. "I'm out," he said.

Yes! I'd been waiting for those words, waiting for Goliath to fall! I was on the verge of planting a congratulatory kiss on Milena's lips when the dean shuffled back into our circle, his cardigan damp with drool. For some reason he clutched Haxby's shoulder.

"Middlemarch!" he shouted.

No one laughed out loud. There wasn't time. Haxby turned and thundered: "Sit down, you perishing idiot—the game is over! Do you understand?" The whole room fell silent. "And let go of my jacket. Will you please let me go!"

The dean smiled, but did not release his grip.

"Will you please . . . " Haxby tried to jerk his arm free, twice, three times. "You . . . you blubbering fool, let go!"

The dean continued to smile. "I'm sorry?" he said, "I'm afraid I'm a bit hard of hearing!"

Haxby and Milena spoke at the same time, Milena the loudest. "He said you've just won the game!" she cried.

"I've just *what?*" said the dean. He released his grip.

Milena stood up. "You're the winner!" she spoke into his ear, her hand resting on his shoulder. The old dean looked at her, at all of us, with incomprehension. Philippe rose, then Barbara. We all got up to congratulate the dean, pumping his hand, patting him on the back. Now he understood. He grinned, then beamed, his eyes brimming with tears. Milena kissed him on the cheek.

Haxby, a look of disgust warping his features, grabbed his briefcase and mumbled something complicitous to me about "dimwit dykes and novelettes."

"Fuck off," said Barbara, who had overheard. Haxby glowered but made no reply. He examined a rip in the shoulder of his jacket before leaving to join the third and last group.

ೞ

Milena and Barbara, as the evening regressed, were getting on like a house on fire. Barbara drew up a timetable of her courses and invited Milena to audit any or all. As they laughed together I laughed too, not knowing what was so funny. Barbara, I was fully aware, was the only reason Milena accompanied me to this party. It certainly wasn't to be with me, I've no illusions about that.

I wish *I* had told Haxby to fuck off. Damn it. I would have, I'm almost positive. Given enough time, I would have walked right up to him and told him just to fuck right off. Or I would have phoned him. Faxed him. Left a message. Shit.

"Pardon?" I said. Milena was looking at me, an empty glass in her hand. Barbara was no longer beside her. "More wine?"

"Did you say your thesis was on *A Yorkshire Tragedy*?" she replied.

"Yes, I said that."

"Who wrote that?"

"Shakespeare."

"He did? How'd you end up choosing that? Because you're from Yorkshire?"

"Because of the Page."

"The page?"

"It's a long story. Do you want to hear it?"

"No. I'll have more wine though."

"*Moi aussi*," said Philippe as he plumped down beside me.

In the kitchen, as I searched for a corkscrew, the Director ambushed me from behind. "Ah, Davenant," he said loudly, as though challenging me to deny it. "How's that thesis coming along?"

"Finishing up, final sprint."

"I enjoyed your article on the Dark Lady, by the way."

You bullshitter, you just glanced at my (inflated) résumé. "Oh, thanks very much. I'm glad you—"

"That was your last publication, I believe. Quite a long time ago."

"Yes, well actually I'm now—"

"You know, I was thinking about you the other day. We have more and more black students in our department, particularly from Haiti, and we should probably do something in their honour. Africa would be good, wouldn't it?" He spooned some caviar into the hole in his beard.

"Well, I . . . " Africa would be *good*? What are you talking about, you bald trout. "Yes . . . I think you're right."

"Did you happen to see Victor Toddley's column this week? In *Barbed-Wire*? There's a conference at York University next semester. On the French-speaking theatre of West Africa. Perhaps we could schedule the same guest speakers. What do you think?"

I think you've had too many fish eggs. "Good idea."

"And I think you're just the man to represent our department. Present a paper, an introductory sort of thing, start the ball rolling?"

"Me?"

He wiped his mouth and whiskers with a tea towel. "You went to school there, did you not?"

"Yes. I mean no. The school was . . . is . . . in South Africa."

"And you've taught African literature before, have you not?"

"Well, yes but . . . I'm not sure that . . . you see I just did one guest lecture. On Bantu literature. On the praise poem."

"Good for you. I'm glad that's settled. It's at the end of January. Lots of time to prepare. Perhaps you could contact Mr. Toddley for more information."

"Mr. Toddley. Right, but you see I know nothing about West African theatre, and I'm on sabbatical next year—"

"Corkscrew in the second drawer." He walked out of the room.

I brought back two bottles of wine and set them on the coffee table. Barbara had returned and was telling a story to Milena and Philippe. Like a waiter, I began filling glasses. Maybe I should empty the ashtray too. When I sat down next to Philippe he held up his glass, which I mistook for a toast, clinking air as he took a sip.

After a few seconds of looking back and forth from Barbara to Milena, pretending to follow the conversation, Philippe asked me a question. I now turned to talk to him. It may have been the wine but I suddenly found him interesting and witty, and began to doubt whether he was ever attracted to me. He was just a nice soft man, which for some reason makes me uneasy.

"There's something I probably shouldn't tell you," he confided in whispered French, after emptying his glass. "But I'm too drunk to know any . . . No, never mind."

"Tell me."

"Well, it's about Jacques de Vauvenargues-Fezensac."

"You've got a crush on him."

Philippe looked at me with surprise, then smiled. "As a matter of fact, I do. He's quite something. You're his best friend, aren't you?"

"You're welcome to him, if that's what you're getting at."

Philippe laughed. "Thanks. But that's not what I wanted to tell you." He paused to refill our glasses. "Haxby was the one who got Jacques fired."

"So I heard."

"You didn't hear all of it. I was working on a project with Haxby around that time and we were exchanging diskettes a lot. One time, late at night, I took the wrong disk off Haxby's desk while he was in the john. Guess what was on it."

"What?"

"A letter, from a student, complaining of Jacques' offer of marks for sex."

"Haxby wrote that letter? Are you serious? And you didn't report him?"

"Shhh. I made a copy. And then told Jacques, who said not to breathe a word of it. That he'd make Haxby pay. And I think he did, literally. Haxby's got a shitload of money, remember. Well, less now."

I looked across the room, towards the man in question, wondering how I could use this information. "What did Haxby have against Jacques?"

"Lots of things. His review of Haxby's translation in the *Wire*, for one. And his jokes about Haxby's collection of fireman paraphernalia, for another. But they were always fighting. Jacques was the only one who'd ever stand up to him."

"Haxby collects fireman paraphernalia?"

"Once, before you were hired, Jacques told Haxby to 'make like a coprophagous insect.' At a faculty meeting, in front of everybody."

"Jacques actually said that? To Haxby? Are you serious? That's . . . hilarious." I began to laugh. "What does that mean exactly?"

"Eat shit."

"Right."

"Haxby can't bear to be insulted, least of all publicly. And he's a vindictive son of a bitch—with a hair-trigger temper."

"I saw flashes of it tonight."

"And he obviously thinks Jacques is gay, which is another strike against him. Haxby doesn't approve—on religious grounds, I think. 'Adam and Eve, not Adam and Yves,' is how he once put it. He probably thinks you're gay too, since you hang out with him so much."

"*Is* Jacques gay?"

"I hope so. Come, I want to show you something."

Milena, while talking to Barbara, smiled at me as I got up to follow Philippe. The guests had reached the stage where they were getting louder and friendlier, all notes of earlier discord lost in the sweet harmony of inebriation, and we twice had to stop to feign interest. The old dean, his long johns showing below his cuffs, was now mingling, a drink in each hand, shaking his alligator face and shock of ghost-white hair, making comments that stopped all conversation. I followed Philippe into the hallway. Next to the bathroom, on what looked like an old ecclesiastical bench, Haxby was asleep, ruffled and snoring, his burgundy briefcase beside him.

"One or two drinks and Haxby's in the bag," said Philippe. "Never fails. What should we do to him?"

"What should we *do* to him?"

171

"We must avenge his treatment of the dean—and of Milena."

"Yes, you're right. I was planning on . . . doing something."

"Now's your chance."

"You mean like tie his shoelaces together?"

"That's elementary school, Jeremy. We're in a university now—more is expected of us."

"Pour wine in his briefcase?"

"No . . . but we could try to open the thing up. I heard he carries an antique derringer inside."

"Are you serious? Loaded?"

"Apparently. I know he has a collection of handguns, including a Rivière. Let's see if this thing's locked." Philippe squatted beside the briefcase as I looked around fretfully, grinding the fillings of my teeth. "No use," he whispered. "Combination lock."

"What's a Rivière?" I asked. "Is that what firemen use?"

"No, it's a duelling pistol. I think Poe had one."

"Great. Maybe we should just forget the whole—"

"We're not going to forget anything. Think of something."

I sighed. "I don't know. Set his tie on fire?"

"Not bad, but he'd wake up right away."

"Stuff his coat pockets with ice cream?"

"No . . . "

"Crazy-glue his fly?"

"Glue it open, you mean? Not bad, you're on the right—"

"What are you fellows up to?" said Daphne's Major Hunk, coming out of the bathroom. We smiled. He walked on. I flapped at the air.

"I've got it," said Philippe. "I unzip his fly and you take his cock out."

"Excellent!" I laughed. "Perfect. He's in an ideal spot, right next to the bathroom, everyone'll see him before the evening's out. He's a real prude; he'll hate that. He'll never live it down. Except I undo the fly, you take it out."

Philippe shook his head. "No. You have to take it out."

"Me? Why me? It was your idea."

"Exactly. My idea included you doing it."

"But why me?"

"Why not you?"

"Because you've had more experience."

"This is your chance to gain some." Philippe looked both ways and then deftly unzipped Haxby's fly. Haxby didn't budge. "It's your move, Jeremy. Go for it."

"Philippe, I'm serious, I can't. I would but I . . . just can't. The thought of handling that squirmy . . . wrinkled . . . thing . . . it's just . . . it's—"

"Don't be such a fucking wimp."

I looked at Philippe, who was no longer smiling. This is no game, his eyes were telling me, this is no joke. I bit my bottom lip, looked around, waited for the Director's wife to pass. As she closed the door of the bathroom I whispered, "She saw us, she's knows we're up to something! I can't do it while she's in there—"

"We'll wait till she leaves. Then I'll keep a lookout. Just do it."

The music from the living room was getting louder and people were starting to dance. To Céline Dion. I was breathing heavily. The alcohol had not given me courage; I needed much more of both.

"Get me a drink," I said.

Philippe put his hand to his mouth, stifling a belch. "Get it yourself."

In the kitchen I met Daphne and her hunk who, with their tongues in each other's mouths, were unable to express much of a greeting. I looked around for clean glasses, without success, and ended up drinking from the bottle's neck. When I returned to the (potential) scene of the crime, Madame Sobranet, with more powder on her face and more scent, was closing the bathroom door. She looked at my wet shirt front and then at the sleeping Haxby. With a faint smile forming, she paused as if about to say something, but continued on her way.

"She knows we're up to something!" I slurred. "It's obvious! She's going for her husband!"

Philippe was casually twirling a pink party streamer round his finger. "Just do it."

"I can't believe I'm even considering this. If anyone sees me, you're dead." I took a deep breath, felt the room start to move. I gingerly pried opened Haxby's fly and peered inside. Boxer shorts. Thank God for small mercies: Y-fronts would've been tricky. I reached in. Haxby stirred. I withdrew my hand as if I'd touched fire.

"He's waking up!" I said.

"No he's not."

Haxby had moved slightly, more onto his side. The angle made things a bit easier. I reached in again and with a safe-cracker's agility pulled out Haxby's limp, squirmy, uncircumcised Oxonian tool. This time the only movement he made was in his face: a hint of a smile.

Philippe grabbed me by the shirt sleeve as I was about to flee, then calmly tied a phallic bow, or what could pass for a bow, with the pink streamer. We ran like schoolboys—Philippe one way, I the other—and then collided in the living room, where we mingled with our colleagues, roaring with drunken laughter at everything said to us, booming with laughter, aching with laughter.

ᘯ

When our taxi pulled up the tree-lined triple driveway, the four of us—Barbara, Milena, Philippe and I—were sitting in the front garden, arms entwined, singing crambo ballads amidst the autumn crocuses. None of us could remember what a crambo ballad was; we simply made lots of rhymes. Philippe swore he knew some good ones in English but no one could understand him. His meter, I believe, was anapaestic, so they may have been filthy limericks.

In the back seat of the cab we continued to rhyme, each of us providing one line: "We're driving in a car / Not very far / On roads of tar / To get to a bar." Philippe, who delivered the last line, got out a few seconds later, hand over mouth. I said I'd call him. I was now in the middle, my arms around two wonderful women. I closed my eyes. When I opened them Barbara and Milena were hugging across my lap, exchanging wet kisses and phone numbers. Barbara then bussed me on the cheek as I tried to kiss her on the mouth.

Milena and I continued on, getting out in front of her apartment. Her lights were on. "You only went because of her," I mumbled. "Didn't I. I mean you."

"Huh?"

"Barbara. You wouldn't have gone with me . . . otherwise, right?"

"Let's go to your place," she said.

This next part I remember well. We stumbled through the alleyways, past walls of urban scrawl, our drunken shadows growing and fading from one illumination to the next. Near Denny's window I kissed Milena on the mouth for the first time. Our lips—hers so exquisitely soft—moved on the moisture of our mouths as I pulled her body close to mine, as I soared into another realm, an upper realm, leaving time and earth below. When I dreamily fumbled with the buttons of her blouse, she took my hand away, motioning towards my apartment. "Let's go up," she whispered. She looked desirable, and desirous.

We slept together that night, in the literal sense. When I came back from the bathroom Milena was sound asleep, and there was nothing I could do to wake her.

ల

In a dream I ran with Milena through mountain fields near my mother's tombstone. It was near midnight, according to a clock of stars, when we stopped at a kissing-gate covered with moss. Without a word Milena pushed open the creaking gate, grabbed my hand and guided me along an overgrown path with occasional sunken steps to a garden that turned into the bed of wildflowers beneath my balcony. Amidst the towering plume poppy, goat's beard and meadow rue, under a cluster of pale stars and crescent moon, we made fiery love till dawn . . .

I woke up to the sound of Milena throwing up in the bathroom.

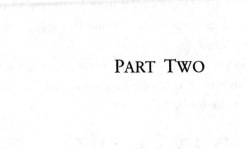

PART TWO

Twelve

I am mad to think that moon was mine . . .
—A Yorkshire Tragedy

On William Shakespeare's forty-first birthday, a brutal and depraved gambler named Walter Calverley stabbed his wife and murdered his children in a manor in northern England. A version of this rake's progress into infanticide was told three years later in an odd one-act play called *A Yorkshire Tragedy*. Its title-page looked like this:†

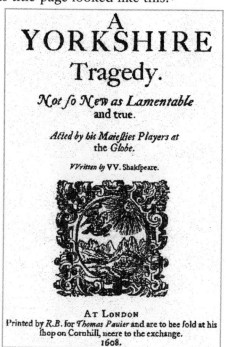

A
YORKSHIRE
Tragedy.

Not ſo New as Lamentable
and true.

Acted by his Maieſties Players at
the *Globe*.

VVritten by VV. Shakſpeare.

AT LONDON
Printed by *R.B.* for *Thomas Pauier* and are to bee ſold at his
ſhop on Cornhill, neere to the exchange.
1608.

I heard the name Calverley for the first time when Gerard took me to the Castle Museum in York. I must have been seven or eight. Stuffed horses, fire buckets and old muskets come streaming back, but what stands out most are the "old gaols" where, according to Gerard, Walter Calverley was "pressed to death." With images of an electric iron in my head, I remember thinking "what a way to go." "Why would they press him to death?" I finally asked.

"For incest and murder," Gerard replied.

I don't remember anything else.

My second encounter with Calverley took place a year or two later, around Hallowe'en. Gerard and I had been to the racecourse at Pontefract, in West Yorkshire, where we had won (in my eyes) huge sums of money. Some of it—two fist-fuls of coins—I had won myself, on hunches. But I tried to remain calm. "You must keep up a gentlemanly dignity," Gerard advised me, more than once, on our way back to the car park. The cold wet grass was littered with discarded race tickets and programs, and the bookmakers were taking down their stands. "Only the rabble jump up and down. A real gentleman should not show excitement—even if he loses his entire fortune."

In the car, a battered black Rover, Gerard wrapped me in a woollen blanket while talking about the Druids, a favourite theme. The coins jingled in my pockets as we threaded our way through narrow by-roads and windy moorland tracks, my eyelids getting heavier and heavier. "Fish and mistletoe were sacred to them, you see . . . And they'd ignite these mammoth bonfires at Hallowe'en—bone fires, actually, since they burned the bones of their near relatives . . . "

†In the Stationer's Register of 2 May 1608, the author was listed as "Wylliam Shakespeare," and in the quarto of 1619 as "W. Shakespere." The Bard himself spelled his name at least a dozen different ways (an anagram of "William Shakespeare," my uncle pointed out, is "A weakish speller, am I?")

The next thing I recall is the sound of branches brushing against the windscreen. When I asked where we were, Gerard put his finger to his mouth and whispered, "Do you believe in ghosts, Jeremy?" I remained silent. "Fancy seeing a haunted house?" he asked. I nodded yes, but was thinking no.

We got out of the car as quietly as possible, Gerard signalling me not to slam the door. Hand in hand, we walked through a small thicket to the edge of a marsh, where Gerard stopped and pointed. A large solitary house with ill-kept grounds stood shimmering, mirage-like, in a sunset of orange and plum.

"Calverley Manor," Gerard explained. "Old Calverley's ghost has been seen in these very woods, galloping at night on a headless horse."

I squeezed Gerard's hand harder, my heart galloping wildly.

"Oh, there's no fear of meeting it now, lad. The ghost has been laid and cannot reappear, as long as hollies grow green in Calverley Wood."

As long as hollies grow green in Calverley Wood. I looked at the house, at the woods behind us, at Gerard. "Are there any holly trees growing around here, Uncle Gerard?"

"Not that I know of. Let's see if old Calverley can be persuaded to come out. Shall we give it a try, lad?"

I didn't answer. I clutched Gerard's hand white as we walked around stagnant pools of water and beds of decaying vegetation. Our shoes crunched on a disused gravel path that led to the rundown but not ruined manor. Near the front entrance, on the weeded gravel, Gerard placed his gloves and trilby hat and asked for my gloves and cap as well. "Gimme yer titfer," he said. He arranged these, along with some gravel and stones, in the rough shape of a pyramid. We then joined hands while Gerard incanted a strange refrain:

Old Calverley, old Calverley, I have thee by th' ears
I'll cut thee in collops unless thou appears.

With prompting, I eventually joined in. As I whispered these words alone, Gerard produced from his mackintosh an amber bottle and drank its dregs. The empty bottle he laid gently on the ground before smashing it with a rock. He spread the shards of glass around the pyramid, and then tramped on these, round and round, while repeating the refrain.

On tiptoe we crept towards the house, to a large mullioned window. Gerard lifted me up so I could see in. The glass was almost opaque with grime and it was pitch black inside.

"I can't see anything, Uncle."

"Are you sure?"

"Yes, quite. You can let me down now."

It was Gerard's turn to look. "Oh yes," he said. "Absolutely. That's him all right. My word! The furniture's moving round in a circle, Jeremy! He's coming our way!"

We ran back to the car, Gerard laughing devilishly. I wasn't laughing at all. We got back into the car, slammed the doors shut and quickly locked them. Gerard began to cough, a long deep-lunged hack.

"You're a brave lad," he said into his handkerchief. "Very brave indeed. Now let's see what we can find under here." He reached under his seat and pulled out a paper bag. "Shall we have a touch, then? Celebrate our winnings?" He held up a bottle of what he said was champagne, and then opened it with a corkscrew from a knife with lots of attachments. "We shall toast the goddess Fortune in foaming goblets," he said while filling two streaked plastic cups. He laughed and so did I. We touched cups, Gerard emptied his, and then said he had to go "micturate". The moment he disappeared from view,

I opened my door and poured my sparkling wine onto the ground. It tasted dreadful. I locked both doors and waited.

When Gerard emerged from a bush seconds later I quickly unlocked his door, not wanting him to think I was a coward. He got into the car and told me that in the jungles of Zululand he'd almost died of blackwater fever.

"What's a blackwater fever, Uncle?"

"It's a disease, Jeremy, that turns your urine black."

Gerard started up the engine and we were off again. I finished my cup of wine, which Gerard had replenished, and the bog and ling and black rock began to swim before my eyes. I soon fell asleep, my head on a pillow on Gerard's lap. Back in York, each morning in the bathroom and each night in bed, I had images of black pee in my mind. It lasted quite a while.

ଔ

My third Calverley encounter took place in North York, not long after the move. I was in the York University library, among grown-ups, researching the seven entries on the Page. A woman who looked like Claudia Cardinale with glasses was putting away books, and when she came to clear off my table I nervously asked her if there was a way of looking up specific words in Shakespeare. She smiled and said "Come with me."

After a period of amatory distraction I set to work, paging through the Shakespeare concordance she gave me. Among other things, I discovered that one of the entries on the Page, **shaking palsy**, appeared in only one play . . . *A Yorkshire Tragedy*. It was, moreover, a central metaphor:

> *'What is there in three dice to make a man draw thrice three thousand acres into the compass of a little round table. and with the gentleman's palsy*

in the hand shake out his posterity. thieves or
beggars . . .

I see how ruin with a palsy hand
'Begins to shake the ancient seat to dust.

In my convoluted logic of youth I attached great significance to this "coincidence"—and to the fact that the father,
like Gerard, wagered away his family lands:

My lands showed like a full moon about me. 'But
now the moon's i' th' last quarter. waning. waning.
and I am mad to think that moon was mine. 'Yours
and mine and my father's and my forefather's gener-
ations' generations. 'Down goes the house of us:
down. down it sinks.

I asked Claudia if the library had an original manuscript
of the play. Unlikely, she thought, but she would do some
research if I liked. Yes please. When I returned the next day
as arranged (it was like a date), she said that there was a good
first quarto in the Newberry Library in Chicago.

At least once a week after that I asked my parents if I could
go to Chicago; at least once a week I was told I could not.
But I ended up going anyway, about a year later, when my
geography class went on a field trip to a nickel mine near
North Bay. They were away for a long weekend and Ralph
thought I was with them. Mother knew I was not.

My train was an overnighter, a milkrun, during which I
slept no more than an hour. I kept busy with a detailed map
of Chicago, with bus and El routes and tourist attractions and
a big red circle around 60 West Walton Street, the site of the
Newberry Library. By the time we pulled into the station, I

knew Chicago like the back of my hand. But I got lost anyway, too shy to ask for directions, and ended up taking a cab.

"You sure the library's open on a Saturday, bossman?" the black cabby asked me, avuncularly. I just grunted; I hadn't thought of that.

The library wasn't open. At least not yet—I had an hour to wait. On the steps of the triple-arched entrance, squinting in the midmorning sun, I put on a jacket and tie, tied my hair at the back and stuffed it under my collar. From my breast pocket I pulled out a letter of recommendation from my English teacher, Mr. Gilburne, which I'd written on the train. I didn't want the Newberry librarian thinking I was some nutty vandal.

But the librarian was a kind and trusting soul, and he smiled as he read my letter. He ushered me into a reading room, switched on lights that flickered and fizzed, and told me that the Newberry was Chicago's first electrified building. He also said it contained twenty-one miles of books. I nodded, not knowing what to reply. Eventually, as I waited in the shadowy room, alone with palms dripping, he brought me a slender volume bound in red morocco. "This is a good first quarto," he assured me. "I know," I said.

I waited for him to go, but he didn't seem in any hurry. He hovered close before sitting down across from me. He picked up a random book on the desk and swung his gaze from it to me, his bifocaled eyes darting up and down. What was he worried about? That I'd use a highlighter?

My heart was pounding as I held the smooth leather book, wondering how many dead hands had turned its pages. I counted to eleven and opened it. The inside front cover bore the armorial label of one William Gott of Armley House, Leeds, and on the fly-leaf was a handwritten summary of the facts based on "Stowe's Chronicle", anno 1604:

Walter Calverley of Calverley in Yorkshire Esquier. murdred 2 of his young children. stabbed his wife Phillipa into the bodie with full purpose to have murdred her. and instantly went from his house to have slaine his youngest child at nurse. but was prevented. The reason the Murdrer gave for the act was that hee perceived and conjectured from his Wife's conduct that his children were not by him begotten. At his triall in Yorke hee stood mute. and was judged to be prest to death at the castell of Yorke.

I turned the page and began the play, though I'd read it many times before. With its old spellings and script (and with the librarian watching me), it was more difficult than my copy—more mysterious and frightening as well. Slowly I pored over each word of this macabre tale, uncertain of what I hoped to find there. Confirmation that Shakespeare had written it? I didn't need any.[†] More clues about Gerard's gambling disease? No, I think I just wanted to hold it. I eventually dozed off, exhausted from my train ride, and woke up in a tug-of-war, the librarian trying to pry the book from my arms.

ଓ

My final visit from Calverley's ghost took place in Paris, in my last year of school. I was in the Bib Nat (you can call it that if you've been there twice) just before closing time when

[†]Alexander Pope described *A Yorkshire Tragedy* as "a wretched play . . . that cannot be admitted as Shakespeare's." Among those who accept the work as canonical are Steevens, Ulrici, Fleay, Ward, and J.S. Moore. Moore has gone so far as to say that "[the play's] stark realism, its unremitting dramatic power [. . .] distinguish *A Yorkshire Tragedy* and set it among the few truly great domestic tragedies of its age." (*Shakespeare Pseudographia Society Newsletter*, Montreal, Fall 1993).

I fortuned upon a doctoral thesis called *"Une Tragédie york-shirienne' de Shakespeare: canonique ou apocryphe?"* It was written by a certain Jacinthe Amyot and published by the Université de Champagne-Ardenne—in the year and quarter of my birth. To this coincidence I ascribed a fatalistic relevance—the promptings of chance could not be ignored. The next day, accordingly, I returned to the library and copied the 186-page thesis from microfilm to shiny wet paper. Over the next couple of weeks of missed classes I feverishly translated it, and then modified the contents of the cover page. I've not submitted it yet, and trust I never will (especially now, with the cat out of the bag).

Thus equipped with a shaky licence and shakier *diplôme d'études* from Paris, a doctored thesis from Ardenne and blank doctorate from North Shrewsbury, I returned to North York in Canada. I arrived on a Saturday and left the next. As Ralph, in his panelled basement refuge, cocoa and Fig-Roll biscuits at his side, watched men talking about zinc futures, I rounded up a few essentials and fitted them with jig-saw precision into my mother's blue Colt, which had been sitting, sad and unridden, in the driveway. At midnight I headed east along the 401 and arrived in Lower Canada as the sun came up. A few rudderless, compassless years later, I applied for a teaching post at a French-speaking university.

THIRTEEN

Why, he's married, beats his wife, and has two or three children by her.
For you must note that any woman bears the more when she is beaten.
                                                            —*A Yorkshire Tragedy*

"**D**id your father beat your mother?" It was the morning
after the faculty party and I put this question to
Milena the moment she opened her eyes. Rain lashed against
the bedroom window and the sky was shaking. I should have
felt excited, ineffably romantic, but I didn't. I felt wretched
from undersleep and nightmares—in one of which Milena's
father rode up and down my street on a headless horse.

Milena glanced at me for a second's lapse, said no, then
disappeared into the bathroom. She was there a long time,
at least long for her. When she came back to bed she lit a
cigarette, dropped the spent match into a glass mug, took a
few long hauls and said yes, he did. I waited for her to tell
me more; she asked if I had any coffee. With a smile and split-
ting headache I got up to make some.

At opposite ends of the chesterfield we each had two cups
of coffee and two aspirin with codeine. I waited, as my head
gradually cleared, for Milena to tell me about her father. She
remained silent. "Did your father beat *you?*" I asked.

Milena scratched at the label of the aspirin bottle and then
stared at a plate of butter that had been sitting on the coffee
table since two breakfasts before. It was half-wrapped in
aluminum foil, with scrapings from toast adhering to it.

"When I was around ten," Milena eventually replied, "I dropped a dish of butter like that onto the floor. It was during supper. Just my father, my sister and I—my mom had died a few weeks before. It was a hot summer night and the butter was soft and runny and it splattered when it hit the floor. Must have been half a pound of it. I laughed, nervously, and so did my sister. My father looked down at the floor, poured himself another drink, then told me to get down on my knees and lick it up."

"*Lick* it up? Are you serious? The bastard! And did you?"

"He pushed me down, hard, by the back of the neck. I was on my hands and knees, staring at the butter, not knowing what to do. And then whack! My father smacks me on the behind and goes, 'What're you waiting for? Do it!' So I did it. Or tried to. It was not only sickening, but hard to get in my mouth. But I bit into a big chunk of it, stood up with butter smeared all over my face, and looked at my father. And then at Violet, who started to cry."

"Oh shit. And then what? What happened next?"

"I looked back at my smirking father, and then spat the butter in his face."

"Yes! All right! And then you ran like hell, right? What'd *he* do?"

"He grabbed me by the hair and swung me till my heels left the ground and didn't let go till I started screaming and Violet started screaming and he was left with strands of hair in his hands."

03

After sitting alone on the balcony Milena got dressed, said she didn't feel like going out for breakfast, but didn't seem in any hurry to go home either. She sat back down on the sofa, fired up another cigarette, and looked blankly at the wall in front of her. I went to make toast and devilled eggs, which Milena didn't touch. In a dense Virginia fog we sat.

"Your father," I blurted out, "was a jealous husband, right? Always thought your mother was playing around?"

"Well, yeah, but how—"

"And he thought that his children weren't really his?"

"How'd you know that? I mean who told you that?"

"I have my sources. And your father's name is Walter, right?"

"Jeremy, what are you—"

"Did your father ever . . . abuse you? I mean, sexually?"

The ash of Milena's cigarette fell onto her lap and she quickly brushed it off. "That's none of your business," she said, staring at the grey streaks that remained. "But no, he didn't. Although someone else did."

I watched Milena, waiting for her to continue, emotions rippling inside me. The grandfather clock ticked away, a steady clop like horse's hooves, as loud as my heart. The phone rang and I let it ring. The answering machine clicked on and off and Milena looked up at me and sighed. "A friend of the family . . . " She stopped to pour herself more coffee but didn't drink. She stared at the butter dish, far away in thought. A full minute passed, maybe more.

"If you don't feel like talking about it, Milena—"

"You don't know what territory you're entering . . . A friend of the family, and I use the term lightly, 'took advantage' of my sister and me. Years ago. I know it happens a lot. I hope you're not thinking—not another one, not another one in this age of victimology, scapegoating, shifting the blame—"

"I'm not thinking that at all."

"I know that lots of women, men, have dealt with things like that. And I think I've dealt with it, put it behind me. But

189

in our case there was something else that made it harder, much harder to deal with."

I waited, thoughts wheeling like bats, hardly breathing.

"I don't know why I'm telling you all this, I really don't, you don't know where this is going. We were . . . well, lost. By my father."

"*Lost?*"

"In bets. Gambled away. He'd give us to this friend of the family to cover his losses. Addicts like him will bet anything—whatever's handy."

"You can't be serious!" I exclaimed, inadequately. "Your father *gave* you away? To do what? Who to? Who was this friend of the family?"

"No one you know. Or ever will know."

"Who was it? What's his name?"

Milena held smoke in her mouth before releasing it in short puffs. She looked me in the eye and paused. "Denny."

"Denny? Your friend who hanged himself?"

"He was my father's friend, not mine."

"Jesus! So he committed suicide because of what he did to you?"

"That crossed my mind—but only for a second. It's not something he'd regret. Besides, it wasn't . . . At first I thought it was some sexual game gone wrong—autoasphyxiation or something. But when I opened the door for the police—my father refused—I noticed his hands were tied behind his back."

"Yeah, I heard . . . Jacques mentioned . . . So it wasn't suicide."

Milena shrugged her shoulders. "There were signs of a struggle. As they say."

"So you're the one who discovered the body? The day I moved in I saw you going into his apartment . . . "

"I went in a few days later because Denny had some things that belonged to my mother—also gambled away by my father. And he had other things too, things that belonged to me."

"Shit, how do you deal with something like that? You must have nightmares and . . . I don't know . . . "

"About seeing the body? His grimy, stinking body? Not at all. Although his face was almost black, his tongue sticking out—"

"No, I mean about the . . . whatever he did to you, the abuse."

"I did have lots of nightmares, yeah, but it was never the abuse I saw, which wasn't exactly abuse in the physical sense . . . Well, I suppose it was. I mean, he just told us to do things, took polaroids of me, of my sister, of us together. And sometimes he tried to slip us roofies, in our cokes, which never worked, we were on to him. But posing was really horrible, humiliating, I was so shy about my body, in some of the pictures I had tears rolling down my face . . . When you saw me going into his apartment—I might as well tell you the truth—I was really going back for those pictures."

"Oh God. That's so . . . awful, I don't know what to say. I hope you found them."

"Yeah. And lit a match to them, then and there. If I hadn't found them, I'd have burned the fucking house down."

I nodded. "Did he . . . you know, do anything else besides take pictures—touch you, molest you, rape you?"

"My father gave us to Denny under one condition—that he never lay a hand on us. That he would kill him if he did."

"Did he? Lay a hand on you?"

"Once."

"Did you tell your father?"

"Yes."

"Shit. And did your mother know what was going on? Did you notify the police?"

"My mother was dead when it all started. And no, we didn't phone the cops. I don't know, my father was very powerful, we were afraid of him. Plus he said if we didn't help him—help him with his debts—then some thugs would come and kill him, and we'd be left all alone, in an orphanage. And later I have to admit I felt sorry for him in a way. He had a rough life in Europe, family life, and he was persecuted, beat up, stuff like that. He was from the north—north of Prague—which is where the worst attacks take place. And he had this paranoid obsession that we—my sister and I—weren't really his. As I guess Vile told you. In many ways his life's been rougher than mine. Denny's a different story . . . In any case, when I think about what happened, when something triggers memories of it, I don't really see Uncle Denny, or anything else. It's hard to explain but when that happens my mind suddenly goes all red, like an explosion of red, which isn't all that bad because it somehow stops me from thinking, from feeling, from wanting to kill myself—"

"Kill yourself! Christ . . . "

"I really don't why I'm telling you all this, I never mention it to anybody, I don't even know you. But I'm not going to talk about it again. I'm OK now. I'm definitely getting to the stage of leaving it behind, of letting go. I can't even remember quite a lot of it now. But now that you know, I don't want you to be different towards me, or pity me, or stop telling your stupid jokes or whatever. And no one else needs to know, ever, OK?"

Milena left without another word, without saying when or if she'd be back. I tried to remain calm as she shimmered down the stairs and out the door. After watching her disappear, from the balcony, I got into bed and pulled the covers over me.

ɔ೩

I remained in bed all day, sick as a dog, waiting for my buzzer to sound, my phone to ring, for Milena to come and cure me. At night, I stumbled in nausea and insomnia up and down the Boulevard; with bloodshot eyes I looked not at women's bodies but at men's faces, looked deep into their eyes and souls. If only sexual assault could be read in the face as fever and disease can! How about you? What dark secrets do *you* have?

Another day of sickness—fever and vomiting from devilled eggs—followed, with no sign of Milena. At night I walked again in circles, where men looked warily at *me*, as if they knew I knew. I arrived home to the chimes of midnight and fell asleep on the living-room rug, images of Calverley and his terrified children swirling through my brain.

My buzzer, I don't know how many hours later, jolted me awake. Seeing no light outside, I turned over to go back to sleep, sure it was some wayward drunk, some sardine-eating Latino. It groaned again. Milena. How could I forget? It's Milena! I bolted out of my makeshift bed and fevered bedclothes, out onto the balcony in boxers. It couldn't be Milena. I looked down. It was! She was descending the stairs.

"Milena! Milena! I'm home. I'll be right down!"

I raced into the bathroom to adjust my hair, splashed on some Andron, leapt down the stairs. I took a deep breath, tried to compose myself. One, two, three . . . I threw the door open. Before me stood my Dark Lady, in a rumpled blue raincoat, her wet hair streaming from her head in crooked curls. I looked into her eyes, deep into her heart-stoppingly beautiful eyes, and it was all I could do to stop myself from proposing on bended knee.

"Oh, it's you," I said coolly. "You're back. Come on up."

We walked up the stairs, Milena behind me, into a sick living room in disarray. "Can I get you anything?" I asked, scooping up mugs and magazines and analgesics, kicking aside clothes and Kleenex and Kaopectin. "Have a seat. Beer? Cigarette? I don't have either but I could get you some. Would you like a sardine? Or I might have some Lucky Charms or—"

"Jeremy, take a Prozac. I just came to get the tape."

"The tape?"

"The video."

"The video? Right, of course. The video." I sat, slumped on the rug.

"Friend of mine wants to see it."

A *friend* wants to see it? At one in the morning? Victor Toddley perhaps? Some bard from the developing world? "I'll get it," I sighed.

"Sorry if I got you out of bed, I should've called. Are you sick?"

"No, no. I was . . . I'm fine." I wiped my forehead with a used Kleenex.

"Why don't you put on some pants. And make me a coffee. If you feel like one yourself."

I looked down at my bare legs. "I do feel like one, I was just about to make some, the kettle's boiling, I mean the coffee maker's boiling . . . on."

Milena, still in her faculty-party clothes more or less, was sitting on the sofa and reading a New York magazine called *Bomb* when I emerged from the kitchen with a Bodum container of triple-strength coffee, two mugs and a one-pound bag of sugar. Milena pushed down the plunger of the coffee maker with both hands, as if detonating dynamite. She then shovelled in the sugar. So did I. We sipped in silence. She picked up her magazine; I punched the TV remote. *Three more . . . two more . . . now one more . . . and switch . . .* Zap. *. . . to a recent poll, 37% of all Americans would throw their pets off a cliff for $1 million . . .* Mute. Why did Milena come back? Surely that means something. No. She just needs the tape. A "friend" needs the tape. I turned on the radio. *Most of the music said to be by Pergolesi was not in fact his, but posthumously attributed to him by profit-hungry publishers . . .* Why do we have nothing to say to each other? We haven't enough conversation to cover a coffee. Why can't I be more like Victor? Milena will never fall for a bore like me. An academic fraud like me, incapable of political thought. What have I got to offer? She's probably got men like Victor crawling all over her. Or women like Victor. *A good deal of Pergolesi's success can thus be attributed to his premature death . . .*

In minuscule increments I edged my way closer to her. I drank coffee in nervous gulps and half-listened to a piece that was not by Pergolesi. In a sudden, impulsive gesture I moved my head to within a hair's breadth of her temple. She froze as I breathed in the scent of her hair and body, her unique, maddening scent. I kissed the side of her neck, her ear, her cheek—but lightly, almost imperceptibly. She let me, without shrinking, without encouraging. Her thoughts seemed elsewhere. She remained perfectly still, her magazine open on her lap. I paused, wondering what to do next.

"Why don't you just pounce," said Milena, "and get it over with."

I pressed her body close to mine, hard; she placed her hands on my back, lightly. The magazine fell to the floor. She looked down. I leaned back on the sofa and pulled her towards me, feeling her body tighten and resist, hearing her heart through the thin wall of her chest.

"Everything all right?" I asked.

"I guess so. I mean not really. I . . . I don't feel right about this."

"I understand." You want to be Platonic friends. You're on your way to see Victor. Enjoy the video.

"Would you mind if I stayed the night, Jeremy?"

Yes, I knew it, she *does* want to stay! "Yes, of course. I mean no, I wouldn't mind . . . "

"I mean, on the sofa? I haven't paid my bills in a while. They've shut off my electricity."

FOURTEEN

Travelling the sky, hardly touching earth . . .
Nothing stays distant, and nothing near.
                                              —*Shakuntala*

B oth my alarm clock and I failed to wake Milena for work
the next day. Milena slept soundly, comatosely, as if
hiding in a cave from daylight hours, making up for unslept
time. It took much persuasion, verbal and physical, to get her
to open her eyes. When I suggested she phone the restaurant she said "fuck the restaurant" and went back to sleep. I
did the same. We spent the next nine days together: nine
vertiginous days, at least for me.

"Milena, it's a beautiful day," I whispered into her ear, on
my third attempt to rouse her. "The sun's shining—let's rise
before it sets." No reaction. "Milena, I'm lighting a cigarette
for you."

At this she half-opened her eyes and emerged from sleep
as if climbing out of a deep well, a dark zone full of spider-
webs and bats. Only after strong filtered coffee and strong
filterless cigarettes was Milena ready for speech.

"So where you want to eat?" she said dully, through
smoke.

In a strict routine we ate breakfast on the Boulevard on
each of these nine days, at one of three places: a Québécois
greasy spoon that served bacon and eggs and "godlike
patates" all day long, the best place to find out who was

197

sleeping with whom; the French *charcuterie*, where the owner from Nancy continued to look at me mockingly; and an Italian pasta place that was good, cheap, but fluorescent.

On the street, men would often turn to look at her, which Milena, the rare times she noticed, couldn't stand. She couldn't stand men in general (all Montreal men, she once told me, were "hockey fans, liars or dolts"—I'm not sure to which class I belong) and certainly made no effort to attract them. Which of course attracted them all the more.

Past the dying tradesmen we would walk, towards the cat bookstore, which Milena would reflexively enter, as much for the animals as the books. She was the pied piper, leading a parade of adoring cats up and down the foul aisles. Ernst Kesselstadt, the dour German philosopher-proprietor, seemed to like Milena as well, perhaps the only human in the world he did like. On one occasion, while looking shyly at Milena (and never at me) with tired green eyes, Ernst told us a "joke" he had made up. "In a youth hostel," he said in a voice with no inflection, "two travellers get sheets for their bed. They're given a set of disposable paper sheets, ya? As they're lying in bed reading, one says 'These are hard covers.' The other says 'Shall we take the paper back?'" Ernst here let out a quick gunshot of a laugh, more like a bark or quack, without smiling. I had doubts about his sanity. Milena laughed. "Booksellers love that joke," he added before returning to his world of styrofoam cups and rolling tobacco and umlauts.

As Milena began to stroke two brindled tabbies vying for her affection, I discovered a curiosity on the bookshelves: a locked diary bound in pink plastic, with an inlaid photograph of daffodils and ceramic ducks. On its spine were pink carnations, a pink cup and saucer, and the word "Dream". Inside, once you opened it with the attached toy key, were more flowers, kitchen utensils, pots and pans. The pages were heavily perfumed and made me sneeze. On the frontispiece was a poem:

> *A good woman is like a good book—*
> *Entertaining, inspiring and instructive;*
> *Sometimes a bit too wordy, but when*
> *Properly bound and decorated, irresistible.*

While Milena was conversing in feline, I paid for it. A dollar fifty, a steal. "Could I have a bag?" I asked. "You don't need bag," said Ernst.

I handed the diary to Milena. "A gift."

"It's not wrapped. Cool. I used to have one like this." She read the poem, frowned, and then rummaged in her bag. In the "This Book Belongs To" square she wrote this inscription:

Jeemy,
will you be one of my good friends and be the
take good care of you Jer, And now I Jill.

It was at this time that I learned what Milena wanted to do in life. On our way out she said, "This is what I always wanted to do—own a bookstore. Sit and do nothing except read with animals, drink coffee, smoke cigarettes . . . and maybe paint."

☙

Awkwardly, all three restaurants took us past Cinéma La Chatte, the "L" of whose neon name was formed by a pair of women's legs, splayed, and the phone number of which ended in ♋. Once, to my surprise, Milena stopped and examined posters for a Shakespearean double bill: *Othella, the Whore of Venice* and *Venis in Uranus* ("𝕴 𝕷𝖔𝖛𝖊𝖙𝖍 𝖙𝖍𝖊 𝕾𝖒𝖊𝖑𝖑 of an Older Man's Balls", said one of the captions). Milena thought the place should be bombed for "eroticising dominance and submission," while I thought of Milena's past and of what Jacques had said—about the theatre being set on fire, possibly by her. The walls of the entranceway were still blackened by smoke. "Porn is the theory, rape the practice," Milena muttered as we walked on. I agreed that pornography was a venal, despicable business.

After our three o'clock breakfasts we would return to my place (Milena didn't like the sun) to do nothing in particular. Once, on the balcony, in Indian-summer twilight, we drank wine from my mother's silver goblets and Milena wore one of my shirts. When the wine ran out I proposed we play the child's game—although adults can play too—of spin-the-globe. Wherever your finger stops the spinning world is your ultimate destination in life. Milena spun the globe and put her finger on Hell-Ville, the capital of Nosy Be, an island off the coast of Madagascar. She seemed pleased. I spun the globe and put my finger in the Arctic Ocean.

After poring over the globe, rotating it slowly, Milena looked up towards the mountain. I asked her what she was thinking.

"About how fantastic it would be to go away. Far away from this fucking city."

I followed her heavenward gaze, saw the shape of a heart in a fleece of clouds. We could go away together. I pointed. "What does that cloud look like to you, Milena?"

"Which one? That one? I don't know. A pig's head, with bulging eyes?"

"Right. You know, I'd like to get out of this fucking city too."

"You've got things keeping you here—a job, for example."

"I can't stand academia, never could. Academics are full of crap; they don't live in the real world. Maybe we could go away together, Milena. Just get up and go. Just fuck right off. To England, to Ireland, to York!"

Milena smiled bleakly, shook her head. "I'd love to go to England or Ireland, I really would. But I can't. I've got debts that'll take years to pay off. And there's . . . other things."

I had no money to lend her. "I'll lend you some money."

"No. It's out of the question."

"We'll buy lottery tickets. No, the Casino!" I regretted these words the moment they left my mouth.

"Don't be stupid. I already told you, I'm anti-chance, I hate anything to do with gambling."

In a patch of silence we watched Lesya tend her garden and then the Parks Department plant a row of trees down the street. They had state-of-the art equipment and planted each sapling in a matter of seconds. I now had a tree right in front of my balcony. It was the shortest and spindliest of the lot.

I turned to Milena and said, out of the blue, "*Je t'aime.*" (In French, this doesn't sound so bad, not as jarring as the English, just as *Gott ist tot* doesn't sound so bad in German.) When I looked Milena in the eye, she may have thought I was expecting her to reply in kind.

"What do you want me to say?" she replied. "I plight thee my troth?"

I looked down at the balcony floor. "Well, yes," I mumbled, too soft to hear.

 જી

On our last night together, while Milena was showering, I saw someone sitting on the curb across the street: a thickset man with bad posture and a pale fedora cocked over his eye.

Someone I'd seen before. He appeared to be staring up at the balcony, and didn't avert his gaze when I stared back at him. For some reason I felt fear. He was like Death's grim-visaged messenger. But it was dark outside—was he really looking at me?

I went back in, shaking my head at my silliness, and waited for Milena. She eventually emerged wearing a towel, like Doris Day, and said she had to go back to her place to "pick up some more things." I surreptitiously watched her dress, admiring her willowy, callipygian form, then followed her down the stairs and out onto the sidewalk. "He sleeps in that hat," Milena muttered.

"You know him? I think it's that same guy who was staring up at your apartment the other day. Remember?"

"Yeah, I remember."

"Who is he?"

"My father. I'll call you in an hour or two."

Fifteen

This mounting joy breeds months of pain."
—*The Rape of Lucrece*

Milena didn't call in an hour or two. She didn't call in a week or two either. How could she do this to me? Why? Hadn't we spent nine vertiginous days together? Days in an upper realm, in a world without gravity? Evidently just one us had. In my mind I played back our time together, sifting through her words and gestures, trying to understand why she'd bailed. Because she regretted confiding in me? Because of my Gallic words of love? Because her electricity was back on? Or was there a sordid third party involved? Victor? An abductive father? She wouldn't let me into her apartment—who was she hiding?

I dialled her matchbook number again, but this time got a woman's recorded voice: "I'm sorry, this line is no longer in service." I dialled the operator, who wouldn't tell me when or why it was disconnected. I suddenly became anxious, anguished. "But . . . but something may have happened to her. She hasn't called me in days, she may have amnesia. I mean her father . . . her father may've kidnapped her. No, she's killed herself!" "Do you want the police?" I hung up, my head aflame. Milena! I saw her chalk outline on the black of the alleyway, saw her white lips in the Saint Lawrence waters, saw her rotating, her neck in the hemp.

I made photocopies for lamp posts: MILENA MODJESKA. TALL, JET-BLACK HAIR, DEEP TROUBLED EYES, LARGE DISDAINFUL MOUTH, LAST SEEN ON RUE VALJOIE WEARING WHITE T-SHIRT, TORN GREY VEST, FADED BLACK JODHPURS, BROWN BOOTS. REWARD. I didn't put any up, of course. I slid messages through her mail slot, ran after tall dark strangers, scoured the Page for clues. What would Shakespeare have done? Shakuntala? Shaka? Well no, we don't want to know what *he* would've done. Should I phone the police?

Of course not. Because Arielle had seen her with Victor Toddley. *Victor fucking Toddley.* This is when reality set in. And self-pity and jealousy. I'd been removed, I was one of Milena's removals, another face airbrushed out of the picture, another stat in *Men Women Leave*. It happens all the time; it's happening every second all over the globe. She's totalled up my pros and cons, and I'm out. Where are you Milena?

"I often take the alleyways home," she once said. "It's the best way to avoid people you don't want to meet."

I roamed the alleyways, through miles of darkness and debris, to ask for a recount. I demand a recount of the pros and cons. There's been a tragic mistake in arithmetic.

"But it's dangerous to do that," I replied. "You should be careful, stay on lit streets."

The danger was no deterrent; on the contrary, she did it to prove a point—that no man was going to stop her, etc. I fantasised about rescuing her from dark-alley aggressors, even thought of bribing some thick-headed thug to waylay her. "Unhand her, villain!" I would say, springing from the shadows, in a cape, a rapier in either hand. It was the same fantasy I had with Bernadette when I was twelve.

One night, after miles of vain search, I saw someone—or rather something—familiar. Under a bald yellow light bulb, against an alley wall, I spotted a leopard-skin top—of the kind worn by Milena's sexy sibling. She appeared to be in the middle of a twenty-dollar upright, a vertical liaison with a short individual in gargantuan running shoes. He had his back to me; hers was up against the wall. She turned her head and looked me in the eye. I discreetly reversed my direction.

"Jeremy?" she said languidly.

I turned and watched her disentangle herself, leaving the gentleman with his pants around his running shoes. "*Crisse de tabarnac*," he muttered. She walked towards me, smoothing out her skirt with empurpled fingertips.

"Hello Vile," I squeaked.

"Jeremy, I need money. Bad. You got to help me. I'll like, pay you back."

I looked into her unfocusing black-lined eyes. Of course I'll help you. You're Milena's sister. Name the amount. I pulled out my wallet. "Have you seen your sister lately, by any chance?"

"How much you got?"

"Looks like about sixty, seventy bucks. I haven't seen her for ages. How much you need?"

"Twice that," she replied, looking not at me but at my wallet. She smelled of sweat and beer and her cosmeticised whiteness, smudged with black, looked ghastly in the sallow light. As my gaze shifted downward, towards the cleft of her breasts and black bra, a flapping sound came from behind. Her companion was walking towards us, high-top shoes unlaced, tongues wagging. I smiled idiotically at him. He placed a gold-coloured cigarette-holder between his lips.

"I could go to the bank machine," I said. "There's one around the corner."

Vile shot an interrogative glance at her friend and he nodded. "Oh by the way, this is Rodrigue." Rodrigue, who ignored my hand, had a moustache that was one step away from being waxed, the kind worn by those who tie women to railway tracks. His hair was oiled and curly, short at the front and disproportionately long at the back. Slurring his words, as if suffering from dementia pugilistica, he told me he wanted an extra "*32 piasses pour les niaiseries*," which I guess meant for the coitus interruptus. It was a curious amount to ask for: an imperial measure.

They waited outside as I punched in my numbers. I opened the glass door and handed a sheaf of crisp notes to Vile, wondering how this loan was going to help me with her sister. As she leafed through the bills, Rodrigue drew designs on the plastic neon bank logo with his car key.

"Here," she said to Rodrigue. "And here's a hundred if you got anythin' else."

Rodrigue counted the bills, lips moving, and then paused for an anal explosive, lifting his leg like a dog. Apparently satisfied, he removed a cigarette pack lodged under the sleeve of his boy's-small T-shirt. On his biceps was a tattoo of a woman with flaxen hair swirling into the image of a devil. After tossing Vile the cigarette pack, which hit her in the forehead, Rodrigue strutted over to a yellow car that was parked, coincidentally, in front of the bank. It had a large spoiler on the back. He rolled down the window as if to say goodbye, spat on the sidewalk instead, gunned his engine, and left us rubber and a cloud of foul exhaust.

"A close friend?" I asked, flapping my hand at the air.

"Yeah, right."

"Not exactly from the deep end of the gene pool, is he."

"What?"

"He's not a future Nobelist."

"Neither are you."

"Do you know what that spoiler on his car is for?"

"No," she replied after a few seconds, "but you'll tell me." She was examining the contents of her package and likely hadn't heard the question.

"It's to prevent the car from becoming airborne at speeds over 180 miles an hour."

"What's the number of your house?" she replied.

"Thirty-nine eleven."

"I'll bring the money over to you, maybe tonight, maybe tomorrow. Can I like, slip it through your mail slot?"

"No problem." I paused, wondering how to pilot the conversation towards her sister. "Vile, you haven't seen . . . how's everything goin' these days?"

"Don't ask."

"How are things with what's his name? The musician. Drew."

"It kicks ass. Except I'm real nervous around him. He makes me real fuckin' nervous or somethin'."

"So what do you like about him?"

"That."

I nodded, in perfect sympathy.

"See you around, Jeremy."

"Wait, Vile. You . . . you haven't seen your sister around, by any chance?"

Vile frowned, shook her head. "Nope, ain't seen her for a while. Wait, I think I did see her—yesterday at the pasta place. Having breakfast, with Victor."

Victor. The Italian restaurant. *Our* restaurant. Breakfast, for Christ's sake. "Right, I know . . . she said she was . . . If you see her again, tell her to . . . c-call me."

"You want some free advice, Jeremy? Milena's not . . . It's not gonna be easy with Milly, if you know what I mean."

"Well, no relationship's easy—"

"There's some things you should know about her . . . Nah, forget it, it's none of my business."

"What? Tell me. About what Denny did? About—"

"Milena told you about all that? Well well, aren't you the lucky fucking confidant. But no, it's got nothing to do with that . . ." Her voice trailed off as she turned her head towards the bank. A faint clicking sound, like cleated footsteps, echoed in the alleyway. When it stopped I said, "Vile? What does it have to do with?"

Vile's eyes were now wandering and her mind seemed to be doing the same, as if uncertain about my question, or even my identity.

"Vile? What should I know about Milena?"

"I gotta go, I'm gonna puke."

ଔ

My foghorn buzzer interrupted a dream in which I was gliding, stark naked, in a kind of large chariot with both horses and oars, over the treetops of Arden and Illyria and Renaissance Italy, with an equally naked Rosalind and Viola and Juliet and Portia and Beatrice and Desdemona . . . I stumbled out of bed and onto the balcony, and looked down. It was Vile.

"I need more money it's mega-urgent, just fifty, I'll pay you back like, tomorrow, guaranteed, I get paid like, tomorrow!" Her words were slurred.

"Hold on," I sighed. "I'll come down."

I opened the door and tried to impress upon her that she had already borrowed a hundred and fifty dollars and that money didn't grow on trees. Vile, pale as a corpse, looked at me and smiled. I looked down, down towards her change of outfit: a vulcanised rubber micro with a wide steel zipper running up the front.

"I can like, pay you back right now if you want," she said.

"Well if you can like, pay me back right now, why do you need more money?" I looked at her, ingenuously, for an explanation. Milena once said I was "educated but ignorant—invincibly ignorant."

Vile smiled again and raised her gloved hands, as if in surrender. With sleepy eyes rolling, she then grasped the zipper of her skirt and slowly slid it upwards.

No, you can't be serious. I can't go along with this. Ravishing you is a major fantasy of mine, a trio with you and your sister is too, but this, this is too . . . real. It's surely a trap of some sort. You've been around the block a few times; I haven't. No, I can't accept this . . . barter. It won't exactly help my chances with Milena, will it. I glanced at her sheer black tights, thigh-high and torn, stared at her white underclothes. White like her sister's.

"Come on in," I said.

In the bedroom Vile unzipped her skirt the rest of the way, bisecting it, letting it fall dramatically to the floor. "I think I been here before," she said, looking around. "Right, Denny's neighbours' place, the crazy Costa Ricans or Panamanians or whatever. Fixed up, kinda. So what do you want me to do? You want pictures too?" On the bed, sitting with her back to me, she removed her ankle boots and then top, revealing a range of body art in the form of tattoos, branding and scarification. *Now* I remembered where I'd seen her before: in the polaroids! She calmly turned to face me, full-frontally.

"What's-a-matter?" she said as I stared rapaciously. "You look like you seen a zombie. Never seen a nipple ring before?"

"Y-yes, I have. It's not that, it's just . . . "

"Got a ring down here too."

"I'm sure you do. It's just that I'm not sure whether, you know, the timing . . . right now and everything . . . seeing I've sort of . . . well, promised my body to your sister."

Vile laughed. "Good luck. With Milly you'll need it, believe me, you'll really fuckin' need it."

"How much you say you wanted?"

"A couple a C's should do it."

Vile was grinning as she put her clothes back on. And laughing hysterically by the time we reached the bank machine. A side-effect of the drugs in her veins, obviously.

SIXTEEN

Both in tune, like two gipsies on a horse . . .
                                    —*As You Like It*

It was about a week later that I once again saw Milena's father—we were clearly in each other's orbits. I was thinking, oddly enough, about my encounter with his youngest daughter, wondering if it was going to be one of those missed chances you regret for the rest of your life. He was leaning against a maple tree, a cigarette stub in his mouth, squinting up at my window. He ignored me—even when I remained standing with a scowl in front of him—as if I were a rock or post. What the hell did he want? What further damage was he planning?

The phone was ringing as I stepped inside the door. It was Jacques, on a cell phone from a girlfriend's rooftop garden in Quebec City. At least I think it was a girlfriend—some elderly European countess no doubt. "*Quoi de neuf?*" he asked with his usual lukewarmth.

While looking down onto the street, I said my latest bit of news was that a degenerate man in a fedora was staring up at my apartment, planning to kill me. When this met with bored silence I recounted, in bare outline, my misadventures with Vile.

"Takes one to blow one," said Jacques.

"No, I didn't . . . she didn't—"

"No? Your British gallantry never deserts you, does it Davenant. Just as well—she'd devour you. The woman's a forni-cat, a fellatrix of demonic insatiability."

"How would you know?" I glanced down at Vile's father, who was walking briskly away. "She's just got a bit of a drug problem and besides she had a rough child—"

"A bit of a drug problem? A *bit* of a drug problem? Are you intellectually unemployed? She's a professional coke-slut, Jeremy, an angel-dust whore. They'll bury her in a Y-shaped coffin."

"She'll shake the habit, you'll see."

"The only thing she'll ever shake is her ass."

"Jacques, why are you so—"

"How are things progressing, by the way, with her gloomy sibling? Is Pandora's box officially open?"

"Fuck off, Dion." I slammed the receiver down. "And don't call me again—ever."

Head aching, thoughts whirling like a dust storm, I trudged off to feel sorry for myself amidst the pigeon-fouled statues in the park, under a sky that seemed ready to collapse under its weight of leaden grey. Things were not "progressing" with Milena, oh no, things were circling the fucking drain. The relationship's dead, we're incompatible in every way . . . I had barely sat down when I spotted, across the soccer field, a portly policeman or policewoman closing what appeared to be Milena's gate. I sprung from the bench and went from trot to gallop, anxious to know more, but could only watch the cruiser pull away.

For at least an hour I paced back and forth near Milena's house, carrying with me a willow branch, the emblem of forsaken love, and smoking fag after fag, a new vice of mine. With the stub of a mown pencil I'd plucked from the grass I began writing a tragic love sonnet on my Player's package,

on the back of the sailor cameo. What rhymes with "valentine"? Aquiline, lifeline, intertwine; undermine, incarnadine,
disentwine. And with "marry"? Hairy, axillary, sanctuary;
lapidary, lachrymary, mortuary.

I mounted Milena's front stairs and slipped my ode
through her slot; as it hit the ground the door magically
opened. Before me stood my slum goddess in mauve and
mourner's black. I stared at her in mute agony, wracked, rent,
heart jounced off its track. Haloed, squinting into the sun,
Milena smiled softly. "Jeremy. It's good to see you, I . . . tried
calling you."

I tried to respond but my English was handcuffed, bound;
why does Milena turn me into a stammering serf?

"Pardon?"

"Erghh."

As my heart bounced erratically in my chest, almost as it
does in a cartoon, Milena apologised for her vanishing act,
but offered no explanation. She had "some things to clear
up—no big deal." It took a Herculean effort for me not to
make a big deal of it.

"Hey, n-no problem," I said, with a chuckle. "Forget it. I
have."

"Oh by the way, I just talked to my sister. Thanks
for . . . well, for rescuing her."

"It was nothing."

"I know she'll pay you back."

"Right." I wondered how.

As if divining my thoughts, Milena described her sister's
sex and drug habits—which so far had produced two abortions and a jail term. Was this a warning to stay away? A
marking of territory? Probably not.

"I think your sister wanted to warn me about something.
Like . . . I don't know, like you have an insanely jealous

boyfriend or a criminal past or an incurable disease or something."

Milena raised her eyebrows. "None of the above, although I'm sure there's lots of other things you should be warned about. Listen, Jeremy, I'd invite you in but I really can't, not now, the place's a bit of a mess . . . "

From inside, swells of putrescence hit my nostrils, while the stairwells, painted in blood orange, assaulted my eyes. "I didn't want in, I just wanted to . . . see if your electricity's back on and leave you . . . " I nodded towards the ground.

As Milena stooped to pick up the piece of cardboard, I looked down the billowing front of her dress, at the drooping lines of her cleavage, at her neither round nor full breasts and huge dark areolae. I could feel, in my boxers, some preliminary erectile hoist.

"What this?" said Milena as I darted my eyes back to hers. "Oh I see, it's a poem. Looks . . . interesting. Lots of rhymes."

"I just dashed it off."

"Really? That's hard to believe. I like it where you've rhymed 'bliss amidst the ruins' with 'the Boston Bruins'."

"Well, what that symbolises—"

"And 'none but Milena' with 'nuts macadamia'."

"It may lose something in translation."

Milena exploded into laughter. "What language does it sound better in?"

"Sanskrit."

"What are you doing tonight?" she said, after another detonation.

I had two classes, neither of which I could possibly miss. "I'm free as a bird," I said.

"Want to go for supper?"

"What time?"

"Sevenish?"

My second class started at seven sharp. "Perfect," I said. "Where do you want to eat?"

"I'll drop by your place and we'll decide, all right?"

I wanted to leap heavenward, wanted to kiss Milena on the lips, put my hand down her blouse, go down on my knees before her (not for forgiveness). "Whatever," I said, with an unflappable calm.

"I'll see you around seven, OK?" She kissed me on the mouth, closed the door, ode in hand.

I headed back home, no longer with dragging steps but treading on air. Inside, after pulling all the blinds, I stripped naked, put on Irish bagpipe music and the Screaming Moist Accountants, and pogoed round the room. I raised clenched fists aloft. She suggested we go out; I didn't say a thing. Cool as hell. The poetry was an inspired idea. Kicked in rather nicely. Boppa-boom boppa-boom boppa-boom. A slight problem with my lecture, though. I turned down the music. I'll have to pin some lie to the classroom door. Unless I ask someone to replace me. But who?

"Vauvenargues-Fezensac," said Jacques, after the tenth ring.

"Jacques, I've got a lecture tonight. You have to do it for me."

"I don't have to do anything of the sort."

"It's on Sonnets 57 and 147."

"I've not read either."

"Liar. What you do is look at three translations of each, discuss their merits if any, poll for a winner. I'll give you my notes."

"Please don't."

"Will you do it or not?"

"What's in it for me?" Jacques was bluffing. He'd filled in for me before; he missed hamming it up, missed captive audiences. The only hitch was that he was officially barred from campus.

"Visvamitra, on me." Chez Visvamitra was a restaurant whose dishes were Indian and prices Himalayan. "I'll come over with the material in about an hour."

"What time are you seeing Milly?"

"How do you know I'm seeing Milly—Milena?"

"I know everything."

"She said sevenish."

"Ah, the latitude of the 'ish'. That means she'll arrive when, around nine?"

"If at all."

C8

Jacques' Apartment Beautiful, in a fashionable area on the other side of the mountain, was like a library in miniature. Burdened ceiling-high bookshelves, with volumes arranged alphabetically, dominated every room, kitchen and bathroom included. Jacques knew the precise location of every author. "Céline? Over the toilet." Woe betide he or she who dealphabetised.

Sharing the apartment with Jacques was an animal, a Maine Coon cat named Juvenal who behaved like a rabid rat. He was fearless of visitors (though brontophobic) and greeted you with claws or teeth in the ankle. He was also relatively famous, having appeared in a fifteen-second catfood commercial—an attempt on Jacques' part to extend Warhol's theory to animals.

"Pray step into my inner sanctum," said Jacques in his plummy tones, while rubbing his hair with a purple bath towel. He was clad in a red silk dressing gown with gold tassels, like a cardinal's chasuble minus the nether layers. Juvenal was up on his hind legs, swatting at the oval hem of

Jacques' gown—or perhaps at his dangling tool, it was hard to tell. The beast glowered at me as I removed my coat, but did not attack.

Jacques motioned me into the living room with a head jerk and then sank into a capacious chair of jade-green leather worth double my earthly possessions. He put his feet up on the ottoman, whose surface had been savaged by the cat's claws, and didn't ask me to sit down. On the wall above him was a brass-framed picture of himself.

"You look a bit like my Uncle Gerard in that pose," I remarked.

"Really? How is the sinister kinsman, the infamous quester after women?" Jacques looked comfortably majestic, like an off-duty pharaoh.

I sat down on a steel chair. I was happy to talk about Gerard because Jacques contended that he didn't exist, that he was a figment of my imagination, like Milena. He said that Gerard sounded "too stock to be real," that he made "no attempt at divergence from type." But Jacques said this about most people. "That's the way he really is," I protested. "Honestly." But was it? Who was he exactly? Beyond his passion for wordplay, women and wagering, beyond his interest in things exotic, erotic and demonic, Gerard was a cipher to me. He was not given to talking about his private life—at least not truthfully—to me or anyone else I knew. Like spreading aniseed to confuse the hounds, Gerard misled and deceived those who were getting too close to him, shrouding everything in fantasy, old-soldier fables, lies. My image of Gerard was a distorted magnification; I saw him about as clearly as I saw Milena. The less you know the more you idolise. I guess what I'm saying is that Jacques was basically right.

Untypically, my host was all ears as I recounted the last bit of news I'd heard about Gerard: his highly-successful defence against the charge of forging French lottery tickets. Jacques only stopped listening when I steered the conversation towards Milena, my *féministe fatale*, as he called her, my lost but worthy cause.

"The 'bicycle theory', as you probably don't know, says that if forward motion is maintained, one will remain upright. You, Davenant, who are going backwards with your foot caught in the chain . . . "

As Jacques inveighed against her, against us as a couple, I had my second inkling that he was jealous of Milena, jealous of the time she and I spent together, or worse, that he might ruin our relationship forever. I put the thought out of my mind. Just more of my paranoia. I focused my attention on the opposite wall, a delicate duck-egg blue, on which a series of drawings depicted extreme forms of Tantric orgiasticism.

" . . . You're shovelling shit against the tide, Davenant, can't you see that? You're wasting your time putting your finger in the dyke. You'll be bedlamised by the experience. And besides, I'm bored with the whole thing—"

"*You* are bored? What the hell have *you*—"

"She's turned you into some grovelling whiny-assed hand-jobber—"

"I'm not asking for your fucking advice. I have a feeling it can work out."

Jacques nodded. "And your shit-clear chimp-brained reasoning for that would be?"

"It's a feeling, all right? It's unlikely you've ever had one."

"Remember what happened to your ex-neighbour."

"What's that supposed to mean?"

"You could be next. I've been doing a bit of research—some people, not the least of whom the police, believe that Milena killed Denny."

I was used to this kind of thing from Jacques; he was always dramatising, always trying to shock; I knew how to take these things with a grain of salt. "Milena killed Denny?" I screamed. "Jesus Christ, Dion, you're fucking delusional! Denny committed suicide, for Christ's sake. You'll say anything to get me away from her. I know you don't like her, but I do. So fuck off."

With a tolerant smile Jacques pushed some buttons on his remote-control panel. Music was the result: Schubert's "Death and the Maiden".

Milena kill Denny? "Don't forget those nine days Milena and I spent together," I said, voice quavering, as Jacques cranked up the volume. "Consecutive, joyful, vertiginous days . . . "

"She's obviously forgotten them. You maudlin idiot."

"I'm trying to rekindle—"

"You're trying too hard. You put too many logs on the fire and it goes out." He sat back in his chair and smiled. "That's rather clever, isn't it?"

"The thing is, I have a feeling she likes to be with me, that she's happy, or happier, when I'm around. But won't admit it, or can't express it. It's not easy for her to trust a man, get intimate with a man, I know that. It seems like one guy after another has let her down, brutally, including her father and mother's ex, both gambling addicts, alcohol addicts and violent human beings. Milena and Vile were both runaways, and their father didn't want them back. It's hard to recover from things like that. Look, I've tried to give up on her lots of times but I can't, I just can't help gambling on her, can't help falling, spiralling, melting into adolescent worship every time I see her. I'm not in control of this."

Jacques rolled his eyes. "Yeah, she's the flame, you're the moth. The scorched victim."

"Bugger off." I said this not to Jacques but to Juvenal, who had by now discovered my socks, his red flag. When I tried to bat the mad cat, he scratched me across the knuckles. "You mangy bastard!" I yelled. "If I get tetanus . . . "

With an exaggerated sigh, Jacques rose from his emerald throne and opened a suede cassette box inlaid with mother-of-pearl. While his back was turned, while he hummed along with the music, I prepared to kick the cat into the ceiling. One, two . . . Just before three, a loud clap of thunder came booming out of quad speakers. Panic-stricken, Juvenal jerked his claws from my socks and scurried out of the room, his paws spinning cartoonishly on the wooden floors.

"It's the only way," said Jacques as he relapsed into his chair. "Brontophobia." We sat, without speaking, listening to the sounds of a thunderstorm. Minutes passed. Jacques' face disappeared behind a book bound in maroon Nigerian goatskin, while I for some reason thought of Clyde Haxby. Should I tell Jacques what Philippe had told me at the party? No, it was said in strictest confidence.

"By the way, and I know this is none of my business, but was it really Haxby who got you fired?"

Jacques slowly lowered the book to reveal his eyes. "Who told you that?" he asked calmly.

"Philippe."

"That babbler, that sieve, that slack-jawed faggot . . . "

"He was drunk—and he told me not to mention it to anyone."

"So you're as tight-lipped as he. Don't breathe another word to anyone, not a syllable. I would have told you about it myself, but silence was part of the deal. I'm quite satisfied. My reputation isn't important to me. For the chance to be idle, I'll take a blot on the old escutcheon any time."

We sat. I looked at my watch. "I'm gone," I said. "Here's the stuff I told you about. Would you like to see my article on the Dark Lady?"

"What on earth for?"

I got up to leave. Jacques dropped my notes onto the floor and measured me with dispraising eyes. "Nice look," he said.

On my way to retrieve my coat, I paused to look at my myself in Jacques' hall mirror: white T-shirt, grey silk vest, torn black jodhpurs, brown boots.

"If you can't have her, *be* her," my host shouted from the other room.

From the bottom corner of the mirror, Juvenal looked up at me with fat agate eyes, patronisingly, superciliously, trying to one-up his master.

SEVENTEEN

Tall men can scarcely reach the fruit:
A dwarf, I stretch my arms in vain."

— *Kalidasa*

I arrived back at my apartment at exactly five to seven; Milena pushed my buzzer at exactly five to nine. Compulsive punctuality meets compunctionless erraticism.

"Hi Jeremy, ready to go?" she said.

No apology. No explanation. Ever. She claimed that all her friends were like her—what's my problem? *My* problem. Arielle once excused her by explaining she was on "Caribbean rhythm", where time was more elastic. Now this I could understand: it was the pace Sabrine and I got on in Jamaica after sunstroke and ganja smoke. "Okay, fine, I can accept that," I said to Arielle. "Okay, let's go," I said to Milena.

As she was low on funds we decided, despite my objections, to go to a Portuguese restaurant where three ninety-five plus tax could be exchanged for a plate of shit. Where the lighting and decor (fluorescent and yellow) were as hard on the senses as possible, as if the waiters were going to interrogate us all. Beside the cash register were tins of aspirin. It was one of those places that stacked the chairs at closing time to give the impression the floors were going to be washed. But for Milena and her circle it was cool, unbourgeois.

We sat down at a ripped leatherette booth near the back. The table was covered with our predecessors' crumbs and ashes and possibly their predecessors'. I asked Milena about her last few days. She said things were not going great, that she slept most of the time, and that she was proposed to.

"Really? Who proposed to you?" Victor?

"Some visiting relative of my father's."

"You're kidding. What's he like?"

"Like a bull. Charging with lowered horn. He said he loved me, that he'd marry me even if I didn't have a Canadian passport."

"So when's the date?"

"Thirty-second o' never. I explained to him that the only animals that bond monogamously for life are the California mouse and the wave albatross. I don't think he understood."

"Would you marry *me?*"

Milena looked at me blankly, straight through me. "Waiter," she said.

Milena ordered a lamb brochette and I something fish-sounding and the soupe du jour. The nature of the soupe du jour depended on which insects had fallen into it. The lamb and fish tasted about the same. Burnt woodish. Milena didn't seem to mind.

"Everything all right?" asked the waiter.

"Couldn't be better," I said. "But next time I'll go for your fabled *bisque homard* and swordfish *amandine.*"

"Pardon?"

"Very funny," said Milena. "Don't mind him. He's being an asshole."

The thing I remember most about the conversation that followed is the frequency and intensity of Milena's use of the word "fuck". Nothing unusual about that, except we were next to an après-glee-club group who kept raising their eyebrows for our benefit. On their way out, one of them paused in front of our table. "May I remind you this is a non-smoking section," he said snippily, arms akimbo. He had a marsupial pouch over his loins, and Ken-doll hair.

"Oh fuck," said Milena. "Not another one. I'm sick of this decafeinising of the world."

"The owner should be informed of your foul language," he added, clucking his tongue in disapproval.

"I wouldn't get upset. When I say 'fuck' it's with a 'ph'."

"Next time, and I mean this, I'm going to lodge a complaint with the owner." He turned, with a flourish, towards the door.

"Fuck the owner," said Milena after him. "And fuck you too."

"It's time to order dessert," I said cheerily.

"Don't bother," said Milena. "I have something for you. From Prague." This she pronounced Praha. Out of her knapsack she pulled a tinfoil package and handed it to me. I opened it. It looked like a poppyseed sandwich. "It's called *makový koláč*. My aunt sent it to me. She's a great cook."

The waiter pushed my burnt offering, my prison food, to one side and set a cup of coffee down in its place. The saucer, which held as much coffee as the cup, bore the mark of the waiter's thumb.

"Do you cook?" I asked.

"Hardly. I can't stand cooking."

"If you had a choice of one of the following, which would you choose: a full-time cook, chauffeur, or housekeeper?"

"A cook. No question about it. I'd marry someone who was a great cook. How about you?"

I have to admit I was surprised, make that stunned, by what Milena had said—the matrimonial part. I stared at my coffee for a few seconds before saying, "Well, since I already cook, I guess I'd choose a chauffeur."

"You cook? Really? How come you've never cooked for me? What are your specialties?"

"I'll cook for you tomorrow night if you want. What kind of stuff do you like?"

"I'm not fussy. What kind of stuff do you do?"

I took a long sip of my brackish coffee. "Well, you know, the standard stuff."

"The standard stuff?"

"Well, you know . . . the French stuff, French cuisine."

"What kind of French stuff?"

I paused again. "Well, you know, French stuff like . . . boeuf bourguignon and canard à l'orange and . . . coq au vin, bouillabaisse . . . coquilles Saint Jacques . . . that kind of stuff."

"God, you sound like a serious chef."

"I wouldn't go quite that far. It's a hobby."

"And you just do French dishes?"

"Well . . . right."

"I'd never have guessed."

"Yeah, I suppose I'm a bit mysterious. Do you want to come over tomorrow night for dinner?"

Milena laughed. "Well . . . I guess I could. I mean, if you're sure you want to go to all that trouble."

"No trouble. What would you like?"

"I'll leave it up to you—you're the expert."

I concurred with silence. We had another saucer of coffee and then left. Milena said she had to go see her sister (her Bunbury), but that she would definitely be over the next night for dinner.

"You have to be on time," I said. "The timing is crucial."

"No problem. What time?"

"Seven?"

"Fine."

"Not sevenish. Seven."

She smiled. "I understand." Always more affectionate when parting than when arriving, Milena put her arms around me and kissed me. She then walked towards her sister's—if, that is, she circumambulated the globe. I walked towards seven o'clock.

ଔ

On my way I got a haircut by mistake. I was passing by a new high-tech salon on the Boulevard named Chez Délilah and decided to enter, partly out of curiosity but mostly because I envisioned them making me handsomer for Milena. I said I wanted an appointment "sometime in the near future" and they said they had room for me in the immediate present. Everyone was bubblingly polite and wearing cellophane name badges. I was relieved of my coat and served a cappuccino. After my first sip I was led to a small room and instructed to take off my shirt and put on a flowered red frock. This I did, with a certain loss of dignity. I next found myself on a padded reclining bench, between two recumbent women whose heads were resting in black enamel sinks. There were two shampooers: I got "Jean-Marc", who washed my hair with probing fingers in circular slow motion. It was more a massage than a shampoo and it left me in a narcoleptic state. "I'll be back tomorrow," I said, slurring my words, as Jean-Marc woke me up.

Weak-kneed, I followed him to my cutter. "Yvan", whose name was pinned to his spandexed thigh, had alternately long and short hair, half black and half yellow, and at least four chained earrings running up the helix of each ear. He wore a vest with nothing on underneath and a pair of tights that made him look like a trapeze artist. I said that I wanted just a little trim, half an inch off all around, and he replied that he was from Saint-Tite. He studied me in the mirror before starting, scissors poised over my head.

"OK? À *l'attaque?*" he asked. I nodded.

Whenever I get a massage, a shoeshine (once in New York from a cool dude around eighty), a fitting for clothes, a haircut, I get into this floating nirvanic state. There's something about a stranger servicing you. I closed my eyes and drifted off. When Yvan said something (not to me), I opened my eyes and looked at his leotards in the mirror. I reclosed my eyes and drifted into a movie I saw at the old Tower Cinema in York, when I was around eight. It starred Burt Lancaster and Tony Curtis as trapeze artists. It was about how they depended on each other, how Tony was trying to do a difficult stunt, a triple I think. After seeing this picture I had a recurring dream of flying through the air without a safety net, trusting my partner to catch me. But I always woke up as I saw the outstretched hands. It wasn't that I was afraid I wouldn't be caught: I knew I wouldn't be caught, because it wasn't just a difficult stunt I was attempting, it was an *impossible* one. It was one of those Sisyphean dreams where you struggle to make the impossible possible. I get them all the time.

I opened my eyes. Yvan was puffing on a four-paper joint. I closed my eyes then quickly reopened them. The person next to him in the mirror had a haircut similar to his. No, couldn't be. I suddenly felt hot. Beads of sweat welled up from my hairline. Yvan offered me a toke on his dynojoint.

"*Ça va?*" he asked.

"Well, no, not really . . . This is not exactly what we agreed on, this is not what I ordered—"

"You can handle it. You got the features. You can swing it, man, believe me—not many could, but you can. With your features, you can handle it no problem. I understand hair, I understand *your* hair."

"But I thought I said half an inch. Didn't I say a half an inch, *un demi-pouce?*" I slid my arm out of the frock and showed him, with thumb and forefinger, how little this actually was.

"*Excuse-moi.*"

I looked into the mirror again. There must be some mistake. That can't be *me*, surely. It's somebody on the other side. I wiped away the sweat from my hairline. No, that's me all right. With a cruel variation on the crewcut, a vicious denunciation of sideburns, and a cartoonish tuft of hair at the front like a rooster. A practical joke perhaps. Is there a camera behind the mirror? Come on out, Alan Funt. "Cut, that's a wrap"—somebody please say it. And then call makeup and remove this. Or play the scene backwards. Oh shit. Oh no. I want my hair back. I want it back, right now, do you hear me? Yvan, put it back. Please. I'm a teacher. Write on the blackboard one hundred times: *I will never disobey instructions I will never disobey instructions . . .*

I looked down at the floor, at my former hair, and almost asked for a doggie bag. I walked robotically to the change room and sat on a bench in semi-darkness, stunned. When I finally emerged, someone pointed out that I was still wearing the flowered frock. I removed it and someone held a bowl of candy under my face. "No thank you," I whispered. At the spaceship cash-bar I saw my face in the mirror, the white stick of a lollipop hanging out of my mouth.

"And two makes fifty," said the cashier, placing my change on the counter. "Enjoy your hair."

愈

I took the alleyways home, out of humanity's sight. I got into the shower and re-shampooed, piling on a blend of conditioners and creams in the hope of increasing my hair size. With a blow-dryer I rearranged, re-styled, stretched and pulled. I looked in the mirror again and almost broke it. Milena would find this very funny. And naturally like me less. Our dinner date would have to be cancelled.

I took two of Milena's antidepressants on my way to the kitchen and turned on the gas, not to commit suicide but to see if my stove worked. It did. It also smelled—the former tenants may have used it for curing or synthesising. In my hall closet I found some recipe books among my mother's things. Out of desperation, at 5 AM York time, I rang my guardian angel.

"Gascoigne residence." The voice was crystal clear.

"Uncle Gerard! How have you been? What are doing up at this hour?"

"Jeremy my boy, how lovely! Good to hear from you! I was just doing a bit of nambling. Where are you, at the Cock?"

The Cock and Bottle is a pub in York by the Ouse, near Skeldergate Bridge. Haunted, according to legend. Gerard had been drinking.

"No, I'm in Montreal. What's 'nambling'?"

"Gambling on the Internet."

"You've got a computer?"

"Of course not. But a friend does."

I laughed. "Aren't you supposed to be coming to Montreal? I got your letter. When are you coming?"

"Soon. Would you like me to place some bets for you on-line?"

"Uh, not tonight no, I'm kind of in a hurry. I need some advice. What should I cook to impress the shit out of someone?"

"Interesting choice of words. How about prunes?"

"No, seriously."

"Italian or French?"

"It has to be French."

"Go with the King or the Queen of entrées—Tournedos Henri IV or Chartreuse de perdreaux."

"Hold on, I'll write that down. Tournedos Henri IV, Chartreuse de perdreaux. Where the hell am I going to get a partridge?"

"You can use other game birds. What do you have in Quebec? Any beast of warren will do. Who's the guest of honour?"

"Milena, my potential fiancée. She said she'd marry a good cook—"

"Marry? I hear the rattle of chains. Marriage is not a word—"

"It's a sentence, I remember."

"*I would be married, but I'd have no wife, I would be married to a . . .*"

"*Single life,*" we said in unison.

"Woo, woe. Fiancée, fiasco . . . "

"Thanks Gerard—see you soon."

"Married, marred . . . "

"Goodbye, Uncle."

"Holy deadlock . . . "

I scoured my books for the King and Queen, in vain. I went to bed, got up, swallowed three Dormex, went back to bed, and dreamt of partridges. Somewhere high on a mountaintop an old peasant who looked like my landlady offered to sell me a partridge, but only if I wrung its neck and plucked its feathers. I recoiled at the thought but agreed. I asked her if she knew my Queen recipe and she said she did, but judging from her description I think she mistook perdreaux for pierogis. She also suggested it be served with pears. "Plant pears for your heirs," she thrice declared, laughing each time the hideous laugh of a sorceress.

Not since my Saturdays in York have I exactly sprung out of bed, but I did so on this morning. I threw on my clothes and took a cab to a large French bookstore called, falsely, La Plus Grande Librairie au Monde. After waiting outside in the cold for the shiftless bastards to open up, a drowsy salesman with a key ring directed me to another bookstore, La Cuisine Classique, a specialty shop in the west end. I got in another cab and eventually found a book with both recipes. It was simply meant to be.

"Henri IV": grilled beef fillet slices topped with artichoke bottoms cooked *à blanc* and filled with *sauce béarnaise*, and served with neatly-stacked *pont neuf* potatoes. "Chartreuse de perdreaux": partridges moulded with cabbage and decorated with vegetables (alternating rows of green peas and turnip, string beans and carrot strips), crowned with sautéed onions and garnished with slices of sausage and bacon. I decided to go for the Chartreuse. Milena was a Marxist feminist—a royal male would simply not do.

At an indoor market called Les Nouvelles Halles I managed to procure my partridges (frozen), as well as every other ingredient bar none. From a florist I bought a bouquet of white gypsophilia and feathery pink spiraea, commonly known as bridal wreath, along with some love-in-idleness because, according to Puck, if you pour its juices on a woman's sleeping eyelids, it will make her madly dote on the next living creature she sees.

In my homeward cab I reflected on the wording of our announcement in *The Gazette*, and then saw myself, a gardenia in my buttonhole, walking up the middle aisle. I began to whistle Mendelssohn's "Wedding March" from *A Midsummer Night's Dream*:

The Haitian cabby hummed along with me, bobbing and grinning at me from his rear-view mirror. I gave him a titanic tip.

I puttered about in the kitchen, turtlelike, from eleven in the morning to six-thirty at night. The oven was roaring like a blast furnace. *Double, double, toil and trouble, fire burn and cauldron bubble.* I even prepared a salad (with rosemary and rue) and a dessert: Poires Bourdaloue (poached pears with frangipane cream). When my clock struck the quarter, I realised in a panic that I had no wine, and that the Société d'Alcool had just locked its doors. I ran to the local *dépanneur*, where one of the owners persuaded me to buy an "extremely excellent" local wine called Harfang des Neiges. In the aisles were boxes of the stuff, stamped with what appeared to be a Best Before date. I bought a case.

While looking for a corkscrew in my "liquor cabinet", I found a forgotten Bordeaux that Sabrine's mother had sent me as a birthday present. It had been standing upright, which they say is not recommended. Château Chasse-Spleen, 1983. Perfect. I left the dust on.

The background music, I decided, would be French, fin de siècle, tonal impressionist. The mood would be magical, enchanting, transcendent. If that failed I'd put on the Sinfonia in F by Fux.

It was now quarter after seven. Milena, exercising the privilege of a bride, was late. I had left the downstairs door open with a message: ENTER. As I was setting the table I realised this might be misconstrued by people walking by. Like the fish bandit. Before I could change it Milena shimmered through my unlocked door like a dream.

"Smells great," she said, gliding into the kitchen. "Sorry if I'm late."

I looked her in the eye, soulfully. "Milena, love means never having to say you're sorry."

"Right. Silly me. How could I forget? God, I hope you didn't go to too much trouble. I'm not fussy. It looks amazing. Nice flowers. I should've brought some wine. What kind of vegetables are those?"

"Let us turn up and pee."

Milena grinned and grimaced at the same time. "Never too late to have a happy childhood, I guess. Sometimes I think . . . oh never mind."

"Sometimes you think what?"

"That you secretly wish you were back in grade three."

"Not secretly. I admit it openly."

"I bet you were a riot in elementary school."

"Well, Miss Gurney seemed to think so."

"I knew it. You're returning to past glories. She encouraged you, probably thinking you'd be quite clever when you grew up. She didn't know you'd peaked."

I laughed. So did Milena. "I don't think I've ever seen you in a baseball cap," she remarked, while looking in the vicinity of my late sideburns. "Or any hat, for that matter."

I shrugged, backing away as she drew closer. "Yeah, it's uh, a special cap . . . "

"Did you get your hair cut, Jeremy?"

" . . . that I got from my uncle. An old cricket cap, actually, that he—"

"You're not going to show me your haircut, right?"

"My haircut? It's more of a trim, really. I'll show it to you later—after our second bottle of wine."

"OK." Milena narrowed her eyes then burst out laughing. "What's this called?" she changed, nodding towards my *pièce de résistance*.

"Chartreuse de perdreaux."

"I really didn't know you did this kind of thing. I'm impressed."

"Don't be," I said modestly. I could hear Mendelssohn again. "I whipped it up in a few minutes. Hope you're not one of those who think cooking's an art. You just follow instructions in a book."

"Someone's got to come up with the recipes. That takes some creativity."

"Trial and error. Is chemistry an art? Let's sit down."

I opened the wine, which I had forgotten to let breathe; when I apologised for this, Milena said it was all bullshit anyway. As I turned the corkscrew, the dried-out cork disintegrated into the bottle. I poured Milena a glass of swimming particles. I switched glasses and poured again. Same result. I went to get a tea strainer.

The salad was all right, the main course imploded in the dish as I went to serve it, the meat was overcooked, the vegetables undercooked. Milena got a mouthful of string. I knocked over the vase of flowers while straining wine through a tea towel. Milena asked me to change the music because it was "depressing", said the meat smelled like hashish, and hardly ate a thing. She did say, however, that the second bottle of wine, the Harfang, was "very good". The dessert did not look like the picture in the recipe book, but was sweet. When we finished I looked at Milena and she burst out laughing. I gathered up the dishes and trudged back into the kitchen. As I scraped the plates into Mr. Tuffy, I felt Milena's hand on my shoulder.

"I'm sorry, it was really good," she said. "It really was. And I know you put a lot of work into it. I appreciate it, I really do."

We watched a video that night, after pulling out the sofa, and I can't remember which one it was. Milena made a good start on a bottle of whisky from the Inner Hebrides and ended up falling asleep in my arms.

EIGHTEEN

Never, never discharge that weapon into that soft body,
like fire into flowers . . .

—*Shakuntala*

"Milena." I gently caressed her cheek, and in her ear whispered softly: "Milena, we should go to bed. It's quarter to six. Milena?"

She grunted, shifted her position.

"Milena, I'm going to kiss you if you don't get up. On the lips." No reaction. "Milena, I'm serious." I counted to eleven and then leaned over, awkwardly craning my neck, and kissed her on the lips. She opened her eyes and instead of recoiling gave me a sleepy look that was hard to read. When I kissed her on the neck she started to cough, a genuine cough I think. She extricated herself from me, took a sip of scotch, and when she set her glass down I kissed her again. Lightly, ever so lightly, I began to caress her face, shoulders, arms.

"What are you doing?" she said into my lips, when I cupped her breast.

"We don't have to go any further."

"I know."

"We can stay on first base."

Milena's forehead puckered. "We can what? I think I just had an out-of-decade experience."

"Fifties?"

Milena nodded. "So what can I expect at second base?"

"A three-way sandwich. My friend Jacques' coming over."

Milena smiled. "Very funny. I won't ask about third base."

I turned the peak of my cap around and tried to kiss her again; she turned her head and said, "I'm not on the pill or anything."

You won't need contraceptives for what I'm about to do. I dropped to my knees before her, unlaced her boots, ran my fingers over her ankles, the bare skin of her calves, her knees and thighs, rested my head on her lap. *I'll make my heaven in a lady's lap.* I unbuckled her belt and looked up. Milena was smiling nervously (was it a smile?), her head turned away. I slowly undid her zipper—a tantalising sound—and pulled her jodhpurs down below her knees. Old-fashioned white cotton panties, low on the leg, high on the waist. So what now? As light as air, I grazed her inner thighs with my lips. Once more I paused to look up: her eyes were closed, her expression enigmatic. What was she thinking? I unlaced the legs of her jodhpurs, slid them off slowly. I prised her legs open. My mouth went higher and higher.

I was soon whirling in a merry-go-round of sensations, every sense filled to the brim. Every sense but one, that is— she made no reassuring sounds. She pulled me back up, to her other lips, and placed her hands on the bare skin of my back.

"Do you want to go the bedroom?" I whispered, a few dizzying moments later. I had to repeat it.

"I don't know," she replied.

"If you feel uncomfortable—"

"Let's go."

I took Milena's hand and led her to the bedroom, awkwardly, unable to believe this was happening to me, to us. On soft down we lay haunch to haunch, heart to heart.

"Go slowly," Milena said, as I nervously unfastened buttons. "I haven't been able to do this in a long time."

Throughout my invasion Milena lay motionless. She tried—or rather I made her try—to get on top of me, but her attempt was half-hearted and my member half-willing. My condom felt like a tourniquet. After much toil I ended up on top, holding her hands back behind her head, the better to see her dark underarms. I knew I shouldn't be doing this—too male-dominant, too missionary—but did it anyway. I forced my way into her like a thief. When I gazed into her eyes she looked away, at the wall. It was not the way it was supposed to be, not the way it happened in movies. I felt like such a novice.

We were lying on our backs a few minutes later, side by side, in darkness. While I strained to think of something romantic to say, sifting through worn phrases of love, Milena fell asleep. I lay awake for what seemed like hours, watching her silhouette in the pale-green glow of my clock radio. In a sudden spell of post-coitum triste, I tiptoed to the kitchen and ate half a jar of olives. I botched it, a D minus, one and a half stars. In the living room, sitting on the floor, I opened and closed my pocket *Shakuntala*. I set the book down and tiptoed back to the bedroom.

Milena was still sleeping, the sheets and blankets now in a twisted pile on the floor. I strained to see her naked body in the semi-darkness. My statue come to life, my Indian queen, is that really you? A shaft of sunlight came blading through the slatted blinds and crossed her perfect form. The chemicals of my brain would fix this image forever. I crawled in beside her.

∞

We spent the next six days together, warm and affectionate

days, albeit without making love again *per se*. The last of these was one of my working Wednesdays, and while I worked Milena waited for me like a housewife. In the taxi to school I had that warm inner glow that comes from knowing your beloved is home waiting for you; I then flashed to her rifling through my closets and Book of Saturdays. In the classroom, on the podium, I pictured Milena lying naked in bed, her long midnight tresses touching the floor. How dark and mysterious she is! How beautiful! "In this lecture I would like to discuss . . . "

On my way out, after two classes in which my students were unpunctual or unpresent, two abbreviated classes in which my students were engrossed by my hair, I met Clyde Haxby, who was on his way in. "In a hurry, are we then, Davenant?" he said feudally, glancing at his watch, blocking the doorway. "What in the world happened to your head? Have you joined a cult?" I grunted, tried to walk around him. "I have not finished," he added, barring my way with his arm across the door. "I believe we have a little matter to discuss. My humiliation at your hands—"

"For insulting a friend of mine."

"A friend of yours? Now which one would that be? The slovenly mulatto girl? A touch of the tar brush in that one. Or are you referring to your other friend—or is it lover?— that snide pederast Jacques de Vauvenargues-Fezensac?"

I looked at Haxby's formal attire pressed and pleated with military precision, at his starched face and hornet eyes. I could feel myself growing hotter, feel the urge to slap him. My hands clenched and unclenched.

"You guessed our secret, Clyde. Jacques and I are lovers. In fact we fantasise about you standing in front of your mirror, dressed up in your fireman's rubber overalls, playing with your hose."

Haxby's nostrils flared. "Now look here, Davenant. Two can play at this game, I'm warning you. I'm still checking up on your credentials—"

"Fuck you."

I decamped, through his arm and out the door, in search of a cab. One approaching. I waved my arms but stopped when I saw a group of four up ahead, who were just as eager to get the driver's attention. I turned round to see if Haxby was watching. He was. He was still in the doorway, his brief-case resting on the heater vents, his fingers fiddling with the combination lock.

Inexplicably, the taxi passed the group of four and stopped at my feet. I got in and the driver drove as if possessed, screeching his tires, jerking in and out of lanes, careening down the mountainside like an ambulance. Which was fine with me. For my raven-haired love was waiting—and raving Clyde, I was sure, was going for his brace of pistols. The driver, who had the look of a disturbed offender, seemed to know all this. Through a smoked bulletproof barrier he looked back at me from time to time, to the general detriment of his driving, all the way to rue Valjoie. I jumped out, slammed the door, and was halfway up the stairs when the driver bellowed at me. I walked back down and passed cash through his window. His tires screeched as I flew up the stairs.

I knocked on the higher door three times. No answer. I unlocked it and yelled, "Honey, I'm home!" Still no answer. "Milena?" Ominous silence. An acrid smell pervaded the apartment. "Milena?"

"I'm in the bathroom," a muffled voice replied.

"Can I come in?" I asked sheepishly. "I've got something to tell you, about Haxby. It's quite funny."

"No."

The door was open about an inch. Naturally, I peered in. Milena, her back to me, was standing in front of the sink and mirror. Her hair was a froth of black, and dark streamlets ran down the side of her face.

Sitting in the living room I mechanically paged through the newspaper, with hardly a syllable registering. Have I been deceived? Is Milena not my true Dark Lady? How could that be? She's Indian, for God's sake, her pubic and underarm hair are black. Or does she dye that too?

Milena emerged from the bathroom, her wet hair streaming like Medusa's, and without a word sat down opposite me. I didn't look up from my paper. At least not right away. I eventually peeked over and saw Milena, a cigarette between her lips, reading a beaten paperback, I couldn't tell which one.

"What are you reading?" I asked nonchalantly.

"*The Story of My Life*. George Sand."

I nodded. "Did you know she translated Shakespeare's *As You Like It*?"

"Yes."

"I'll dry your hair if you want."

"Don't bother."

I went to get a towel and a hair dryer and began to dry her hair. I asked if she wanted me to brush it and she didn't say no. And so I brushed and brushed and ran my fingers through the glorious waves of her hair. At first she continued reading but then closed her eyes and book.

"You dye your hair, right?"

Milena jumped slightly, as if roused from sleep. I had to repeat the question.

"That's right," she replied.

"Why? Isn't it naturally black?"

"Yeah, but I'm prematurely grey. And vain, I guess."

"You? You're the least vain person I've ever met, which is one of the things I like about you. One in a constellation of things." From behind I put my arms round her neck, buried my face in her shiny blue-black mane. Like a Harlequin Romance heroine, I hoped that somehow, against astronomically long odds, we could make it together.

ങ

That evening we stayed in, ordered out, and suffered through hours of two-dimensional shadows. During a commercial for frozen french fries involving a champion figure skater, Milena asked me about the cool mood ring I was wearing. After slightly overestimating its worth, I removed it from my finger and slipped it on hers. *With this ring I thee wed.* It went from blue-green to black.

"I want you to have it," I said.

She slipped it off. "I don't want it."

"No, really. I want you to wear it."

"I don't want to."

"I'm serious."

"So am I."

"I insist."

"So do I."

"Please."

"No."

Milena went back to the commercial; I continued to stare. She turned to me with a sigh, shrugged her shoulders and put the ring on her middle finger, making a rude gesture in the process. Now, I thought, I can monitor her moods. Not so. She lost the ring the next day—while taking a bath, she thought. *While bathing, Shakuntala loses the ring . . . CAUTION: Ring Should Not Be Immersed In Water.*

ങ

On our second night together, as Milena was reading beside me, leaning against me, I asked if she felt like playing tennis at the university sports complex. Maybe I could flash my fac card and bump some student. I asked again. She turned her head and raised her eyebrows. I guess not. When I suggested a Canadiens-Red Wings game, she laughed. Sports, for Milena, were "silly" (no argument there) and "dominated by males" (nor there). We have all known Milenas in high school: the ones who watched gym class from the sidelines, in street clothes, who smoked in the toilets while the others were changing.

"Do you ever do any exercises?" I asked.

"Never. I read that exercising just increases the number of free radicals in the body, and free radicals cause cancer, heart disease and ageing."

I laughed. "So that's why you don't like sports?"

"I hate all the rules and ranks and everybody shrieking at you what to do and where to be. Plus I basically don't like running after balls."

"I've noticed."

"Some of the lone-wolf sports are all right, I guess. Like long-distance running."

"You were a long-distance runner?"

"Once. My smoker's lungs practically exploded and I screwed up both knees. But I like the concept—running far away."

I cast about for something else to do and eventually proposed some dance-theatre called *The Survival of the Luckiest*. No rolling eyes, no burst of laughter this time. "No, I don't want to go," she said simply.

Unless it was to drink espressos on the Boulevard, the slightest act of relocation loomed up in Milena's mind as some colossal enterprise, like climbing Everest. This may, incidentally, explain her chronic lateness.

"Let's go," she said suddenly.

"Let's go where?"

"Where do you think?"

At the theatre, Milena insisted on paying for both tickets, despite my token objection. We then walked across the street to buy cigarettes, the lack of which may have sparked our evening out. I didn't ask. Milena speed-smoked half a cigarette before flicking it into the gutter.

Inside, the red velvet seats were unreserved and the majority unoccupied. "Let's sit by the aisle," said Milena, "in case we have to bolt."

We sat by the aisle and watched semi-nude bodies throw themselves at each other for sixty minutes in six inches of water. At the end, after partisan flurries of applause from relatives and friends, Milena said she enjoyed herself— immensely. Surprise surprise. The more she heaped praise on the show the more I began to like it. "Yes, I agree . . . That's actually what I thought too . . . Right, that's exactly the way I saw it . . . " As she spoke of sexual-political symbols of oppression, I pictured bare breasts. "Yes, I was about to say the same thing . . . " We both liked the lead dancer, an athletic platinum blonde who could have tossed me like a javelin across the room, and who winked at me—or perhaps at Milena—during the performance. On the way home, dreaming of an orgiastic triangle, I remarked that the dancer was beautiful. Milena replied, "So what?" An argument about beauty ensued, during which I devised a compelling theory while in the act of speaking.

"If Woody Allen, say, had been handsome," I ended, "he would never have been as creative, as funny. If Margaret

Atwood had been beautiful, she wouldn't have written about the same things—in fact, wouldn't have been a writer at all."

"Bullshit."

"She'd have been spoiled from day one, made a fuss of, given in to, granted favours. She'd have traded on her looks, had no motivation to write. 'A beautiful woman should break her mirror early,' as Graciàn once—"

"I thought you said that dancer was beautiful."

"Well yes, but I—"

"And what do you mean by a 'beauty'? That's a subjective term, isn't it? I happen to think Margaret Atwood is beautiful."

"Well, yeah, so do I . . . I mean yeah, but I think we all know what *really* beautiful means, I think, even though it might, you know . . . change or—"

"So you're saying there's never been a beautiful woman author."

"No, I'm saying—"

"You're saying you can't be an artist if you're beautiful."

"Well no, I think that, sometimes, there are . . . exceptions or—"

"You're full of shit."

We walked down the Boulevard in tense silence, stopping at Noctambule for an espresso, which Milena could drink by the gallon, whatever the hour. I swallowed three cupfuls while she talked to some friends at the next table about gender politics, Internet porn, and lesbian parenting. Drawing on my store of knowledge in these areas, I remained silent.

On a cold toilet seat, wincing from coffee's colonic corrosion, I gazed at exaggerated drawings of private parts, and then at political graffiti (FREE QUEBEC — IN EVERY BOX OF CHEERIOS / IF AT FIRST YOU DON'T SECEDE, TRY TRY

IMPROVES) which brutal French obscenities had almost oblit-erated. I flushed, washed my hands with pink granulated powder, and strained to think of clever ways to enter their conversation. When I got back to the table I said something lead-balloonish that Milena covered up with, "Ready to go?"

We walked to my apartment. In the dark I fumbled opening the downstairs door, putting in wrong or upside-down keys. I could feel Milena's impatience welling up behind me, impending over me. I fared little better with the upstairs lock. When I finally found the keyhole and pushed, I got a spooky surprise—the door moved no more than two inches, the length of the chain lock.

"What the hell . . . " I looked at Milena and then peered through the opening. All the lights were on. I never leave my lights on. There were also the faint sounds, believe it or not, of a couple making love. We looked at each other, not knowing whether to be amused or afraid. We decided on the latter. We walked back down the stairs and ran to a phone booth, where I dialled 911.

⅓

Two policemen arrived minutes later. They were oddly alike, each about 6'2" with moustaches of identical dimensions and hue. One of them knew Milena. I briefly explained the situation, after which we went to ask my landlady to unlock the back alleyway gate. She said no, and shut the door. We rang again; she opened the door again. Milena calmly explained the situation and Lesya, after muttering "Trouble, dey make trouble," went to get the key. The five of us—Lesya, Milena and I and the two policemen—then walked Indian file around to the back, where Lesya opened the gate. She headed back home, muttering to herself, while the rest of us climbed up the fire escape. My back door was wide open.

The police entered first, hands on holsters. The lights were on in every room, as I mentioned, and the television and VCR were on as well. The video was at the end, in the blue scramble zone. I pressed EJECT to examine the tape; I slammed it back in and hit OFF.

The bedroom, which Milena and the blue twins were now examining, was a tornado alley: the contents of my closet and chest of drawers had been emptied onto my bed and magazines and polaroids littered the floor. In a swamp of embarrassment I tried to kick some of the more explicit or identifiable ones back into the closet as Milena watched in silence. The policemen watched me as well; one of them even stooped to pick up one of the magazines.

The only items that were missing, or so it appeared, were some videos and a vintage leather jacket from Amsterdam; on its former hanger was the burglar's coat, made of vinyl. (My address book, I discovered days later, was also missing.) The thief or thieves were evidently looking for cash or jewellery, because none of my consumer durables were missing. I immediately thought of the former tenants, the Aztec savages, and felt my first surge of anger. Or was it the fish-foraging Latino, whose first visit had been a reconnoitre, a case-job?

After a jealous examination of the site, and reasoning in the deductive mode, the officers determined that a break-in had occurred. "He—or they—climbed over the alley fence, walked up the fire escape and then through the unlocked door."

"Once inside," added the other, "they fastened the chain lock so as not to be caught in the act."

The act of burgling, officer, or beating off?

"Why didn't you lock the back door?" his partner asked. Twice. I didn't answer.

"In the future I'd keep the back door locked," said the other, fondling his furry moustache, staring at my haircut. "If I was you, that is."

The only clues, apart from the vinyl jacket with pungent armpits, was a turd in the toilet that wasn't mine, and two cigarette butts on the carpet, filtered Lucky Strikes that Milena said weren't hers.

"Can't you do a DNA test on the feces?" I eagerly asked one of the officers. He looked at his partner, muffled an explosion of air, and began writing up his report. "Or at least dust the butts for fingerprints?" I persisted. This too went down very well.

"Right, we'll just check with the boys at the crime lab," he replied, lips tightly closed. "And while we're at it," his partner added, "we'll get them to dust the magazines for prints." I found this very amusing.

"You said you heard some people in the apartment?" asked the other. "Like they were making love?"

"Uh, yeah, I guess it was the . . . TV." I glanced at Milena. She was the mannequin in the store window, inscrutable. I felt like holding out my wrists for the handcuffs.

NINETEEN

True, I talk of dreams; which are the children of an idle brain,
Begot of nothing but vain fantasy.

—*Romeo and Juliet*

Milena never confronted me, never let on that anything was wrong; on the contrary, she was full of comforting commiserations. She understood, she said, how it felt to have one's space raided, ransacked. But she didn't stay with me that night, or the night after, or the night after that. Clearly, my stock had plunged: Davenant Preferred down, way down. I was not gold, but tin, not a dollar but a zloty, a gourde. The days turned over like decades. I knew I would never see her again.

But of course I did see her again. We were walking on the Boulevard a week or so later, on opposite sides and in opposite directions. I had stopped to kiss Arielle, who was about to board a bus, when I spotted her in the distance like a rainbow. Arielle waved, Milena waved back and the bus rejoined the traffic. I imagined Milena running, in soft-focus slow motion, into my arms. I ran towards her; she seemed to recede. I passionately embraced her; she held me with humiliating restraint. I took her hand tenderly in mind; she released it. Reversing my original direction, I accompanied her up the street. "I'm going this way anyway," I said.

We walked in near-silence, Milena stopping once or twice to drop coins into baseball caps, until we reached her sister's cross-street. "I turn here," she said in a voice as lively as Mount Royal cemetery. I nodded, sighing, and watched her walk away.

"Look, Milena, we might as well do it now and make it official."

Milena stopped, turned. "What?"

I took a few steps towards her. "This whole thing's driving me nuts. You're so closed, so cold. I don't think we have much in common anyway, so let's not see each other any more. It was doomed from the start. So goodbye. And best of bloody luck." It was now my turn to walk away, which I did with drama, my throat tightening.

"Jeremy."

I swivelled on my heels. "Yes?"

"You doing anything tomorrow night?"

"Tomorrow? Tomorrow being . . . Tuesday? No I'm not . . . well, yes actually, I have a date but . . . "

"Fine. With Arielle?"

" . . . but you could join us. I'm dining at my landlady's."

"What about tonight?"

"Tonight being . . . Monday? I think I'm . . . disengaged."

"Mind if I drop by? Around eight?"

I shrugged. "If you like."

In near-aphasia I watched her lithe, pantherine movements as she headed towards her sister's. If I wasn't doing anything later? I crossed the street in a state of abstraction, heard a truck horn possibly meant for me, narrowly missed a roller-blading couple with slipstream helmets, and then stood idly in front of Cinéma La Chatte. It was the blackened walls, I think, that acted as a chemical reagent on my brain. They gave me an idea in other words. A way to prove that I was upgradeable. I walked up two blocks to the Portuguese gift shop and looked into its window, where most of the cuckoo clocks said ten past four. I had almost four hours. At the local dépanneur I made a pit stop for some starter-fluid, which they gave me on credit, then jogged home. I paused in front of my landlady's, looking furtively this way and that, before seizing her decrepit barbecue.

As I was setting things up on my perilous balcony, a voice from below called out my name. I looked down. Amidst the towering plants I made out the ruddy cheeks of my land-lady, who was shouting out something that made no sense. I smiled and waved. She said something else—louder, something involving the word "trouble"—while flailing her arms about, semaphoring her displeasure. I moved the barbecue back into the house. Shit. I'll have do it in the alleyway. I looked out the window and saw Victor sweeping leaves off his patio. No, I couldn't let Victor see me going into the alley with a barbecue—he would have burst with curiosity and saliva. How about my back fire escape? I went out onto it and looked down: my Italian neighbour, as usual, was puttering about in the sunless courtyard. Shit. I went back out the front door, ignored Victor's greeting, and walked quickly to the Greek hardware store, where I bought a roll of butcher cord.

In my bathroom I attached the cord to the barbecue and lowered it into the alleyway, across from my ghost neighbour. I ran down the fire escape, opened the fence door with Lesya's key and unfastened the barbecue. I ran back up the fire escape, filled up a green garbage bag, noosed it, and then lowered this down too. I ran back down and then back up because I'd forgotten the starter-fluid, and then back down.

Sweating like a hog, I moved everything into the narrow half-alley behind the house, between a rotting mattress and a rake with large gaps in its front teeth. In the barbecue I made a pyramid-shaped mound of paper, doused it with fluid

251

and threw a match on it. It exploded into flames (the fluid was overkill), the pages writhing at Fahrenheit 451. One by one, I tossed in celluloid tapes, each melting and crackling in noxious black fumes. The flames rose higher and higher as I fed my funeral pyre with more and more glossy paper and polaroids. It was beautiful, symbolic, Druidic. Well, maybe not Druidic. As the last pages curled and died in embers, a police cruiser passed through the adjoining alleyway. It braked and backed up. I thought it might. Shit, what if it's the same two sarcastic cops? After back-pedalling onto rake prongs, I ran, and didn't stop running until I reached the park.

At the foot of Mount Royal I chatted with a pair of squirrels, recounting, in outline, what I had just done. One of them was clearly intrigued, advancing closer and closer, hanging on my every word. She looked pregnant. I gave her the only food I had, a Rolaid. She ran one way and I the other, she up a tree and I back home, back to the scene of the slime. From behind a brick wall I peered into the alleyway. The mattress and rake were still there but nothing else, not even my landlady's barbecue.

To complete the rite of purification, I luxuriated in a raspberry bubble bath—like washing myself clean in the blood of the lamb, I thought. But I hardly felt purged. What a child I am to think this burning sacrifice will set everything right! Why didn't I just leave everything in a bag for the garbagemen? Why this *coup de théâtre*? Why must I dramatise, symbolise everything? And who was I offering this burnt sacrifice to anyway?

My brass-faced longcase announced, with one stroke, the half-hour. Half-past seven. I bolted out of the tub. Milena, you recall, would be over "around eight". Should I tell her what I had done? Had I done it for her sake or mine? Doesn't matter.

At nine I was cool. People wait for their dates all the time. Nothing unusual there, doesn't mean a thing. I can read a murder mystery, listen to Beethoven or Betty's Not a Vitamin. Doesn't have to be wasted time. She doesn't share my obsession with punctuality, that's all. I should loosen up a bit, learn from her, relax.

I selected a CD track and pushed pause. Vile once told me that Milena liked a My Bloody Valentine song called "Touched"; the next day I acquired their entire library, imports and vinyl included. The song was cued up: when Milena knocked I had only to push a button.

Glancing restlessly from dummy book to grandfather clock, I listened to the annoying sound of time passing. Ten . . . We are all clocks, ticking away towards death, I thought. What crap. Eleven . . . Something has happened to her, I can feel it, her antidepressants have given her amnesia! Twelve . . . Red knave on the black queen. One . . . We count the faults, according to the French proverb, of those who keep us waiting. Two . . . Milena has no faults. I put my hand on the swinging pendulum and stayed its movement. I had to find her.

While closing my front gate I heard a gratingly familiar voice. Across the street, under the lurid light of a street lamp, I discerned a large purple butt compressed into spandex bicycle shorts. It belonged of course to my charismatic neighbour, who was closing his front gate. If he remarks on this coincidence, I'll snap. If he says something Elizabethan, I'll kill.

"What ho, milord!"

Should I get my Swiss Army knife? If only Toddley could be fast-forwarded. And muted. Maybe he'll slip through a manhole. But hold on, maybe he knows where Milena is. I'll be casual, roundabout.

"What a co-inkydink," he remarked, "us both closing our—"

"Have you seen Milena?"

Victor crossed the street and offered me a warm pudge of a hand. "Closing our gates at the same time. So you're up burning the midnight oil, I see."

"No, I have electricity."

"Good one. Hey, like your new haircut! It works for me, it really does." He smiled at me, conspiratorially. "Get a load of this."

He handed me a "humorous" postcard, one of those all-black affairs that used to be found in every city of the world. MONTREAL BY NIGHT, it said. As Victor grinned, waiting for me to soil myself, I simply stared at the card, drawn into its blackness, lost in vagabond thoughts—on the beauty of dark cities, cities in the dead of night, when you glimpse what a city could be, should be, without all the fucking cars, the exhaust, the blare, the hazardous waste of space . . .

"Uh, Earth to Jeremy. Earth to Jeremy. Come in please."

"Sorry, I was just . . . " I handed back the card.

"I know it's late and everything but I just had to send this card right away."

"I understand."

"This is rare for me because I'm usually up early, because I'm a sunrise freak—it's great when you're jogging. I'm usually up with the sun."

"I with the moon. I don't think I've ever seen a sunrise."

"You've never see a sunrise?"

"I saw one on TV once."

Victor smiled. "You're pulling my leg, Jer, I know you can be a card sometimes. Hey, that's a pun!" He punched me playfully on the shoulder with one hand and held up the postcard with the other. "We were just talking about, you know . . ."

As we walked together to the mailbox, my sides heaving, I tried to steer the conversation back to Milena. Victor, however, was more interested in his dream novel, his nocturnal emissions. He had found a *very* interested publisher: Presto Press. According to Jacques, Presto published two types of manuscripts: vanity and purloined.

"I'm calling it *Such Stuff*," said Victor. He paused, giving me a kind of nudge-nudge with his eyes. "Do you get it?"

"Yes."

"'We are such stuff as dreams are made on . . . '"

"Yes, I'm familiar with—"

"'And our life is rounded with a sleep.' It's from *The Tempest*. I have to thank you, Jeremy, because if it wasn't for you I would never have thought of taking a title from Shakespeare."

"It's 'our *little* life'."

"I'm sorry?"

"Nothing."

"I've got a whole new batch of dream images that I'd like to try out on you, if you're game. They're metaphorical or symbolical but I'm not really sure what they're metaphorical or symbolical of. There's three of them, a triumvirate of images in your parlance. I call them 'oneiric metaphors'. They may be elusive of precise interpretation."

"Ambiguous."

"Exactly. The first one is when you come out of the shower and you look in the mirror and you don't see your face because the mirror's all clouded? Know what I mean?"

I nodded.

"So you get your hair dryer and you zap the mirror—whsssh, whsssh whsssh—and the mist goes away and your face reappears."

I waited for him to continue. "Continue."

"Well that's it. What do you think?"

"What do I think?"

"Yeah."

"Well it's . . . hard to say." I strained to think of something pithy to say, befitting a Shakespearean scholar.

"Can I take a stab at it?" said Victor.

"Do."

"I think it's like discovering your other self after living in a fog. Or it's like technology eliminating mystery—technological demystification. Is that what it says to you?"

"Yes."

"The second one is when you're crossing a street but there's a car blocking you, stopped, waiting to make a turn? Know what I mean?"

I nodded again.

"So you walk around it, behind it, right? But by the time you've started your arc the car has moved on, so you've actually walked around something that's not there. You've walked around empty space! For nothing! That's ironical, is it not? What do you think that's metaphorical of?"

"Well, I'd have to—"

"I think it represents the paradox of life, or imagined barriers or something."

"Good."

"The third one is when you take your *last* green garbage bag out of its package and the *first* thing you put into the garbage bag is . . . the package. The *package.* So the container has now become the content. Container-content, content-container, bag enclosing bag, an alligator swallowing his tail. Or her tail. What do you think?"

I think your record of unblemished imbecility is intact. "Very nice." We stood, awkwardly, in front of the mailbox, poised to part in different directions. I wanted to leave, but couldn't. Not yet. I needed information about Milena, about her whereabouts, about her relationship with him.

"What time is it, Jer? I should probably get back, catch a few z's. I haven't being doing all that well in the sleep department."

"I know what you mean. Listen, if you happen to . . . you know, see . . . Milena, tell that I . . . tell her that . . . well, say hello."

"Okeydokey, artichokey." Victor kissed the card and slipped it into the mailbox. After shaking my hand with his sausage fingers, he pottered off and I boarded the conveyor belt.

The conveyor belt, as Milena called it, was a kind of moving sidewalk, a vicious circuit of four or five bars hopped by her and her aimless crowd. At each of them I bought drinks for anyone who remotely knew her. After last call I stumbled home, dead-drunk, taking a long-cut through the Milenian fields.

TWENTY

A reflection cannot form while a mirror is beclouded with grime.
—*Shakuntala*

"So Milena's anorgasmic?" said Jacques, into the phone.
"What?" I wiped the sleep from my eyes. "I never said
that. What do you mean?"

"She's frigid."

"I never said that."

"It was implied."

"By who?"

"By *whom*. You."

"Bullshit."

"You spoke of passiveness, unresponsiveness, vaginismus."

"I did? I said all that? What's vaginismus?"

"You said she would tighten, lock up, that penetration was
practically impossible."

"You're delusional. When did I say all that?"

"Last night, four in the morning. You phoned me in a
pathetic drunken stupor."

"Oh shit. Did I really? Christ." I rubbed my forehead. I
was in the grip of a punishing hangover, so he may have been
right. I looked at the clock—my clock was stopped. "What
time is it, for Christ's sake?"

"'*The bawdy hand of the dial is now upon the prick of
noon.*'"

I closed my eyes, suppressed an urge to vomit.

"You OK?"

"No, I'm not OK." But I described anyway—wearily, without interruption or sabotage—my break-and-enter, broken *rendez-vous* and broken heart. Some moments elapsed before Jacques said anything. "Jacques? Are you listening?"

"I'm coming over to lift your spirits. Tonight, seven o'clock."

"I'm eating at my landlady's tonight. Want to join us?"

"Nine o'clock." Click.

႙

At exactly nine o'clock that evening, Hallowe'en, Jacques emerged from his Hemlock cab clothed entirely in grey— shod and gloved in grey as well—and holding an incongruous brown paper bag in one hand. After examining his reflection in a car window and straightening a coat of irreproachable fit, he looked up towards my balcony and greeted me with a few amiable obscenities. I stood motionless, my eyes riveted to the spectacle below.

"What are you gaping at, Davenant? Let's go. And bring those Superclown 2000s you've been jabbering on about. And something to write with."

I left my remaining miniature Life-Savers and Oh Henry bars on the landing, testing the restraint of those next to arrive, and then ran to catch Jacques. We walked towards the Boulevard, past window skeletons, pumpkin lanterns and a scarecrow sitting in a chair; we walked in and out of Bar None, Noctambule and Pablo Fanques Fair. No sign of Milena. At Dame de Piques we saw Astérix, Jean Chrétien and Captain Cook, Mata Hari, Cleopatra and Captain Hook. But still no Milena.

"Here," I said as we sat down, "a Hallowe'en present." I placed before him my (bonus) Supersound 2000, of which I was pardonably proud.

Finger by finger he drew off his kid-leather gloves. "You rob me of words. I've something for you too. A way of dealing with your pathetic plight." From his paper bag he extracted two bottles of some no doubt well-vinted, well-matured wine.

"Where'd you get that?" I asked.

"Found it in my Christmas stocking."

"We can't drink that here."

"Jeremy please, act like you've been somewhere. Waiter! Corkscrew!"

As I smiled at Jacques, I wondered for the hundredth time if he were handsome. Sabrine said he looked *déchu* (fallen), that he had some bygone disease like gout or scurvy or absinthism (she also said she wouldn't mind bedding him). To give Jacques his due, his hair was vigorous—long and flowing, ash blonde, rakishly falling over his forehead—and his battleship-grey eyes were alive with lights and shadows. Intelligent eyes. All the famous marksmen in the American Civil War, I've been told, had grey eyes since they were thought to be the keenest. It was Jacques who told me this.

The waiter, as commanded, uncorked both bottles. Jacques poured out a lavish stream while explaining that I was suffering from "nympholepsy". When the waiter left I denied this adamantly, and a day or two later looked the word up: *Frenzy caused by contemplation of, or furious desire for, an unrealisable ideal.* I still deny it.

"Let's walk around," said Jacques. "In different directions," he added when I started to follow. "And get everything down."

Most of the voices I overheard were distorted by loud music whenever I got too close to a speaker, and by feedback whenever I cranked up the volume. Here's what I salvaged, some of it translated. I started with a table of backward caps:

So it just pissadeared.

What?

She disappeared.

So tie into somethin' else. You didn't like her anyway.

Yeah. I've had better head from a lettuce.

There's a flower that needs arranging.

Where?

I'd spit out half the teeth in my head for her.

Where?

On TV.

Look what she's wearing, eh?

Slutfest.

I looked up. A row of monitors projected women modelling bathing suits—the high-cut versions which, I don't know about you, but I find slightly repellent. Sabrine had one. It's not so much the string through the gluteal folds, not so much the unaestheticness, the vulgarity of it all—it's what must be worn underneath: a genital Mohican plume. An apology should be beaten out of the inventor.

I moved on, to bearded graduates:

You're not aware of it? By jumbo, it's well on its way to becoming a Canadian classic—don't forget it was shortlisted for the Iris Lumby Award.

True. What's that prize worth now, by the way?

A hundred dollars and a painting from the federal Art Bank.

So you were saying it finds what is transsubstantial in the consubstantial?

Exactly.

To a man and a woman:
Were you looking for any artist in particular?
No, not really.
Any period in particular?
No, not really.
So you're just going to look around till a painting strikes you?
Well, I've just had my place redone. In berry and écru. What painting would go with that?
To two women:
So how's that whole thing going?
I don't know, I don't think we have much in common . . .
My breathing stopped. I was sitting at the bar, suffocating, palsied. The last two comments came from behind my back.
And I think he expects to see me every day or something.
Oh no.
And he's a bit of a pornographer . . . like Denny.
He's what? You're kidding!
No, I'm not. He got robbed a few days ago and . . .
Their voices died as I slithered off. My instinct, unfortunately, was to flee; I wish I'd stayed to hear the rest. By roundabout means I made it back to our table, where Jacques was sitting alone. I sat down, pretending to be fine. Jacques was writing and didn't look up. I pulled out my set-piece Sonnets and drank my wine in gulps, trying not to shake. It was only soft-core, I would tell her, innocent erotica. Which is now ash. It belonged to the former tenants, I would explain, I was just safeguarding the stuff . . .

When Jacques began reading out his eavesdroppings, nothing registered—I could only see his lips moving. I tried to laugh on cue. "I heard nothing of interest," I said. A woman came with a basket of roses. A man came and stood at our table, jittery and jack-in-the-boxy, febrile and neurotic, selling alcohol from a suitcase, talking well beyond the point anyone was listening. Jacques told him to shut up and then nodded towards the door. Milena was on her way out.

Through a window obstructed by heads I watched her and her silver-haired friend—Barbara Celerand!—chat with the flower girl outside. They kissed her on both cheeks. "Five bucks, final offer," said the seller of spirits. Milena and Barbara disappeared up the Boulevard.

I was up and out of my chair as if launched. I ran after them as if my life depended on it—but stopped a few feet away and watched them recede. And then ran after them again, unseen, stopping only when they reached Milena's apartment. As they entered I hid behind a tree out front, the same tree her father used, wondering what the hell I was doing. I couldn't come up with an answer so I left.

I unlocked my front door but then quickly shut it. I had to go back. Some voice was telling me to go back. Yes, I would knock on her front door, Milena would invite me in, we'd have a grand time! I'd amuse them with my Supersound 2000!

At Milena's front door, poised to ring her bell, I lost my nerve. So I went around to the back, into the alleyway, and looked through the slatted fence. Milena's was the only light on in the building. *Go home go home*, another voice was telling me. I climbed over the fence and up the fire escape, tiptoeing like a burglar. I peered through her torn curtain and almost opaque window—the glass had been partly painted over—into her living room, I guess. As I took in its contents, short of breath, I began to understand why Milena wouldn't invite me in. She lived in a sty. It was like my place before I moved in, or after Milena had been there a day. The furni-tureless room, whose walls bore the faint red tracks of a roller-brush, as if the paint had run out, was littered with stepped-out-of clothes and underclothes (male as well?), pizza cartons and crusts, a pan of rice-krispie squares baked in the '80s, crushed beer and Coke cans (who drinks Coke?— not Milena), overflowing ashtrays (with plain *and* filtered cigarettes), punctured and shrivelled balloons (what was she celebrating?), and an overturned can of Ajax (what was this for?). When I heard voices, women's voices, I jerked my head back. I strained to hear more, to hear what they were saying about me, but heard only the beating of my heart. I put on my Supersound 2000. It's come to this, I said to myself, the low-water mark of my self-dignity, the last ignoble act. *Go home go home.* I turned up the volume. I looked through the window again and glimpsed Barbara Celerand, or at least the back of her. She was sitting alone on a blanket, drinking what looked like red wine out of a glass tumbler. When I contorted to see more, I kicked over an empty beer bottle but caught it as it rolled towards the stairs. In my headphones it was thunderingly loud. "Did you hear something?" said Milena. I could hear the clomp clomp clomp of approaching footsteps, as in a badly-dubbed movie.

I stood, with arrested muscles and respiration, pressed against the wall, beside the door, praying they wouldn't open it (those who look behind doors have been there themselves, says the French proverb). They didn't. Their voices were suddenly indistinct and distorted—is there a guarantee on this machine? The sound of a television followed, clickings of a video machine. *Go home go home.* I peered back in. Again, the back of Barbara's head was visible but not Milena—at least not right away. She came into my frame of vision suddenly, pulled into it by Barbara's bangled arm. Milena looked directly into my eyes, or so it seemed. I ducked back. I crouched in the shadow, inert, heart pounding like a jackhammer. When I looked in again, the bangles were moving around in circles, the hand above them caressing Milena's chest. *No! It's not written on the Page! The Dark Lady wasn't gay!* I ran down the fire escape, clang-clanging on the iron steps, sweating like a terrified beast.

ɔ઼

From the other side of the mirror, my turbid bathroom mirror, a progeric, sad-faced stranger watched me soliloquise about love and death. Love is a vacuum world, I concluded, a world of vortexes and downward spirals; death is an escape. The relationship is now dead. We are sundered for all eternity. I'm so relieved. I'll clean up the apartment, rid it of her traces, expunge her scent, exorcise her ghost. I'll do it tomorrow.

"If you brush your teeth with your wrong hand," Milena once told me, "you will look like a child." I picked up my toothbrush and saw her in the mirror standing behind me, watching. I closed my eyes. When I reopened them Milena was gone and my hair was streaked with toothpaste.

I crawled into bed and lay in darkness with my eyes open, fearing for my sanity, until the morning traffic lulled me to sleep. I dreamt I was an encyclopaedia article: *DAVENANT (Jeremy). Another name for an idiot. See FOOL.*

TWENTY ONE

O gull, o dolt, as ignorant as dirt!

—Othello

On a late afternoon in late fall I am sitting at a picnic table not far from Milena's apartment. Possibly a week has passed, or more (my Book of Saturdays is unclear). It is a windbreaker autumn day, leaves are shedding their trees, clouds are chasing clouds across a brilliant sun. The mountain's kaleidoscope of red-brown-yellow is in gentle movement and the air is filled with the scent of mown clover. I just made all this up—my journal's empty, my mind a blank.

I sigh, histrionically. A stack of papers in front of me awaits red ink, but it's too cold to correct, my fingers are numb, my thoughts elsewhere. Two of the papers fly off the table as I gaze at the cross on the mountain. As I retrieve them, the others rise up like an accordion and scatter with the wind. Jerry Lewis-like, I embark on a paper chase, trying to stop the flight of leaves first by stepping on them, and then by lunging and belly-flopping on the grass. I manage to corral them all—except one. I watch it tumble across the soccer field. I'll say I lost it. "You have another copy? No, don't worry about it—I read it, really enjoyed it. Gave it an A." As I am saying this aloud, I hear an achingly familiar voice.

"Hello Jeremy."

I make a sound unlike any known word, like the bleating of a sheep.

"How's it going?" says Milena. "Who were you talking to? Anyone I know?"

I nod. Milena smiles. With volts of electricity passing through me, I try to play it cool. Don't press. Stay cool. Or should I stay hot? I'm mad at her, remember. Not for what I saw through her window, but for her *default*. Her eight-o'clock default.

"I saw you from my front window," she says, smiling. "It was quite a show you put on."

I am waiting for an apology. I am not saying anything until I get one. I demand an apology. I take a deep breath, clear my throat.

"Are you all right?" says Milena.

I try again. "Yeah fine I guess it was quite a show I did it on purpose do you want to go eat at the Italian place?"

Milena laughs. "Well, I suppose we could. Later."

I take another deep breath. "I saw you, uh . . . " *Why* does Milena make me stutter and falter and flutter? " . . . a few nights ago."

"When?"

"The night after you were supposed to come to my place. At *eight*."

"At eight? I was supposed to come to your place at eight?" Oh don't give me that. "Yes."

"Really? Sorry, guess I forgot. So you saw me the other night? Where?"

"It was . . . at your house. I was taking a walk. You were going into your place. With a friend. A girlfriend."

Milena looks at me without blinking. "Yeah. It was a strange night. We had a lot to drink."

"Why strange?"

"I don't know. It just was."

"You made love with her, right?"

267

Milena is calm, singularly unruffled. "I don't think that's any of your business. Who told you that?"

"No one. So what happened?"

"I told you—it's none of your business." She squats down and rummages through her knapsack. "Nothing happened."

"Nothing?"

"Does it matter?"

"Yes, it does." We look at each other. "OK, it doesn't. It has nothing to do with me." Logic and emotions, each side struggling for mastery, scramble my brainwaves. Did she make love with her? Does it concern me? Am I jealous? Do I care? Who am I?

"Nothing happened . . . of any importance," says Milena, striking a match. "I was drunk, she was drunk. Have you ever tried it?" She cups her hands round a cigarette.

"Tried what—making love with Barbara Celerand?"

"No, braindead, making love with someone of the same sex."

I take my time before saying, "Once."

"What happened?"

"I don't feel like going into it."

"Fine."

We sit in silence, neither one of us knowing how to break it. I sigh, she blows smoke rings that lasso the errant clouds. I can't articulate what I'm feeling. I don't want to say I'm jealous, don't want to talk about our "relationship", demand explanations. Milena is not one to be called to account. I don't feel like telling sexual self-discovery stories either. The silence is unbearable.

"I . . . really don't mind, Milena, if you make love to other women. In fact, as long as—"

"As long as you can watch, right?"

"Well . . . right."

"All men are the same. But it's nice to have your permission."

"Was the other night your . . . first time with a woman?"

"No."

"How many . . . I mean when was the first time? How old were you?"

"I don't feel like going into it either. It's a boring story anyway."

"Fine."

More than a minute passes.

"Did you know," I ask nonchalantly, "that the original title of Baudelaire's *Les Fleurs du Mal* was *Les Lesbiennes*?" This was one of those conversational nuggets that both fascinate and redound favourably upon the fascinator. But not in this case.

"Baudelaire was an ass. Lesbians for him were decadent, deformed by their genes, doomed to loneliness."

"Verlaine thought lesbianism was beautiful. In one poem he calls it *"le glorieux stigmate"*."

"Good for him."

"They say that women are *naturally* more bisexual than men."

"Who's 'they'?"

"Well, people. Baudelaire. You wouldn't agree?"

"I think more lesbians have had sexual relationships with men than gay men with women, yes. I also think that women can be better partners for each other—sexually and emotionally."

"Then why aren't there more lesbians?"

"More than what? Gay men? If there *are* fewer lesbians, it's probably because women are more repressed—sexually, economically—and because of that are less . . . willing, or confident, to explore new possibilities. Sexual possibilities."

As Milena speaks I watch the animated movements of her hands and fingers. "I think most women still feel they have to have a man around to survive—not another woman. Plus women are conditioned to want and need motherhood more than men are conditioned to want and need father-hood . . . Are you listening to me?"

"Of course."

"Then why are you looking down my top?"

"I wasn't. I was looking at your hands."

"What was the last thing I said?"

"That . . . women are conditioned to want and need moth-erhood more than men are conditioned to want and need fatherhood."

Milena raised her eyebrows in surprise. "Very good."

"Arielle's always complaining about a 'male shortage'. I suggested lesbianism."

"Well done."

"And why aren't there more feminists—why hasn't femi-nism really caught on in a big way? Why is the movement spinning its wheels, and why the backlash from women?"

Milena holds smoke in her mouth and then releases it in short puffs. "I guess because there are just as many stupid women as stupid men."

"Arielle said you were a Next Wave feminist. What's that?"

Milena laughs. "A lesbian, I think."

On one side of us, a young couple is amorously entangled on a cold bench. On the other, two dog owners—one wearing a Baggie on his hand, the other holding a trowel—yell at each other as their mismatched dogs copulate.

"Milena, why didn't you tell me you were . . . interested in women?"

"I thought you knew. Everyone else does."

"Well Jacques mentioned . . . Vile said something . . . I guess I didn't want to hear."

"Or you thought you could convert me? That lesbianism's a temporary phase, that all women would prefer men if they had the opportunity?"

"No, not at all. I thought our problems had something to do with, you know, your past . . . "

Milena sighs. "Everybody assumes there's an automatic connection. That all lesbians are that way because of some trauma caused by men, or by a faulty environment that brings out a woman's homosexual side. It's not always like that. Sometimes it's a political act, a rejection of patriarchal values, an acceptance of woman-identification."

I have no idea of what she's talking about. "I understand perfectly. I'm sorry, I feel really stupid."

"So do I, for not making things clearer. Maybe things aren't clear for me either. Despite everything I just said."

I sigh, stand up, sit back down. "So you prefer women . . . sexually? I mean—"

"Yes."

"Exclusively?"

"I have my occasional lapses, as you may have noticed. But you're the first in a long time. Of either sex."

"So you're sort of . . . sitting on the fence or . . . "

"In almost every imaginable way, Jeremy, I've spent my whole fucking life sitting on the fence."

Minutes pass as we both fidget, I looking at the clouds, she at the ground. Milena's mingled blood, I reflect, is half serene Indian, half spirited gypsy. Or is it? The gypsies' roots are in India. I nervously light up a cigarette, or at least try to. Milena snatches the matchbook and cigarette from me and, cupping her hands against the wind, expertly fires it up. "Tell me what happened," I exhale, "the first time you made love to a woman."

"No."

"Fine. I don't want to know anyway."

Milena laughs. "You're like a sulking child sometimes, aren't you. But I'll indulge you. It's not much of a story, really. It happened with a friend I was very close to in high school, and then lost contact with her when she moved to the Prairies—Saskatoon or Swift Current or . . . doesn't matter. One day we ran into each other at Noctambule and after that we started to see a lot of each other. I knew she was a lesbian, but never felt like she was trying to convert me or anything, although she was always very touchy—affectionate. One night after a few drinks, *many* drinks, we ended up at this bookstore to get some book she was raving about. The store was closed but she had a key. She knew the owner, I think, or used to work there. Anyway, as we're paging through this book, she suddenly kisses me on the lips then asks me if I want to make love."

"Just like that?"

"Just like that."

"That's very male."

"Is it? I thought it was just honest."

"How'd you react?"

"I laughed. I thought she was kidding, but she wasn't. Nope. Quite serious. I didn't really say anything. She took my hand, led me out of the store and then up to her bedroom, which was above the bookstore. That's it."

"What bookstore?"

"What difference does it make?"

"None."

"Fleur de Lysistrate. Any more questions?"

"So you made love?"

"I said I did."

"Did you enjoy it?"

"It was kinda weird. I was confused. I went to *high school* with her."

"Is she still in Montreal?"

"No."

"Where is she?"

"What difference does it make? I think she's in Windsor now. Someone told me she was actually married. Briefly."

"The merry wife of Windsor."

"Married, not merry—one precludes the other."

"You'd get along with my uncle. Is she pretty?"

"What the hell's that got to do with anything?"

"Did you go down on her?"

"Christ Jeremy, you're unfuckingbelievable. Everything's got to be graphic with you men. You're all a bunch of pornographers."

"So did you?" I redden at her allusion, but brazen it out.

"Let's go to the metal angels."

I do not feel like going to the "metal angels", a square at the foot of Mount Royal where lions and angels grew green. The statues are fine; it's the clustering tribes of atavistic rhythm-keepers that have to go. When Milena and I arrive, a dozen Piltdown men are beating away on the skins of dead animals. As I sneer and scoff Milena says, "What a fucking snob you are."

"Last resort of the artistically inept," I reply.

"What is—snobdom?"

"No, percussion."

"Don't be stupid."

"A last-ditch attempt, once they realise they've got no talent, to hitch a ride with music. I can't see any skill or art involved in pounding, can you?"

"Yes, the rhythms are intricate. And it's raw and real—primordial."

"It's in the same league as photography."

"What *are* you talking about?"

"Push a button and pray."

"Jeremy, do I bring out your idiot side? Do your thought waves slow down when I'm around? Let's get out of here."

We walk back across the park in silence, which is argument sustained by other means. "Look, is that Victor?" asks Milena.

It is. Captain Empathy himself, Protector of Womankind, Human Air-Bag, alone in the middle of the soccer field, in a quietistic trance with his gut hanging out, performing the slow-motion movements of Tai Chi. Wearing ball-hugging lycra tights and a hat he should be ashamed of.

"Yeah," I say. "That's Brother Teresa all right. Wanker extraordinaire." Milena gives me a sharp look of reproval, which I ignore. "He's hasn't got an original thought in his fat fuzzy head. Does all the trendy things, supports all the trendy causes in his loser-friendly column. I see right through the bastard."

"Oh you do?" Milena flares back. "I see. Fighting for women's rights, fighting for the oppressed is trendy, is it? Thanks for the insight. I happen to think he's sincere and does a lot of good. And I support all the 'trendy' causes he supports, by the way. He's also a great journalist."

"Toddley, a great journalist? Toddley shouldn't even be a journalist. He should go back to his old job, pulling poo out of pipes as a plumber."

"He also happens to be a close friend of mine."

"How close?"

"What's that supposed to mean?"

"How goes it, people?" Victor twitters. Under a yellow nylon jacket with red piping he is wearing a T-shirt that says ☺ IF YOU LOVE SUMMER. On the ground beside him is a tam-tam.

Victor gives Milena a long, overly-familiar bear hug, begins a playful sparring with me, then slaps me on the back with the warmth of long-lost brother. His frenzied enthusiasm makes me wonder if he needs a rabies shot. He and Milena engage in a lively conversation of which I am not a part, punctuated with peals of hee-hawing laughter. What—would someone please tell me—does Milena find so amusing about Victor? He's about as funny as Zeppo Marx. Milena congratulates Victor for winning some journalism award, and Victor tells a story about a landed immigrant who was denied a federal grant to write poetry in Punjabi. "Sure, I'll sign the petition," I say. He asks me if I'm going to the protest against poker machines, casinos and pathological gambling. "Of course I am," I say. Milena cocks an eye in suspicion. Victor turns to Milena and says, "Are we still on for tonight?" Milena nods yes, while looking at me. Victor's purring is almost audible.

"Want to tag along, sailor?" he says to me. "Meet the staff of *Barbed-Wire?*"

Sailor? Why was he calling me a sailor? "Uh, no. I don't really like staff parties. I mean I've already made other plans for tonight. For supper, at a restaurant, an Italian restaurant. With a *friend*." I look Milena in the eye.

"Which way are you two going?" says my benighted neighbour, writhing like a Uriah.

"I'm on my way *home*," replies Milena, returning my stare.

"So am I," I counter.

"I'll walk with you, Mil, I'm going that way," says Mr. Award-Winner.

"OK, well I guess I'll see you guys later then," I say, looking at the ground.

"Milena's not a guy," says Mr. Lard-Ass.

"Right. Sorry."

They nod goodbye. I watch them walk away (waddle in Toddley's case), Milena chattering away non-stop. Obviously about yours truly. And me without my bloody Supersound 2000.

On my way home I step in a dog's ordure. After sliding my foot against the grass and then on the curb outside my house, I pound up the stairs and slam as many doors as possible. I kick-throw my malodorous shoe down the hall, storm into the bathroom and look into the mirror. A sad sweating face, red as rhubarb, looks back at me. How can she not see that Toddley is mentally arrested? I must give her a pair of spectacles. He doesn't have a brain in his space-helmet head. How come no one sees this except me? His mother must have dropped him when he was a baby. You hear of things like that. Journalism award schmernalism award. It's over, I'm ending it right now, breaking it off, giving Milena the brush. She'll regret this. She can beg on bended knee but I will not budge. Because the sad fact is we have nothing in common. Absolutely nothing. The gap between us is as big as Asia. She's a dyke feminist, I'm a straight smuttist; she's politically enlightened, I'm a politico-idiot. Misunderstanding people is becoming a habit of mine. I really have to cut down. There's got to be someone better for me, more suited. Arielle, for instance. Thoughtful, considerate, pretty, heterosexual Arielle. Yes, she's ideal! Why didn't I see this before? I will simply transfer my affections to her!

I run into the living room, pick up the phone and punch the preselect. I put the phone down. Why mar Platonic perfection? *Sabrine.* Yes, beautiful Sabrine! I'll give it another shot. A reconciliation! People do things like that all the time. You get divorced and then you get married again. It's like a cycle. You change your mind, that's all. Admit you were wrong, go back to a period that wasn't as bad as you thought. Pre-Milena was not so bad, not really. I punch in Sabrine's number and hang up well before the first ring.

TWENTY TWO

Like a right gypsy hath at fast and loose
Beguiled me to the very heart of loss. What, Eros, Eros!
—*Antony and Cleopatra*

The next morning, elevenish, I was roused by the sound of my own voice: " . . . *un message après le ton sonore. Please leave a message or fax at the sound of the tone . . . *" Why can't I remember to turn the fucking volume off, I muttered to myself, it's really not that difficult. Any ape could do it. I rolled over to go back to sleep.

The caller's voice was melodious, thespian, familiar: "*Jérémie, c'est ton oncle . . .* " I went from anger to elation at the speed of sound. Finally! I leapt out of bed and lunged for the phone. "Uncle Gerard! Where the hell have you been?"

"Good man. I loathe those machines. Are we recording? How are you, son?"

"Wait till I turn the damn thing off. Hello? Gerard, you still there? Shit. Gerard? OK. Where've you been? Gerard? You were supposed to be here a month ago. Where are you calling from? When are you coming? Your room's all ready for you."

Gerard laughed. "No need for that. Wouldn't want to strain the old household."

"When are you coming? Where are you now?"

"Long Island. Yorkshire country, Jeremy."

278

"Yorkshire?"

"Given to the Duke of York in the 17th century by Charles II."

I smiled. "So you're inspecting our subjects?"

"No, on my way to a race. A friend of mine who mucks about in the stables, when he's not behind bars, strongly advised me to put my shirt on Roam Barbery in the third. Want in, lad? She's a real beauty, held back all summer. Worth a wager."

"Put me down for a hundred."

"Pounds or dollars?"

"Neither, I was joking. Well, all right—pounds."

"Money for jam, lad. Cable me the sum as soon as you can. At the American Express in Elmont? Wouldn't want the odds to shorten now, would we?"

"So when are you coming to see me? Right after the race? I sort of . . . need you, need to see you."

"Anything wrong?"

"No no, I'm fine, everything's fine."

"Sorrows of the heart?"

"You could say that."

Gerard laughed. "I'll be there as soon as I can, right after a visit to Saratoga. I'm staying at a friend's cottage nearby. Awfully nice of her, actually. Be a bit rude to rush off—break her heart, poor thing." I could hear a woman laughing in the background. "I'm using my friend's car phone, so I mustn't ramble on. Should I be wishing you a happy birthday?"

"No."

"Right, then, I'll see you soon. I understand Montreal has a new casino—we can meet there."

"Drive carefully," I said as he hung up. He sounded well into the breathalyser red zone.

Despite a chronic lack of sleep and a ringing in my ears, I was now feeling euphoric. The prospect of seeing Uncle Gerard cancelled everything else, cleared away the cobwebs and crap. He couldn't have phoned at a better time! I was in the mood to make a new beginning. A fresh start. I turned on "Télérencontres" (lifestyles of the rank and file) to find my dream woman. A man with a moustache the size of a hedge was looking for a woman with "a sense of humour." I turned off the TV. I'd go out and meet someone new. Right on the street. Someone nice. A blonde! I'd improve my hair, splash on some Andron, meet some buxom blonde. I could already feel Milena's power ebbing, her force field fading. The time and hope I had squandered on her! On a boyish infatuation! A boyish infatuation with a lesbian! I'm a new man now, emotion-free. Ice Man. I jumped down the stairs three at a time, onto the sidewalks of freedom, exhilarated at the thought of removing Milena from my life. Milena the millstone, the fool's gold. *A witch, a quean, a cozening quean!* I was no longer under her crushing weight, her radiant spell, her curse.

With my eyes trained on the sidewalk I walked directly to the feminist bookshop. Fuck the new beginning. I had to *understand*, goddamn it. Milena is the right one, the only one for me. Milena is one in a million. Our union, I repeat, was preordained.

og

Two saleswomen were chatting behind the desk when I arrived. "Can I help you?" asked one of them, perhaps sensing I needed a lot of help.

"Do you have this month's *Asian Assmaster*?" is what Jacques would have said. "No, it's all right, I'm just browsing thanks."

I went to the far end corner—away from the three female customers in the store who watched me from under lowered scornful lids—and picked up a Dictionary of Feminism. I stuck my finger in at random. In the C's:

> *Cunnilingus: Yet another power exercise performed by the male which reinforces the female's socialisation to passivity.*

Oh no. You can't be serious. I didn't know! Shit, why didn't someone tell me? Why didn't Milena tell me? Why didn't we discuss this? I read the entry again. But this doesn't make sense. Power? Passivity? What if she's riding atop, rodeo-style, holding your hair as reins? Is this passive? And what do lesbians do, for Christ's sake? I thought of Shakespeare's Adonis grazing on greater and lesser lips— what were my female students thinking? What was Milena thinking as I performed the "power exercise"? It was suddenly very hot in the store. Should I ask someone? Is there a book that elaborates? I looked for the entry on "fellatio"— not there. I walked up and down the aisles, book in hand, thoughts whirling like a helicopter. In a pubescent voice I asked a saleswoman if there were any "beginner's books" on feminism.

"Any what?"

"B-beginner's books on feminism, or lesbianism. Like a *Cliff's Notes* or—"

"I could check. Nerissa, Nerissa! Do we have any beginner's books on feminism? Or lesbianism?"

"Any what?"

"No no," I mumbled, "it's all right . . . "

"Beginner's books on feminism or lesbianism! Like a *Cliff's Notes*!"

Every head in the store turned. "Or maybe intermediate level," I mumbled. "I . . . do have some knowledge."

Nerissa, who was wearing a name tag that said "Lesbians Ignite", led me to a shelf marked GENERAL without recommending any book in particular. I was positively radiant with ignorance. After much page-flipping I settled on three volumes, each with "power" in the title: *Beyond Power; Passion and Power; Sex, Power and Pornography.*

"Are there any lesbian clubs for men?" I asked in a near-whisper, while paying.

"Any what?"

"Nothing."

On the street, I discarded the plastic bag and positioned the books so as to make their titles conspicuous. I looked in all directions for Milena and who should I see but . . . Arielle, pedalling furiously towards me. She skidded to a stop and in lieu of a greeting said I looked sick. "You look like a beat dog," she said.

"A beaten dog."

"You look like a beaten dog."

"You look stunning."

After examining my haircut, with no verbal reaction but lots of facial, she cocked her head to read the book titles and laughed out loud, I don't know why. My casual explanations ("Yeah, doin' an article on Victorian heroines . . . ") were met with a nodding head and knowing smile, that knowing smile that mothers and wives have as a birthright.

"And this has nothing to do with you know who?" she asked.

"Who? You mean Milena? Of course not, give me some credit."

"Maybe you should get *The Bluffer's Guide to Feminism.*"

"Does that exist? Do you have a copy?"

This broke Arielle up, for the second time. "I was pulling your leg."

"Right. I knew that. Very amusing." I tried to laugh along.

"Jeremy, I know I should mind my own onions, and I don't want to be a spoke in your wheel or a monkey wrench, but, well . . . "

"But what?"

"It's just that Milena . . . she's a difficult person. She's nice and everything, she's smart as whip and gorgeous, but she's . . . "

"A lesbian, I know. And you're having an affair with her."

"No, stupid. It's just that you get could tons of woman. I know tons of people who like the cut of your jib."

"I'm sorry? They like my what?"

"Your jib. The cut of your jib."

"Well, that's . . . very flattering." Memo to myself: buy Arielle an updated book of idioms. "But you see there's only one person I want, even if she doesn't want me. There's no logic to these things, Arielle. And that, as they say, is that."

"Whatever you say, boss. Listen, I got to go now. Call me sometime and we'll go out, OK?"

As she pedalled away, someone in a car (possibly male) yelled out: "Hey babe, I wish my face was your bike seat!"

"Fuck off," I said. Loudly, but to myself.

ಔ

When I arrived home the next evening, after another stuffing at my landlady's, there was a taped message from Gerard waiting for me. He had suffered "a mild setback" and wouldn't be able to make it to "la belle province" after all. He'd phone back. At first I thought he said "mild heart attack" and nearly had one myself. I was disheartened, to put it mildly, and worried. What if he had a drunken accident?

I phoned the American Express on Long Island. No, he hadn't picked up the money. No, he hadn't left a forwarding address.

Over the next three days, while waiting to hear from Gerard and Milena, I read my Power books, or portions thereof. Within their distressing pages I hoped to discover clues to understanding Milena, or myself.

On Guy Fawkes Night I wrote a letter to Victor, summarising my discoveries and making a few modest proposals to help women, ending with the suggestion that child-abusers and rapists be treated in the same way as chickens, where the immature males (cockerels) are castrated chemically with hormones that atrophy the testicles.

In a frantic rush I typed everything up boldface. I was so excited. Finally, I thought, someone's come up with some answers—me. If I'd waited until the next day, I might not have done what I did next: I ran madly across the street to Victor Toddley's house and slid an envelope through his mail slot.

Before I could disappear into the night I heard the sound of his door, and mouth, opening. "Halt. Who goes there? Jeremy? Is that you? Approach, sirrah! No really, come on in!"

I reluctantly obeyed. While closing the door behind us Victor spotted my envelope on the floor. I reached down and grabbed it but he snatched it from me like a junkyard dog.

"Caught me in my jimjams," he said breathlessly.

I eyed his burnt sienna shortie-pyjamas. "Sorry to get you out of bed."

"I wasn't in bed." In his other hand he held up a magazine called *Man! Men's Issues, Relationships and Recovery.* "I was reading. So what can I do you for? Is this from you?"

Feeling awkward and embarrassed, I almost asked for the envelope back. "Well, I just jotted down I mean typed up a few ... ideas for your next article. They're probably old hat, now that I think of it. And they may not exactly get at the root of the problem. Maybe you shouldn't even open it ... "

Victor tore open the envelope, put on his glasses and, with his closely-barbered head bowed, pored over my words. I could hear, from a back room, the sound of humpback whales.

"Look," I said, "I've got to go, we'll talk about this later, OK? You haven't seen Milena, have you?"

"Looks good, buddy, real good. Mercy buckets. I need all the help I can get. By the way, I'm writing an article on the drummers and dancers at the statues. If you have any insights, let me know."

"Will do."

I scuttled back home, convinced I'd made a complete ass of myself. Two weeks later my proposals were published in Victor's column, edited (vastly improved) by him and source acknowledged. *Barbed-Wire*, November 21-28, 1996: you can look it up. I'm not bragging, mind you—*Barbed-Wire* is no *Village Voice*. Besides, my motives are not hard to disinter, are they. I, fond fool, was using feminism to seduce. At least that's what Jacques said. What do you think?

TWENTY THREE

Give me your hand. I can tell your fortune. You are a fool.
—The Two Noble Kinsmen

Given my truant education and the diligence with which I would avoid classes and libraries, it is ironic that I should now be giving classes and practically living in libraries. The mountains of books, the millions of words, were my refuge whenever I felt unmoored, adrift in a Milenian sea, which was most of the time. When I wasn't staring at the walls of books I was doing research on the Dark Lady, trying to determine whether or not she was a lesbian. After one blind alley after another I phoned Women's Studies, who gave me enough leads to keep me in libraries for years.

Like many a jilted lover, I also went on a series of archaeological digs, gathering relics from another time. When the libraries closed I retraced our steps, looking in the same store windows, pausing at the same restaurants, thinking of what I should have said or should not have said, trying to re-architect the past, change what was unchangeable, relive what was dead. I rode the conveyor belt, I interrogated and re-interrogated her friends after plying them with drink. I was the newest, and most generous, member of the Boulevard club of runners-on-the-spot, turnstilers and rutting animals in ruts. I know what you're thinking, because I was thinking the same—it's time for a checkup.

JEFFREY MOORE

Like her grim-visaged father, I stared up at her window. Her building—it too—was giving off waves, rays. But her lights were now off, curtains cruelly drawn. Was she staying somewhere else? With someone else? One evening, at dusk, I saw a black cloth hanging from her fire escape, flapping in the wind. It was like a black flag, the ensign of pirates: "No mercy to be looked for here," it said, "no quarter to be given."

I was helpless, in thraldom, her dumb thrall. Over and over, from every angle, I tried to conjure up our days together. What happened? Nothing and everything. There were no walks by mountain streams, no moonlit exchange of vows, no passionate, bed-rattling sex. We slept, talked, read, hung out. We followed a banal routine that never once seemed banal or routine. Time moved differently then—the clock's hands were more relaxed, supple, like a child's made of plasticene. The days were unentangled, uncalendered, uncluttered by anticipation or nostalgia. It was the happiness of my Yorkshire youth, when days slipped by like hours and weeks like days.

But that was then. Now the clock's hands were rigid again, stiffly jerking forward, loud reminders that more time was grinding on without her. "We are all clocks, ticking away towards death," I thought, again. "We are all clocks ticking away towards death!" I screamed. "Where the *hell* is my uncle?"

☙

The next day I went to see a doctor. At a CLSC, a local rabble clinic where I had no appointment and no doctor, I sat in a pale-green waiting room with artificial plants and memories of pain, wondering what diseases I was contracting. It wasn't my obsessive behaviour, my impending nervous breakdown that I wanted checked out; it was my heart. It was simply too loud—I was sure everyone could hear it. A tell-tale heart. Between my buzzer and Milena, it had taken quite a beating over the last few months, volted and jolted and pierced by arrows.

I waited and waited, watching morose faces, holding my breath as much as possible. A Chinese baby with a pacifier stared at me the entire time, unblinkingly. After an hour and three quarters, my name was called.

"I'd just like a checkup, doctor. A top to toe physical. The last one I had was at birth. Pay particular attention to my heart."

Dr. Chiron smiled and then ran the gamut of tests. She poked and prodded, checked pupil and pulse, and wrote down numbers on a clipboard, as if measuring me for a coffin. She listened to my heart again, and even called for a colleague (mortician?) to come and have a listen. They had a few words out of earshot, after which Dr. Chiron said I had a slight murmur. "If I were you, I wouldn't worry about it too much." You wouldn't worry *too much*? "Everything seems to be fine." *Seems, Madam*? "Naturally, we'll have to wait for the blood and urine tests." Naturally. "Anything else you'd like to tell me about?"

In my ear a siren roared, my mind was dark as a dungeon, my heart like shattered glass. "N-no," I said. "Nothing."

"Would you like me to recommend you a psychologist?" Now why would she say that? "No need," I said.

"Take this number anyway."

"Oh, I almost forgot. I black out sometimes."

"Do you suffer migraines?"

Only since meeting Milena. "Yes."

"When you close your eyes do you see a brilliantly-lighted image or aura? In the form of a zigzag or throbbing line?"

Not really. "Right."

"I'll prescribe you something. It's a condition known as scintillating scotoma, or migraine aura."

"There's something else, Doctor. A friend of mine sometimes get these explosions of red in her mind when she . . . well, thinks of certain things from her past. Her whole mind goes red. But it's not anger or anything. In fact she says it helps her, it does her good. Do you know what that's all about or what's it's called or what it means?"

"No."

"Do you think she's . . . never mind. Can you prescribe me some good sleeping pills while you're at it, Doc? Some really potent, dynamite ones?"

"No."

An administrative foul-up ensued, I think, because when I phoned back two days later they asked me to come in and redo the tests. Fuck that.

ᚼ

When a woman recounts how her best girlfriend has been left for another woman, this other woman—a complete stranger—is usually referred to as some "floozy", some "nympho predator". Or worse. When a male friend has been left for another man, this other man becomes "some skirtchaser", "some slimebucket". I attach no profundity to this; I mention it only to explain my reaction to learning, fourth-hand, that Milena had gone to Europe with an attractive goth-vamp named Véronique. Véronique was a choreographer, intelligent and charming, and I rather liked her. *Liked*, past tense. Now, if anyone asked, she was a nympho predator, a skirtchaser. When I saw her two weeks later, however, she explained that she had merely taken the same plane as Milena, that they had parted at Warsaw International

Airport, that Milena, after getting a free ticket from a stewardess friend, was on her way to visit a relative. At least that's what she said.

Confirmation came from Vile. I stumbled across her in a bar Arielle had recommended to me (to find someone new), a black-walled maze of "techno trip-hop/ industrial goth" with a portcullis and gallows known as The Hangmen's Ball. In torn thigh-highs and kinderslut frock, Vile was lying on the floor of a small room that had all the atmosphere of a cement bunker. She couldn't talk, literally. Her friend Drew could, but barely. He asked me if I wanted to "chase the dragon," which I declined with thanks, unaware of what I had declined. I watched him place some white powder on a strip of foil while Violet, after several misfires, lit a match underneath. From my vantage, it looked like she was lighting Drew's fingers. With their mouths in an "o", they then chased the burning trail of smoke, reaching a state in which they were asleep with their eyes open. I asked Vile if her sister was in Poland. Twice. With a limp smile Drew suggested I consult her some other time, preferably by phone. Neither responded to my request for her phone number, but Drew, while examining his red fingers, seemed to remember where she worked: "God's Hotel." This made no sense. When I asked for clarification, glancing from one to the other, they looked at me with glazed immovable eyes, like fish.

I went to the bar for a draft and, after screaming to be heard, floated a five-dollar bill on a pool of beer. As I looked around, scouting half-heartedly for a new girlfriend, a gaunt man with white suspenders tapped me on the shoulder and asked me if I wanted some "E". I shook my head, wondering why he'd be selling vitamins in a bar. "How about some LoveStone? Very reliable. Made from toad slime. You rub it on your genitals. I'll show you." I moved on, briskly, into an

L-shaped room in which people were sitting cross-legged on polished cement, some watching soundless cartoons, others watching the walls. One gentleman, conservatively dressed in a three-piece suit, was vomiting into his hat. In a larger, louder room, in clouds of tobacco smoke and dry ice, I watched multi-pierced, poly-tatooed dancers sway to menacing fin-de-siècle music, entropic fragments wedded by shotgun: Rudy Vallee and jackhammers, Gregorian chant and chainsaws, Scarlatti and Accidental Goat Sodomy. Everyone seemed to like it.

ഗ

That night I dreamt of God's Hotel. When I rose from my bed at the crack of noon, things were suddenly clear: Vile worked at Hôtel Dieu, the local hospital. That had to be it. And so there, without a particle of indecision, I went.

At the personnel office a tough old dame with aluminum hair and high-cut basketball shoes informed me that Violet worked ("when it suited her") in the cafeteria. She was supposed to be in that day ("unless of course she phoned in sick"). I thanked her and headed towards the cafeteria ("Thank God for unions," she muttered after me).

In an unlocked room near the kitchen I found Vile sprawled out on a table, dressed in a short, drab-green frock and black Mountie boots. At her side lay a red-stained butcher knife. Foul play? With a surge of adrenaline I raced to the table and discovered, on the other side of her motionless body, a mound of diced beets.

"What the fuck's goin' on? Who the hell . . . Jesus Christ Jeremy, you scared the livin' shit out of me. Give me that for Christ's sake."

I handed her the cleaver. "Sorry, I . . . Drew told me you worked here. I didn't know where else—"

"How the fuck you get in here? What'd I do? Do I owe you money?"

"Do you know what's happened to your sister?"

"What's happened? What happened to Millie?" Vile was shouting, and waving the knife in my face.

"Nothing's happened. Calm down, and put that down. I was just wondering if you knew where your sister was."

"Jesus Jeremy. You're scarin' the livin' shit outta me. Right fuckin' out." She shook her head and sighed before sitting down on the table cross-legged. This was distracting. "You're always asking me where my sister is. Why don't you like, put a cowbell round her neck."

"Do you know where she is or not?"

Vile set the knife on the table and began rubbing her eyes, spreading mascara over her cheeks. "Yeah, I got a card from her. I think she's in Poland."

"Did she leave an address?"

"On the card you mean?"

"Yes, on the card."

"No, but I know someone's who's got it." She smiled.

"Who? Victor?"

"No. Your ex."

"Sabrine? Sabrine has Milena's address? They don't even know each other."

"I introduced them."

"How the hell do you know Sabrine?"

"I already told you. I know her boyfriend, Bonze, your favourite night porter—"

"Right. So why would Sabrine have Milena's address?"

Vile shifted her position, rubbed her hair vigorously with both hands as if dislodging fleas, then held her knees up to her chest. Her mesh stockings contained self-inflicted holes at the knees and thighs. "Because Sabrine knows somebody cool in Poland that Milena can crash with, before she goes to visit our aunt. Somebody named Madame Zoom?"

"Zoumromski. Shit." I knew her all too well. "Do you know when Milena's coming back? Are you going to write her?"

Vile overcame a yawn. "I never write nobody. And we don't get along all that well anyhow. Milly can be a weird sister sometimes. Don't you think she can be weird?"

"No, I think she's perfectly normal. Especially considering . . . you know."

"Considering what?"

"Well, you know, her . . . what happened to her and everything—"

"So something did happen to her—"

"No no, nothing's happened to her. I mean not recently. But, you know, in the past, when she was . . . you know—"

"What the fuck you talking about?"

"When you guys were . . . abused."

Vile, her black-lined eyes narrowing, picked up the cleaver again with a multi-ringed hand. "Right, I forgot, you're mister fucking confidant. It's none of your fucking business. I can't believe she told you all that."

"Don't tell her I mentioned it. But do you think that having to pose together like that might explain, you know, why she's . . . "

"Gay?"

"Well, no. Why you two—"

"We didn't just pose together. Is that what you want to know? We made love to each other, OK? Did she tell you that? Denny gave us money, and drugs, to lick each other's cunts. Did she tell you that?"

Oh, hell. "Yes. I mean no, sort of. I'm sorry, Vile, I'm really sorry to bring it up. But I'm trying to understand . . . So is that why you two don't get along that well, why there's a distance?"

"Jeremy, I don't know why the fuck we're talking about this, I really don't. But when two people go through shit, you either end up with a bond or a wall. We got a wall, OK?"

"Because the other person reminds you of what you'd like to forget?"

"Bingo."

"Milena likes the colour red, paints everything red. Do you know why? Is there any connection or . . . "

Vile shrugged her shoulders. "Red charges the field, the *chakra*, it burns out cancer, warms out cold areas."

"I see." I had no idea what she was talking about.

Vile was abstractly carving letters into the wood table. "Jeremy, I know you're like, in love with my sister and everything, which is not a smart idea by the way, but why are you asking me all these questions? We're not in high school, for Christ's sake."

"Did Milena kill Denny?"

Vile jumped. "*Milena* kill Denny? You're fucking joking, right?"

"Right."

"Any more stupid questions?"

"How are things going with Drew?"

"You're always asking me that. Fine, things are fine. He fucks like a Tantrist."

ೞ

I phoned Sabrine and was relieved to hear her recorded voice; I left her mine. I then wrote a long effusive airmail letter to Milena which I delivered, piecemeal, into the vortex of the toilet.

In the early hours of the morning, my mind leadened with three sleeping pills, I heard the fragmented voice of Sabrine: *... qu'elle va traverser la frontière après, mais elle n'a pas dit laquelle ... Est-ce que ça veut dire que tu va tuer Milena? C'est drôle, n'est-ce pas ...*

I leapt out of bed, panic-stricken at the words *tuer Milena*. I fumbled with buttons and knobs, forgetting how to work the answering machine, how to go backwards in time.

... Are you interested in long-distance savings? Well have we—

... elle voulait l'adresse de Madame Zoumromski à Crakovie. En passant, tu sais qu'elle dit que c'est écrit dans ton destin, tu tueras ta prochaine amante? Est-ce que ça veut dire que tu va tuer Milena? C'est drôle—

I hammered down the stop button and went back to bed. I was livid. Me kill Milena! Madame Zoum! It wasn't my first collision with the witch.

One fall evening when I was living at a higher elevation, Sabrine informed me that a friend of her mother's, *une dame merveilleuse, une gitane* from Krakow, was coming for dinner and staying one night. Madame Zoumromski arrived with two Persians in a box and stayed two weeks. Because she was a vegetarian, we ate a lot of vegetables during this period. One night, at the dinner table, our guest began to act strangely.

"Your mother ... your mother is dead, Jeremy ... I know this ... I feel this ... " (Yes, and you may have heard it from Sabrine, too.) "I knew her . . . many years ago I knew her . . . " (This shocked me, at least at first.) "Eons ago I knew her ... through the mists of time ... I see an accident, I see other accidents ... I see red streams and blue skies and a floating body ... You ought to know ... you ought to know ... " (I ought to know what?) "You're a Libra."

"No I'm not," I said.

"You're a Libra just like me . . . "

"I am not a Libra."

She nodded sagely. "I see a number . . . fourteen . . . thirteen . . . You ought to know . . . "

The upshot of all this was that I, like my mother, was going to die in an accident (I was reading between the lines, mind you) by falling off our fourteenth (really thirteenth) floor balcony. As she continued to receive and transmit signals, one of her cats lapped soup from her bowl. Sabrine laughed out loud but the cat, perhaps thinking I was the one who had laughed, paused to glare at me. I suddenly felt the urge to flee. Which I did, but not before telling Madame Zoum she was out of her fucking tree.

Her mantic illumination that I would murder Milena was perhaps some cheap revenge on her part—or perhaps on the part of Sabrine. And now Milena was going to stay with the nutter! Or was already staying with her, and had already learned that I was to be her murderer. Christ almighty. I don't need this.

I went to get my atlas, to see which border Sabrine was talking about. Sprawled across my bed, I opened the book at random—at the map of Poland—and discovered that the two countries closest to Krakow were the Czech Republic and the Ukraine. The Ukraine! **Shakhtyorsk!** Of course! I must look to the Page for guidance! As I circled it in the atlas, an idea was forming in my mind, an idea so crazy and exciting I can hardly wait to share it with you.

As soon as I got up the next day I went looking for my landlady, who was not far to find. She was standing out front on the sidewalk, in the freezing cold, mittenless, looking like a lost little girl, her cart next to her, empty, with one broken wheel. The scene was simply heartbreaking. I walked quickly down the stairs and asked if she was all right. She replied in gibberish, and I asked questions that were gibberish to her. Eventually, things became clear: she had locked herself out. She had also picked out all her groceries, set them on the counter, and then discovered she had no money to pay for them.

"You poor thing," I said. "Does anyone else have a key? Key, you know, key." I made turning motions with my hand.

"Woly."

Yes, but Wolodko is dead. "Any one else? Sister, brother, daughter . . . "

Lesya bit her lip, shook her head. She was shivering and her hands were red with cold.

"Well, let's see what we can do." I put my shoulder to the door and pushed with all my might, without the tiniest measure of success. I then started smacking the door pane with the heel of my boot. "Don't worry," I told her as she tried to restrain me, "I have some experience in these matters." The glass cracked in a perfect diagonal across the bottom corner. I pushed it through, struck my arm through the hole without mishap, and released the bolt.

Inside, after I set her cart down in the hall, Lesya grabbed my arm and said "Sit." Like a dog I obeyed. She stuffed a plastic bag into the hole in the door pane, bustled off into the kitchen, and after a clatter of dishes returned with a tray so full that I wondered if she had mistaken me for a party of Ukrainian wrestlers.

"Have you ever been to Shakhtyorsk?" I asked between mouthfuls of cabbage. "You and Wolodko were born there, right? Shakhtyorsk? Born?"

Lesya smiled and pushed more pierogis and chicken breasts at me. I gave it another shot in my best Ukrainian accent, which involved pronouncing Shakhtyorsk the same way but louder. When Lesya shrugged her shoulders I wrote it down on a piece of paper. She examined it with a puzzled expression; I remembered her upside-down books on the shelf.

I stood beside her faded map of the Ukraine, and put my index finger on the city in question. "You were born here, right? This exact spot?" Lesya gave me a vacant look, the same one my students give me when I ask questions. I repeated the question, in a variety of forms.

"No," she eventually replied. "Nozdrische."

I shook my head. "No no, you . . . you must be mistaken." I pointed again. "Shakhtyorsk."

"Nozdrische."

"Shakhtyorsk." I sighed. "You may not have been born there, but you lived there, right? Or Wolodko lived there, am I right?" As I pointed and gesticulated, Lesya went from smiles to giggles to great peals of laughter. What was so funny? I waited for her laughter to subside.

"How do you get to the Ukraine, Lesya? Where do you land?"

"How go Oo-crane?" she asked, wiping tears from her eyes.

"Yes."

"Boat." She re-exploded into laughter.

"Thanks, Lesya. Look, shall I do your shopping for you?" I pointed to her empty cart. She stopped laughing, shook her head. "You sure? OK, listen, I have to go now, I left my door unlocked and I have to make a phone call." I made a telephone with my thumb and little finger. "I'll be over tomorrow— Tuesday—for dinner as usual." I tapped my fingers to my mouth. "Dinner, eat? Tomorrow? Don't make anything special, just heat up the three meals left on my plate, OK?"

Lesya was now turning her purse upside down. She gave me a look that melted my heart as she handed me two quarters.

"No no, it's OK," I protested but she slipped the coins into my breast pocket.

"Thank you, Lesya, but it's really not—"

She handed me something else: a door key.

"Oh, right, good idea. Thanks again for lunch, it was delicious. See you tomorrow. Take care."

"Same time to you."

Back at my apartment I phoned my travel agent, who told me to leave everything to him, be back to me in ten. He had a special "Ukrainian connection". I hoped it wasn't my landlady. The phone rang exactly ten minutes later, but it wasn't my travel agent.

"Jacques, I can't talk, I'm on my way to the Ukraine."

"Say that again."

"You heard me."

"No one goes to the Ukraine, Jeremy. Not by choice. How'd you choose that—spin the globe?"

"Guess."

"Milena? Christ. Pack a Geiger counter. But wait, that sounds like a good idea. You can check out Soci—it's a resort on the Black Sea."

"Bye Jacques."

"S-o-c-i. It's Russia's sex capital, where you can get more tail than a toilet seat."

"Jacques—"

"You read today's *Devoir*? Some bureaucratic berk from Ottawa was walking out of his hotel in Soci and gets stopped by this tart offering 'personal services'. One of those no-request-refused deals. Twenty-four hours for twenty-four American dollars—about a grand Canadian. Then it goes

299

down to ten, then to a 'gift' from the hotel shop, then to just dinner or breakfast. He bought her breakfast. Jeremy, this is no joke, now's the time to go—it's a crippled economy. Take advantage, lay some pipe."

"I appreciate . . . lay some pipe?"

"Five rubles should do it. Or even three, if you play your cards right. That's sixty cents, for Christ's sake."

"Got to go—"

"And it beats ramming a tailor's dummy, which you—"

I slammed the phone down. It rang seconds later. I picked it up. "Fuck off!" I cried. "Just fuck right off you evil bastard!"

It was my travel agent. Who as usual said everything was booked, then quoted a ridiculously expensive price, then "found" a cheaper price. My itinerary: Montreal-Warsaw, Warsaw-Kiev, train to Shakhtyorsk, three days at the city's only "Western-style" hotel for foreigners called Inn Biggest Top. About two days of travel and two grand. I'd need a visa. And Visa.

"How far is Soci from there?" I asked.

"How far is what?"

"Never mind. Thanks for your help."

PART THREE

TWENTY FOUR

What folly I commit, I dedicate to you.
—Troilus and Cressida

It was the Christmas holidays. Mirabel Airport, normally one of the emptiest in the world, was thronged. I was sitting with my feet up in the departures lounge reading *Marxist-Lesbianism*, trying to ignore a loud Ukrainian contingent who all wore the same yellow and blue jackets, obviously a team of some sort. There was also a long line of wheelchairists, all young males, and also jacketed. Neither group appeared to understand English or French, for after every announcement they scuttled towards the embarkation door, shouting and elbowing and spinning their way to the front of the line. Each time they were turned back by patient airline personnel. But with the very next announcement—"Would Marie Mountjoy please report to the information desk . . . "—the process would begin anew. The delay was now approaching an hour and a half, so they were getting a decent workout. Maybe they'd sleep on the plane.

Shakhtyorsk. I took out my fountain pen and began scrambling the letters, ending up with: SHAK. YORKSH. T. "Shakespeare, Yorkshire Tragedy!" I said aloud. Pertinent. Then "MILENA": I'M LEAN (pertinent); NAIL ME/ANIL ME (impertinent); I AM LEN and I'M NEAL. Shit! Milena is Len Neal! Leonard Neal! He was in my Grade 3 class! I suddenly felt hot. Why am I doing this? Why am I sitting in an airport?

I wiped my brow, unbuttoned my shirt. What at first seemed like a dramatic gesture, as bold as it was inevitable, now seemed silly. Why am I going to Shakhtyorsk? Please tell me again. Because of the Yorkshire Page. Because I have to stop Milena from killing herself (unhappiness and self-homicide ran rampant in her circle), because I have to tell her I've read some books on power. That I understand, or rather understand more. No, I have to tell her I'm sorry. For what? For being of the unfairer sex? For my paper harem? What the hell am I going to do when I get to the Donets Coal Basin? Would she be at the "Inn Biggest Top"? I've got Madame Zoum's number, I'll phone her when I land, she'll know where Milena is. My plan is sound. Unless the plane crashes, which it probably will. But it's out of my hands now, there's no drawing back, all for love and the world well lost, faint heart never won fair lady . . .

In the wisdom of the ages I took comfort, and when that comfort subsided, in alcohol. "I'll have whatever they're having," I mumbled to the waiter, nodding towards two well-lubricated executives, each crumpled with laughter as cell phones rang in their pockets. They were having "boiler-makers", as it turned out, shots of Crown Royal chased by Boréal Noir. After two of these I was convinced I was doing the right thing. Convinced there was a tide in the affairs of men which, taken at the flood, leads on to Shakhtyorsk.

From a hollow aluminum cone I retrieved a newspaper stained with ashes and oranges, and turned to the horoscope. This would confirm everything, I said to myself. Everything.

You are inclined to be obsessive, blind and infan-tile, which leads you to make the same mistakes repeatedly. Everyone thinks you are a complete fuckwit. There has never been an Aquarius of any importance. Most of them are murdered.

I had to find a phone. Two behind me, both being used. I circled each, sighing, drumming my dirty fingers on things metallic, bouncing up and down, trying to secure eye contact. One of the men was speaking in a foreign tongue, perhaps Ukrainian, while the other said "Really?" nine times in a row. Hang up, you idiot. Yes, really. Get on your fucking plane. I need encouragement; I need support and understanding.

"You're going where?" Arielle screamed into the line. "*Es-tu fou?* Are you cocklemany?"

"We don't use that word anymore."

"Don't go anywhere, *bordel de merde.* I am trying to call you since three hours. I just saw my sister who just saw Sabrine who say that a friend of Drew say that Vile say that her sister say that she will be back in a week or two. Or so. She phoned her."

"I haven't understood a word you've said."

"Milena will be back in the middle of January. She phoned Vile. And told Vile to tell you."

"Tell *me*? Really? When?"

"Last night, night before."

"She called from the Ukraine, right? From Shakhtyorsk, in the Ukraine?"

"Prague."

"Shit."

I hung up and ran to the LOT counter. My father had just died of blackwater fever, plus I had to donate both lungs to my kid sister. Would it be possible to have a refund? I had only a carry-on bag, and no luggage checked, so surely it would be possible. (It would not.)

"Do you fly to England, by any chance?" I sighed.

"Not from Canada."

"No, I mean from Warsaw."

"Once a day—to London Heathrow."

"Okay. I'll keep this ticket to Warsaw, cancel the return portion, and apply it to the Warsaw-London trek. Can I do that? Yes, I'm still talking to you. Do you understand what I just said?"

"I understand. But I don't know." He shrugged his shoulders and looked down at his desk.

"What do you mean you don't know?"

He started doodling with his pen. "I don't know. I don't think so." He looked over my shoulder to a jittery customer behind me.

"I lost my bag near the carousel and—"

"Wait a minute," I said to the customer. "Hold on. Excuse me? I'm still talking to him; I'm still being looked after. Thank you." You look like a lost bag yourself. "What do you mean you don't *think* so? Do you have a supervisor? Excuse me, I'm still talking to him. Can you ask your supervisor? Yes, you."

The "supervisor", a perspiring man with a dented cannon-ball of a head and squat silver suit, eventually appeared, looking like someone with unhealthy sexual ambitions. While he made a steeple under his nose with his hands, I explained the situation three times before he made his (probably improvised) ruling: "No."

I bought another ticket, on a borderline credit card, then ran to make a last-minute phone call. To York. No answer. I ran through shaking corridors to the plane, whose wheels turned as I fastened my seatbelt.

 ଔ

At the first phone I saw at Heathrow I called Gerard collect. Still no answer. So what now? At the Duty Free I sampled and re-sampled scotch from the Isle of Skye; at a souvenir shop I bought my landlady a St. Paul's thimble, Arielle a Handbook of Modern Idioms, Milena a postcard of Big Ben. For myself I bought a green phone card and again called the cathedral city. I walked, exhausted, toward a line of taxis.

"Where would you go," I said as I climbed in one of them, "if you were just arriving?"

"Where in London?"

"Yeah."

He eyed me in his rear-view mirror. "Soho, Greek Street. That's what's your lookin' for, innit guv?"

"I'm looking for a hotel, not a prostitute."

"Mayfair."

"Go to Bloomsbury," I said.

In a jet-lag fog I got out at Cartwright Gardens and checked into a hotel with a tennis court but no net. A voluble man with a stoop and thinning hair swept up from his temples and creamed onto his pate showed me to my room. As we walked through the corridors, I heard a periodic sibilant sound. "Showers down the hall [psss, psss], breakfast between seven [psss] and nine [psss]. Leave your key at the desk if you're [psss] going out." With the last spurt I glimpsed an inverted can of Glade up his sleeve. In my room I sneezed several times in rapid succession before lapsing into perhaps the deepest sleep of my life.

I came out of this dreamless coma about three hours later, after which I stumbled downstairs to the lobby phone, where I again tried to send my voice northward. In vain. I went back to bed and woke up the next morning not knowing where I was or when.

Alone in the basement dining room, last to be served, I sat in a mindless state, staring at a papered wall of cavorting nymphs and satyrs while Andy Williams sang "Chestnuts

Roasting" on a lo-tech radio. I took a sip of coffee that may have been dredged from the Thames and then fled after seeing my eggs and sausages afloat in oil.

Nauseous and vaguely depressed, I ended up in Tavistock Square (a "Dog Free Area") without the faintest idea of what to do with myself. At a statue of Gandhi I examined morbid bouquets of flowers wrapped in cellophane and flashbacked to me, lost little me, placing gladioli on the grave of my mother. I saw her cameo brooch, her double necklace of pearls, her long dark hair spread out like a fan on white linen pillows, her cheeks the colour of cement . . . I ran my fingers along her tombstone of polished black glass . . . She wasn't instantly killed, she hung by a thread for weeks . . . I wanted to jump down, drag the coffin back up, lift the lid, say "You mother. It's *you* I loved the most . . . "

Except for the stench of asphalt and oxides, the only thing I remember of the blind wanderings that followed is the British Museum, of sitting on its steps, blankly watching the hordes going in and out. Like counting sheep, it had a sedative effect, and my eyelids gradually closed. When they opened minutes later I was looking at a blinding sun and cirrus clouds and my head was resting on cement. Obeying a voice in a dream, I suddenly leapt to my feet and ran through the museum's portals, straight to the statue of Shakespeare. I stared, trancelike, into his stone grey eyes, thinking not of him but of his mysterious Dark Lady, trying once more to imagine her. She had dark eyes and colouring, hair under her arms—this much we knew. She was aloof, dissatisfied in love, musically accomplished, and her name (most believe) was Emilia Bassano, the illegitimate daughter of an Italian musician. Emilia—an anagram of Milena! No it's not.

Music, Indian music, gradually infiltrated these thoughts. On my way towards it, lured inexplicably towards its source, I passed a row of large posters, all the same, announcing a special exhibit on THE SHAKESPEARE OF INDIA: KALIDASA. The music was getting louder. I continued on, hypnotised, and who should I see, sitting on a bench at the gallery's far end, but a dark-haired lady! Yes, it's fate, she's here, she has to be here, we'll spend Christmas together, how utterly romantic! My heart was beating like a tabla as I walked closer to Milena.

It was not Milena, of course. How could it be? It was a beautiful young Indian woman, elegantly dressed and bespangled, who ignored me as I lingered near, pretending to be lost. When I asked if she had the vague impression someone was staring at her, her face creased into a smile. I couldn't help it, I explained, I was drawn to her like iron dust to a magnet (I being the dust, I added). She remained silent, eyes downcast, with the ghost of a smile. I apologised, mumbling that I was just an innocent sleepwalker, and continued on, towards the mummies and sarcophagi.

"To exchange a look is not innocent."

I stopped dead, swivelled on my heel. "I beg your pardon?"

"To exchange a look is not innocent. The visual relationship transmits energy. It is what we call *darshan*."

I didn't know quite what to say to that. "When I saw you I was thinking of Shakespeare's Dark Lady. The Shakespeare of England. Do you play a musical instrument by any chance?"

"Did the Dark Lady play an instrument? I play a percussion instrument—the tabla."

"Do you consider that a musical instrument?"

"Yes, naturally. Percussion is the heartbeat of music. Listen, you can hear one now."

I listened. "Yes, it's very beautiful," I said. "Percussion is important, isn't it? But I don't really understand what's going on in Indian music. There doesn't seem to be any . . . key. It just seems to meander all over the place."

"There is no key, and no harmony. The music is based on note complexes called *rags*. The musician's art lies in exhibiting, with many nuances and ornamentations, the full range of the note relationships admissible within the structure of the chosen rag. The *rags* are classified into ten *thats*. Each *that* comprises many *rags*, and each has a *rag* chosen as characteristic of its *that* . . . But I fear I'm losing you."

"No, I'm with you. Do you work here?"

"Yes." She smiled again. "But not today. I start in one month's time."

"Please continue."

"Well, each *rag* has its own emotional character, and is associated with a particular time of the day. The one that's playing now, for example, is an afternoon *rag*."

"What happens if you play a *rag* at the wrong time of day?"

"There is a well-known story about Tan Sen, a court musician of the 16th-century emperor Akbar, who sang a night *rag* at midday with such force that darkness fell on the place where he stood."

"No kidding?" I listened. "And what emotion does this one convey?"

"It is inquisitive, with a mixture of joy and affection."

We listened together. "Yes, I believe you're right," I said. "Definitely inquisitive—and yet affectionate."

She smiled. We gazed at each other in silence. "Do you intend to see the Kalidasa exhibit next month?" she asked, averting her eyes. "Are you familiar with Kalidasa?"

"Yes. Shakuntala, in Hindu mythology, daughter of Visvamitra and Menaka, and heroine of Kalidasa's erotic Sanskrit drama *Shakuntala* (c. AD 400). In this idealised tale of love lost and regained, which many regard as India's greatest literary achievement, the infant Shakuntala is abandoned on the banks of the river Malini and raised by the hermit Kanva. While hunting, King Dushyanta watches the maiden from behind a tree and falls irretrievably in love with her. After days of indecision and heartache he seduces her, asks for her hand in marriage, and gives her a ring as pledge before returning to his throne. A son is born of their union, whereupon mother and child set out to find the king. While bathing, Shakuntala loses the ring and King Dushyanta, enchanted by a curse, does not recognise her. The ring is."

"Such erudition! Please continue, I'm impressed. Is what?"

"I'm afraid that's all there is. Do you play tennis?"

"I'm afraid I do not."

We went back to my hotel to play tennis. We stood on the decaying courts, watching the swaying trees and twilight skies of violet and rose. Since Purinima was wearing ankle boots and tight slacks, and since we had no rackets, balls or net, she finally suggested we go back to my room. "It is getting cold," she said. "And darkness is falling."

I was only her second lover. Her first was her husband, who had betrayed her on many occasions. She was making love to me out of revenge, I gathered; I too confessed to betraying someone.

ଔ

"We are like the sheldrakes of Indian mythology," Purinima

said softly as I walked her back to her cousin's flat in Bedford Square. "Lovebirds fated to separate at night."

"Can't we see each other tomorrow?"

"Tomorrow I leave for Hastinàpura. When I return, you will be in Montreal. Give me your address, I will write."

That night I saw Purinima pleading with her husband, saw dreadful flames, saw her writhing in the fires of self-immolation. I could feel the heat—I was in there with her!—and woke up in the grip of a death sweat. With no hope of getting back to sleep, I dressed and tiptoed down the stairs, breathing in the warring scents of Glade and fumigant.

In Bedford Square at quarter past six I stood below Purinima's balcony—or what I felt might be her balcony— and gazed up like Romeo. She'd be leaving soon for the airport—should I go with her? Don't be mad; she's married and I'm practically betrothed. A black cab stopped at the house next door and a couple with canes got out. I ran over to take their place, instructing the driver to take me to Eastcheap, where Falstaff caroused, and then on to St. Olave's Church in Cripplegate, where Shakespeare stayed. The driver was mystified so I instructed him to drive wherever he felt like driving. I closed my eyes, nauseous from watching London through the flickering frames of the cab window, and reopened them only to check the ticking metre. At the £8 mark, near Lancaster Gate, I got out.

It started to rain, ever so gently. From inside a red call box I watched the fine mist creep over the trees in Hyde Park, feeling that London at this instant was never more beautiful—it was romantic, rapturous, ineffable. In a daze I gradually shifted my attention to the glass walls of the call box, on which fluorescent orange, raspberry and lime stickers made a pretty, childlike mosaic. Each sticker contained a message:

MUTUAL CANING!!   344 0337
RUDE GIRL DESERVES BOTTOM MARKS   629 9913
SCHOOLGIRL CORRECTION: FIRM HAND NEEDED   742 8847
FRENCH LESSONS   937 3300
HOW TO BUILD YOUR OWN COFFIN   629 0375

I phoned York again. Busy. Good news. I tried again. Still busy. Hasn't England got call-waiting? I counted to sixty and dialled again. An elderly voice answered.

"May I speak to Gerard please?" I asked.

"Sling yer 'ook," the lady replied with a voice like a shaking fist. Click.

I pushed my green card back into the slot and redialled, but this time asked for Uncle Gerard. A brief silence followed. "'Os't then, that's askin' fer im? An' doant try ti pull t'wool over me eyes!"

"His nephew from Canada. To whom am I speaking?"

"Julian iss't then?"

"No, it's Jeremy. Is that you Mrs. Kern?" Madeleine Kern (or Mad Cur as we called her) was from a dairy farmer's family up Richmond way, and lived on the second floor. She was Gerard's landlady or charlady or mistress, I'm not sure which.

"By gow! Jeremy! Weer 'as ta bin, lad? America?"

"No, Mrs. Kern, not America. It's nice to hear your voice again. Is my uncle there by any chance?"

"That bummerskite? 'E's gallavantin' again. 'E's down south, lad."

"London?"

"Aye."

"Do you know where he's staying, by any chance?"

"Some knockin' shop, more 'n likely."

I laughed. "Is he staying at a hotel?"

" 'E's 'appen gone to t' Pilgrim."

"The Pilgrim. Do you know where that is exactly, Mrs. Kern?"

"Nay, 'aven't the foggiest."

"Thanks, Mrs. Kern. Hope to see you soon."

The rain began to fall, harder and harder. Sardines could have swum through the air. "It's fair silin' it dahn!" I exclaimed à la Mrs. Kern while paging through the tattered phone book. There was no hotel in London called The Pilgrim. Maybe there's another word, before or after. "Passionate", for example. Yes, there's a Passionate Pilgrim off Cromwell Road, on the other side of the park.

∜

The walk across Hyde Park was magnificent. And I had it all to myself, almost. Despite the pelting rain, I took a winding route, past the Fountains, along the Serpentine, to a pair of swans under the canopy of a tree. What if it was here that Shelley's teenage pregnant wife drowned herself? At the Round Pond I paused to read an underwater newspaper and watch a solitary boy and his floundering sailboat. Then along Rotten Row, the Flower Walk, across High Street Kensington, down Gloucester Road to the Cromwell Road.

My shoes were squishing like a five-year-old's as I walked up the steps of the hotel, which was larger than I expected and a bit of a dive. Groups of giggling schoolgirls in navy blue dresses and berets stood in the lobby amidst mounds of luggage. I shook myself like a dog before making my way through the obstacle course of suitcases and uniforms.

The receptionist, who sounded East European, was extraordinarily unassisting. Because I looked like a swamp rat, an escaped con? "Room 44," she eventually said, possibly to me. I looked at the board: the key was on its hook. "Could you call him?" I asked. No response. "Excuse me, could you call Room 44?" A chain of laughter spread from schoolgirl to schoolgirl. "Is it raining out, by any chance?" asked one of them, to the squealing delight of all.

The lift was broken so I ran up four flights, trebling my pulse in the process, then wandered through labyrinthine corridors with threadbare carpets that ended in one cul de sac after another. I asked a young cleaning lady, who spoke no English, French or Latin, for directions. I flashed four fingers twice. She shrugged her shoulders as if to say "I don't work here," and walked away. Was she the receptionist's daughter? A few wrong turns later I found Rooms 43 and 45, and an unmarked door in between. I knocked on it. And knocked again. The cleaning lady reappeared at the end of the hall. I whistled casually, hoping I wasn't knocking on a closet door. When she disappeared I tried the door and it yielded.

The room was full of mist and I could hear someone humming softly in the shower. Sitting on the bed, holding a hand mirror with a rope coiled loosely round her wrist, was a very black black woman, very very attractive. A bright orange sari-like affair covered her nether regions, but not her upper. She looked at me appraisingly, with neither apology nor embarrassment.

"I'm sorry," I mumbled, lingering a moment before closing the door. With a tightening in the groin and images of dark areolae in my brain, I ran back down the stairs and verified the number with the receptionist. It was 44 all right.

"Is it possible the number on the door is missing?" I asked, panting. I had to repeat the question.

"In this hotel, *anything* possible." Another gale of laughter broke from the schoolgirls.

"Could you call him? Excuse me, could you call him?"

314

The frowning receptionist took off her glasses and sighed. Every customer, every inquiry, she took as an insult. But she eventually complied, plunking down an antique receiver on the desk, which I picked up and listened to ring five or six times.

"Yes?"

"Uncle Gerard, is that you?"

"Jeremy? Is that you son?"

"Yes, it's me!" I was shouting, unnecessarily, as if we were on two cans and a string.

"Well bugger me sideways. How's the bardolatrous boy, the son of York? Where are you calling from? Canada? No? How'd you arrive—magic carpet? How in the name of bleeding Jesus did you track me down?"

"I'm at the reception desk! Mad Cur told me you were here!"

Gerard laughed. "Madeleine, bless her heart. Jeremy, can you give me a few minutes to . . . tie up a loose end here? Shan't be long. Let's see . . . there's a place just opposite, one of those dreadful wine bars. Powder-blue sign. Shall we meet there at say, half four? Is that all right?"

"Fine!"

"No, on second thought we'd best not—I may have misbehaved there last night. Even better—half a mile east on the Cromwell Road, near the underground, on the left. The Phoenix and Turtle."

"I'll find it!"

"At half past, then?"

"Right!"

"It's lovely to hear your voice, Jeremy."

"Likewise!"

"Clogs'll spark toneet, lad!"

❀

The Phoenix and Turtle was a great barn of a place, with a barn's charm. In one corner was a red-and-white shirted, pot-bellied darts team and in another an antique colour television with a picture that rolled badly. This didn't seem to disturb its viewers, three drowsy old men with dark pints close to their lips. At the bar I asked not for beer but for wine, took the litre and two glasses to a table by an open window, and drank large gulps while breathing in the flatus of a caravan of idling double-deckers.

"Terrific pot," said the television announcer. I looked up. Snooker. A team championship: Northern Ireland versus Canada, with Canada in the lead. At the end of a long run by one of the Irishmen, a steel-haired man in his sixties stood in front of the TV and adjusted the horizontal. Gerard.

Wearing a kilt. I was not surprised by this—on our Saturdays he often wore one. "For comfort," he said. He also said that all women fancied men in kilts. All women. I wonder if Milena does. I stood up and waved him over. We hugged and slapped, after which he stepped back and eyed me appraisingly. And then burst out laughing.

"You're a Davenant all right—face like an angel, impeccably ruffled, thin as a rake. And leading a rake's life I'll wager. Got your mourning weeds on, I see. Always someone dying—got to be on the ready, what? Or is it self-mourning? What are we drinking then, a bit of the old Château Ausone '59?"

"No, I think it's a British vintage." I poured him a glass, not his first of the day, which he raised with a shaking fist.

"Alcohol is the anaesthesia by which we endure the operation of life—Shaw." He winced as he drank and then asked the waiter for "something better, labelled, sharp as you can." To me he said, "So what in the devil brings you to London?"

As I explained about Milena, about her disappearance, about Shakhtyorsk and the Dark Lady, Gerard went from a faint smile and gentle laughter to a fit of wheezing and coughing. Pulmonary gasps. He then stood up and did a kind of Cossack dance which, in McLeod tartan, looked rather funny. But it was hard to laugh, because at the same time I saw how slow and awkward his movements had become.

"I'm sorry lad, but the Ukraine? You must have it badly—to want to go half-way round the world like that. She's struck you moon-mad. Just like that pretty Irish girl back in York—remember her? Bernadette, was it? When you couldn't eat for two weeks? Oh well, *semel insanivimus omnes*, I suppose. What's the dark lady's name again?"

"Milena Sarakali Modjeska."

"How beautifully exotic. Slavic? Indian? So how long have you known this Milena creature?"

"Five months, three weeks, one day."

"Oh I see. She hasn't given you time to fall out of love. To discover that passion never lasts, like a horse burning itself out in the first lap . . . "

With a sigh I stopped listening and gazed at the television screen, which was rolling again. I tried to smile but no smile came.

"Well good for Milena," Gerard changed, seeing my expression. "So what if you're mad about her?" He put his hand on my shoulder. "So what, eh? Hope to meet her one day myself. Attractive, is she?"

"Hellishly."

"I'll bet she is. I'll bet she's bright as brass too."

"She is, you'd like her. She's an artist—a painter. Or at least she would be if she could afford to go to art school, or let me buy her some materials. I'm sure she's good; she's been to hell and back."

317

"She should go to school here in London. Or York. I'll see what I can do; I happen to have a bit of pull at the—"

"She wants to live here. We both do."

"So why don't you?"

"Well, we aren't really . . . Milena doesn't have any money. And I won't either after I quit my job. But I don't think she'd live with me anyway. She's sort of . . . sapphic."

Gerard laughed. "Sapphic? The dark lady's a lesbian? How lovely, how exciting. So you're trying to convert her? I mean, even Sappho was married, and in love with another man . . . "

"No no, I just . . . Well, I suppose I am, in a way. I like her a lot—you would too."

"I like her already. She's the one, after all, who drove you here—here to spend Christmas with me in merry dissipation. I told you that Page would guide you, didn't I? It brought you back to your uncle, didn't it? Didn't it, lad?" He laughed and ruffled my hair as if we were Saturday in York. I smiled, this time a real one, and couldn't get the smile off my face. I just grinned and giggled as he talked and talked. "You're just like your mother, lad, same nose same eyes. Take me right back, you do. Image of your mother . . . "

As the wine worked I began to laugh from my belly at the slightest provocation: when he imitated my Canadian accent; when he spoke Cockney with the Cockney waiter; when he concluded some lubricious tale of conquest with "What is home without Plumtree's Potted Meat?" I was a boy sliding down banisters and Gerard was sliding with me. He was acting as young as he felt—somewhere, I would guess, around thirteen.

After hot whiskeys with clove and lemon, and after drinking the health of everyone in the room, individually,

Gerard exclaimed above the din of the room, "How are you feeling then, lad?"

"As happy as a sandboy."

"As a pig at a trough. Aye. And tomorrow will be even happier—we'll win a few quid for poor Milena."

TWENTY FIVE

Let us sit and mock the good housewife Fortune from her wheel.
— *As You Like It*

The receptionist, later that night, assigned me a room down the hall from Gerard's that commanded a view of a brick wall. It had a low toy sink, evidently designed for a smaller race of people, along with a convict's bed and bumpy wallpaper with the kind of patterns you get when you rub your eyes too hard. My shower, one floor below, in a communal bathroom whose lightswitch I was unable to locate, had a nozzle that sent an errant stream of water over the curtain and onto any clothes hung on the back of the door. Making up for this, however, was a marvellous old bidet, whose jet of water was not only true but furious. I spent many a giddy moment thereon.

We spent the next three days together, Gerard and I, from the 24th to 26th. Whatever plans he may have had he adjusted, except for Christmas Day, when he wanted to see something called the Peter Pan Cup, a swimming race in the icy waters of the Serpentine. "I won it, lad, when I was your age." This was to be followed by a visit with a distant relation of his—a great-aunt or great-cousin named Mrs. K. or Mrs. Kay—who was old, otherwise relationless, and the owner of a substantial house near Cadogan Gardens. I was instructed to wear my "second-hand Camden Lock mourning clothes" for luck. "Cross your fingers, lad—perhaps by year end we'll peal the jolly knell. What's an anagram of 'funeral'? 'Real fun'." We ended up missing the swimming race—it began at nine and we both slept till noon—but we did make it to Mrs. Kay's residence. On a quiet street with wrought-iron fences and Victorian red-brick facades, it sat a bit taller than its neighbours, its arms folded proudly across its chest. Gerard was not the only one who admired it: when we made our entrance a roomful of guests were circling round Mrs. Kay like carrion birds. It took some pushing and shoving to join them.

A baroque organ droned plaintively from a 1960s reel-to-reel that might have been playing at the wrong speed. Heat seemed to emanate from the walls and ceilings, as in a kiln. And no alcohol in sight. When I was finally introduced to Mrs. K. or Kay, she said it was lovely to see me again, as it was of course every year. Would I like to see the album photos of Christmases past? "Yes, I'd love to see the photos," I said. "And we'd love a drink even more," said Gerard, behind his hand. She didn't appear to hear either of us, for she began talking about china cabinets with some sycophant named Alistair who was bent at the waist, clicking a lighter under her cigarette-holder. As he produced only sparks, Gerard leaned over with a safety match, ignited from its friction against Alistair's rear end. At least this was how it appeared— Gerard lit the match himself then ran his nail down the man's buttock. While Alistair snorted and sniffed Mrs. Kay laughed and laughed, which caused her huge, seemingly inflatable bosom to quiver and shake. She held Gerard's wrist and winked at me, and it was in that brief instant that I realised she had no intention of shuffling off this mortal coil anytime soon.

I expected enormous turkeys, acres of pound cake, mince pies, plum pudding—and the Queen's speech at three. But it wasn't to be. When a sallow-faced scarecrow of a man with muttonchops and wide garish tie entered (looking like he came to pinch the spoons), Gerard tiptoed out of the room, beckoning me to follow. On our way back to the hotel, he explained.

"Nicky Greville. He's one of those dogged . . . things you can never quite shake, like a paparazzo."

"He's after Mrs. K's money too?"

"No, he's after me. I welshed with his winnings—or rather his employer's winnings—from the Breeder's Cup, which is one of the reasons I'm down here. It was getting a bit hot up in York."

"The Breeder's Cup? The race on Long Island?"

"The very one."

"Did you get the money I sent? How'd we do with your tip?"

"Yes, I got it all right. Thanks very much lad, I suppose I should've mentioned it earlier. I owe you a bit, don't I?"

"Did our horse win? What was his name?"

"Her name. Roan Barbery. Oh no, we didn't win, far from it."

"Then you don't owe me anything, do you."

"You're a good man. You know you sent me more than your wager."

"Is that why you didn't come to Quebec to see me— because you lost everything at the track?"

"It was a tragic day at the races, Jeremy, a real . . . tragedy. And not only for me—oh no, not only for me." He shook his head and heaved an exaggerated sigh.

"What happened?"

Gerard cleared his throat while pulling out a small metal flask from his inside breast pocket. He shook it, and shook it again. Grimacing, he slid it back inside. "I hardly know where to begin. In the very first race, the Sprint, I'm on Mister Quince—*we* are on Mister Quince. They're coming up near the turn at the end of the backstretch, everything's fine, we're looking good, right where we want to be. But you'll never guess what happened next."

"The horse died."

"So you read about it—"

"No, I—"

"A few furlongs from the finish, Quincy rears in front and plunges to the track."

"Clipped?"

"Heart attack."

"What?"

"Mr. Quince had a heart attack. The horse we bet on had a bloody heart attack. In mid-race. What are the odds on that? The jockey—a mate of mine from Norfolk—went down with him and broke his collarbone. Capilet and Doctor Butts also went down—the latter broke his spine. Destroyed straight away, poor thing."

"But . . . I don't understand. How can that sort of thing—"

"It happens, it's a pity, but it happens—especially nowadays. But that's not all. Oh no, this was just a portent. In the third race, the Distaff, the finest on the card, I've got a small fortune on Roan Barbery. A can't miss. The horse is a real beauty, lad, and so is the race—an absolute classic, a duel between her and White Surrey. They're side-by-side in the stretch, side-by-side, when Roan Barbery inches ahead just a few yards from the finish, and then . . . I can't bear to think of it."

"What happened?"

"She stumbles—goes down in a dreadful somersault. The jockey's flung face-first into a patch of dirt—not ten yards from where I'm standing! The poor beast gets back to her feet—fractured foreleg dangling—and then staggers to the finish line on three legs. And then collapses again! It was dreadful, pathetic. I was right on the rail, lad—the sobs and gasps were horrifying."

"My God. But how could a horse just . . . fall like that? Foul play?"

"No, I don't think she was nobbled. Just one of those things, I suppose. The horse's leg gave out, simple as that—cannon bone, ligament damage. Put down straight away. She was a real beauty, lad. And like many a beauty, she cost me a fortune."

We walked in silence, Christmas decorations blinking here and there, people with parcels breathing vapour. It was now "snowing", the flakes melting the moment they touched the ground. London snow is rarely deep and crisp and even.

As we walked up the steps of The Passionate Pilgrim and into the lobby, I noticed for the first time Gerard's stooped posture and shuffling tread, which he may have been trying to hide. Hesitating before the broken elevator, Gerard said he was going back out to see his "South African friend". He looked old. And his handshake wasn't what it used to be. A wave of anxiety washed over me.

"Are you OK, Gerard. I mean your health, is it OK?"

"Fine, just fine. A touch of the shakes now and then, that's about it. Nothing to worry about."

CB

I got halfway up the stairs when I turned round and went back out the door, too upset to sleep. I walked around in circles before hopping on three random double-deckers that took me past, among other landmarks, the shimmering fluted columns of Selfridges on Oxford Street, Hamleys toy shop on Regent Street, and the huge Norwegian Christmas tree in

Trafalgar Square. Here I boarded another bus and remained on the top deck, alone, until the end of the line, Elephant & Castle.

Here, through brown-walled detours on floors of muddied plywood, I made my way to lifts that were not in service, though zombies stood and waited. Large tiles had been ripped off the stair walls and rusty streamlets of water trickled down the steps. Near the end of my descent into the Elephant's bowels, I was detained by a scraggly-bearded Scot who grabbed my lapels with the dirtiest hands I have ever seen—as if he'd been digging a tunnel with his bare hands. "You look like a French pirate prince," he remarked matter-of-factly. "All you need's a white horse." I gave him 50p to take his hands off me.

The train, possibly the last of the evening, was waiting with doors open. I sat down in an empty car, the next-to-last, and put my feet up. Straddling the next doorway was a couple, an elderly black man with soft eyes and gentle manner, and a slightly younger white woman, dyed red perm, fiftyish, matchstick legs. She was clinging to him with long nails like talons; he was reassuring her that they would see each other again. The doors closed and it was all he could do to wrench himself free. He sat down with a sigh. She, sobbing, ran beside his moving window before disappearing into the black torrent of the tunnel.

I went back to the hotel and pulled the covers over me without undressing. I dreamt, not for the first time, of my first visit with Father Christmas in a dark dank mine near Wakefield. Except this time it looked more like Elephant & Castle. With a shaking hand Father Christmas gave me a red children's book that was not a children's book at all, but rather a lost play of Shakespeare's. Its fragile pages were covered in coal dust and pine needles. There was a scary banging sound at this point, as if the mine/tube station were caving in. It was Gerard knocking on my door.

"Fancy a walk in the mist and the rain?" he asked, poking his head in and flicking the light on and off. "Not asleep, surely?" It was two in the morning. As I put my shoes on he pulled out a replenished flask from his tired tweed jacket and poured its contents into a filmy hotel glass. "*It nearly broke the family's heart,*" he began to sing, "*when Lady Jane became a tart . . .* "

As we passed the ailing lift, I banged the down-button out of frustration and the door miraculously opened. We made our slow, bumpy descent. "The service here is not what it used to be, Jeremy, not by a long shot." On the front steps of the hotel we paused, not knowing which way to turn. The snow had turned to a thin sleet, and I remarked on its beauty. "Aye, it's a fine neet," said Gerard, lapsing into dialect, gazing up at the frozen skies. We crossed at a zebra where a black-clad motorcyclist, watching us behind tinted plastic, revved impatiently. We went right and then left, towards Hyde Park, and walked perhaps half a mile before anyone spoke.

"Gerard, do you remember when we went to Pontefract? To the racecourse?"

"Aye, and a fine outing it was," he said, blowing his nose into a handkerchief monogrammed with someone else's initials.

"Yes, I remember we won some money. But do you remember after the races, when we went to a haunted house nearby? Was that the site of *A Yorkshire Tragedy*?"

"The Calverley murders. I used to work nearby as a lad, at the racecourse—"

"Yes, I know. What were those words we were chanting?"

"Let me see. 'Old Calverley, old Calverley, I have thee by th' ears, I'll cut thee into collops unless thou appears.'"

"Yes, I remember those, but there were others."

"Were there? I don't know any others."

"Well, it must've been when we went to the Castle Museum."

"Did we go to the Castle? I can't remember . . . hold on." Gerard stopped and looked high above us, searchingly, as if the vaults of his memory were in the heavens. "Calverley was executed at the gaol there. Pressed to death. 'Lig 'em on, lig 'em on Walter de Calverley.' Were those the ones?"

"Yes, that's it. What does that mean?"

"*Peine forte et dure* it was called. The prisoner was stripped naked and laid on his back on a board with a sharp stone or spike on it. This entered the spine, you see, and then weights were piled on the body until the prisoner's ribs were broken—until the life was crushed right out of him. An old servant, so the story goes, attended Walter Calverley as they were putting the stones on his chest. Calverley begged him to put him out of his misery by sitting on the stones. 'A pund o'more weight lig on, lig on . . . '"

"What does that mean, 'lig on'?"

"Lay on."

"And did the old servant do it?"

"Yes, and was later hanged for his pains. Calverley's dying words became a sort of children's rhyme. The boys of the village would gather in the porch of Calverley church, form a circle, throw their caps in the middle and chant: 'Lig 'em on, lig 'em on Walter de Calverley . . . '"

"And what was that thing we did with the pyramid of broken bottles and everything. What was all that about?"

"Nothing. I just made it up. We had to do some sort of ritualistic hocus-pocus, didn't we?" Gerard let out a loud guffaw.

"He killed two of his children—"

"But was prevented from killing the third, who was at nurse."

"What ever happened to the third child? I've never been able to find out."

"Lived on for over fifty years, in the very same house."

We continued on without speaking, and then lingered under a tall chestnut until the icy rain stopped. I looked up. The moon was a pale vapour, flickering in and out of the dark lacery of branches.

"Did you have lands, Uncle, that you wagered away?"

A look of exasperation, or loathing, contorted Gerard's features. "Oh God, not that old story again. Made up by that cretinous bookkeeper Ralph Stilton, who couldn't find his arsehole with a mirror. If I had any lands, they weren't much. Nothing much to speak of. We weren't landed gentry or anything. I didn't deprive anyone of anything, make no mistake about that, lad. A bit of marsh and an outhouse, that's about it."

"But Ralph always claimed that . . . Would Mother have stayed with you if you hadn't gambled it all away?"

"Well, I think that . . . she may . . . that is, we'll never really know, will we?"

No, I suppose not. I looked up towards the moon. "Is there another reason why Mother decided to marry Ralph? She told me she became afraid of you at one point. And Ralph was always talking about 'evil rumours' about your past. Something that happened in France."

Gerard lowered his gaze and mumbled incoherently to himself. He then looked up at me with something I'd never seen before in his eyes. Fear? Sadness? "Yes, something happened in France. A very dark time for me, that. Do you remember you were always trying to get me to marry your mother? Well, I didn't marry her because . . . because I was already married."

"Already married? You've got to be kidding. I thought you didn't believe in marriage."

Gerard opened his mouth to speak but hesitated, as if grappling for his lines. "Marriage: two cannibals, each waiting for the other to fall asleep." A weary smile appeared and disappeared. "It was a time when . . . my wife had money. I'm a gambler, remember."

"So who's your wife? Where is she now?"

"Her name's Henriette Boyet; she's from Normandy . . . But when I met your mother I was separated—which I hid from her for the longest time, God knows why. I didn't abandon my wife either; she left me because she . . . well, she thought I was having an affair with her younger sister."

"Were you?"

"And then Ralph proposed to your mother, so I filed for divorce and tried to get your mother back and . . . and then something else happened. Bad things always happen in bunches."

"You killed your wife."

"Almost. My house in Normandy burned to the ground. Compliments of that bastard Nicky Greville."

"Nicky Greville? That scarecrow we saw at Mrs. Kay's? The guy you owe money?"

"I owe him nothing. He acts on behalf of . . . disgruntled clients." Gerard ran his splayed fingers through his bushy grey hair. "Henriette wasn't there at the time, thank God, and I was in York, but that didn't stop some people—some of the villagers, the police, Ralph—from thinking I was trying to get rid of my wife. I was charged, and then acquitted, which didn't stop Ralph from trying to pin it on me all his life. Or from spreading rumours about my . . . my relationship with Henriette's daughter. I mean sister. I don't know what your mother believed, but I divorced so I could marry her, and raise you, but it was too late, things took too long, the lawyers . . . it was just too late." Gerard rubbed his eyes, his forehead, forced a laugh, hit me on the shoulder. "You believe me, don't you, Jeremy? I'll make it up to you, you'll see."

છ

Never one to stew, Gerard was in higher spirits on Boxing Day and so was I. His revelation/confession was good for both of us, I think, though we never talked about it again. In the morning he greeted me with a wink and a firmer hand-shake, and a proposal we go to Oxford to see an amateur production of *Love's Labour's Lost*—an irony too obvious to dwell on.

In our first-class carriage that he insisted we ride ("to steer clear of football thugs") Gerard regaled me with stories from his days "treading the boards" as a member of the Lord Strange Amateur Dramatic Society, where he met my mother. He spoke of *Macbeth* and *Henry VI* and *Timon of Athens*, and how he rose through the ranks to play the leads in each. (The original programs Mother gave me listed him, respectively, as the Third Murderer, the Scout, and Another Servant.)

"Oh, by the way," he said suddenly, "I wrote a lovely letter on your behalf. North Shrewsbury stationery. It's all taken care of."

"What's all taken care of?"

"I received a letter from South Africa—forwarded by my associate—requesting information on your 'work in progress'."

"My what? Who from?"

"Your department director, Dr. Haxby. Just some verification, lad. Piece of cake."

"Haxby? He's not my director." That interfering fuck. "What exactly did he want?" Revenge, obviously.

"It's all fixed up. Not to worry."

For some reason, I wasn't about to. I was starting a sabbatical in January—maybe I'd make it perennial.

"I've got a nice anagram for 'William Shakespeare'," said Gerard, while doodling with his fountain pen on page 3 of the Sun. I leaned over, expecting something lewd. In rickety block letters, beside WILLIAM SHAKESPEARE, was I ASK ME, HAS WILL A PEER?

"Good one! Fabulous. And it uses all the letters?"

"Of course."

"But shouldn't it be 'I ask myself'?"

"How about these two?" He tore off a strip of the newspaper and handed it to me: "WE ALL MAKE HIS PRAISE" was followed by "I SWEAR HE IS LIKE A LAMP."

I checked the letters. "These are brilliant—if you thought them up yourself. Did you?"

"Of course I did." He winked and then sat pensively for a few seconds. "We all make his praise when it comes to the tragedies, that is. We all wish Shakespeare hadn't written so many comedies."

"Many seem to find them hilarious," I replied.

"Those who laugh at a Shakespearean comedy are either bloody well showing off their knowledge of what was once funny or clever, or reacting to some slapstick addition by the director. Why, they'll be putting in a bleeding laugh track next. Besides, how can you be funny when you're syphilitic?"

"Shakespeare had syphillis? I know he might've had Parkinson's, judging by the signature on his will . . . "

"You didn't know? Of course he had syphillis. Read the Sonnets, lad. Read *Timon* and *Troilus*."

On the train back to London, after a performance which left the audience rolling in the aisles and Gerard and me stonefaced, I started to ramble on about the Page and how, ever since I had met Milena, it had invaded every aspect of my life.

"I know you'll think it's pure coincidence, Gerard, but this last year has been full of . . . well, connected events. Almost everything that's happened to me since meeting Milena—the meeting itself—has somehow related to the Page. Don't laugh, I swear it's true. I know it's just a game we were playing years ago, but it's become much more than that, somehow. It's really gotten out of hand. And I didn't force anything either, really. I suppose the first sign, the first omen, I got was . . . "

Here I recreated the mesh of chance and mischance, the chain of symbols and portents which had Milena for its final link. " . . . And so you see, not only is Milena the Dark Lady and Fair Em, and Indian like Shakuntala, and not only does she wear an assegai cape-pin and have a book of Bantu literature, and not only is her father named Walter, as in Walter Calverley of *A Yorkshire Tragedy*, a gambler who beat his wife and thought his kids weren't his just like Milena's father, but there's, well, lots of other things. There's the mood ring, like Shakuntala's ring lost in the river Malini, which Milena lost too, just like in the story, a story of love at first sight—"

"Jeremy, I think—"

"And the Page moves from violence and death to happiness and marriage—just like Milena and me are going to . . . move. And there's lots of other stuff too, shaking palsy, the Ukraine, I could go on and on. So you see, Gerard, it's not as silly as it seems—that Page *was* in some ways magic, as you . . . "

"Codswallop."

" . . . said it would be. I beg your pardon?"

"Absolute rot. I've never heard such bilge."

"No, I'm serious." I looked at him. Was he drunk?

"It won't wash, lad. There were no magical symbols, no omens. You provoked everything. That page could've been an advert for toilet-bowl cleaner and you would have somehow connected it to your life."

Was this an impostor before me? "I know it may sound silly or irrational, but this year everything has finally connected, everything has somehow coalesced or—"

"Coalesced, my arse. When you're in love everything coalesces, everything becomes symbolic and fatidic. The Page gave your life a pattern, a connect-the-dots picture, an explanation for all the things in life that make no sense. The human mind dislikes disorder, randomness—"

"I swear . . . "

"Besides, I rigged it."

" . . . to God. You what?"

"I exchanged books while you were blindfolded."

I looked him in the eye, waiting for him to break into laughter. Surely this was a joke, a leg-puller. His face remained stern. What was going on? Had someone switched uncles on me?

"You bloody well did not," I said calmly.

"I did indeed." He was in dead earnest.

"You did not."

"Believe what you want to believe."

"You c-couldn't have, you didn't, I saw the book, you're lying! It's . . . impossible!" I could feel my face filling with blood.

"I had to give you something, lad, something to remember me by. So I thought and thought and decided in a moment

of illumination, or perhaps drunkenness, on a 'Map of Life'—
which is how Dr. Johnson described Shakespeare's plays. I
just wanted to steer you in the right direction, lad, a gentle
little nudge, with a little magic thrown in."

"You . . . but . . . that's impossible! You would've told me
years ago!"

"I was afraid to tell you earlier—I thought you might turn
against the Bard, or worse, against me." Gerard cocked his
head, winked at me, shifted to a lighter tone as I gaped
stupidly. "Let's just call it a long-term experiment, shall we,
chance versus determinism? Or a kind of performance we
were creating together, a life-poem taking shape over the
years? 'Mock Tudor' we'll call it."

"All tickets please," cried the ticket-collector.

"And was there any damage done?" he continued. "I mean,
apart from the way you made an ass of yourself with Milena.
Look where the Page put you; look what you've done in your
spare time instead of watching the telly like a moron. I
couldn't let you choose just anything now, could I? What if
you'd chosen, I don't know, a page from a manual for dental
surgeons or *Knave* magazine . . . "

"You bastard!" I cried. "You didn't exchange books! You're
a liar!"

" . . . or the black page of *Tristam Shandy*? Don't get in
such a paddy. No harm done. It's the only thing I had to give
you, Jeremy. It's all I had. It's all this world has, the Bard's
the only religion we've got—"

"Shakespeare offers no religion, goddamn it."

"In this secular world Shakespeare is our bible."

"But what about all the other stuff on the page? Was that
supposed to be a fucking guide too?"

"I never thought about all the other rot—the Zulu king
and Indian queen and Lord knows what else."

"You . . . you phony! I . . . I almost ended up in the U-fucking-Craine because of you!"

"Steady on, Jeremy, no need to raise your voice. Yes, I know you did—almost—and I also know it's because of me you've read every word of Shakespeare. And made jars of money in the process."

"But you were using me—"

"Don't be so dramatic."

"For one of your stupid fucking experiments, one of your . . . your crooked lotteries. And stop smiling, it's not funny, damn you. It's that . . . c-corroding passion for play of yours—"

"You sound like Ralph—"

"It just makes me sick. And it's not funny! I hate you!"

A few hushed moments followed. Through the streaming frames of the train window I stared sightlessly, smouldering. Miles of dark landscape went by.

"But I thought I was fulfilling my fucking destiny with that page!" As soon as these words came out I knew how silly they were, and I didn't need Gerard's tightly-pressed lips to tell me this. "Well what book did I choose, for Christ's sake?"

"Something to do with horses, I think."

"Shit."

"I'm sorry, Jeremy."

I, sad fool to a northern king deposed, sat silent and brooding for the remainder of the trip home. My whole world began to rearrange itself before my eyes. My life, I now saw clearly, was a farce from beginning to end—conceived by mistake ("carelessness," said Ralph), programmed as a practical joke, planted with targets I would inevitably miss. His power ebbing, his numinosity lost, Gerard left me alone to brood as he pored over his football pools and racing columns. He offered me a toasted Danish blue sandwich and ploughman's pickle, both of which I suggested he shove up his arse. He said he might be able to accommodate the latter but not the former. I wouldn't laugh.

Gerard left the next day for York. With a sly grin he said he was preparing "a special gift" for Milena and me, and that he hoped to be back in America in May for the "Run for the Roses." But I never saw him again. When we parted on the hotel steps, my eyes suddenly filled with hot tears, and I struggled in vain to conceal them. With my eyes riveted to the ground I tried to laugh. The Page? Kidstuff, a load of rubbish, a tempest in a teapot.

"I was only joking about that stupid page, you know."

"Of course you were, lad."

"It doesn't matter a bit."

"Of course it doesn't."

"You don't think I took it seriously, do you?"

"Of course not, lad."

TWENTY SIX

O, I am a feather for each wind that blows.
—*The Winter's Tale*

I was in the air when another year came barging through.
Bury your dead days, bring on the new. To dampen the din
of celebration, the stewardess-enforced fun, I turned up my
Discman and closed my eyes.

When I opened them minutes later a plastic glass, filled to
the brim with what looked like champagne, was inches from
my nose. It was offered by my bespectacled neighbour, who
grinned from ear to ear and said something I couldn't or
wouldn't hear. I wearily took off my headphones. "Hap-py
New Year!" he cried. Blah blah blah. He was from Leeds, "the
home of Yorkshire Television." "I know," I said. And on his
way to a conference in Quebec City on "emporiatrics". "Do
you know what that is?" No, but I will soon. "It's the study
of travel-related diseases." His wan wife leaned over and
smiled at me; on her lap was a barf bag. They were going a
week early because they had heard that Quebec was the
oldest and loveliest city in North America. He was all right
I guess. He continued to talk even after I put my headphones
back on.

I thought of Shakespeare as he prattled on, as the year
turned over, and of Shaka. Both suggested that our fears and
anguish in life come from the realisation that our future is

not determined, but must be freely chosen . . . I drifted into sleep as my batteries died.

On my threshold, while struggling to unlock the door, I sensed an important letter was waiting for me. I opened the door and it pushed a large envelope. My heart was racing as I took it upstairs into my bedroom and watched the characters swirl and slide into Milena's sinister hand. I opened it. It was Victor's article on bongo drummers.

I rewound my answering machine, listening to the high-pitched squeals, and sensed it was the sound of Milena's voice backwards. It was not. It was the sound of Jacques' voice backwards. There were also messages from Arielle, from the Director's secretary about some conference, and from Philippe, who asked me to sub for him in a grad seminar while he went off to frolic with some Aztec adonis in Acapulco.

CS

The month of January, the beginning of my unpaid sabbatical, was cold and long. It was one of the coldest months on record, in fact, and my heating system, a small gas furnace, was not up to the task. I was living in an igloo. I shivered under blankets, unable to sleep, venturing out only for sugar and pharmaceuticals. I popped Morphodex and Sominex and Lethenex, trying to kill time with edible bullets, but I may as well have been popping adrenaline. I was lost in Milenaland, a cold queendom where sleep was forbidden but dreams allowed, where day was dark and time moved backwards.

In my Book of Saturdays I drew up a list of pros and cons regarding our "relationship". I drew a line down the centre of the page and itemised the pluses on the left-hand side, the minuses on the right.

Although the minuses won out quantitatively, the pluses won out qualitatively. The overriding plus: "in love with her". But why in love? What exactly had I seen in those first moments? A look, a smile of complicity? A kindred spirit, someone I knew already, someone as lost as myself? I'd seen something like that when I met Jacques. Yes, that was part of it. And like Jacques, Milena was smarter than I—was that the attraction? The dim in search of the bright? The weak in search of the strong? Love, says Plato in *The Symposium*, involves the imperfect searching for the perfect.

Was it love at first sight? Doesn't exist. A jolt of adrenaline and testosterone, nothing more. I don't think women ever feel it—at least not as much as men, who if they go out at all, feel it hourly. Marlowe was exaggerating wildly. And *Romeo and Juliet*'s a crock. It's simply impossible to fall in love before words are spoken—otherwise it's lust, not love. Or are the two inseparable? *Love*, as everyone knows, is derived from the Sanskrit root *lubha* (to desire, to inflame with lust).

Did I want Milena because I thought I could help her? Was I the Good Samaritan or Florence Nightingale or Carl Jung? (To desire a woman is to desire to save her, says Updike.) Perhaps that was part of it. I would be her copemate, her crisis counsellor; I would make love to my companion/patient and make her forget everything. What crap.

Milena was passive, Sabrine was passive: there is a pattern here. Does cold make me hot? Is it possible to enjoy sex knowing the other person does not? Yes, I'm afraid to say. Milena was the passive prostitute or innocent child-bride; I was ravishing her, she was saying "Do what you will with me . . . " Was that it, the passion of power? No. It was more like entering, against all odds, an impregnable island fortress.

It was the thrill of arriving at some sequestered place where luck had led you, or where you shouldn't be.

Jacques had other reasons for my attraction. "First, she treats you like shit. Which you see as a sign of superiority—and unattainability. Second, all women become more desirable as you're getting dumped—rejection as aphrodisiac. Or in Kierkegaardian terms, love and attraction are only possible when there's resistance—lesbianism, in the present case, being the ultimate form of resistance. Third, you want to be seen with her, thinking she reflects flatteringly on you, that it's a feather in your cap to fuck a feminist . . . "

After I called him an asshole he advanced some psychological theory he was reading about or made up to suggest that the whole thing boiled down to a sexual memory seeded deep in my childhood. "Look at Nietzsche," he said, misquoting Tama Janowitz. "Beaten and raped by a viscountess when he was fourteen. A few years later? *The Will to Power* and the Superman. Examine your past, dredge up your first sexual experiences, find the aetiological correlative, the *incitamentum*. What about that pubescent Irish girl you've fantasized about ad nauseum? And wasn't your old lady dark and thin?"

After closing my eyes and muttering another obscenity, I insistently denied any link between Milena and my past. "A thing is likely to be true," Jacques replied, "in direct proportion to the insistency with which it's denied." When I accused him of idle, unscientific psychology he countered, "Is there another kind?"

CB

On a freezing afternoon in late January I was standing in my kitchen, slicing an overripe tomato with the Swiss Army knife and debating whether it was nobler in the mind to suffer the slings and arrows . . . Put another way, I was debating whether or not to slash my wrists. The phone rang and I almost sliced off a thumb.

"What are you doing?" said Jacques.

"Committing suicide."

"What method?"

"A Swiss-Army slashing of the veins."

"It's more effective in a piping-hot tub."

"So I've heard."

"Remember though what Brutus said—that suicide is 'cowardly and vile'."

"He said that shortly before killing himself."

"True. Why don't you try ceremonial *seppuku* instead?"

"Any particular reason for your call?"

"Yes, it concerns your flame-retardant friend."

"My what? Milena? You've seen her?"

"Yes."

She's back! Christ. Why hasn't she called me? "Where?"

"On the Boulevard."

"Fine. Bye. I've got someone on the other line. Hello? Great, how are you? Noctambule? Right now? Sure, I'd love to but . . . Is it anything . . . serious? OK, great, see you then."

What's going on? It was Barbara Celerand.

Like an Olympic walker, puffing and sweating, I swivelled my way to Noctambule. What could Barbara Celerand have to tell me? That I'm getting sacked for the North Shrewsbury charade? For my party piece? Why couldn't she tell me over the phone? I ordered a cappuccino and sat, my fingers drumming on the round metal table, my knees pumping beneath it, waiting for I knew not what.

What seemed like a day later, Barbara entered with her usual poise, removed her snowy wool hat and brushed her hair back with one hand. "I was at this very table with a friend of yours last night," she said.

My heart sank as we kissed à la française. Christ, everyone's seen Milena except me. What am I, nineteenth on her list? "Yeah, I heard she's back in town." I let out a sigh. I'm beginning to understand what this is all about. Barbara's going to tell me that that the two of them are moving in together. "And she's not called me yet," I added, "so I guess it's over between us. Milena must have told you that."

"No, as a matter of fact she didn't. Why do you think it's over?"

I said something vague about opposite directions and X-rated literature, which she had heard about. To vindicate myself I also described the barbecue episode, the burning of the visible harm. Barbara burst into laughter at this, I don't know why. "I'm sorry," she said, composing herself. "I suppose that's commendable."

"The videos belonged to Jacques, the magazines to the former tenants. All I owned was a bit of historical stuff— vintage sepia art shots." Again, Barbara crumpled into laughter, as if I were doing stand-up.

"And not all post-feminists are against . . . adult entertainment, are they."

"No. I'm not. Neither is Milena."

"But she said . . . I thought she tried to burn down Cinéma La Chatte?"

"She did? That's news to me."

I glanced at Barbara's long silver hair, at the medley of bracelets round her wrists. "Are you having an affair with her?"

Barbara's expression changed. "No, Jeremy, I'm not. I'm really not. We sort of . . . it never felt right. I felt badly when

I heard you found out what happened that night—which was nothing, really nothing. I'm sorry, I didn't mean to hurt you."

I looked Barbara in the eye, which is the only place a person can't disguise what they're really thinking. "Well, our relationship was kind of open; we never had any understanding about . . . other people, other lovers. In fact, we never had a relationship."

"I'm not sure Milena would agree. She's often asked for my advice about her relationship with you. She's confused, we both know that."

"So what advice did you give her, if you don't mind my asking."

"No offence, but I do mind. That's between Milena and me."

Then why did you mention it, for Christ's sake? "I understand."

"Jeremy, we've been friends for a long time. We've always liked each other. So you can imagine what I . . . Basically, I told Milena that I thought you might be good for her, knowing you as I do."

I looked down, feeling like I'd received the best compliment of my life.

"And I will say one thing about our conversation last night—the subject kept coming back to you. She even called you a kindred spirit. I'll be right back."

Kindred spirit. It's not over! This is why Barbara had to see me. What a great friend! What a nice thing to do! What would I do without her and Arielle? Barbara returned with a sheaf of napkins and wiped up some cappuccino I seemed to have spilt.

"Is Milena at home now?" I asked.

"No, she's in the Laurentians. She gave up her apartment."

"The Laurentians? The Laurentian Mountains? Now? Why'd she go there? Why didn't she call me before she left?"

"She's working there. I think she did try to call you. Why don't you call her—Victor can give you the number."

Victor bloody Toddley. "Great."

"Milena's an entrancing woman, a delight, she really is. She's honest and bright and complex and I can understand your obsession, even if others can't." Barbara paused to look at her watch. "But Milena's not the only reason I wanted to see you, Jeremy. I wanted to warn you about Clyde Haxby. I overheard him talking about you, to the director. He had some vicious things to say about you."

"Such as?"

"Well, I suppose it all stems from your parlour trick, Clyde's dangling participle—"

"I was grotesquely drunk, I hope you realise that."

"And your missing that conference on West African theatre last week."

"Last week? Sobranet never got back to me on it!"

"He said you failed to show up for some ten o'clock meeting."

"I haven't been up at ten since high school. And besides, I'm on my fucking sabbatical."

"I know, but for our dear director that's no excuse. Anyway, Clyde ended up doing the introduction."

"So what'd he say about me?"

"Basically, that you were a discredit to our department, a disrupting influence, in league with that 'reprobate' Vauvenargues-Fezensac. He said he was going to take matters into his own hands, fix your wagon, that sort of thing. Oh, he also said he was 'on to you'—whatever that means. I just wanted to tell you to be careful. Maybe you should talk to somebody, someone in authority, lodge a complaint."

"Oh, I don't know about that. I don't think I want to do that."

Barbara glanced at her watch again. "Clyde scares me sometimes. He's becoming more and more . . . unpredictable. Maybe he'd back off if you made an official complaint."

"Or maybe he'd go the other way."

"It's up to you. If you need someone to back you, vouch for you, I'll be happy to do it. I think I owe it to you. Listen, I've got to run, I'm late for class."

I walked Barbara to her car, a vintage Volkswagen bug. Through its window I brushed her lips with a goodbye kiss and thanked her for all she'd said and done.

"Oh, by the way," said Barbara, "how's that dream journal of yours coming along? What's it called again? Such Stuff? Is that it?"

"Yeah, that's it," I said glumly.

ɔ

OK. Such Bloody Stuff is a book *I* am working on, or was. It's a book of dreams, written in second person. With oneiric metaphors. It's all crap. Do you see now why I'm setting down this story? I'm a failed noctuarist who's turned to memoirs, the hack genre that any clown can do. Especially when it's ghosted and glossed by Milena. *Such Stuff*: I fobbed it off on Toddley because he represents everything I despise. Well, not everything. One thing. He's hand in glove with Milena—they talk non-stop about God knows what; they're thick as bloody thieves. I gave the book to Victor only to give a better idea of what a fool, what an impostor he is. Sometimes you have to garnish the truth to get the right effect. And besides, it's hard to be honest about everything, it really is.

ɔ

Only because of what Barbara had said, I decided to give it one last try with Milena, one last shot before the fitting for a straitjacket. But before doing anything I had to find her.

My first step was to find Violet, who was not at Hôtel-Dieu; according to the aluminum lady with basketball shoes, she had phoned in sick ("Surprise surprise," she said). My second step was to find Victor, which proved much easier: he was out clearing snow with a red plastic shovel, wearing a fun-fur hat with lowered flaps and a snowsuit that made him look like an astronaut. After painfully beating about the bush, I was informed that Milena had indeed gone to the Laurentians, to work at a ski resort, which made no sense. Milena does not ski, nor does she mill with jockstrappers. "Which resort?" I asked. Victor shrugged his eiderdown shoulders.

My third step was to scour the Page for clues, which I did until my mind turned to porridge, until the only words I could see were *"stabbed to death"*. My final step was to double-click Help on my computer and punch in "Milena"; it sent me to the closest match: "Mistakes, undoing."

The next day I went back to step one and Hôtel Dieu. Vile, while sleepily stirring a vat of soup, gave me a story that conflicted with Toddley's: Milena was in the Laurentians all right, but not at a ski resort. She was in a *maison de santé*— a sanatorium, a nuthouse. She had snapped. And not only that. Her father was driving up to see her. I knew this boded ill. I had a hunch, a gut feeling that Mr. Modjeska was going to kill his daughter.

"What makes you think that?" said Jacques, who had waved me into a bar on my way home.

"Horse sense. And because it happened in *A Yorkshire Tragedy*. Remember? The jealous husband beats his wife, kills two of his children? Milena's father beat his wife and one of Milena's sisters is already dead—obviously killed by her father. Milena's next."

"Milena's *next?* Well I have to bow to the logic of that. Airtight, that. Obtained through, let's see, a ouija board? Animal entrails?"

"And—get this—what do you think Milena's father's name is?"

"Modjeska?"

"His first name."

"Astonish me."

"*Walter.* As in Walter Calverley! And look at this." I handed him a page from *The Gazette* and pointed. "Read it out loud."

"I'm not going to read Sydney fucking Omarr, least of all out loud."

"'Psychic impression proves prophetic—heed "inner voice". Taurus involved.' Taurus! Milena's a Taurus—and so's Shakespeare and Calverley and Shaka!"

"Shaka? The Zulu chief?"

"Yes!"

"Jeremy, make an appointment, this afternoon. You're seriously undermedicated."

"'And these do I apply for warnings, and portents, and evils imminent . . . '"

"What are you now, a soothsayer? Is this a career move?"

"I was quoting Julius Caesar."

Jacques closed his eyes. "Go. Check yourself in. Go to the brain college, the cracker factory, it's where you both belong."

And he was right, as it turned out—or at least half right. Surely it was madness at this point (at any point) to look to Gerard's Page for guidance. Hadn't he already told me that it was all rigged, all a big sham? Yes, but so what? He was *destined* to rig it: the Page, despite everything, was still a treasure map. Nothing had changed. It was just a matter of reading its clues correctly.

And so, with the fire of a new resolve, I set out. In a rented white Stallion (on whose glass flank a Disney animal was barnacled) I sped north, up into the Laurentian Mountains. The trip, on a frosty winter's afternoon that became frostier and frostier, is now and was then a white blur. I remember leaning over the wheel, my foot to the floor, my upper torso rocking, urging my steed to final effort. Rented cars are great because you can drive the shit out of them. I shot past cars and trucks as if they were stationary, past police cruisers who didn't seem to mind. I killed kilometre after kilometre, mile after Milenian mile. I listened to Purcell's *The Indian Queen* and *The Tempest*, fast-forwarding, rewinding, humming along out of key. After an hour or two, as I approached a steep winding slope, it occurred to me that I had come up that slope before, whereas now I was going down it. Two gas stations sent me in polar directions. As I pulled out of the second, the car heater went dead. My breath was soon visible, the windshield white. With no scraper in sight, I clawed at the frost with my fingernails.

Daylight was waning and the winter sky red as I entered the grounds of the asylum, a beige hive of New Brutalist buildings called "Belleforêt". At the main entrance were the remnants of a picket line—two or three stragglers leaning on placards—and multi-coloured union stickers plastered all over the doors. A VISITEURS sign with arrows led me to a lobby festooned with drawings, or rather with colouring-book pages, as in a kindergarten classroom. In one of them Santa's whiskers had been coloured green, and blue devil horns stuck out of his cap.

"*Je peux vous aider?*" said the receptionist with a Haitian accent. I asked for the room number of Milena Modjeska. "*Chambre cent soixante-six dans l'annexe sud deux,*" she replied rapidly, looking at a computer printout and never at me. As I thanked her a white-coated attendant shot by, obviously on his way for some chloroform and a net. "*Suivez-le,*" said the receptionist. I followed his comet tail down a long hallway and somehow ended up in another building. And then another. I went right, left, up, down, in one ward and out another. I caught a digital-lock door before it shut and went astray in a maze of maniacs.

"Stop!" said one of them, a ruffled man in a striped bathrobe who held up his hand like a traffic cop. "He holes the troubadour. Went like two of had."

I nodded.

"Pocket Rocket," he added. I nodded again. "Poc-ket Roc-ket," he repeated, louder, stressing each syllable through gritted teeth.

"Jeremy Davenant," I replied, tentatively extending my hand.

"Pass!" he shouted, ignoring my hand and stepping aside.

I passed, quickly, towards a lady in a Merry Widow who was rocking something in her arms while singing tunelessly: "One two three four five six seven, Lucy Ann Morgan goes to heaven, one two three four five six seven . . . " As I got closer I noticed it was a plastic doll being rocked to sleep, a doll with lipstick that went well beyond the boundaries of her mouth, wrapped in a sort of fishnet body bag. I managed a tense smile as I walked by; she stuck her tongue out at me. Or perhaps at someone just beyond me: an elegant, distinguished-looking lady in a forget-me-not dress who was wandering the halls, talking to no one in particular:

"Cocksucking son of bitch of a swinefucking bastard, I'm going to squeeze your motherfucking little cock in a vice . . . "

On I went, through a narrow hallway, down a downward slope. Life is a long corridor, so they say, with death waiting at the end. At the end of this particular corridor was a large room with a pool table, reeking of disinfectant and incontinence, and a dozen Fellini faces staring up at me. As I gingerly glanced from side to side a barely human cry rent the air, a kind of war cry, which scared the shit out of me. It came from a man of uncountable years in a tartan robe, a near-contemporary of King Duncan I. Another sound. Off on her own, a woman was leaping lissomely to and fro, as if in slow-motion, periodically spreading her arms for applause.

The tartaned man, much less spry, shuffled towards me at a glacial pace, both hands clutching the eight ball. When I put my hand out to accept it, he dropped it onto the floor. We watched it roll, he took my arm, and then together, my pace suited to his, we inched our way towards a long narrow window with iron bars at the bottom. Everyone in the room, I could feel, was watching us, waiting.

The old man pointed with a big blue-veined hand. "Do they . . . you know . . . make soup . . . out of those . . . those . . . "

I gazed up at the twilight sky and focused on a set of fresh vapour trails. I looked back at him. His leathery face, as wrinkled as a walnut, was contorted in concentration as he tried to find his words.

"Do you mean do they make soup out of those vapour trails?" I ventured.

He nodded, piercing me with youthful, luminous blue eyes (which saw things I may one day see myself). I looked back at the others, who also seemed to be waiting for an answer, some smiling, some nodding, as if to say "Yes, good question."

"As a matter of fact," I said finally, "they do . . . make soup out of them." I smiled, hoping this would satisfy everyone. "Oddly enough." I tried to move on, but was prevented by my questioner, who grabbed my coat sleeve with shaking hands.

"Is it a big . . . "

A big what? "Industry?" I suggested.

He nodded again, his eyes boring into me. "It's being downsized," I replied.

He chuckled knowingly, as if this corroborated some inside information he had. Someone else began to chuckle, a soft sound that spread contagiously until they were all laughing like fiends in hell.

I hurried on, into another hallway, where a bare-chested man was bent over, wobbling, struggling with an article of clothing. He was trying, not entirely successfully, to wear his pyjama top as bottoms: both legs were in the arms and he was finding locomotion difficult. It was funny and sad at the same time. I laughed. Not something to joke about, touch wood. I helped him out as best I could.

Room 164 . . . 165 . . . 166! I took a deep breath, rapped faintly on the door. And then waited, listening for sounds inside. I knocked louder. "Oh shit, don't tell me I came all this way . . . " I looked right, left, then bent down to look through the keyhole. There was no keyhole. There was no doorknob either—it had been removed, violently by the look of things. I pushed on the door, which in turn pushed something on the floor on the other side. I peered through the half-open door. "Hel-lo-o? Milena? Are you there? Oh shit . . . "

I was plunged into a vortex of déjà-vu as I examined the cyclone zone before me. Even by Milena's standards, the place was a mess. Clothes, shoes, books, cutlery, food were scattered over the floor and bed, along with the contents of desk drawers, manilla envelopes, accordeon files, garbage pails and slashed moving cartons. A mattress leaned against a wall, draped with torn sheets. As I took a few steps closer to see if these things were Milena's (they were), I heard a familiar yet startling sound: the gurgling of a toilet. "Milena?" I croaked. I stood there, rooted to the spot, waiting to see who flushed it.

The door swung open and a dark, thickset man stood before me, his eyes showing as much surprise as mine before narrowing into slits of hatred. We stood mute, staring at each other. He wore a black leather coat that was comically long and tight, and his hair was obviously dyed, slicked back like an old movie star, a ladies' man past his prime. It was *him*. The queue-jumper in the *dépanneur*, the hatted man behind the tree, the Grim Reaper staring up at my apartment, Walter Calverley . . .

Milena's father was now striding towards me as these connections flashed through my mind. I braced myself, fists clenched. "I'll cut thee into collops!" I cried. He stopped in his tracks, puzzled, then struck a pose with his finger under his coat, simulating a gun. I should have been petrified—to this day, I don't know why I wasn't, or why I did what I did next. Perhaps the image was too preposterous, too archetypically cheap-crookish, for me to react normally—or perhaps I realised he was wearing my (burglared) leather coat. What I did next, in any case, was calmly walk over to him, slap down his fake-gun hand and shake him by the lapels, my lapels, repeatedly, like a frothing asylumite. Even if I had understood what he was bellowing at me, even if the

Mounties had ordered me to let him go, I wouldn't, couldn't, have released my grip. I was in an altered state, an unreachable zone. There's only one voice, I think, that would have registered amidst the shouting and struggling that followed.

"Jeremy, what the hell . . . "

I released my grip. I was on the floor, still holding the lapels of my coat, but no one was inside it. I looked over towards the voice. Milena was standing by the door, dumbstruck, taking in the spectacle before her. Her father made it to his feet. "*Gadje!*" he spat at me, before lisping and growling at Milena in Romany or Czech or West Bohemian. He grabbed a leather sack on the bed and strode towards her, past her. "*Gadje si dilo!*" he spat back at me before flinging the door open, crashing it against the wall. "*Pampuritsa! Kurva!!*" Outside the room the hall echoed with a clicking sound, as if his shoes were cleated.

"Jeremy, are you all right? Your eye . . . Did my father do all this?" Milena stood, hand on her forehead, looking around the room. "He did, didn't he. Shit. Just like your place. Goddam it . . . I can't believe this . . . "

I rose to my feet and made my way to the bathroom, where I wiped a rivulet of blood from my eyebrow and cheek. Milena came in to help, as close to tears as I've ever seen her. She asked if he'd hit me with the butt of his gun, which was lying on the floor next to my leather coat.

ଔ

If ever there was a time to propose to Milena, I thought as I lay sprawled across her box spring, waiting for her to return, this would be it. But as usual, I misread her mood. When she re-entered the room with first-aid supplies she looked as if she wanted to strangle me with the gauze and tape.

"Why?" asked Milena, after stinging me with alcohol and sticking a bandage over my eyebrow. "Why? Because he's broke, because he's sick, because he owes money to people who can hurt him, that's why. He wants some things of my mother's. He thinks they're his, or rather he thinks they're valuable—especially a brooch and this ring. They were in the pocket of his coat, I mean your coat."

She showed me the pieces in question, raising the lid of a small black jewel box. "Thanks for stopping him, I . . . I appreciate it, I really do."

The brooch was mandala-like in shape with a green thunderbolt at its centre. The ring had a deep indigo stone and two diamonds. "These are wonderful," I said. "Incredible. Is this a sapphire?"

Milena shrugged, her eyes trained on the ring. "So I'm told. I don't care what it is. It was my mother's. She gave it to me and her grandmother to her. It's from India." She closed the lid and then her eyes.

I looked toward my leather coat, which was now lying at the foot of the bed. "What was your father screaming at me?"

Milena shrugged. "Does it matter? He was just . . . explaining that you were a non-gypsy fool and a homosexual. And that I was a slut."

"Is he . . . mentally unbalanced?"

Milena opened her eyes. "He's got problems."

"Is that why he was excommunicated from his band?"

"Probably. That and stealing. I hate to say it, but in this case the gypsy stereotype holds. Except he stole from his own people."

"Did he stab your mother? And kill your sister? And try to kill you and Violet?"

"No! My sister . . . Where'd you hear that? From Violet? My sister drowned."

"Your sister drowned? Are you serious? Calverley tried to drown one of his children!"

"Jeremy, what the hell . . . why are you shouting? Who the hell is Calverley? Why are you always digging into my past? And why are you here exactly?"

Isn't it obvious? "Well, I heard your father was coming up and I thought . . . I guess I'm a bit superstitious sometimes, irrational." I shook my head, trying to shake the Calverley nonsense out of my brain. "I'm sorry. Barbara told me that you . . . I don't know why I came, really."

"I'm the one who's sorry. I should've thanked you for coming, not ask why you did." She kissed me on the forehead, put her arms around me briefly, then began the long process of putting things back where they had been.

ა

I sat up in bed and surveyed the damage, my gaze resting on the far wall. I stared at it for minutes before realising it was bright red, the same colour as her living room and stairwell. The colour that swims before the eyes in violent emotions.

"Did you paint that wall, Milena? Why do you paint everything red?"

Milena was stuffing papers and photographs back into a manilla folder. "Who said I did? I explained it to you before—for some reason red makes me feel better."

"But why? What associations does it have? Why red?"

"Who knows? Maybe because it was my mum's favourite colour, or because of a red sari she gave me when I was a little girl, which I never wanted to take off. I really don't know." Milena picked up a tarnished kettle off the floor, filled it with water, plugged it in. "You want a coffee?"

"Did you know that Shakespeare's favourite colour was red? That it appears in his works more than any other colour?"

"Yeah, because it's the colour of blood."

I rose from the box spring and walked over to the upright mattress. "How was your trip, by the way? I almost forgot to ask. You see your relatives?"

"It was all right. Seeing my aunt was good. She's cool, she's a *phuri dai*, the head woman in her band. We got along really well—she wanted me to stay."

"But you explained that you'd miss me too much."

"I like their attitude towards time. No one seems to give a shit if you're late. And work isn't a fucking existential thing like it is here. Gypsies work only to get their needs of the moment. I like that. Except women do most of the work—the men do almost nothing, apart from yacking all day."

"But what about the gypsy attitude towards . . . isn't the notion of luck central to gypsy culture? Everything's determined by fate?"

Milena sighed. "Yes."

I dragged the mattress over to the bed and toppled it back onto the bed. "Did you manage to meet Madame Zoum, the fortune teller?"

Milena half-smiled. "Who told you that? Sabrine? Vile? Yeah, I stayed one night with her, it's all I could stand. She kept insisting I was a Libra. And that I drink coffee and tea, mixed half and half. The woman's mad as a brush."

"Did she tell you her prophesy—that I was going to kill you?"

"No, she said I was going to kill you."

"And are you?"

"I will if you don't stop asking questions. You want a coffee or not?"

"Got anything stronger?"

"I think there's a bottle of wine somewhere. Almost full. At least there was. You want it?"

"Yes." I watched Milena glide over to a miniature fridge and begin rooting around inside. "So how long are they keeping you here, Milena?"

"Keeping me here? No one's keeping me here—I work here. This room is where I happen to live now."

"You work here? Doing what?"

"I work in the cafeteria. Violet got me the job—Siberia, they call it back in Montreal."

"But . . . why'd you want to come to Siberia?"

Milena handed me the wine bottle without a glass, then poked her finger into an ashtray beside the bed. "I had to get away . . . from everything. I needed a break, some fresh air, a haven. I was on the brink." She plucked out a cigarette butt and lit it.

"And working here, in a nuthatch, is going to help? It won't push you over the brink?" I took a slug of white wine.

"This isn't a 'nuthatch', as you so delicately describe it. That's in the next compound—and how did you get in here, anyway? Everything's closed to visitors today—the employees are on strike. And yes, working here is going to help. I like the elderly. I feel an affinity."

"You feel an affinity? With mad cadavers? You should have seen some of them on my way in . . . "

Here I described some of my encounters, at the end of which Milena gave me a frosty look and a scowl. "You like to take cruel advantage, don't you," she said.

"I what?"

"You make jokes about serious things, about dark things."

"People laugh at funerals, cry at weddings."

"You're always making jokes at other people's expense; you're sarcastic about everything."

"I know, like at the faculty party, you already told me."

"Jokes are disguised forms of aggression."

"No they're not. Not always. Sometimes they're just funny."

"And your attitude is ageist."

"Ageist? Oh fuck." I walked over to the room's only window, bottle in hand, shaking my head. Through the frosted pane, black trees against the banking clouds swam before my eyes. "So did you come here to get away from me too?" I said finally.

Milena sighed as she put tubes of paint back into a ripped shoebox. "From everything. I don't know you well enough to need to get away from you."

Milena was always saying this sort of thing. Once she said there were never any "interruptions" in our relationship because that would imply, rather presumptuously, a relationship. When I asked her if we were drifting apart, she asked if we were ever drifting together. Milena was not afraid to give me the unvarnished truth—she knew I'd varnish it myself later.

"You just hate my politics—or lack thereof—and my *particeps criminis?*"

"Your what?" Milena screwed her face into a derisive grin.

I poured more wine down my throat. "My partner in crime, my main confederate. Jacques."

"Then why don't you just say that? I'm not one of your fucking students. You're always tossing in some Latin phrase, always quoting somebody—usually Shakespeare. Why is that? What are you trying to do? Be smart by association? Seduce with some dead language or someone else's wit?"

I held the bottle up to the light and looked through it, towards a distorted Milena. "Any harm in that? Sometimes I can't help it—sometimes it's like the Bard's whispering to me from the prompter's box. And I guess I got some of it from Gerard, who was always—"

"I don't want to hear about your fucking uncle or what he used to say or how he 'influenced' you. He sounds like a chauvinist swine, by the way. And he's a fucking gambler, and you know how I feel about that. I'm sure he's hurt a lot of people. Maybe even you."

I looked towards the window, heart pounding like a jungle drum, but saw only my reflection. I downed the rest of the bottle. "You have no right to criticise him." I wiped my face with my sleeve and turned to face her. "You don't know a *fucking* thing about him."

"Maybe you don't either."

"And what about *you?*"

"What about me?"

"You're . . . " Milena's glassy stare made me falter. You're unreliable, thoughtless, sanctimonious, ungrateful. "You never express your feelings."

"I just did."

You're hypocritical—you stand up for minorities, but let your friends down. "You never think you owe an explanation to *anyone*."

"Continue. This is interesting."

"If someone loves you, you feel threatened—so you become cold and hypercritical, or else run away and hide."

"Thank you, Dr. Davenant. I'm amazed at how much you know about my personal—"

"You only fall for people who don't fall for you."

Milena raised her eyebrows. "You sure you're not describing yourself?"

"Me?"

"But what's this got to do with what we were talking about?"

"What were we talking about?"

"Jacques."

"Right, another person you treat like shit, my *particeps criminis.*" I spat this out at her.

Milena gave me a look—dim, imperturbable—which was hard to read. It wasn't anger. She looked away. "I don't exactly like Jacques, but I don't hate him either. He's just a highbrow sneerer, relatively harmless. Victor says he's a sheep in wolf's clothing; that he actually does some good from time to time."

"No he doesn't."

"He gives huge amounts to charities that Victor raises funds for."

I was in no mood to hear Jacques praised. "He doesn't give to beggars or Greenpeace because they don't give tax receipts. And he told me that his donations were merely, quote, 'hush money to my conscience.'"

Milena laughed. "So what?"

"Jacques thinks you're mixed up in Denny's murder. I mean suicide. Is that why he doesn't like you?"

"Maybe. Partly."

"Did he ever come on to you?"

"Yes."

"The bastard. I knew it. When?"

"Years ago."

"And?"

"And nothing. He told me it was love at first sight. Asked me back to see his collection of rare books after putting his hand up my skirt."

"It's quite a collection, isn't it."

"Very funny."

"So what'd you do?"

"I grabbed his hand, crushed my cigarette against it, then sprayed him with beer."

"Christ. Well done. So that's what he has against you?"

"Unlikely he'd remember it, the state he was in. No, he doesn't like me because I'm with you."

"You mean he's in love with you?"

"No, doorknob, he's in love with you."

This made me stumble, I admit. "Oh come on, don't be . . . I don't think . . . " Could this be true? "What about Victor?"

"What about him?"

"He's in love with you, right? You've slept with him?"

"That's none of your business."

I stared at the floor, my head feeling heavy and light at the same time, like I was about to black out.

"You all right?" said Milena.

"Fine." I sat down on the bed and noticed something on the bedtable. The lost ring. *Shakuntala.* "Milena! The mood ring—you found it! Excellent. This is a good sign, trust me, a very good sign."

Milena stared at me with the look she gets when watching television.

"What's that behind it?" I asked.

"What's it look like?"

It looked like a photograph of a nude woman. "Where'd you get it?"

"Found it in my Christmas stocking. What are you, a prosecuting attorney?"

"I thought you didn't like nudity."

Milena sighed. "I've got nothing against nudity—I'm not a fucking prude. And I don't care if you have polaroids of my sister."

"Your sister? Right. But you see they weren't actually mine, I was just safeguarding . . . I burned them."

"I don't care. And I don't think you're evil or corrupt—which is what Barbara said you thought I thought. I respect you enough to know that porn probably won't harm you. I just hope you're aware of what it does to women—and men's attitudes towards women. You may not know this, but the majority of women who pose were abused as children."

As Milena spoke I was lying on my back, staring sightlessly at the ceiling tiles, picking the skin at the side of my thumb till it bled. Milena stirred her second or third instant coffee while I walked over once more to the window. Frost had begun to paint palm trees on its pane. I tried to look through it but saw only blackness. Milena said something I didn't hear. I asked her to repeat it.

"I asked if you've lost weight."

I had. Jacques remarked on it too. He said I was like the mayfly, which lives only for a few hours with no mouth or stomach, devoting its brief life to a single desperate mission: finding a mate. I watched Milena slip out of her black skirt. "Is there any point in me running after you all the time?" I asked.

"Depends what you want from me."

Come live with me, and be my love. "Come live with me."

"Don't be mad."

"You can live in the spare bedroom. Think of the money you'll save."

A double funnel of smoke streamed from Milena's nostrils. "Forget it, there's not a snowball's chance in hell of that happening. I'll be in the ground before I live with a man."

I could feel my blood pressure rising. "All right, for fuck's sake, I'll leave you alone. Is that what you want?"

It took a while for Milena to answer. She stood beside a chest of drawers, one hand wrapped around her coffee mug, the other crushing a filter into an already full ashtray. I looked at her vintage cotton briefs and athletic bra, once white but now stone grey (Milena was not one to separate whites and colours in the wash), then turned towards the window. My hands were moist, my mind malfunctioning. Milena would have shrieked with laughter if she knew my real feelings—that I wanted a house in the country with her as my wife.

"Yes," she said, from the other side of the room. "I want to be left alone. I need to be left alone. I don't think I can make it work—with you, with any man."

I put my hands on the window sill, for support. I looked up at the dark winter sky and a cold wind swept through me.

"I have to go to work now," said Milena, "I'm already late."

I tried to calm myself but couldn't, tried to smile but no smile came. "Really?" I turned around to face her. "I fucking marvel. *You* late?" My voice rose; I felt sweat on my forehead. "You're *always* fucking late. You know why? Because you don't give a shit about anyone but yourself. I came here to help you for Christ's sake."

Milena shrugged her shoulders before rummaging in a drawer. I slumped into a plastic chair. "I'll walk you to the parking lot," she said calmly, while throwing on a ratty fur coat. "It's a shortcut to the building I'm going to."

"Don't do me any fucking favours."

On our way out we were met by some guy, some raving heterosexual with a goatee and a brass ring in his ear, a colleague of Milena's named Roch. They seemed to get on rather well (Roch has an earring, Victor has an earring—there is a pattern here). As they chattered away I threw in the odd forced smile, Shaka smiles. Roch, the pride of some jerkwater town nearby, said he was on his way to clear the parking lot with a snowplough. Maybe he'd use his bare hands. He had the arms of the village blacksmith. And thighs like York hams.

Outside it was cold as an Eskimo's grave, twenty-five below with a wind chill factor of twenty-five hundred below. I was wearing a down parka with hood up, a virgin-wool scarf wrapped round my throat like a noose, Scott-of-the-Antarctic boots and gloves like oven mitts; Roch wore a short leather jacket, open at the front, and black running shoes. He had muscles and a cigarette to keep him warm. We made our way onto the one walkway clear of snow, wide enough for two abreast. We walked three abreast: Milena in the middle talking to Mr. Cool on her right; I on the left, off the path, in the snow, sinking with every step, rubber-arsing to keep up, pretending everything was fine.

I *am* fine, I said to myself as I broke away from the pair, walking backwards against the wind towards my pale horse. I'm free again. With open highways ahead of me. A ramblin' man. I looked towards Milena and muscleman, who were watching me, obviously talking about me. A patch of bare ice ahead gave me an idea: I would slide across it, laughing all the way, to show them my carefree spirit. I ran madly towards it. It was a patch of bare concrete.

I got up so quickly they probably hadn't seen me go down. The ground shook with silent laughter and the frozen trees mocked me as I clawed the ice off the windshield and climbed in behind the wheel. The engine kicked over on first try. Purring like a kitten. I revved her up and spun my tires. And spun and spun. In my rear-view mirror I watched Roch get bigger and bigger, watched his grin grow. He pushed me onto the service road with his bare hands.

With no red tail lights to guide me, the trip home was like falling through a black sky; I could feel my altimeter needle spinning round and round the dial towards zero. I went twenty miles, at twenty miles an hour, unable to see. It wasn't the frost on the windshield, wasn't the darkness that blinded me, not really. It was a stinging in my eyes. I stopped at a motel called Le Doux Paradis and lay awake on a double bed till dawn.

ᝯ

A union is preordained. Milena, the lottery ticket in the gutter, is found by Jeremy, the loser who plucks the torn ticket out, dreaming like a five-year-old there's still a chance to win. Milena's the fool's gold, the alchemist's gold, the glittering gypsy siren; Jeremy's the fool, the gull, the fall guy, failing, flailing, falling . . . Oh I deserved it, I had it coming. She warned me, others warned me, but I wouldn't listen. Because I was in love, in blind, mad love. And when you're blind and mad, things tend to go badly, don't they. Circumstances conspire, lives collide; I, Jeremy, mistook Milena for my bride.

TWENTY SEVEN

Roses have thorns, and silver fountains mud . . .
—*Sonnet 35*

In desolate February I did nothing but wait for God only cares, for letters that never came, for a phone that never rang. Life in enforced bachelorhood was one long wait, my apartment the grim waiting room on some phantom line. It was reverting to the state in which I found it; it was a fucking mess and so was I. Even my appliances, my servants, were breaking down one by one.

I got into February without anyone mentioning my birthday—at least there was that. Birthdays are a bugger; milestones down Rue Morgue. As a child I had never liked being born on the last day of January, I can't remember why. Perhaps because it was too close to Christmas or too cold or because, as Gerard liked to remind me, it was the day Yorkshireman Guy Fawkes was hanged. When I arrived in North York I changed my birthday to the 23rd of April, Shakespeare's birthday, and even got gifts that day, though never from my parents. Later, I claimed I was conceived on Shakespeare's birthday. It's possible.

My conception. I've often wondered what happened that day or night. Haven't we all? What if my father, my brute phantom father, raped my mother? It could have happened— whenever I mentioned him Mother would start to cry. He

366

scarpered, in any case, the fucking coward. I rarely think of him. I always had Gerard. And now . . .

Absence filled the space of my apartment. Reading or research was impossible—words whirled and hazed and did not mean. My few scribblings were entombed in dead letters of mourning; the ink from Milena's messages grew fainter; my Book of Saturdays remained locked in its drawer. Although I knew that time would heal and time would cure, I also knew it was unlikely to happen in my lifetime.

Those rare times I overcame sloth or the effects of supine drinking, I wandered in vagabondage through Fleur de Lysistrate or Mount Royal Cemetery. Once, at the former, I spotted voluminous Victor doing some erectile browsing in the gay porn section, amidst *Aussie Boys*, *EndGame* and *Power Tools*. Ever striving for new lows in tastelessness, he was wearing . . .

But I thought I was going to stop this. Victor was not there that day—it was someone who looked vaguely like him. And while we're at it: Victor is not particularly fat or fatuous, not the master of the obvious, the rent-a-clown I've turned him into. His clothes? They're fine, better than mine.

Starlight and shining crosses lit my loneliness. On Mount Royal at midnight I walked over burial plots and untrodden fields of snow, the stones of the graveyard standing out strangely in the rays of the moon, the dead all around me— lives once filled with as much worry and yearning and self-importance as my own—underneath the snow and clay. At Wolodko's headstone, my *memento mori*, I would linger, puzzling over the Ukrainian inscription, straining to read the secrets of the grave. God is really all the dead, I thought, all the dead organisms of the earth. When you pray you are asking the dead to help you live. Which is why I've been summoning dead England, India, Zululand, Ukraine. But enough. My problems are infinitesimal. Why would anyone listen? I shouldn't be acting this way, shouldn't be affected so deeply. Something's wrong; I am not well.

On Valentine's Day, in a field of virgin snow that glistened like feldspar, I footprinted MILENA in letters fifty feet tall. Why? Did I think she'd see it from her madhouse tower? Was I making it easier for the dead in heaven to see my plight? On the bridge of the "A", lying on my back on the cold ground, I gazed up at the glittering sky. Gerard once explained to me, as we looked through his telescope, that a wish made on a falling star would always come true. He also told me about the Dark Star, the member of a binary star system that is invisible. It's up there somewhere, he said, burning bright, but not for you or me.

೧

I didn't see Milena in February. Or March. And then everything happened at once. On the first of April, in the season of fools and resurrections, I got a call from York. Mrs. Kern calmly informed me that Gerard was dead.

"Last week per'aps the week before . . . an accident . . . 'E's breathed 'is last, poor bugger . . . "

I hang up and the telephone rings. I see the red rings emanating upwards, in spirals, and the air is tinted and glazed. My answering machine will not answer. I listen to the phone ring and ring. It's like a phone waking you from a dream, except I can't tie it into the plot. I know I'm supposed to do something, but what? I pick up the receiver. A familiar voice, a lover's voice, says something I don't understand. I speak of Gerard perhaps, or cry like a child. There is a dial tone then seconds or hours later another beckoning sound. Again, I'm expected to react. Is recess over? Do I go to homeroom? I think of Jacques and Pavlov's bell. I pick up the phone and say hello but the phone is dead. The sound is repeated. It passes through the air in violent waves. I say "hello" into the air. "Hello!" I scream. I sit on the floor. It's coming from below. I walk down the stairs and open the door and look at my bare white feet as Milena takes me in her arms.

Twenty Eight

O! call back yesterday, bid time return.
—*Richard II*

We flew to Heathrow the next day, arriving with the sun, entering my other time zone. A taxi, floundering in stinking chaos, took us to King's Cross, and an express train to York.

"London is hideous," I said as we roared northward.

"On the plane you said it was beautiful," replied Milena.

"It's a huge fucking lunatic warren. The new buildings are mind-bogglingly ugly. It's fucking depressing. The IRA should blow them all up. Or else line up all the architects, shoot the bastards, throw them in the grave of Mies van der Rohe."

"Are you saying this because of your uncle? Didn't he feel the same way?"

"And the cars! Buckle up, everybody, get into your rubber and steel straitjackets. It's so obvious cars have killed London, killed the world. Why do we put up with them?"

"Are you saying this because of your mother's accident?"

"That has nothing to do with it."

Milena soon fell asleep. As I was trying, with gymnastic gyrations, to read the open diary on her lap, to read what she'd written about me (what else would she write about?), I felt a hand on my shoulder that practically ejected me from my seat. Milena woke with a start. Across the aisle, a man with a face as lined as a map and an eye that was difficult to

370

meet offered to trade newspapers with me. I agreed even though I hadn't started mine. My mind was racing as Milena stuffed her diary back into her knapsack, as I paged through the man's *Yorkshire Post* with almost none of the words registering. I was thinking of what I saw in Milena's diary. Beneath a fine sketch of a burning cigarette I made out these fragmented words: " . . . *dangling on his side . . . quicken, kill together* . . . "

I continued leafing through the newspaper. *Dangling on his side? Kill together?* When the man said something about India and a new outbreak of mad cow disease I said, "May I rip something out of here?"

"Certainly," he replied with a wink. "That girl in the negligee advert?"

"No," I replied. "An obituary."

It was cold and windy in York, which was fine with me. On Mrs. Kern's door I knocked with a gentle rap and then with a loud banging before she finally emerged with a ring of keys in her hand. She was much smaller than I remember, having carried some twenty more years on her back, while her head was much bigger—a real task for her neck. Her face was bloodless and hair so sparse you could see her scalp. It was only her eyes that hadn't changed: as darting as a rabbit's, they gleamed in their hollows the way they always had.

"Coom yer ways in," she said excitedly. "Ah'se reet fain to see you! These are hard times for ailin' folk. Eh! T' wind is in a cold airt, Ah'se thinkin' it 'ull freeze afore morn . . . Ah must say yer a right nice-lookin' young couple. Aye. Afore we speak of t' matter 'at weighs heavily on our hearts, we'll have a sup o' tea."

I introduced her to Milena. "Tha's not Yorkshire, Milena, tha canst tell me nowt. I'll bet me Sunday rubbers . . . "

"I think we'll go straight up, Mrs. Kern," I said. "If you don't mind, that is. We'll have that tea later."

With heavy baggage and whispers of the past echoing through the stairwell, we lumbered up the stairs. I opened the creaking dungeon door, not needing the key, and broke down—from sadness, from exhaustion, from knifing nostalgia. Memories came welling up in a fountain of tears I couldn't stop. Milena left me alone, for a smoke in the frozen rain.

The flat, icy cold and in the same state of conglomeration more or less, seemed hardly to have changed—it still had its musty smell and creaking boards and darkened areas around door handles, its tilting walls and sloping floors and stalactites of peeling paint. Though the toucans had flown, the toys and rocking horse and books still had their homes. I made a quick search for the encyclopaedia volume with one page missing and found it easily. Had Gerard known I was coming? Here, then, is the end of **Shakuntala**:

> subsequently recovered by a fisherman from the stomach of a fish. When the king sees the ring, he recognises his wife and proclaims her his queen.

Cold rain began to beat and lash on the windowpane. I opened it all the way to let the water in. I picked up the terrestrial telescope on the ledge and looked through its filmy lens.

"But everything is fuzzy, Uncle Gerard." "Turn the sleeve to the right, lad, that's it." "It bring things very near, Uncle!" "Look over to the right, just above the chemist's— that's where Richard of York's head was stuck on a pike." "Did you see his head, Uncle?" "Just missed it, I'm afraid." "Have you a photograph?" "Look over towards Shambles, Jeremy, beside Smith's? That's where Guy Fawkes plotted." "Why are there so many Smiths, Uncle?" "Because in days of yore women

*wore chastity belts, and everyone wanted to be a smith—a
locksmith." "What's a chastity belt?" "Can you see the sweetshop, lad? W. H. Auden was born down that street on the
left . . . Wystie was a dear friend of mine." "Uncle Gerard, I've
decided I'm not going to school anymore." "Excellent idea,
lad." "It was a hard decision but I've finally made up my
mind." "That's the spirit. Can you see the Tower, son? That's
where all the nagging wives were locked up." "Is nagging a
crime, Uncle?" "One of the worst." "Is that why you won't
marry Mummy?" "My word, look at the charlies on her!"
"But is that why you won't marry Mummy?" "Give me that
spyglass, Jeremy, quickly." "What are charlies?" "You'll find
out soon enough, lad . . . "*

I shut the window and collapsed on Gerard's second-best
bed. In the haze of twilight sleep I felt the soft pressure of
Milena's breasts against my back; she was coiled around me
in a spoon position. In French, the verb *lover* means "to coil,
wind around."

In a daze I whispered, "Milena, why did you come to York
with me?"

"I already told you."

"Tell me again."

"I came because you asked me to. And because you paid
for my ticket."

"I didn't pay—it was an air-miles ticket. So otherwise you
wouldn't have come, that's the only reason—"

"Are you fishing for flattery? Of course that's not the only
reason."

"Was it because of Barbara?"

"Barbara? What's Barbara got do with it? What'd she say?"

"Nothing really."

"I came because I wanted to, OK?"

"Yes, I'm sure you did. But I thought you said you couldn't live with a man, make love with a man, that I was just a lapse, that you were sitting on the fence."

"Making love to anyone, male or female, was a lapse. I almost never made love. And I'm still sitting on the fence. But maybe my legs are dangling on your side."

Dangling on my side. "So that's . . . so you came with me because—"

"It was right after Belleforêt, believe it or not, that I . . . that things became clearer. I know I wasn't very charming, friendly, grateful, whatever. That period was one giant dark patch, one of the worst I've ever had. After you left I had some time to think about things. About your attempts to understand me, about some things I'd discovered about you . . . Oh what the hell, I might as well tell you. I read your diary, or whatever it is."

I sat bolt upright in bed. "You read my Book of Saturdays? You read my Book of Fucking Saturdays? How dare you? When? What did you read? All the things I wrote about you?"

"I read parts of it while you were in class one night. You left it out. I'm sorry, I really am. I didn't know what it was at first. But then it was . . . unputdownable."

"Shit. I can't believe you'd do that. That's . . . criminal. Unbelievable."

"There was a folded page inside. All creased and worn—"

"You read it?"

"Glanced at it," she lied.

"You actually saw the Page? I can't believe that."

"Why, what is it?"

I hesitated. "Well, it's something that Gerard . . . It's a long story. It's like a treasure map, one that takes years to read. It basically says that we're going to get married and live happily ever after—like in *Shakuntala*, like in a Shakespearean comedy. I haven't figured out yet where all the happily-ever-aftering is going to happen—England, India, South Africa or the Ukraine. But it will happen, trust me, it's fate, destiny. The dice were thrown years ago—it's just a matter of waiting, waiting to read their fall."

What I first thought was a smile forming on Milena's lips was more of a scowl. "Jeremy, sometimes I really don't know when you're kidding. You *are* kidding, aren't you?"

"Well, sort of . . . I don't know anymore."

Milena shook her head. "There's no such thing as fate or destiny—a fool's excuse for failure, nothing more. I think we've been on this treadmill before."

I sighed. "I think there's more to it than that, Milena. More to it than just failure, as you call it. There's also something called bad luck . . . " Here I stopped, Milena's words wrapping me in a chain of questions I couldn't answer. Failure. What happened to Milena as a child, was it a failure on the part of her father and father's friend? Or what happened to me as a child, or to my mother as an adult . . . Isn't failure or success allotted to people by their stars? Sometimes, isn't it just grievously bad luck? Her dad's bad luck and Denny's and Milena's and Violet's? The wicked wheel of fate? I mean, what can you do when the gods say no?

"Things happen," Milena continued, "cruelty and violence happen not because of fate or destiny but because of other people, all right? And because of situations created by other people. It's not just bad luck in a world of fucking chance."

I paused again, eyes downcast. "You could be right," I said, surprising myself as much as Milena. "I know I've let chance, superstition run my life."

"You're not alone, believe me."

"I really can't help it."

"I've let things run my life too. But I'm trying to move on. Which is one of the reasons I came to England, I guess."

"What are the other reasons?"

Milena smiled. "The reasons that have to do with you? I guess there were a lot of little things building up. At first I thought you were just a little boy—superstitious, insecure, silly—and now I . . . well, I still think the same way. Let's see, what do I like about you? Maybe that. Oh, and the way you treated your landlady, the fact you helped her out, had dinner with her when you couldn't understand a word she said. What else? I was impressed—make that shocked—by the way you stood up to my father at the hospital. By your courage, or madness, I'm not sure which. I've never seen anyone stand up to him like that. I thought he was going to kill you."

"Kill?"

"And I have to admit . . . no never mind."

"Tell me."

"Well, I have to admit I was a bit jealous."

"Jealous? You?" I thought that was my domain. "Who were you jealous of?"

"Arielle. You two seemed to get along so well that I assumed—"

"Arielle! Are you kidding? It was your sister I was after."

Milena hit me in the shoulder with her fist, playfully I think (it left a bruise), and I grabbed her around the waist, sweeping her off the ground. She hit me again, hard, in the shoulder blade as we toppled onto Gerard's bed, I hitting the back of my head against the wall. As I lay totally inert, dying, Milena lit a cigarette.

❧

The next morning I made inquiries. Gerard had indeed had

an accident: according to the French consulate he had drowned in the Atlantic, a few kilometres off the coast of Normandy, near Saint-Aubin-sur-mer. He went out in a borrowed sailboat, it seems, and never came back. The boat had been recovered but not the body. There were witnesses who saw the boat capsize.

Surely it was a scam, perhaps Gerard's best yet, his crowning achievement—an insurance dodge, an alimony duck, who knows? I half expected him to show up at any minute.

That night a 1940s-style Parisian gendarme with white *képi* waved a traffic ticket at me which turned into a registered letter. In typical French fashion he broke three seals and asked me to initial three different documents, each on thick sheaves of carbon. With cars and mobylettes whizzing by on either side of us, he then handed me a letter typed with the punishing hammer-strokes of Gerard's typewriter.

```
Dear Jer. ,
Full fathom five- thy uncle lies .
Inside your toy box is an indigo tie.
In the lining of the tie...Send half,
when coast is clear, to C.P. 55,
Saint-Crispin-sur-mer. Sorry if I gave
you a scare.
    Love, Ger.
```

I felt happiness, relief—and anger. The bastard, for putting me through all that. The rest of the dream is blurry, except where I opened the toy box, pulled out the tie and discovered not money or insurance policies but Moon Traveller fireworks. I must have yelled out something at this point because I woke up Milena, who as you know is the deepest sleeper in the world. "You all right?" she asked, in a sandpaper voice.

I asked her if we got a letter from Uncle Gerard. "Gerard is dead," she replied, turning over to go back to sleep. But I wouldn't let her; I insisted on relating my dream. Before the end she said, "Wish-fulfilment. But maybe it's premonitory. Good night." "Yes, goddamn it—it would be like him, wouldn't it?" I said. "That beautiful fraud!" I was suddenly buoyed; I ran downstairs in my underwear looking for the morning mail. There were three letters, all addressed to Gerard, all bills by the look of them. I trudged back to bed and slept, without dreaming, until three in the afternoon. Milena was still asleep when I opened my eyes. I woke her up by making love to her—by descent, and consent.

While eating Indian take-away hours later, sitting leggily cross-legged on the floor, Milena said she wanted to live in York. "I want to live here," she said simply.

I tried to remain calm during this earthquake. "What . . . exactly do you mean?"

"Which word is giving you problems?"

"You mean live here? *Here?* With me?"

"Yes, unless you don't want me to."

"Of course I want you to. *Us* to. But how . . . I mean, why now . . . why here?"

"I can't go back, I can never be happy back there, I realise that now. I should've left a long time ago, I don't know, I'm just happier here, much . . . calmer. And besides, the police are driving me fucking crazy."

I stared at my plate, fiddled with my papadum and mango chutney. The *police* are driving you crazy? "Are they . . . still checking out Denny's suicide?"

Milena took a drag from her Silk Cut cigarette. "You could say that."

I stared at the ground. "Did your father do it, Milena?"

"Do what?"

"Did he kill Denny?"

Milena bowed her head. "I don't know. The cops talked to him, even took him in, but never laid charges. They also suspected me. Still do. They know what Denny did to me and my sister."

"You told them?"

"My father told them."

"*Did* you kill Denny?"

Milena sighed. "No."

"Of course you didn't. Sorry for even asking." I lit up the wrong end of a cigarette and walked to the window. The sky was interstellar black and the spires of the Minster invisible. "Milena, was it . . . could it be that out of guilt, or revenge, your father killed Denny? To show you he was sorry, ashamed of what he did to his own daughters?"

"I doubt it. If he killed Denny Tyrell, then he has more guts than I thought. Besides, Denny had a lot of weird friends—women included—who might've wanted him dead."

"So now you want to get away from everything and live here in York . . . permanently?"

"What does permanently mean?"

Well, permanently means a long time. "Nothing," I said. "Permanently means nothing."

慓

We booked a cheap charter from Belfast, of all places, a direct flight to our distinct society that coincided—I made sure of this—with Gerard's (bodiless) funeral service. On our way out the door Mrs. Kern said, "An' so thoo's trapesin' off agen, just like yer uncle . . . "

"We'll be back soon, Mrs. Kern. We're just going to tie up a few loose ends in Canada—"

"Just like yer uncle, trapesin' off agen . . . "

"Wasn't the Titanic launched from Belfast?" Milena asked, and none of us knew.

At the airport, on the runway, aboard the plane, I eyed Milena suspiciously, afraid she'd renege, afraid she'd skip out on me when we touched down. And I had a dread feeling that some tragedy was about to occur—in Northern Ireland, over the Atlantic, in Quebec. On the shuttle, in the washroom, by the luggage carousel, I looked over my shoulder for hidden assassins; I saw forms passing through the draperies, saw shadows towering over us. "*All pregnant women were slaughtered . . .* " warned the Page. Was Milena pregnant?

In the taxi from Mirabel, Milena asked what was wrong. "Nothing, nothing at all," I said. "Why do you ask?" "Tell me the truth," she said. I told it. Milena said not to worry— she was not pregnant and my forebodings of disaster were "a hundred percent unreliable." She was not entirely accurate, as it turned out.

☙

On my answering machine were several messages from the Director's secretary, Madame Plourde, and one from the man himself. He said it was "urgent" I get back to him. Had I been found out? Sacked? There was also a large envelope in the livery of my former school, also from the Director, with this inside:

> *Mr. Davenant,*
>
> *Since you have responded to neither Mme Plourde's calls nor my own, I have no recourse but to write this letter, a copy of which I have forwarded to Dr. J.C. Provost, Dean of Arts & Science. In part, it concerns your student evaluations of last semester (enclosed). As you can see for*

yourself, the epithets chosen to describe your lectures include 'impromptu', 'incoherent', and 'half-ass backwards'. It has also been drawn to my attention that you took it upon yourself to cancel or greatly abbreviate several, if not most, of your classes . . .

I skipped to the last paragraph:

But there is a much graver matter to be discussed, as you can see from the enclosed photocopy of a formal complaint received one week ago today, in which Dr. Clyde Vincent Haxby accuses you of falsifying your academic credentials, and of unprofessional involvement with one of your students (Ms. Arielle Castonguay). He has furthermore accused you of sexually assaulting him last October 6, and of subsequently issuing threats involving fireman's apparel . . .

I crumpled up the page and punched in Philippe's number. "Doesn't surprise me," he said in French, after peals of laughter. "I think he's lost it. He came to work last week sans Hush Puppies and briefcase, for the first time in his life, wearing wellington boots and gardening clothes, smelling like a compost heap. And he's a man obsessed—he can't stop ranting about his 'penile humiliation'."

"He's not very big, is he?"

"As the entire department saw. He called you a 'disgusting unregenerate homosexualist.' I decided, by the way, not to confess my role as accessory to the crime."

"Accessory? You masterminded the whole thing."

"They're your fingerprints."

I paused to mull this over.

"Listen, Jeremy, I hope you don't plan on doing anything . . . rash, like confronting him or doing what Jacques did, or giving him your address or anything. He's starting to scare me. I hope he doesn't follow you to York—you know he spends his summers Wordsworthing it in the Lake District."

I chortled with exaggerated unconcern. "No fear. Listen, would you mind clearing out my office for me?"

"No problem. And I'll keep you posted. I'll talk to Sobranet, try to calm down Haxby."

"You're a good man, Philippe, I always knew you were."

"You're full of shit."

"So I'm told. Come and visit us in York—you're welcome any time."

❤

I filled only one suitcase—I don't remember packing the Swiss-Army knife but pack it I did—and threw out bags and bags of stuff, the clogging impedimenta of my past. To Arielle I left my apartment and what remained in it, with the rider that she have tea with my landlady at least once a week. Arielle, I thought, would be my sanctuary (and insurance policy—mustn't get carried away with this Platonic business) should things go awry.

When I went to see my landlady for the last time, and explained that Arielle was moving in and I moving out, she seemed to know everything without my saying a word. She started to quiver, then cry, and long tears ran down her cheeks. Which of course started me up. I hugged her tight and then went to get something I'd almost forgotten about: the silver thimble I'd bought at Heathrow. I slipped it onto her finger. With a sad smile she bustled off to get something for me, something infinitely better: a *pysanka*, a brilliantly-coloured and intricately-patterned Easter egg which, Milena told me later, was like a Valentine, a gift of the heart, made especially for me.

I phoned Sabrine (and baby daughter) to say goodbye, then Victor, and in a moment of weakness even phoned Ralph in North York. He seemed genuinely happy to hear from me and (less genuinely) sad to hear that Gerard had "crossed the great divide." He also said he would send me money—tainted money, Mother's insurance money—which I said I still wouldn't touch, but he insisted; I hope he didn't think I was angling for it. "I know," I said, "I know her death was an accident."

I did not phone Jacques; Jacques phoned me. "So how's Ms. Right? How goes the taming of the shrew? You get my postcard?"

"Why don't you take a flying fuck, Dion?"

"I'll be in York next month. I'll take it there. I've heard some alarming news, by the way, about Milena and—"

I hung up. Milena, second-sighted on such matters, knew who had called. "What did Jacques want?" she asked. "Your face is all red."

"I don't know what he wants." To drive us apart? "He says he is coming to see us in York."

"How did he get our address?" *Our* address, she said.

"I don't know. But I don't want to see him again."

"Let him come. I don't mind."

TWENTY NINE

I bring you good news. You shall soon be married.

—Shakuntala

In York I began dealing with the tedious affairs of Gerard's estate. Mrs. Kern said, "Your uncle's worth a seet of brass, 'e's made 'is pile, 'e can give you baith a 'elping 'and." Which was, it appears, his intention: in a large envelope addressed to "Jeremy and Milena" was a last will and testament dated 31 January of that year, in which I was named the principal beneficiary (Milena was left Gerard's art materials, a cheque covering two years of art school, and a spurious reference letter). I wondered if all this would hold up in court, as there were others with stronger claims. Gerard owned the building in which he lived, which was a surprise to me, but apart from that he didn't appear to own much. A letter from a firm of solicitors in Peckitt Street contained guarded statements about the size of the legacy and frequent allusions to "outstanding settlements"—gambling debts, in all likelihood, and overdue alimony ("back salary," as Milena put it). Gerard's periodic trips to France and South Africa, according to Mrs. Kern, coincided with visits to England by predatory ex-wives (Gerard was a multiple divorcé or bigamist or both, agreed Ralph and Mrs. Kern). Milena urged me to see that this back salary was paid.

A life insurance policy, a gift from beyond the grave, was made out to me. Milena found it inside my toy chest. Mrs.

Kern's nephew, who worked for Great Northern Life, offered to look after the insurance part of it—at least she said he offered—and warned there would be adjustor queries and death duties and trouble from the former wives. The phone rang a lot around this time, but whoever was calling—the merry widows? Jacques? Haxby? Milena's father?—hung up.

The days turned over. My records of this period are sketchy, probably because I had so little to lament. Things were going shockingly well. I was unalterably in love with Milena, though careful never to say so; she was clearly fond of me, though never said so either. She was starting to feel, I think, that living with a man could be tolerable, that it wasn't a contradiction in feminist terms or a knife that turned in her past. She had survived the past, I believed.

Sexually, things were not as they were in Canada, where my fondness for oral foreplay and coitus uninterruptus clashed with Milena's for abstinence. In England, we made love till the cows came home. And I wasn't always the one to start the ball rolling. A case in point: one night, after I showed her the entry on cunnilingus in *The Feminist Dictionary*, Milena said, "Jeremy, feminists are just like everyone else—they don't all agree and they're not always right." A few minutes later, as if to demonstrate her point, she stood before me as I was reading in bed and asked for part of my *Yorkshire Evening Press*. When I handed her a section she remained standing, looking down at me. Maybe she wanted another section, I reasoned. When I asked her she made no reply, staring strangely at me instead. "Is there anything—" I was cut short by the sight of Milena hiking up her skirt and straddling my chest. With Cleopatran eyes boring into me mercilessly, she reached back and caressed my thigh as I stared at her most biblical of zones. With her other hand, and then both hands, she clutched my hair as she slowly advanced towards me.

Milena no longer locked up when making love: on this occasion she trembled while I was inside her, cried out for the first time, a wild and inarticulate cry, and for a second I thought of phoning Jacques. Instead, I pulled a woollen blanket over us and slid into a spiralling state better than sleep.

Something else had changed: Milena was no longer distant, silent. When we awoke she talked expansively about her past, her feelings, the injustices of the world; I, enraptured, listened. She was in unnaturally high spirits. She no longer felt like she was "sinking", no longer "locking doors" on herself. "But I don't know if I have the strength to do anything in life," she added. "I've always been an expert in taking things lying down."

"Things will change for you in York, I know it. I sense it."

"I hope you're right."

I gazed at her in silence, lost in her unfathomable eyes, and felt once again this ridiculous urge to propose. "Will you take me, Milena, for thy lawful wedded—"

An explosion of air interrupted me. "As Mae West once said, marriage is a great institution, but I'm not ready for an institution."

"You're sounding more and more like my uncle."

"I may have to marry you—so I can stay here legally."

ೞ

The happiness of these spring days is hard to describe. We read together, in long stretches of silence, I her favourite books and she mine. She listened to my stories of my uncle ("whose death brought us together," she remarked) and told me stories of her mother ("she left her village in a biblically

JEFFREY MOORE

old cart, a musical instrument maker's cart, I think, hidden under sugar cane, cocoanut shells, donkey-tail hairs and God knows what else, along with two large lizards called goannas"). Twice, to my surprise, Milena roamed beyond the limits of York, to the purple moors, alone, "for the air, for the silence." She brought back flowers—dog roses and wild lilac, cowberry and love-in-idleness—and even arranged them in a vase.

Milena did something else out of character: she offered to cut my hair. Containing my surprise, I naturally accepted. Oh yes. Amidst bouquets of wildflowers and Gerard's dusty books, I sat contentedly as she snipped away at my unbrushed, unwetted hair. I closed my eyes and drifted off. Milena was actually cutting my hair, I thought, she was doing something for me, she was saying "I am giving you this look, branding you, writing my signature upon you, you belong to me." Isn't this what she was saying?

"Pardon?" I said.

"I said I'm finished. Hope you like it."

In the mirror I examined her expert cut, feeling inexpressibly moved. "What possessed you to make this wonderful offer?" I asked.

"Because your hair looked like shit."

○3

The lady who lived in the bottom flat when I was a boy had, according to Mrs. Kern, mysteriously disappeared. For several months the place had been empty, except for a few useless items left behind like cleaning solutions and cosmetics. Milena, who made things very clear from the start, would be living there. This was one of her conditions. Did I forget to mention that? (She also said she might entertain women friends there.) So far, in any event, we had spent every night together.

"It's the closest you'll ever get to living with me," she said when proposing the idea.

"Like Allen and Farrow in the early days? Separate domiciles?"

"Yeah, I guess so. Without the kids, though. Definitely without the kids . . . for now anyway." She added the last phrase in the faintest of whispers, unless I misheard.

During the day Milena busied herself with renovations downstairs, sanding and stripping and breathing in poisonous lead paint. Red paint. She insisted I keep out. With a loan I had to force upon her (insurance money) she planned to turn her lower abode into a bookshop, a "specialty" shop specialising in books not written by men. She would have a room of her own at the back, a room to paint in, with a single bed and a chest of drawers with an escritoire top that she'd found among Gerard's things. I suggested she call the shop "Shakespeare's Mother", which Milena didn't officially rule out. It was she who gave me the idea. When I once suggested she didn't read Shakespeare because he was a male, she answered, "Don't be stupid. That has nothing to do with it. Don't forget that half his genes, half his genius, came from his mother. Probably more like nine-tenths."

Mrs. Kern continued to live in the middle flat, and continued to keep things in order, or disorder, depending on your point of view. In this, Mad Cur and Milena saw eye to eye. Chaos ruled. We were invited to motley meals of cod and chips with white bread and apricot jam and mushy peas and tinned pears and Carnation cream, not necessarily in that order. We were both very fond of her, although at first Milena couldn't make out a word she said. Once Milena got used to her broad Yorkshire, she told me she didn't appreciate being called "pet", "girly" or "more bones than flesh". I, on the other hand, didn't appreciate being called "a pretty young laddie, and a sarkey bastard of an adult."

Madeleine was never Gerard's mistress, I soon realised. One day I asked her, teasingly, if Gerard had ever proposed to her. "Go on, ye daft bugger!" she replied. "Ah'll 'ave none o' that—doant try to tell me 'bout romancin', Jeremy-me-lad, 'cos it's all me eye an' Betty Martin. Eh, men's a bother, they are! I'd rather have a good cup o' tea. Yer uncle's a crafty little bugger . . . " She seemed about to say more, then checked herself. "An' b'sides, 'e thought marriage was a sentence, not a word."

"Yes, I know—"

"An' that marriage was like keepin' money in a bank."

"He did?" I hadn't heard that one. "Why?"

"You put 't in, 'e says, you take it out, you lose interest."

There was something in Mad Cur's behaviour that made me think she knew something, knew that Gerard was lying low. When I asked her why she called Gerard a crafty bugger she replied, "Just a guess, lad, but if yer uncle drowned, t'was no accident, 'e knew what 'e was up to if you follow me. Yer uncle was dyin', didn't you know it? 'E had a bad heart—Parkinson's too."

None of this should have come as a surprise—I had seen the symptoms myself—but her words fell on me like a sheet of flame. "Yes, I . . . I knew that," I said, my throat strangling each syllable.

When, later that night, I recounted all this to Milena, that Gerard was dying, that he went to a watery grave to give us insurance money, or even faked his death and might still be alive, just like in my dream, she replied that it was typical of me to think this way, that I was a die-hard delusionist, a hopeless fantasist. Or something like that.

℅

Along the borders of these happy days, anti-Elysian forces seemed to be massing, poised to invade. It was at the library in Museum Street, where I spent most of time away from Milena, that I did most of my sentry duty, my doom-watching, brooding on just about everything—but especially on Gerard and my mother, whose loss York made all the more searing. I began to dread another loss: Milena's. One day as I was leafing through a *Military Medicine* and *Journal of Trauma* left on the table, both of which contained articles on left-handedness, I discovered that lefties like Milena are significantly overrepresented in the following groups: prisoners, delinquent children, alcoholics, drug abusers, manic-depressives, schizophrenics, epileptics, retards, Mensa members, bedwetters, homosexuals, self-murderers. They also don't live as long as righties, in part because they're six times as likely to die in accidents.

I also read the Graveyard Poets. In the past year I had experienced three deaths, two far and one near, and was now haunted by a premonition of a fourth—mine or Milena's, right or left exit, I couldn't decide which. As I walked the Walls, roamed the streets and snickleways of the old city, the nether regions of Back Swinegate and especially my home patch—the old school, the site of the (now demolished) Tower Cinema, the house of (now dead) Dragonetti, the sweetshop (with Cathedral Rock and mint yo-yos still on display)—I wanted to be swept up in a river of nostalgia. But I could never quite manage it. The clouds in the sky, oppressively close, hung over me like shrouds; the waters of the Ouse cast a morbid spell, luring me towards them. I saw Milena from Lendal Bridge, her dark clothes billowing down the river like mad Ophelia's; I saw Calverley being pressed to death at the Castle gaol, saw him stabbing his terrorized children; I saw Shaka, King of the Zulus, being pierced with his own red assegai. I saw lesser ghosts as well: Clyde Haxby, duelling pistol in hand, on the campus of the University of York; Jacques, with a bottle of hemlock wine, on the steps of the Royal York Hotel; Milena's father, a new .44 under his coat, skulking under Skeldergate Bridge.

I also felt pangs of guilt. Horrible as it is for me to say it, I experienced fleeting feelings of joy that Gerard, my broken idol, was gone. I was starting to think that Milena was right, that Gerard had hurt me and others. And yet I still loved him and couldn't shake his ghost, as you'll see. Perhaps from these clashing brainwaves, I was also blacking out from time to time—labyrinthitis? migraine aura?—and sometimes felt that my mind was slowly bending and breaking, that I was trapped in some dark subterranean maze with no way out. I began to realise that I was the sick one, and that Milena, apart from her left-handedness, was practically normal.

On my way home from the library I would often sidetrack to St. Cuthbert's, York's oldest church. Here, I thought, would be a good place to marry Milena before she or I died. *But I will be a bridegroom in my death, and run into't, as to a lover's bed.* Five hundred and two 12th-century Jewish skeletons, according to a plaque, had been unearthed in a burial ground nearby. Beyond this was another of my ritual stops: an antiquarian bookseller named J.G. Trundell & Son—Fine Purveyors of Books. One day, just before closing, I bought a gift for Milena: an early edition of George Sand's three-volume *Journal*, its first English translation and perhaps the prize of Trundell's collection.

Milena greeted me back home with specks of paint on her neck and face, including a red spot in the middle of her fore-head, like the *bindhi* of married Hindu women. "What are you hiding behind your back?" she asked, without looking at me.

"Nothing . . . nothing really. Just some books, I'll show you later."

Milena smiled. "We got a card from Barbara and Philippe. Take a look—it's on the kitchen table."

"Addressed to both of us? What'd they say?"

"Among other things, not to worry about Clyde Haxby. He's now an inmate at Belleforêt."

⸻

At dusk we went for a long walk, hand in hand. Seas of yellow daffodils girded York's grey walls and large green fishing umbrellas dotted the riverside. From the clouds, a dark bird with huge wingspan bore down and skimmed through the mist wafting up from the water. Ducks swam out of the way of sculling schoolboys and the evening star suddenly appeared, hanging low over Lendal Bridge. As we walked towards darkness, a brilliant moon cast lines of shimmering silver onto the water. Church bells chimed. I put my arm around Milena and she put hers around me.

I left the lights out when we arrived back home, and lit a candle in the kitchen. The rays of the giant May moon streamed through the window, falling with a ghostly lustre on the objects within. I asked Milena if I could blindfold her, if we could play the game Gerard and I had played years before. She said no. "Just this one favour," I implored. "Please." Milena sighed as I wrapped one of Gerard's wide ties round her eyes. After a perfunctory ten-second tour she selected a heavy volume at floor level and handed it to me, practically dropping it at my feet. I asked her to put her finger into the book as I turned its pages. She complied. Before she removed her blindfold I set her book aside and substituted the last volume of George Sand's *Journal*. Under the light of the candle we read the end of a ribbon-marked page:

We cannot tear out a single page of our life, but we
can throw the whole book in the fire . . .

"It's for you, Milena. For your birthday, or your bookshop." Milena looked at the cover, shook her head, and with
a devilish glint in her dark eyes said, "You fraud. I want a
divorce. I'm going back to the asylum." She clawed at my
face, affectionately, then put her arms around me and held
me tight, as tight as she'd ever held me.

THIRTY

Fortune, good night; smile once more, turn the wheel.

—*King Lear*

It sounds like we've reached the end here, doesn't it. If the story were untrue, I would end it here. But the story is true, and one episode—of murder—remains untold.

On the first Saturday of the jolly month of June, I left the flat quietly at the crack of doom, leaving Milena's sleeping face buried in my pillow—and on my side of the bed, I proudly noted. On Gerard's antique Rudge I pedalled quickly through the heart of York, a blur of mediaeval and Georgian buildings, zigzagging through lost-looking tourists and lurking louts, down Swinegate, Jubbergate, Shambles, along St. Saviourgate, Pavement, Stonebow, de-cycling first at the gothic grounds of St. Cuthbert's and then at J.G. Trundell's, where I traded some of Gerard's books for others that Milena had shortlisted for the shop. I then stopped at the Market for all the daffodils, tulips and roses I could carry.

Back home, a scribbled backhand message was nailed to the door of Milena's flat: B⅋Cₖ ⅋ ☝ . I tried the door and then looked at my watch: ten past seven. Around eight, when I thought I heard noises from below, I descended with my flowers and books. Her sign was still up. I put my ear to the door. Silent as the boneyard. I unlocked the door and pushed it slowly. "Milena? Are you there, Milena?"

In near-darkness, with the sharp smell of solvents in my nostrils, I stumbled towards the bedroom, towards a spear of faint light from the half-open door. I tiptoed closer, like a jewel-thief, and smiled when I glimpsed what looked like her sleeping body in bed, the sheet pulled over her head. How does she breathe like that?

I was about to lay the flowers down when I saw, next to a desklamp on the floor, a spreading circle of red and within that circle a Swiss-Army knife. Oh God. Oh no! I knew this would happen she's killed herself! I knew she'd do it she's killed herself she's slashed her wrists I gave her the idea! No! Her father! Her father's murdered her! Calverley! My head was on fire and the room's scorching colours throbbed. The flowers and books fell to the floor, into the red puddle I was standing in.

Backing away, I glimpsed open suitcases, drawers and plastic bags. On the floor, bedside the brass desklamp, were white sheets soaking up an overturned can of bright red paint. I picked up the lamp and held it above the bed. Milena was not in it.

On Gerard's escritoire was a fountain pen and leaf of paper, smirched with red fingerprints but surprisingly legible, on which Milena explained that her father had been arrested, for murdering Denny. She had to go back, she really did, right away, not only for that but for her sister too. And sorry about the mess, and everything else. And please—don't follow. Best of bloody luck. Milena.

My hand was shaking as I turned over the page. There had to be more! In a postscript were these scrawled words: *Trust me, Jeremy, there'll be another time, more days for us to quicken, kill together—it's written somewhere on the Page.*

Achevé d'imprimer en septembre 1999 chez

VEILLEUX
IMPRESSION À DEMANDE INC.

à Longueuil, Québec